FIRE AND ICE

Luc wondered what to do next. Gillian looked ghostly pale, as fragile as a porcelain doll, bearing only a vague resemblance to the spirited, opinionated—and often irritating—young woman he had come to know. He should leave. But he couldn't turn his back and ignore the wounded look in her eyes.

He approached her in measured steps, then reaching out, caught her chin between his thumb and forefinger and tilted her face upward, willing her gaze to meet his. "Was your lover worth all the pain?" he asked quietly.

As he watched in fascination, she came to life. Color flooded back into her face. An angry gleam replaced the dull hurt. "How dare you ask such a question!" she flared, jerking away from his touch.

Before Luc could savor his victory, Gillian picked up a small glass paperweight from a nearby table. The missile landed against the door frame, accompanied by the sound of breaking glass.

There was fire beneath the ice. The lady just might survive in the northwoods after all. Fascinated, he watched her eyes darken to the smoky blues of a summer night. She started to speak, but before she could utter a syllable, he silenced her the only way he knew how.

"Just as I suspected," he whispered. "There's fire under all that frost."

WILD AND SWEET

Elizabeth Turner

ZEBRA BOOKS
KENSINGTON PUBLISHING CORP.
http://www.zebrabooks.com

ZEBRA BOOKS are published by

Kensington Publishing Corp.
850 Third Avenue
New York, NY 10022

Zebra and the Z logo Reg. U.S. Pat. & TM Off.

First Printing: October, 2000
10 9 8 7 6 5 4 3 2 1

Printed in the United States of America

For Beth and Greg,
with love

Chapter One

"I hate it. I hate it. I hate it."

The phrase became a mantra as Gillian Stafford pushed through the waist-deep tangle of dried winter grass. Two weeks on this godforsaken island in the middle of nowhere, and still no word from her father. She was tired of waiting, wondering, worrying. In the beginning, she had felt appropriately chastised. Even remorseful, but no longer.

When she did meet her father, she would simply lie and tell him that her visit was prompted by loneliness—or perhaps boredom. There would be no reason for him to doubt her story. Unless . . . Her stomach knotted in fear. Unless, by some unforeseen stroke of misfortune, a letter from Aunt Phoebe managed to reach him before she did.

Impatiently, she slapped a bush out of her way. Seconds later she muttered an oath as her scarlet pelisse caught on a pricker bush. Jerking it free, she ignored the cluster of burrs clinging to its hem and forged ahead. When her father, Captain Randolph Stafford, of His Majesty's 6th Royal Veteran Battalion, finally sent some of his troops to escort her from St. Joseph's Island to Mackinac Island, where he was stationed, she'd explain that her impulsive trip had been a horrible mistake. She'd demand that he allow her to return to England—immediately.

A brisk breeze swept down from the north, tugging a wisp of blond hair from its neat coil. Didn't spring ever come to this blasted place? It felt more like January than April. Gillian tucked the wayward strand behind her ear and kept walking. The small party of soldiers who had accompanied her across Canada had left her in the care of aging voyageur André Tousseau while they proceeded farther west. The fort here on St. Joseph's Island had been deserted by the British at the onset of the war with the Americans. André was one of the few to remain. His constant cheerfulness was wearing on her nerves. How could anyone be cheery first thing in the morning? It was uncivilized. As fond as she had grown of the little Frenchman, she feared she'd go mad if not rescued soon.

Pausing to catch her breath, Gillian turned and tried to gauge the distance she had strayed from the fort. To her surprise, she discovered she had ventured farther than she thought. The sun had already begun to sink in the sky. As she was about to start back, a movement in the tall grass caught her eye. She watched with growing trepidation as bushes and weeds parted in the wake of an invisible predator. Something—or someone—was slowly but definitely advancing toward her.

Stories of wild savages and ferocious beasts flooded her mind. Gillian picked up her pace, glancing back over her shoulder as she did so. Whatever, or whoever, followed quickened theirs also.

Her pulse skittered with fear. Only that morning, André had recounted tales of harrowing escapes from wild animals that inhabited the northwoods. *"She-bears are dangerous in the spring, m'selle. Take care. They will claw your heart out to protect their young."*

With the little man's dire warning ringing in her ears, Gillian turned and fled, not heeding the direction in which her feet carried her.

Her heart slammed against her rib cage. Convinced her pursuer was a bear, she felt the earth vibrate beneath her feet from the animal's heavy tread. Twigs rustled and snapped as it bounded closer, and closer. In her imagination, she could smell its fetid breath as it narrowed the gap between them. Any minute, any second, it would pounce, slicing her to bits with its razor-sharp claws.

The tall winter grass yielded to rockier terrain. Gillian stumbled to a halt at the edge of a steep bluff where the earth dramatically dropped away. Another step and she would have fallen. She teetered on the brink, caught her balance, then stood frozen in place.

Below, on the narrow pebbled beach, stood an Indian warrior. A man with eyes dark as sin and shoulder-length hair as black as a raven's wing. He gazed back at her, his expression fierce, bordering on hostile. He uttered not a single word, but merely regarded her with a scowl.

Gillian bit her lower lip in indecision. She could run no farther. Wild savage, or ferocious beast? Drawing a shaky breath, she made her decision. She gestured frantically toward the direction from which she had just come. "A b-bear . . ."

Her words spurred the warrior into action. Positioning himself directly beneath her, he held out his arms and motioned for her to jump.

She cast a final glance over her shoulder. The brush waved back and forth as the animal darted about. Could a bear sense when its prey was cornered? Did bears toy with their victims before moving in for the kill?

"Hurry!" the warrior urged.

Which danger was greater? Leaping into the arms of a savage, or being ravaged by a wild beast?

"Jump!" the Indian shouted.

Above the frantic thudding of her heart, she heard a deep, rumbling growl at her back. Squeezing her eyes shut, Gillian leaped into space.

The force of her fall sent them both crashing to the ground. Their bodies locked together, they rolled over and over, his absorbing the brunt of the fall. They rolled to a stop not far from where the lapping waves kissed the shore. Gillian lay on top of him, unmindful of the skirts and petticoats twisted about her thighs. Dazedly, she stared into the face of her rescuer. Fascination sparred with fear for dominance. The man filling her vision was intriguingly handsome with a strong jaw, a Romanesque nose, and elegantly sculpted cheekbones. His eyes, instead of black as she had originally thought, were the dark brown of rich chocolate. His hard body perfectly cushioned her softer one.

"Are you hurt, m'selle?"

Gillian was shocked to hear a faint but unmistakable French accent in the deep baritone. A warrior who spoke French? How odd, she mused. Or had she struck her head on a rock?

"Are you hurt?" he repeated.

"No," she managed. She shook her head in answer to his query and to dispel a vague disorientation that seemed to cloud her senses.

Frown lines formed between the man's black brows. Reaching up, the warrior slowly ran his hands down her rib cage, then traced the gentle flare of her hips. Gillian sucked in a quick breath at the intimacy. The man's hands spread heat wherever they touched. Alarmed by her response as much as the action itself, she jerked away.

"Take your hands off me this instant, you . . . savage."

His hands stilled, the frown deepened. "Forgive me, m'selle. I worried you might have broken a bone in the fall."

"My bones are intact, thank you very much." Belatedly aware that she was sprawled on top of him, skirts and petticoats hiked about her hips, Gillian scrambled to her feet. Lithe as a cat, the warrior sprang upright and studied her. Gillian stared back. From his bland expression, it was impossible to guess what was going through his mind.

So, Luc du Pré thought to himself, this was the British captain's daughter. Gillian Stafford was a beauty all right. No doubt about it. Eyes the beguiling blue of a Michigan lake, hair the color of summer wheat, skin like pale ivory. A single look and Luc could see why the old man set better judgment aside. The girl must have her father wrapped around her baby finger. This was the only explanation he could find for allowing a woman to visit a country trapped in the jaws of war.

Luc watched as Gillian brushed dirt from the cherry red wool. He was relieved to note color creeping back into her cheeks and a temper flaring in her eyes. "You're certain you're all right?"

"No, I'm not all right," she snapped. "I've just been chased by a bear, forced to leap from a cliff, my hair is a mess, and my pelisse is torn. Now," she added, giving him a meaningful glance, "I'm at the mercy of an Indian with a French accent."

"I trust you will survive that too, m'selle."

A rustling noise at the top of the bluff drew his attention. Narrowing his eyes, he craned his neck for a better look. The woman had claimed to have been chased by a bear. He waited, fully expecting to see the shaggy head peering back at him. Instead, he saw something totally unexpected. His jaw dropped in amazement. His next reaction was to laugh out loud, but his amusement swiftly changed to disgust. The idiot woman could have broken her pretty neck leaping from the bluff.

"Did you see it?"

"Oui," he said, nodding slowly. "I saw your bear."

Turning on his heel, Luc stalked down the beach. Gillian Stafford might be as pretty as an English rose but, he reminded himself, he had never been partial to roses. Too many thorns to suit his taste.

Gillian stopped flicking off grime from her pelisse to stare after him in puzzlement. Then she angled her neck for a better view of the ledge above. Something up there had caught the man's attention. She had watched his expression change from disbelief to amusement, then to total disdain. But try as she might, she could detect nothing on the cliff above that might have caused the rapid collage of emotion. When she swung around again, her surly rescuer was halfway down the graveled strand.

Hands on hips, she watched his retreating back. "Of all the . . ." she fumed.

With a start, she realized dusk was rapidly approaching. Night would soon cloak the island in darkness. Unless she wanted to scale the sheer rock wall and, perhaps, confront an angry she-bear, she had little choice but to follow the Indian who had rescued her. She lifted her skirts and picked her way along the beach after him.

Not once did the man look back to see whether or not she followed. Indeed, he seemed oblivious to her presence. Indifferent to the fact that she had nearly been eaten alive by a vicious beast. She had been correct in calling him a savage, Gillian concluded. He possessed absolutely no manners. An Englishman, regardless of social class, would have gallantly insisted upon escorting her back to safety.

Approximately a quarter of a mile farther down, the warrior veered inland and began climbing a path along the steep embankment. Gillian trailed behind. Using scrubby bushes as handholds, she made her slow, perilous way upward. Halfway to the top, she paused to catch her breath. The Indian had already reached the summit. Starkly silhouetted against a dun-colored sky, he could have been a figure carved from granite. He stood, arms folded across his broad chest, staring down at her, wordlessly commanding her to follow his lead.

Even from a distance, Gillian sensed the challenge in his eyes.

Afraid? Yes, she admitted inwardly, she was afraid. Many things in this strange new country frightened her, terrified her. Its vast wilderness surrounded, diminished, intimidated. Crude and uncivilized, nothing appeared familiar, everything seemed strange. Even the people added to her unease. The man in front of her was a prime example. Strong, fiercely independent, proud, he made her aware of her shortcomings, her insecurities. She tried to hide these behind a bold facade. Sometimes she succeeded, other times she failed miserably.

An intense longing for home, for England—comfortable and safe—assailed her. She felt lonely and frightened. And worst of all, she knew it was entirely her fault. Her own foolish behavior was to blame for landing her in this predicament. Emotion crested inside her like a mighty wave upon the shore, then receded, leaving her shaken and uncertain in its aftermath.

Gillian closed her eyes against the onslaught of sadness, then opened them, squared her shoulders, and met the gaze of the man on the trail above. She expected to see smug superiority reflected there, but instead she glimpsed fleeting approval before he turned and vanished from sight.

By the time Gillian scrambled to the rocky crest, the warrior had disappeared. The deserted fort and André's cabin were barely visible in the waning light. As she made her way toward them, the entire incident on the bluff began to assume a sense of unreality. A wild animal, an Indian savage, a desperate plunge into a stranger's arms. Everything had happened so quickly, and with so few words exchanged, that it began to seem like a dream. She quickened her step, eager for André's cheery company to lighten her mood.

As she neared the cabin, she detected the smell of wood smoke mingled with cooking odors. Her stomach gave an unladylike rumble of hunger. André was an excellent cook, but she had learned not to ask the ingredients of the savory dishes placed in front of her. Though muskrat, rabbit, and squirrel were dietary mainstays in this wilderness, she preferred to think of them as animals, and not as the evening's menu.

When she entered the cabin, André Tousseau, a short, barrel-chested man, stopped stirring the contents of a huge iron pot. "Ah, there you are, m'selle. I was beginning to worry." His heavy brows beetled into a frown when he noticed her disheveled appearance. "*Mon Dieu!* What happened? Are you all right?"

His genuine concern unraveled her resolve to ignore the episode. "I narrowly escaped being attacked by a bear."

"A bear . . . ?" He shook his bald head in disbelief. "Here, on St. Joseph's Island?"

She nodded emphatically. "In the meadow west of here. The beast chased me all the way to the cliff overlooking the shore."

"You actually saw this creature?"

"Well, no, I didn't exactly see it," she hedged. "But I heard it crash through the brush. And I saw how the weeds and bushes swayed in its path."

"Strange." André scratched his head. "I haven't seen a bear on this island in years. Not since before the British left. It must have crossed the ice this winter when the channel froze."

Gillian began pulling burrs from her pelisse. "Well, there's one now. A big one."

"You were very brave, m'selle." André clucked his tongue sympathetically, then resumed stirring. "And very clever to have escaped with your life."

"Thank you, André," Gillian replied, basking in his praise.

"Tonight, over dinner, you can tell me the details."

"Mmm. It smells wonderful." She sniffed appreciatively. "Will it be ready soon?"

"Soon, m'selle." He pulled a pan of biscuits from the hearth, then gave her a sly smile. "Wait 'til you see the surprise I have in store for you."

"A surprise?" She paused in the act of tugging at a tenacious clump of prickers near the hem of her pelisse.

"*Oui.*" André grinned gleefully.

Just then the door behind her banged open, emitting a gust of cold air. Gillian whirled around. Her jaw dropped in amazement at finding the Indian warrior who had broken her fall—and perhaps saved her life—standing in the doorway, his arms loaded with firewood.

"You . . . !" she breathed accusingly.

"Ah, *bon*, you two have met." Beaming, André rubbed his hands together in approval. "Even though, m'selle, it spoils my surprise."

Elbowing the door shut, the man advanced into the cabin and deposited the newly split logs in a bin near the hearth. The cabin seemed to shrink even smaller with the warrior's presence. He was taller, broader, more muscular than she remembered. In comparison, André Tousseau looked like a wizened gnome.

"Who are you?" Gillian asked, annoyed that her pulse had accelerated at seeing him again. "And what are you doing here?"

André looked in confusion from one to the other. "Ah, I am mistaken, m'selle? I thought you two had met."

With ease born of habit, the Indian lifted the battered pot resting on the coals and, ignoring Gillian completely, poured coffee into a tin mug. "You were right, *mon ami*, the lady and I have met, but we have yet to be introduced."

"Then allow me." André's grin returned as he turned to Gillian. "M'selle Gillian Stafford, meet Luc du Pré. Luc is the finest bowsman on the Great Lakes; ask any voyageur."

"At your service, m'selle." Luc du Pré gave her a mocking bow.

The man was *French?* All this time she had assumed he was an Indian. She had even called him a savage. Her cheeks stung with embarrassment, remembering how she had sprawled wantonly on top of him. "I doubt I shall require your services, M'sieur du Pré," she replied frostily, retreating behind hauteur.

"Ah, but you will, m'selle."

"Your father sent Luc to bring you to Mackinac," André explained, eager to defuse the awkward situation.

Gillian stared at Luc du Pré in amazement. "Father sent . . . you?"

Calmly, Luc sipped his coffee. "You were expecting someone else?"

Disappointment brought a bitter taste to her mouth. Had she fallen so far from her father's graces that he would entrust her safety to just anyone? "Yes," she managed, her throat clogged with emotion. "I expected Father would send a small company of his soldiers to escort me."

"Perhaps he believes I'm better suited to the task."

André went to a cupboard and pulled plates and cutlery

from a shelf. "Your papa could not have sent a better man."

Giving up the chore of removing burrs from her pelisse, Gillian unfastened the buttons, slipped it off, then hung it on a peg by the door. "What qualifies you, M'sieu du Pré, more than a soldier in His Majesty's service?"

"I am a voyageur," he replied with unmistakable pride.

"A voyageur . . . ?" she repeated. That fact explained the man's odd manner of dress. She eyed him thoughtfully. He wore a thick woolen shirt girdled with a gaudy sash at his trim waist. Deerskin leggings tied below the knees with thongs, an azion or breechclout worn by various Indian tribes, and leather moccasins completed his costume. During her brief stay in Upper Canada, she had observed the hardy breed of men known as voyageurs as they paddled huge birch bark canoes heavily laden with supplies and bundles of furs. Their strength and skill had won her admiration.

He seemed to divine her thoughts. "The Great Lakes are as familiar to me as they are to the beaver and otter."

The man's confidence bordered on arrogance. She desperately wanted to put him in his place. "I confess, M'sieu du Pré, the first time I saw you I mistook you for one of the savages who roam the woodlands."

"You were not mistaken, m'selle." Luc's dark eyes gleamed over the rim of his coffee mug. "I *am* a savage."

"Enough, *mon ami.*" André chuckled uneasily as he ladled stew onto the plates. "You will frighten the beautiful m'selle."

"I do not frighten easily."

Luc gave a short humorless laugh. "Liar," he mouthed, loud enough for her ears alone, as she swept past him.

She forced herself to concentrate on setting out pewter goblets and filling them from a small cask of wine.

"Sit, sit," André urged. "We don't want our dinner to grow cold."

Gillian slid onto a bench on one side of the trestle table, and André and Luc sat on the opposite side. Sitting across from Luc du Pré dulled the edge of her appetite. She took a swallow of wine, then speared a piece of carrot with her fork.

Luc, on the other hand, attacked his meal with gusto. "Actually, m'selle," he said, reaching for a biscuit, "I'm only half savage. My father was a French trapper, my mother Ottawa."

"How interesting," she murmured. "You said my father sent you. Does that mean you're employed by the British?"

André shoveled a forkful of stew into his mouth, then used the rest of a biscuit to mop the gravy from his plate. "The British cannot hope to succeed against the Americans without their Indian allies. The Indian tribes, likewise, have become dependent on British traders. They can no longer live without the white man's weapons, cloth, utensils, and tools. So the two work together."

She took a moment to digest the information, then trained her gaze on Luc. "Exactly what service do *you* perform for the British?"

Cocking his head to one side, Luc considered her question carefully before answering. "My mixed blood enables me to travel back and forth between the two parties and to obtain and impart certain information between the Americans and the British. It's an asset that appealed to His Majesty's forces. Unlike you, m'selle, they were most eager to enlist my services."

"You travel back and forth . . ." She stared at him, her meal forgotten, as the full implication of his admission dawned on her. "Between the British and the Americans . . . ?"

André grabbed the handle of the stewpot. "Anyone for more?"

Both his guests ignored him.

"Then you spy for the British!"

Luc shrugged and continued eating. "I regard myself as a . . . courier."

"More wine anyone?" Not waiting for a reply, André refilled the glasses.

Gillian regarded Luc with cold disdain. "Courier, liaison. Call yourself whatever you wish. You are a spy nonetheless."

Luc gave her a thin smile. "I prefer to think of myself as a man who follows the dictates of his conscience."

André ran a finger around the collar of his plaid shirt. "Does anyone else think it warm in here?"

"There is nothing noble about your motives." She angrily shoved her plate aside. "You follow the dictates of the largest pocketbook."

Luc picked up his wine but made no attempt to drink. "Is that scorn I detect in your voice?"

"Scorn?" André boomed jovially. "*Non*, of course not. You two have only just met. It takes months, sometimes years, for scorn to develop."

Gillian was saved a reply by a scratching at the cabin door, followed by an excited bark. André slid out from behind the table and hurried to admit his canine companion. A big dog with black fur and soulful eyes bounded into the room, tail wagging. Spotting Gillian, the dog padded over to her, plopped down on the floor, and patiently waited for any offerings she might send its way.

"M'selle has made a fast friend in Scout," André explained. "The dog follows her all over the island." When neither Gillian nor Luc responded to his conversational gambit, he threw his hands in the air. "Bah! Everyone is much too quiet. Gillian, *ma petite*, tell us about your encounter with the bear."

She shrugged diffidently. "I wouldn't want to bore M'sieu du Pré, repeating what he already knows."

André's head swiveled in Luc's direction. "You were there, *mon ami?*"

"*Oui.*" Luc sliced a piece of meat.

"Tell me all about it." André thumped his fist on the table for emphasis.

Gillian reluctantly recounted her experience on the bluff, along with Luc du Pré's role in her rescue.

"Amazing." André wagged his head at the story's conclusion. "My friend Luc is a gallant knight coming to the aid of a fair damsel in distress." He raised his wineglass in a salute.

Luc shot the aging voyageur a fulminating look. "And you, you bandy-legged runt, are an incurable romantic."

Gillian sucked in her breath at the insult. To her surprise, however, instead of taking offense, André chuckled. She wondered at the friendship between the two men who seemed total opposites. Absently she broke off part of her biscuit and offered it to the dog still lying patiently at her feet.

Scout lapped it up with a single swipe of its tongue, then, apparently eager for more, pawed at her skirt. "I've spoiled you haven't I, boy?" she murmured, running her hand down its thick coat, then pulled her hand back with a frown. "Naughty dog," she scolded. "Where have you been? Your fur is all matted with burrs."

"That doesn't surprise me, m'selle." André rose and began to clear the dishes. "Scout took off after you as soon as you left on your walk."

Guiltily, Gillian's gaze darted to the red pelisse on a peg near the cabin door. It, too, was matted with clusters of prickly burrs nearly the size of walnuts. Burrs identical to e ones caught in the dog's thick fur. Had it been Scout, nd not a bear, who had chased her across a meadow and ent her plunging off a cliff into the arms of Luc du Pré? o, of course not. It couldn't have been. She would never o anything so foolish. Or had she?

But if it had been, it would lend credence to André's atement that no bears had inhabited the island since efore the war. It would also account for the array of motions that crossed du Pré's face as he looked at the m of the cliff. Had Scout's shaggy head peered back at im?

Heat crept up her neck and suffused her face with bright lor. She wanted to bury her face in her hands, sink rough the floorboards, vanish into thin air. Instead she ragged her gaze from the incriminating pelisse to the an seated across from her.

His lips twitching with ill-concealed humor, Luc du Pré nfirmed her worst fears.

His laughter was the final straw. She rose to her feet, lanted both palms on the tabletop and, leaning forward, oked him square in the eye. "I hate this place. I hate verything about it, including you."

Chapter Two

After dinner, the two men excused themselves. André puffed his pipe as they leisurely strolled toward the abandoned fort. Upon reaching his favorite spot and knowing there was no danger of their conversation being overheard, André lowered himself onto a cross section of felled tree that served as a crude seat.

"Imagine," he chortled, "mistaking Scout for a bear." Luc sank down next to him and stretched out his long legs, crossing them at the ankles. He almost regretted his friend knowing the whole story. But if he hadn't, André would have gone to elaborate measures to track the animal.

"Old Scout, here, gave the poor m'selle quite a scare." André affectionately scratched behind the dog's ear.

"That mutt of yours is nearly the size of a bear." Folding his arms over his chest, Luc leaned back against the wooden stockade. For some unknown reason, he felt compelled to come to the girl's defense. The expression on her face had been one of stark terror. She had been thoroughly convinced her life was in danger. He had also watched comprehension register on her mobile features when she realized she had been mistaken. Comprehension that had been quickly replaced by humiliation. He had almost felt sorry for her—almost.

André puffed contentedly on his pipe. "I remember Scout losing a face-off with a skunk." The memory brought renewed gales of laughter. "I swear, it took the rest of the summer to get rid of the smell."

Luc chuckled at the picture André's words created. He could well imagine his friend trying vainly to rid his pet of the pungent odor.

André wiped at tears of mirth with the sleeve of his jacket. "Don't know when I had such a good laugh."

"Gillian Stafford is accustomed to civilization. More than either Upper Canada or the Michigan Territory has to offer." Luc sighed. There, he was doing it again, coming to her defense. What he didn't understand was why. He didn't even like the woman. She had picked a fine time for a visit if she was bored, restless, and in search of adventure. Now that the idea had soured, she had grown irritable, demanding.

André blew out a puff of smoke. "Now that you've seen her, *mon ami*, what do you think of my guest? I told you she was something."

"Oh, she's something all right," Luc agreed.

"What is it that I hear in your voice? Sarcasm? You don't like her?"

"What is there to like or admire?"

"Don't be so quick to judge. You just met her." André pointed the stem of his pipe at his companion like an accusing finger. "I have often told you that you are much too particular when it comes to women."

"It takes more than a pretty face to impress me."

André cocked his head to one side and studied Luc curiously. "What is it that you are searching for?"

"I'm *not* searching." Luc uncrossed, then crossed his ankles. "When I find the right woman, I'll know it."

"It's time you settle down, start a family."

"And you've had too much wine," Luc said with a grin. "It's begun to addle your brain."

André wriggled his brows suggestively. "You and the beauteous m'selle could make fine babies, *mon ami.*"

Luc hooted in derision. "Now I know for certain your brain is addled. Scout here has more sense."

"Don't be so hard on her, *mon ami,*" André cautioned. "The girl has a good heart. She's unhappy right now, a little frightened by this big country of ours. Be patient with her. She needs time to adjust."

Reaching down, Luc scratched the dog's head, then deliberately changed the subject. "You can tell spring is almost here. The evenings are getting milder."

"*Oui.*" André narrowed his eyes against the wreath of pipe smoke to peer at the sky. "The clouds have moved off and the wind has died down. You should have good weather tomorrow for your journey."

Luc nodded. "Soon summer will be here, and there will be hell to pay."

"What do you hear?" This time when André spoke there was no trace of his customary joviality.

Luc hunched forward, elbows resting on bent knees. "As you know, command of the Great Lakes plays a pivotal role in the campaign. The Americans plan an all out naval attack. They are determined to regain Fort Mackinac."

"With the British equally determined to retain it."

"The British know that if they lose the fort, they lose control over the Indian tribes in the northern Great Lakes—and with it much of the fur trade."

The two sat for a while in silence, pondering the ramifications of an American defeat.

André shifted his weight. "Mackinac Island is virtually inaccessible. It sits too high for naval guns to do much damage."

"True," Luc agreed slowly. "It's high on every side—except one."

"But is the fort well defended? Since the Battle of the Thames destroyed Tecumseh's confederacy, the British have been deprived of many of their Indian allies."

Luc nodded. "I'm well aware of that. In spite of a long winter and many hardships, the British have been busy making fortifications."

"Do you think the Americans stand a chance of success?"

"I hope so," Luc replied in a voice filled with fervor. "I truly hope so."

André knocked ash from the bowl of his pipe, then ground it beneath the heel of his boot. "Has it been decided who will lead the American expedition?"

"Not yet." Luc rose and stretched to ease the tension between his shoulder blades. "There is still much to be considered. With many different personalities involved, leadership must still be decided upon. But my source assures me that the Americans will definitely wage an all-out attack."

"It is a dangerous road that you follow." André's brow furrowed with worry. "I fear for your safety."

Luc shrugged off his companion's concern. "As I told the Stafford girl, I have to follow the dictates of my conscience."

"You deliberately led M'selle Gillian to believe you spy for the British when the opposite is true."

"What else could I do?" Luc shrugged. "I could hardly confess the truth. Did you expect me to tell her I hate all things British—her included? That I won't rest until the bastards are driven back across the ocean where they belong?"

Gripping Luc's shoulder, André squeezed. "Like you, *mon ami*, I harbor no fondness for the British. The sooner they are defeated, the better."

"Amen," Luc agreed solemnly. "Meanwhile, I hadn't planned on being assigned the role of nursemaid of the pampered daughter of a British officer."

André arched a thick brow. "What better way to ingratiate yourself into the man's confidence? Or gain information that might interest our American friends?"

The following morning, Gillian woke before dawn, dressed quickly and, after eating a biscuit with honey, finished packing her belongings in the brass-bound trunk. Restless, she slipped into her pelisse and, donning her high-crowned beaver bonnet, stepped outside. The predawn darkness began to lighten to hazy gray. She inhaled deeply of cool, crisp air. A mourning dove cooed, followed by the screech of a gull. The sibilant whisper of wind sighed through the pine trees.

Without conscious thought to her destination, Gillian made her way along a trail leading away from the cabin. A brisk breeze blowing from the north made her shiver. She pulled her pelisse more snugly about her, then fished a pair of kid gloves from her reticule. She wished she had thought to bring warmer clothing. Spring had yet to make its debut in this northern wilderness. Winter lingered like a tiresome guest. Patches of snow still dotted the forest floor while flotillas of ice bobbed among the waves.

She paused to gaze eastward across the North Channel. The sun was beginning to creep over the horizon, but she was too trapped in reverie to notice. Wrapping her arms around herself to ward off the chill, she was suddenly immersed in memories. In England, tender shoots of green would be poking through a heavy mat of dead winter grass. Buds would have already begun to unfurl. City parks and countryside alike would be awash in delicate hues. Soon the sweet scent of lilacs would perfume the air. She longed for the comforts of home, the stately London town houses, the orderly gardens, the endless rows of shops.

Her rash actions had caused her to be banished to a foreign land. Exiled. Desperation eroded her spirit as relentlessly as the waves pounding the shore below. Dear Lord, what had she done? Did a single lapse in judgment merit such harsh punishment? Luc du Pré had proudly stated that he followed the dictates of his conscience. Well, she had followed the dictates of her heart—and learned to regret it. Tears pricked her eyelids. Never again would her heart overrule her head.

"It's time."

Luc du Pré. Gillian tensed at the sound of the velvety baritone.

"Go away."

"Are you always so cheerful in the morning?"

"Yes," she hissed, rapidly blinking moisture from her eyes. "If you knew what was good for you, you'd go away and leave me alone."

"I hope you're not subject to hysterics."

"Hysterics!" she nearly shrieked as she swung around to face him. "I never have hysterics."

"Really?"

The mockery in his tone heightened the color in her cheeks. "Really." Her hands balled into fists at her sides, the nails biting into her palms. She longed to slap the smirk from his face. He seemed capable of bringing out the worst in her.

"Time is wasting. If we hope to reach Fort Mackinac by nightfall, we need to be on our way."

"Don't tell me what to do," she retorted. "You're here to follow orders, not give them."

"Is that right?"

The voyageur's dark gaze seemed to bore straight through her. Smug, arrogant, superior. Smoldering resentment burst into flame. "You report to my father," she lashed out. "He would have you do as I direct."

Luc studied her coldly. "My orders were to deliver you safely. I'll do whatever is necessary."

Whatever is necessary? Gillian suppressed a shudder. She believed he would do exactly that, regardless of how difficult or unpleasant. Steely resolve undermined his words. It wasn't so much what he said—he seemed a man of few words—but what he left unsaid that gave her pause to consider.

Reluctant to challenge his patience further, she raised her chin a notch. "Fortunately, I'm as eager as you to leave this godforsaken place." Without another word, she turned and marched in the direction of André's cabin. Luc easily matched his pace to hers.

"Ah, there you are." André hurried toward them, his red knit cap bouncing with each step. Scout trotted at his side. "I see you have found the pretty m'selle."

"*Oui,*" Luc grunted.

André turned his gap-toothed grin on Gillian. "Your papa could not have chosen a more skilled voyageur to fetch you. Even though he is a big, clumsy ox."

Gillian's eyes widened as she looked from André to Luc, fully expecting him to take umbrage at the disparaging remark, but instead Luc grinned.

André's dark gaze grew sorrowful as he doffed his knit cap. "I will miss your fine company, m'selle. It has been years since a woman as fair as yourself has graced my humble abode.''

"Ha," Luc snorted. "Scout is the best-looking female that's ever crossed your path, you sawed-off midget."

Ignoring Luc, Gillian rose on tiptoe and brushed a kiss across the man's cheek. "Thank you, André. You have been most kind."

A dull red flush stained skin tanned and seamed by a lifetime spent exposed to the elements. "I . . . ah . . . have taken the liberty of loading your trunk into the canoe."

"*Merci.*" Luc slapped André on the back.

"Canoe . . . ?" Gillian echoed, alarm coursing through her.

Luc lifted a dark brow inquiringly. "You have other means of travel at your disposal?"

"Of course not, but . . ." She silently berated herself for not considering the method of travel sooner. She assumed she'd travel by a vessel considerably larger than a canoe. Perhaps a schooner.

"Do not be afraid, m'selle," André consoled. "Du Pré is strong as a bull. If need be, he can carry you on his back. Never has he lost a single load of cargo."

"Cargo?" she repeated, outraged at the comparison. "I'm hardly a piece of freight to be hauled from one place to the other."

Luc hooked his thumbs into the sash at his waist and leisurely perused her. "You're not very big. During portage, I'm accustomed to carrying burdens many times your weight. If you don't believe me, I could demonstrate."

"Certainly not," she snapped. A sudden warmth rushed over her at Luc du Pré's bold appraisal. She found the notion of being held in his arms disturbing.

"Ah, m'selle," André said. "I think you are woman enough to make even a stubborn ox sit up and take notice. My friend here is too long without a woman."

Luc shot him a quelling glance. "Enough, you sawed-off Frenchman, or I'll toss *you* over my back."

André ignored the threat. Instead he kept up a steady steam of chatter as he followed them down a well-trod path leading to the beach. "Your papa will be happy to see you, *non?*" Not waiting for Gillian's response, he continued. "Wait 'til you see Mackinac Island in the summertime. *Magnifique!* It sparkles like a rare jewel."

Gillian privately doubted she'd find anything to admire about the place but prudently kept her thoughts to herself. With luck, by summer, she'd be on her way home to England.

Her feet dragged to a halt as she spied a lone canoe pulled onto the shore. When Luc mentioned a canoe, she had envisioned one of the sturdier versions she had often observed. In contrast, the one before her was much smaller, frailer. It couldn't have measured more than twenty-five feet from bow to stern. Each end was decorated with a colorful design.

"Surely you don't expect to transport me in such a flimsy vessel?" she asked, making a wide, sweeping gesture. "Why, there's barely room for one person, much less two."

Luc gave an indifferent shrug. "I could leave your trunk behind to create more room."

"Surely you can't be serious?" She stared at him, aghast. "Have you taken leave of your senses? Surely you aren't suggesting I travel with only the clothes on my back?"

"I was simply stating choices."

She glanced at André, hoping to enlist his support, but for once the voluble man was silent, avoiding her gaze.

"Very well," she agreed with ill-humor. "Where do you propose I sit?"

The two men sprang into action. André held the craft steady, and before she could divine Luc's intent, he scooped her into his arms.

"Put your arms around my neck and hang on," he instructed.

Gillian cast a nervous glance at the waves curling along the shore. Impervious to the coldness of the lake, Luc splashed through the water and deposited her on a wooden slat in the bow of the canoe. Reaching behind her, he produced a blanket made of animal pelts and draped it over her shoulders.

"Here," he said gruffly. "The wind off the lake can cut like a knife."

"Thank you," she murmured, already grateful for the fur's warmth. And the unexpected thoughtfulness.

In a smooth, practiced move, Luc climbed into the canoe, settling his weight in the stern. The small craft rocked from side to side, then steadied. Luc picked up a paddle, dipped it into the water, and shoved away from shore.

"Take care," André called after them. "Remember, *mon ami*, your enemies are everywhere."

Gillian didn't have time to dwell on the cryptic warning as the canoe sliced through the waves. She sat unmoving, her spine rigid, her gaze fixed straight ahead, as though through sheer willpower she could prevent the craft from overturning. Soon St. Joseph's Island was far behind. Luc expertly steered the canoe through a narrow channel separating an island on the east from a large peninsula on the west. She clutched the fur wrap more tightly as the channel gave way to a vast body of water.

"Lake Huron," Luc announced without preamble. "One of five that are known as the Great Lakes."

Luc hadn't really expected a reply. A frown formed between his brows as he studied Gillian Stafford's ramrod-stiff back. Miss Stafford was scared senseless. Fear was evident in her tense posture, the determined set of her shoulders. She had scarcely flexed a muscle since he had wrapped the fur around her.

With a heavy sigh, Luc raised his face to the wind, invigorated by its cool caress, and let his thoughts roam. What had the British captain been thinking to allow his daughter to visit at such a time? It was nothing short of miraculous that thus far her journey had been without incident. Luc's sources had informed him that the Americans were committed to reclaiming the fort they had lost to the British at the onset of the war. A battleground was no place for an uppity English miss.

Automatically adopting a familiar rhythm, Luc dug his paddle into the choppy waters, sending the canoe shooting forward. Undoubtedly pampered since birth, Captain Stafford's daughter was as prickly as an English rose—complete with thorns. He doubted whether such a delicate bloom would survive in the harsh northern clime.

His attention was captured by a slight movement from his passenger. As he watched, Gillian slowly bent her head and rubbed her cheek against the lush fur wrap. Then, with innate sensuality, she reached out to stroke the thick pelts. Luc's body responded independently of his brain. He felt a tightening in his groin, almost as though that dainty hand had stroked him instead. The force of his response both surprised and angered him.

Clamping his jaw resolutely, he paddled with renewed vigor. Women rarely had this effect on him. Where Gillian Stafford was concerned, he needed to distance himself. Needed to remind himself that she was the daughter of a high-ranking British officer.

And his sworn enemy.

Chapter Three

The setting sun painted the becalmed lake a brilliant vermilion. The birch bark canoe carrying Gillian and Luc skimmed across the water with the grace of a gull. A cathedral-like stillness descended over the scene like a benediction. In spite of the trepidation she felt about seeing her father, Gillian succumbed to twilight's tranquillity.

"Which is Mackinac?" Gillian asked as several islands came into view.

"The one to the right. The Indians call it Michilimackinac or 'Great Turtle' because of its shape."

Mackinac Island grew larger with each stroke of Luc's paddle. Gillian was surprised to discover it only a fraction of the size of St. Joseph's Island, much smaller than she expected. André had informed her that it wasn't size but location that made the island a valuable asset to both England and the United States. Because it was strategically situated at the junction of Lakes Huron and Michigan, he had explained, whoever occupied that tiny tract controlled a vast area from the Georgian Bay in Canada west to the Mississippi.

"There's the fort," Luc announced.

Gillian turned her head slightly. Fort Mackinac perched atop a limestone bluff like a tiara, overlooking the harbor. Towering blockhouses that guarded thick white walls gave the fort the appearance of a mountain citadel. To Gillian's untrained eye, it looked impregnable, safe. Isolated.

Was her father happy stationed here? she wondered. Somehow she doubted it. He had been passed over for promotions in the past with only his fondness for drinking to blame. In all probability, he viewed this remote outpost as another blow to his lackluster military career.

Gillian placed her hand against her stomach as though the action could still its nervous quivering. The prospect of confronting her father was daunting. He could be a hard, unbending man, traits made worse when he was under the influence of alcohol. It had been over two years since they had last seen each other. During that time, she had changed a great deal—and he, in all likelihood, hadn't changed one whit. Therein lay the problem. She was no longer a girl, but a woman.

With a woman's needs.

On the seemingly endless journey, she had repeatedly rehearsed what she would say to him, tried to anticipate his reaction. All her bravado of the previous afternoon had been washed away by the reality of the present. Father would be furious if he knew the real reason she was here. Communication between the United States and England was unpredictable in the best of times. She could only pray he hadn't heard from her aunt. Now that she and her father were finally about to be reunited, she wished Luc du Pré would turn the canoe around and return to St. Joseph's Island. But there would be no reprieve.

Lifting his paddle, Luc allowed the canoe to drift toward

the island. Not waiting for the craft to scrape bottom, he leaped out and dragged it ashore; then, placing his hands around Gillian's waist, he lifted her from the canoe and deposited her on the ground.

Gillian felt her knees buckle, unable to support her weight after sitting in a cramped position most of the day. Instinctively she clutched Luc's shoulders to keep from falling. He tightened his grip, pulling her against him. "Steady now," he cautioned, his voice low, close to her ear.

She raised her head to thank him, but words fled as she found herself mesmerized by the voyageur's exotically handsome features. His mouth, firm and mobile, held the greatest fascination. Thus far, she had watched it harden into a thin line, then quirk with unexpected humor. What would it be like, she mused, to taste its passion?

Shocked by her brazen thoughts, she pushed against his chest, needing distance. "You can let go of me," she said crisply. "I'm quite capable of standing on my own two feet without your assistance."

Luc ignored her request, keeping his hands firmly around her waist. "Ah, Gillian, do you always find it so difficult to say thank you?"

The strong beat of his heart vibrated against the palm of her hand and sent a tingling up her arm. Being this near was having an odd effect on her breathing, leaving her lightheaded, her thinking fuzzy. Or, perhaps it was hearing him say her name? She was behaving like a silly schoolgirl over a man she barely knew. Irritated by her strange reaction, she snapped, "I don't need some half-breed Indian to instruct me on the rules of etiquette."

Gillian watched Luc's expression harden. She regretted the harsh words the instant they spilled out of her mouth. But it was too late to call them back.

"I must have been misinformed." Dropping his hands

to his sides, Luc stepped back. "I thought well-bred Englishwomen were trained to be polite."

She glared at him. "Are you implying I'm not?"

He arched a brow. "Since when has it been considered good manners to hurl insults?"

Color flooded her cheeks. She stared after him, gnawing her lower lip in indecision. For some perverse reason, she felt the need to erect a wall between him and the unwanted response he elicited from her. She had used insults as bricks to construct that barrier. She was suddenly ashamed of her behavior. Picking up the skirt of her pelisse, she hurried after him.

"I'm sorry," she blurted as soon as she caught up to him and before she could change her mind.

"Apology accepted." He acknowledged the effort with a curt nod. "Your father requested that you be brought directly to him."

"What about my trunk?"

"Your things will be brought up shortly. Captain Stafford doesn't like to be kept waiting."

Gillian bit back a nervous laugh. As she had suspected, her father hadn't changed. "I'm very much aware of my father's likes and dislikes."

Glancing around at her new surroundings, she searched for a diversion. The modest little village huddled along a dirt road fronting the lakeshore offered little of interest. It consisted mostly of a small cluster of wood-shingled cottages made from hand-hewn logs. Splinters of light glowed between closed shutters as citizens gathered for the evening meal. One structure, taller and more pretentious than the rest, stood out from the others. "What is that large building?" she asked.

"The fur warehouse. It's the property of John Jacob Astor's Southwest Fur Company. Pelts are stored and processed there before being shipped."

"It doesn't look very prosperous," she observed as they continued walking. "It seems almost deserted."

"The fur trade has suffered since the start of the war."

She quickened her pace to match his longer strides. "Well, the sooner the British defeat the United States, the sooner things can return to normal."

"The war is far from over." He shot a humorless smile over his shoulder. "The outcome could go either way."

She glanced at him in surprise. "Surely you don't believe the Americans could defeat the British?"

"The British were soundly defeated by the Americans on this very soil not that many years ago."

"A fluke," she retorted promptly.

"Spoken with typical British arrogance," he said with a pitying glance. "Is it possible that young ladies in England aren't versed in subjects such as politics or history?"

"Hmph!" she sniffed. "You're a fine one to criticize *my* education, du Pré. Since my arrival, I've found this wilderness populated with illiterate, ignorant backwoodsmen. Be honest—do you know how to read?"

She interpreted his silence for assent. "You don't have to be embarrassed. It's nothing of which to be ashamed. Many people can't read."

The encroaching dusk lent intriguing planes and shadows to his chiseled features. "I never said I was ashamed," he said gruffly.

There, she had offended him again by her thoughtless remarks. "If you'd like, I could teach you," she offered, trying to make amends.

"That's very generous, but no thank you." He veered left and started up a steep incline leading toward the fort. "Knowing how to read won't help me paddle a canoe, portage a stream, or navigate a river. A voyageur needs a strong back and powerful arms, not a head crammed with letters and figures."

She sidestepped a rut in a path that was becoming increasingly hard to see in the failing light. "Ignorance is more curse than blessing."

"I'm content with my lot as an ignorant savage."

"You speak well for a man who is unlettered." She hoped a compliment would soothe the sting from being illiterate. "That attests to a keen native intelligence."

"You flatter me, m'selle." His mouth twisted in a parody of a smile.

"One should always strive to learn, expand one's horizons."

"As a voyageur I am required to know the waterways. That is enough for me. I leave the ciphering to the clerks and scholars."

"Very well," she said with a shrug. "If you are content . . ."

Luc fumed inwardly. Savage, half-breed. Ignorant backwoodsman. The woman's constant barrage of insults and barbs had finally pierced his thick-skinned indifference. The British always acted so superior, one of their many traits that rankled. How condescending. How typical of them to view others from their lofty position. Well, in time he'd prove they weren't nearly as clever, or as perfect, as they thought themselves.

Gillian Stafford was the epitome of what he despised most about the British, and the opposite of what he found attractive in a woman. André had asked him what he sought in a wife. Well, there were a great many qualities to consider when choosing a life partner. Traits such as loyalty, kindness, and sensibility. All of these were far more important than mere physical beauty. Above all else, a woman had to be strong to withstand the rigors of a fledgling country. Not a delicate hothouse flower like the one trudging beside him. Once the war finally ended and the British were

soundly defeated, there would be time enough to select a
bride.

The heavy wood gate of the fort stood ajar. Luc pushed
and it swung open with a squeak of metal. Stepping
through the arch cut into the thick limestone walls, he
inventoried the scene. Sentries patrolled their posts with
muskets slung over their shoulders. Since the dinner hour
had passed, most of the soldiers were in the barracks playing cards, writing letters, or cleaning their weapons until
taps sounded. Reinforcements would be arriving shortly,
Luc knew, and then soldiers and Indian allies would strain
the fort's resources.

"Your father can usually be found at post headquarters."
He turned, expecting to find Gillian beside him. Instead
he spied her still lingering just outside the gate, her face
drawn with tension. Strange, he thought. Rather than eager
to be reunited with her father, she appeared oddly reluctant.

As though sensing his curious stare, she slowly walked
toward him. "How do I look?" she asked, her voice under-
scored with uncertainty.

His dark gaze swept over her. An entire day spent traveling by canoe hadn't affected her appearance in the least.
If anything, it had heightened it. The sun had brought
becoming color to her cheeks; the wind had loosened silky
golden tendrils to frame her delicate oval face. Anxiety
had deepened the hue of her eyes to purple. His brows
drew together in puzzlement. What reason could she have
to be anxious? Isn't this the moment that had prompted
her journey from one continent to another?

"Well . . . ?" she said. "How do I look?"

"You look . . . very pretty."

His grudging answer was rewarded by a fleeting smile.
"Thank you," she murmured, then squared her shoulders.
"I'm ready."

More puzzled than ever, Luc led the way to post head-quarters. Why did Gillian Stafford look as though he were leading her to an executioner? He had assumed the meeting between father and daughter would be a joyous occasion. Had he been mistaken? Casting a sidelong glance at her, he felt a stirring of sympathy.

His knock on the door was answered by a curt command to enter. Luc held the door open and politely stepped aside for Gillian. But once again she froze on the threshold. Her knuckles shone white from their death grip on her reticule, her fine features drawn taut.

And once again he felt an unbidden stir of sympathy.

"For God's sake, girl, don't just stand there like a ninny," Captain Randolph Stafford barked. "Come in, and close the door."

Gillian's stomach clenched into a fist at her father's tone. For a moment, she feared she would be physically ill. She kept a firm grip on the reticule to keep her hands from shaking. The dreaded moment could be postponed no longer.

"Hello, Father." She took a tentative step forward, praying her voice wouldn't quiver. She didn't notice that Luc had slipped into the room behind her.

"Gillian." Captain Stafford slowly rose from his seat behind a map-strewn desk.

She gave him a nervous smile as she slowly traversed the room. "You haven't changed much. Perhaps a little grayer." There were other changes, too. Subtle ones that she purposely failed to mention. Changes such as the spidery network of veins across his cheekbones and eyes that were bloodshot and a trifle glassy.

He regarded her coldly. "You, on the other hand, have changed a great deal since our last meeting."

"I was barely seventeen then. I'm a woman now."

"Yes, I can see that."

Drawing an unsteady breath, she plunged into the speech she had rehearsed countless times in her head. "I know this visit comes at an inopportune time, Father, but I refused to be a burden to Aunt Phoebe any longer."

"A burden . . . ?" He came out from behind his desk. "In what way?"

Gillian detected the unmistakable odor of alcohol on his breath. "Aunt Phoebe has a beau."

"A beau?"

"His name is Bertram Chiltingham. He's a successful merchant with a home in the country. He seems quite smitten with her actually."

"How very nice for my sister." He locked his hands together behind his back and regarded her quizzically. "But I fail to see how that explains your sudden desire to visit Michigan."

"I feared my presence might interfere with Aunt Phoebe's chance for happiness." She made a helpless gesture. "There was nowhere else to go, so I came here."

"It's commendable that you're so concerned about your aunt's future."

"I sincerely hope Aunt gets what she rightfully deserves." Gillian almost choked on the platitude. Phoebe Stafford couldn't wait to wash her hands of the responsibility. She viewed Gillian as a rival and wanted her out from underfoot.

"So you're telling me my sister's love life prompted an arduous journey through a country at war?"

Gillian shifted uneasily. "That plus the fact that I had become bored with London and was eager for adventure."

"Bored, eh?"

Something in her father's tone caused apprehension to flutter anew. Granted, Randolph Stafford had always been considered undemonstrative, but there was a singular lack of warmth in his welcome that frightened her. She moistened her lower lip with the tip of her tongue. "As I already explained, I had nowhere else to go."

"At least that much of your story is true."

She cleared her throat and fought to remain calm. "What do you mean?"

Turning, he strode to the desk and produced an envelope from the top drawer. "This arrived by special courier last week. It was mixed in with orders from the War Office."

"What is it?" The words came out a whisper.

"It's a letter from your Aunt Phoebe." He shoved the missive into her hands. "Go ahead, read it, then tell me if you deny the charges."

Her reticule slipped from nerveless fingers and landed at her feet with a muffled thud. With shaking hands, Gillian withdrew the sheets of parchment and scanned the spidery backstroke. Her aunt spared no mercy. It was all there, all the gruesome details. She felt the blood drain from her face as she read. The room reeled, tilted.

Dimly she felt a strong hand at her elbow, ready to catch her if she fell. With eyes dilated with shock, she saw Luc at her side, regarding her with something akin to compassion.

"Well, girl, is it true? Can you deny that your aunt interrupted a tryst between you and your lover? A lover who happens to be a married man?" Stafford's sharp words sliced through the air like a whip.

"Yes, it's true," she admitted, her voice nearly inaudible.

"Why, you little tramp!"

Gillian flinched at the harsh epithet.

Fury glinted in Stafford's pale blue eyes like the sun glinting off ice. "How dare you disgrace my good name?"

Gillian was vaguely aware that Luc remained at her side, ready to intervene on her behalf should her father's anger escalate into physical violence.

"What?" Stafford raged. He snatched the sheets of parchment from her unresisting fingers and waved them under her nose. "Have you nothing to say in your own defense, girl?"

An icy calm descended over her, shielding her from the burning heat of her father's temper. "There seems little left to say, Father, since you've already passed judgment."

"Was this the first time you offered yourself to a man—or merely the first time you were discovered?"

Numbed by his assertions, goaded beyond caring, she struck back. "What would you say if I told you I've had many lovers?"

"Were all of them married like this one?" Crumpling the incriminating letter into a ball, he flung it toward the fireplace. It missed its target, landing in a corner by the hearth.

"You could send me back to England," she suggested hopefully.

"What! Grant you further opportunity to damage your reputation? Returning to England is out of the question." Turning on his heel, he strode to his desk, sat down, and stared at her across steepled fingers. "In the past I have been far too lenient with you. You shall remain at Fort Mackinac where I can monitor your behavior. Du Pré, here, will keep an eye on you and report any unseemly conduct."

"But, sir . . ."

"Father, really . . ."

"Silence!"

Gillian glared at Luc, resentment simmering. "I don't need anyone spying on me," she returned sulkily.

"Sir, I'm not a nursemaid," Luc informed the captain with indignation.

"My decision stands. Du Pré, please escort the girl to my quarters." He picked up a map he had tossed aside and resumed studying it. Gillian had been dismissed.

Luc picked up the reticule Gillian had dropped and

returned it to her. Her composure dangling by a thread, Gillian turned and walked across the room, her movements stiff, wooden. She had one hand on the door when her father's voice stopped her.

"Should you ever, *ever,* disgrace me again, girl, you'll be dealt with severely. You'll rue the day you didn't heed my warning."

Unable to force a reply past the stricture in her throat, Gillian slipped outdoors where she drank in huge gulps of the crisp night air to steady her nerves. The meeting with her father had been worse, much worse, than she had anticipated. He had been absolutely livid. All her life she had waited, watched, to see her father display some sign of emotion or hint of affection. But Randolph Stafford had kept his feelings well controlled.

Until tonight . . .

Luc took Gillian's arm and wordlessly guided her across the compound and away from post headquarters. The scene between father and daughter had surprised him. Instead of a joyful reunion, he had witnessed a bitter confrontation. No wonder Gillian Stafford seemed unhappy with her new surroundings.

"This is where you'll be staying. It's known as the officer's Stone Quarters," he announced upon reaching a low, two-storied building also made of thick limestone. "Permit me to see you safely inside."

"All right," she murmured, her voice barely audible.

Bounding up the steps and across the narrow porch, he opened the door and stepped inside. He groped around in the dark until he managed to find a flint and light a lamp. Soon the modest dwelling was filled with a soft glow. Gillian entered cautiously, then stood in the center of the room, gazing around with disinterest.

Luc ran his fingers through his hair, ruffling the shoulder-length mane. He wondered what to do next. Gillian looked ghostly pale, as fragile as a porcelain doll, bearing only a vague resemblance to the spirited, opinionated—and often irritating—young woman he had come to know. He should leave. But he couldn't turn his back and ignore the wounded look in her eyes.

He approached her in measured steps, then reached out, caught her chin between his thumb and forefinger, and tilted her face upward, willing her gaze to meet his. "Was your lover worth all the pain?" he asked quietly.

As he watched in fascination, she came to life. In the blink of an eye, all traces of apathy vanished. Color flooded back into her face. An angry gleam replaced the dull hurt. "How dare you ask such a question!" she flared, jerking away from his touch. "Get out of here this instant. Leave me alone."

Before Luc could savor his victory, Gillian picked up a small glass paperweight from a nearby table. He escaped seconds before the missile landed against the door frame accompanied by the sound of breaking glass.

He couldn't help chuckling as he strolled toward the barracks. There was fire beneath the ice. The lady just might survive in the northwoods after all.

Chapter Four

Gillian's rigid control shattered along with the paperweight. She sank down on the floor, put her face in her hands, and wept. For months she had withstood insults and innuendos, humiliation and heartbreak. But her staunch control had splintered with Luc du Pré's cruel jibe.

Was your lover worth the pain?

Hot tears seeped between her fingers. Jeremy Blackwood had told her that he loved her, said he wanted to marry her, but somehow had failed to tell her that he had a wife. Remembering Jeremy's deception, pain washed over her anew. Gillian cried for what she had done—and what she hadn't. She cried for an innocence that would never again unquestioningly trust a man's tender promises. Honeyed promises that turned bitter.

Gradually Gillian's sobs subsided. Using the hem of her pelisse, she wiped the tears from her eyes, then fished her handkerchief out of her reticule and blew her nose. She felt better after venting emotions she had kept locked inside.

No, she could answer Luc's question with brutal honesty, Jeremy Blackwood *wasn't* worth the pain.

He was a scoundrel. She deserved better. Much better. Filled with resolve, she climbed to her feet, already ashamed of her outburst. She would waste no more tears on the likes of Jeremy. Somehow she'd reconcile with her father. Someday she'd return to England. Somehow she'd find a man deserving of her affection. Someday somehow, some way, she'd emerge victorious.

She removed her beaver bonnet, tucked back strands of blond hair that had escaped, then slipped out of her pelisse and set it aside. For the first time since entering, she looked about with mild curiosity. Her father's quarters consisted of a large room that served as both parlor and kitchen. Rustic, spartan, and devoid of personal touches. Except for a faded damask settee, the only furniture consisted of a pair of uncomfortable-looking chairs, a trestle table with a narrow bench, and a corner cupboard with peeling paint. A fire burned low in a blackened stone fireplace. A rusty bucket holding firewood and kindling sat next to it.

To the right of the fireplace was a doorway. Gillian peeked inside and discovered her father's bedroom. A woolen blanket was pulled taut as a drum across an iron frame bed. A pine chest held a few personal items. Curiosity drew her farther into the room. Her hands trembled slightly as she picked up a small silver frame containing miniatures of her mother and herself. Seeing the image of her mother was like looking into a mirror. Only the eyes were different. Those she had inherited from her father. She returned the frame to the dresser and left the bedroom, feeling like an intruder. Knowing her father kept her picture among his treasures buoyed a small kernel of hope that their relationship might be salvaged.

Upon returning to the main room, she noticed a narrow flight of stairs nearly concealed by shadows. Picking up the oil lamp, she cautiously ascended the steep steps and found herself in a loft obviously intended as her sleeping quarters. A crude cot covered with a patchwork quilt stood under the eaves. A washstand with a basin and a pitcher stood in one corner while a small dresser occupied another. Gillian's mouth twisted into a wry smile at seeing the Bible strategically placed at her bedside. Her father evidently thought her in dire need of redemption.

Going to the window, she unbolted the shutters and peered out. From her vantage point she could make out the forms milling about, heard the murmur of voices speaking a strange tongue. Indians from many tribes, du Pré had said, were gathering on the island to lend their support to the British in their battle against the Americans. Even with the knowledge that they were allies, she felt distinctly uneasy under their impenetrable dark stares. And their sheer numbers terrified her. Maybe at this very moment they were watching her stand at the window. Quickly she drew the shutters closed.

A banging from downstairs startled her. Who could it be? she wondered. Her father would never knock before entering his own quarters. She cast a hasty glance in the silvered glass tacked above the dresser. She scarcely recognized the disheveled woman with the tearstained face and hair straggling untidily about her shoulders. The noise sounded again, more insistent this time. There was no time to do anything about her appearance. With a sigh, she tucked a wayward strand behind one ear, smoothed the wrinkles from her dress, and hurried toward the stairs.

Easing the door open several inches, she squinted into the darkness. "Who is it?"

"It's me. Open the door and let me in."

Gillian instantly recognized the voyageur's smooth baritone. "You again?" she asked, angling her body to bar his entry.

"You were expecting someone else?"

"No, of course not." Why did he have to return and find her with her eyes red-rimmed and puffy from crying? She didn't want him to know that his parting words had wounded her. "What do you want?"

"I brought your trunk. Do you want me to leave it on the porch for the raccoons to pry open, or are you going to let me in?"

After the unpleasant altercation with her father, she had completely forgotten about her belongings. Reluctantly she opened the door and granted him entry. Seeing him stooped beneath the weight of her trunk, she was instantly remorseful for her hesitation. It had taken two burly seamen to carry the brass-bound leather trunk from her aunt's carriage up the gangway of the ship.

"You'll strain your back. Was there no one to help you?"

"No," he grunted. "Besides, I'm accustomed to transporting loads heavier than this. Now, where is your room?"

He started toward the back bedroom, but she stopped him midway. "No, up there," she said, pointing at the steps leading to the loft.

"Unless you want me to break my neck in the dark, you'll have to go ahead of me and light the way."

"Very well," she agreed, picking up the lamp and preceding him up the stairs.

He adjusted the trunk slightly to accommodate the narrow passageway, then followed her.

Gillian marveled at his strength as he moved effortlessly beneath the heavy burden. The muscles in his arms and chest bulged from the strain, yet he was able to carry on a conversation without loss of breath, and not a singe drop of perspiration moistened his brow.

"Where do you want me to set it?"

She motioned toward the foot of the cot. "This will do."

He put it down in the place she had indicated and looked around with interest. Gillian felt a flood of embarrassment. Her sleeping quarters here were far different from her luxurious bedroom in London, with its elegant Queen Anne furniture and blue silk draperies and bed hangings. This small room under the eaves was more befitting a convent.

She felt the need to apologize for its simplicity. "It's not much . . ."

"What did you expect?"

She searched Luc's face, expecting cynicism but finding curiosity instead. His question caught her off guard. *What had she expected to find?* "Truth is, I hardly gave it a thought," she replied, dismissing the question with a shrug. "No matter. I plan to return home as soon as I can persuade my father."

Cocking his head to one side, he folded his arms across his broad chest and studied her thoughtfully. "Considering the pending American attack, your speedy departure may have to be postponed."

"I don't remember asking your opinion, du Pré," she said, trying to ignore the flutter of apprehension in the pit of her stomach. "I just need time to convince Father."

He turned and started downstairs. "You'll need more than time, m'selle," he said over his shoulder. "You'll need luck."

Gillian gnawed her lower lip. Though loath to admit it, she secretly suspected Luc's assessment was correct. Her father could be obstinate and, at the moment, too preoccupied with military matters to be concerned with her situation. How on earth *was* she going to survive in this remote outpost for any length of time with her sanity intact? There would be no carriage rides through the park, no leisurely strolls down streets lined with shops, no evening soirees.

No opera, theater, or ballet. How would she wile away long, lonely days? With a sigh, she slowly descended the steps, the lamp held high in front of her.

Luc stood, his back turned, coaxing life into the sluggish flames in the hearth. Grateful for the meager warmth, Gillian set the lamp aside, crossed to the fireplace, and held out her hands. Suddenly she felt overwhelmed with the day's events. The long hours spent in a canoe, her father's vitriolic attack, the grim prospect of having to remain in Michigan indefinitely, all exacted their toll. Her shoulders slumped with fatigue and, in spite of her resolution to the contrary, once more she felt perilously close to tears.

Luc rested the poker against the hearth. "I brought something you might need."

Gillian's glance followed him as he strode across the room, opened the door, and retrieved an object he had left on the porch.

"I thought this might prove useful until warmer weather sets in," he explained as he casually tossed the item in her direction.

She caught it automatically. Instantly recognizing the lush throw he had supplied for the lake crossing, she hugged it to her chest like a long-lost friend. The pelts were luxuriant, thick and soft. Warm. Costly. A knot lodged in her throat at his unexpected thoughtfulness. "These are worth a fortune."

"They're only mink pelts. Beaver and fox are the expensive furs."

"Still, I can't accept . . ."

He cut her off. "Furs are common currency among my mother's people. If it makes you feel more at ease, I'll add them to the price your father already owes me."

Gillian stared at Luc over the throw. The firelight cast his exotic features in intriguing planes and angles. Sculpted cheekbones, square jaw, firm, sensual mouth. His eyes shadowed, his expression shuttered, he watched her with equal intensity. Though still a stranger, she sensed the fur had been offered more from kindness than greed.

She absently stroked the mink throw, trying to find a way to acknowledge his largesse without giving offense. Before she could frame a reply, a knock sounded on the door.

"Private Bunton, miss. Captain's orderly," a young male voice rang out. "Brung yer supper."

Gillian opened the door to find a sandy-haired, freckle-faced youth who appeared to be no more than seventeen. The private carried a covered tray. "Where should I put this, miss?"

She directed the soldier to set it on the trestle table in front of the hearth.

"Nothin' fancy, miss. The fort's low on supplies, but better now since at least one of the supply boats managed to get through. Winter was a bad one, that's fer sure. Thought we'd all starve to death before spring got here."

"I'm certain the meal will be adequate, Private Bunton. Please thank my father for sending it."

Bunton grinned slyly, revealing a wide gap between his two front teeth. "Captain didn't order it, the half-breed did. He told Cook to put together a nice supper tray."

Once again she was in Luc du Pré's debt. Rules of etiquette drilled into her since childhood dictated that she properly acknowledge his effort, yet she disliked being beholden to him. Drawing a deep breath, she began hesitantly, "I appreciate . . ."

Turning, she found Luc already gone. So much for good manners. He already knew she disliked having to thank him. He hadn't even bothered to bid her good night. Oddly, the oversight left her feeling vaguely disappointed.

"If there ain't nothin' else, miss," Bunton said, "Reveille

sounds awful early, seein' how the ol' man's dead set on completin' a new fort on higher ground."

"The old man . . . ?"

Bunton colored. "No offense, miss. That's how some refer to Captain Stafford."

After the young soldier's hasty departure, Gillian removed the napkin from the supper tray. Her dinner consisted of a boiled potato, a piece of fish, and a baked apple, along with a pot of tea. Plain fare, but to her, as sumptuous as a banquet. By the time she finished the tea, she was fighting fatigue.

Picking up the fur throw, Gillian trudged upstairs where she quickly undressed and slipped into a long-sleeved nightdress. She removed the pins from her hair and plaited it into a single braid, then spread the fur across the cot and climbed between the coarse cotton sheets.

Snuggling beneath the warmth and weight of the mink pelts, she closed her eyes and sighed. "Tomorrow," she mumbled as she drifted toward sleep. "Somehow I'll find a way to mend bridges with Father. Tomorrow . . ."

Clouds the color of tarnished silver trailed across the crescent moon, leaving the night swathed in darkness. With a final look to make certain no one observed his movements, Luc slipped inside the narrow opening of Skull Cave.

"What took you so long, du Pré?"

Luc waited for his vision to adjust to the inky gloom. Gradually he made out the stocky figure squatting at the rear of the cave as that of the man who acted as his liaison with the American forces. "I waited to make sure no guards were posted at the new fortification."

"There're no men to spare for the task."

"Yet," Luc corrected. "British reinforcements are expected soon."

"Any word about the new commander?"

"Not yet, but Stafford wants to make a good impression on his new superior."

The man known as Toad spat a stream of tobacco juice on the rocky floor of the cave. "What's the captain's daughter like?"

Luc scowled. How could he describe Gillian Stafford? Haughty? Pampered? An intriguing blend of fire and ice? "She's young," he replied diffidently. "Hardly more than a girl."

"Pretty or plain?"

Luc shrugged. "Pretty enough, I suppose."

"You're a sly one," Toad said with a throaty chuckle. "Closemouthed. Always careful not to say too much, but that's where your value lies. If you admit to pretty, she's probably closer to beautiful."

Wordlessly, Luc sank to his haunches next to Toad. *Face of an angel.* Until now he hadn't even admitted to himself the impact Gillian Stafford had had on him. Seeing her standing on the bluff overlooking the lake had quite simply stolen his breath away. Never before had a woman had that impact on him. He had chosen to ignore rather than explore the incident. It was simpler, safer, that way.

"I want you to stick close to her side," Toad continued. "Make yourself indispensable. Win her trust. She could prove valuable."

Luc shifted his weight, laced his fingers together, disliking the notion. "What importance can a mere slip of a girl have? War is between men. Women and children shouldn't be used as pawns."

Toad regarded the younger man with a jaundiced eye. "In times of war, my friend, man or woman, young or old, makes no difference. One does whatever necessary to ensure victory. You are committed to American success, aren't you?''

"You dare to question my loyalty?" Luc bristled. "I'm willing to do everything within my power to help the Americans defeat the British."

"Good." Toad thoughtfully chewed his wad of tobacco. "Washington is counting on us to relay any new developments. Now that the British have soundly defeated Napoleon, they're free to turn their full attention to war efforts here. Not even the Duke of Wellington can promise success without control of the Great Lakes. That's why it's imperative that the Americans recapture the fort."

"You know I'll do whatever is necessary."

"The War Department is planning an army-navy assault. There are problems, but they should soon be resolved. The plan is to attack by early summer."

"Summer ..." Luc did a rapid calculation. This was already the end of April. The assault could come in as little as two months' time. "The quicker the Americans strike, the better their chance for success. British reinforcements have yet to arrive and fortifications still aren't complete."

Toad rubbed his shaggy black beard. "If the need arises, the Stafford girl might prove a useful hostage. What is the girl's relationship with her father? Is it sound?"

"They're at odds."

Toad's beady eyes narrowed with interest. "Why is that?"

"Some misunderstanding," Luc replied, attempting to keep his tone neutral. "Apparently it involved an incident that happened while she was in London."

Toad dropped his amicable pose. "Give me details, not drivel."

"Surely this can't be of importance."

"That's my decision, not yours."

Luc stared unseeingly toward the mouth of the cave. His conscience wasn't bothered in the least when it came to exchanging information gleaned from the British to aid the American cause. He felt a twinge of guilt, however, at confiding Gillian's personal secrets to the enemy.

"Well . . . ?" Toad prompted.

Luc sighed, despising himself for what he was about to do. "It seems the girl took a lover while in England. The gentleman in question turned out to be already married."

Toad let out a low whistle. "So Stafford's daughter is susceptible to a man's attention." He glanced at Luc speculatively. "I've seen the way women look at you, du Pré, when they think you're not watching. Don't know what it is, but women seem to find you attractive. Perhaps the chit will too."

"Just a minute." Luc held up a hand in protest. "First you talk of abduction. Now you have me seducing the girl. I want no part of either plan."

Toad dismissed his objection with a careless wave of his hand. "From what you've just said, the girl is hardly an innocent."

Luc remained silent as Gillian's face flashed across his memory. Fine-boned features, guileless blue eyes, skin like porcelain. Regardless of past indiscretions, she did, indeed, portray a vision of innocence. Innocence waiting to be awakened by a man's touch. In spite of the English lover, there was a certain purity, a vulnerability, that hovered about her like an elusive perfume.

"We'll meet again soon." Toad climbed to his feet and stretched. "In the meantime, cultivate a friendship with the girl. Learn her habits. You never know if this information could prove useful later. After all, she is Stafford's only child."

Luc rose slowly and watched his contact leave the cave and disappear into the night. Wearily, he pinched the bridge of his nose between thumb and forefinger. How much longer would the war last? And at what cost? How could a new country gain strength with all its resources strained to the breaking point?

When he had volunteered his services to the American forces, he had been told that he would be most useful to them as a spy. His mixed blood provided him undisputed passage between the white men and their Indian allies. His duty was to keep the Americans apprised of British activity, the arrival of reinforcements and supplies, and alliances with various Indian tribes. The British also believed he worked for them. They would be surprised to learn the information he passed to them was essentially worthless. Trivial facts that would soon be considered common knowledge.

Until now he had never balked at following orders, but he found Toad's suggestion of using Gillian Stafford repugnant. He was a descendant of Pontiac, the great Ottawa chieftain. His ancestors had fought face-to-face on a field of honor; they didn't use defenseless women to further their cause.

Luc left the cave. A brisk wind from the north whistled through the barren limbs. Even now the days were perceptibly longer, the nights not as cold. The seasons were about to change as a youthful spring nudged aside an aging winter. Soon, summer would burst forth in all her glory. Luc knew that if he wanted to win Gillian Stafford's confidence, there was no time to delay. Besides, who was he to question his higher command? The Americans insisted he keep a close eye on the English rose.

And he would.

He started down an unmarked path that led to a small cabin situated near Arch Rock, along the island's eastern shore. His thoughts drifted to his last encounter with Gillian. Her eyes had been red-rimmed and puffy from recent tears. What had caused the proud beauty to weep? he wondered. With a start, he recalled his parting thrust. *Was your lover worth the pain?*

Had his query precipitated her tears?

His gut twisted at the realization. The girl must have loved the man who first betrayed her then broke her heart. Knowing he had also caused her pain brought a sharp stab of regret.

He had never meant to make her cry.

Chapter Five

The next morning when Gillian woke, she lay unmoving for a long moment, staring at the exposed eaves above her narrow cot. She had dreamed she was home, surrounded by the familiar, the comfortable, the luxurious. She moved her head slightly, and the fur throw tickled her cheek, bringing a smile to her lips. In England she had had to rely on goose-down comforters for warmth during winter months. Until now, she had never been treated to a covering as soft, or as warm, as the one Luc du Pré had thoughtfully provided.

Dragging it around her shoulders, she swung her legs out of bed, padded to the window, and threw wide the shutters. She could see beyond the fort's thick walls and across the shimmering sapphire waters to a band of virgin forest on the opposite shore. Gulls screeched loudly as they wheeled against a sky such a vibrant blue that it hurt her eyes. She drew in a deep breath of air, crystalline and pure, scented with cedar and pine. A wave of pure pleasure washed over her.

She had no idea how late she had slept. Cocking her head to one side, she listened intently for any sound from the living quarters that might indicate another presence but was greeted by silence. Her father, always an early riser, must have already left for the day. But, she resolved, she wouldn't allow him to avoid her quite so easily. Quickly washing her face and hands, she pulled a burgundy wool walking dress out of her trunk, smoothed out the wrinkles, and slipped it on. After arranging her hair in a neat chignon at the base of her neck, she went downstairs.

As she expected, her father was nowhere in sight. A plate containing a slice of cornbread and a tin of tea, however, had been placed on the table. A kettle of water simmered on the hearth. After breakfast, she spent the rest of the morning unpacking and arranging her belongings. When a soldier delivered the noon meal, she realized that her father had no intention of returning until much later. Bored and restless, she slipped an apple into her pocket, tossed a paisley shawl over her shoulders, and went in search of him.

She found him at post headquarters, pen in hand, bent over a pile of crude sketches spread across his desk. She paused on the threshold for a moment to study him before making him aware of her presence. His light brown hair was now liberally threaded with silver. His patrician face seemed thinner, the lines etched deeper. He looked far older than she remembered. Older, and weary.

She cleared her throat to draw his attention. "Good morning, Father."

Frowning, he glanced up from his work. Eyes the same startling blue as her own regarded her with ire. "Gillian," he said, his voice clipped. "What brings you here? Can't you see I'm busy?"

"We've seen nothing of each other since I arrived."

"I returned late last night. You were already asleep."

Entering, Gillian approached his desk. "I hoped we might talk."

"This is hardly the time for idle chatter." He waved his hand over the mound of paperwork. "I have duties to oversee if the fort is going to be able to withstand an assault by the Americans this summer."

"An assault?" The thought unnerved her. She moistened her lower lip with the tip of her tongue. "Then it isn't just speculation. . . ."

Randolph Stafford tossed his quill down in frustration. "Are you slow-witted, girl? The country is at war. In a few months' time, this fort will be under siege."

She twisted her fingers together to keep them from trembling. Hearing her father's pronouncement added a finality that had been lacking before. "Is there a possibility that the Americans will succeed?"

He sent her a withering look. "Don't be ridiculous. Of course not, but we must take precautions all the same. We won't make the same foolish mistakes the Americans did when we captured Mackinac from them in July of 1812."

"How can you be so certain?"

"A new fort is being erected on higher ground so that it can protect Mackinac where it's most vulnerable."

Gillian released a shaky sigh of relief. Her father seemed to have the situation well under control. Still, a trace of apprehension lingered. She would be glad when she was safely back in England where she belonged, away from this viper's pit.

Randolph pushed back from his desk and, hands behind his back, paced the width of his office. "I wasn't going to discuss this until I saw you this evening, but as long as you're here, we might as well lay down some ground rules."

"Yes, Father," she returned, mentally bracing herself

for another lecture. At least, she consoled herself, her father appeared much calmer—and sober—this morning.

"Since receiving your aunt's letter, I've given the matter of your moral lapse considerable thought."

"But Father . . ."

"Don't interrupt!" he ordered. "Have you no manners?"

"S-sorry."

He scowled at the floor as he paced. "I'm ready to accept partial responsibility for your actions. I've been negligent. In an effort to make it up to you for not having a mother, I've overindulged you. I made sure that you never lacked for anything."

Anything but a father's affection. She bit her lip and kept her rebellious thoughts bottled inside.

"I spoiled you, but that behavior will cease. It's high time you have a taste of life's harsh realities. You're long overdue. Here on Mackinac you'll have duties to perform, the same as everyone else. The care and cleaning of our quarters will no longer be Private Bunton's responsibility, but yours. From time to time you'll be called upon to act as my hostess at social functions. In the meantime, I expect you to make yourself useful every way possible."

"Allow me to return to England. Please, Father." The plea burst out of its own accord. "I'll be the model of propriety, I vow, not a single breath of scandal, not one raised eyebrow."

"Impossible," he informed her coldly. "We're in the midst of a war. And even if we weren't, the idea is preposterous. What do you propose you'd do in England? Who would assume responsibility for you?"

In her eagerness, she reached out and placed a hand on his sleeve. "I'll write Aunt Phoebe and beg her forgiveness. I promise both of you, my behavior will be above reproach."

"Phoebe has washed her hands of you. And rightly so, I might add." He shook off her touch and returned to his seat.

Her hopes dampened but not crushed, Gillian persisted, knowing this might be her only opportunity to persuade her father. "If Aunt Phoebe is unwilling, I have the trust Grandmother left me in her will. I could purchase a town house and hire a housekeeper or a chaperon."

Her father dismissed the notion with a wave of his hand. "In case you've forgotten the terms of the trust, until you reach the age of twenty-one or marry, that money is out of your control."

Gillian hung her head, defeat bitter in her mouth. "I hate it here."

"Consider it penance." Randolph Stafford opened a ledger then picked up his quill, indicating that the conversation had concluded. "If you'll excuse me, I have pressing matters that need my attention."

Aware further argument would be useless, Gillian turned and left. Her throat ached from the effort of holding back tears and her eyes burned. Yet she held her head high as she exited the post headquarters, determined not to betray how her father had wounded her.

Once outside in the bright sunlight, she paused to collect herself. She swept her gaze around the enclosure, trying to decide what to do next. She jumped, startled, as a cannon boomed from the heights beyond the fort. Her heart rate slowed to normal, however, when she noted that, except for herself, no one appeared alarmed by the blast. Feeling somewhat foolish, she realized some of the soldiers were engaged in target practice.

"Hup, two, three, four." The drill sergeant's voice rang out. Gillian turned to watch a group march back and forth on the muddy parade ground in front of her. A tall, gangly private was the first to notice her interest. Immediately, his sullen expression dropped away, replaced with speculation. Distracted, his stride slackened, causing the men behind him to collide into one another.

"You bloody idiots!" the sergeant bellowed at his hapless men. "Can't you dummies walk and think at the same time?"

The private who had precipitated the incident cleared his throat. "Sergeant, sir . . ."

"What the bloody 'ell? Speak up, man! Devil got yer tongue?"

The private bobbed his head sideways. "There's a lady present, sir."

The sergeant whipped around. His complexion mottled with embarrassment as he noticed the captain's daughter quietly standing near the post headquarters. He doffed his hat and gave a short bow. "My apologies, Miss Stafford. I didn't meant any disrespect."

"None taken, Sergeant," Gillian assured him. "Please proceed." Then, not wanting to be responsible for further disruption, she started toward the open gate leading out of the fort. Apparently news of her arrival had traveled quickly. Someone, it seemed, enjoyed passing gossip.

Luc du Pré seemed to materialize out of nowhere and fell into step beside her. "Mind if I join you?"

She tugged the paisley wool more tightly about her shoulders. "Yes, as a matter of fact, I do," she replied tartly.

"I see a night's sleep has left you as prickly as ever," he said, undeterred by her manner.

"Prickly?" Displeased with the comment, she stopped and glared at him. "Is that how you view me?"

Luc solemnly perused her upturned face. "Yes," he answered with painful honesty. "That is precisely what you are."

"Well," she huffed, "you would be, too, given my circumstances."

"What one cannot change, in time one must learn to accept."

"Rubbish!" Gillian scoffed. "I could never learn to consider this place my home. I hate it here."

"Seems I heard the same refrain yesterday." He matched his pace to hers as she marched down the steep ramp leading from the fort's entrance.

She gestured toward the ramshackle jumble of buildings hugging the shoreline below. "How do people tolerate living here? Without shops, the theater, afternoon strolls through the park."

He shrugged. "The island itself is a park. If you'd allow me to give you a tour, you just might have a change of heart."

"Impossible."

"Occasionally even the impossible becomes possible."

"You're speaking in riddles." She stared at the straits, which separated the two great lakes. "I'll do anything to return to England. Anything," she repeated fervently.

"Perhaps you'll feel differently in time."

"Save your breath, du Pré." She gave a humorless laugh. "Nothing you can say or do will convince me otherwise."

"Besides being prickly, you're stubborn as a mule."

She slanted him a look. "You find little to admire in me and much to criticize, du Pré. Surely there must be more enjoyable ways to spend your time than in my dreary company." Then she narrowed her eyes as a new thought struck her. "Did Father order you to follow me about? To act as nursemaid?"

A hint of a smile curved his mouth. "Are you always this suspicious?"

"Prickly, stubborn, and now suspicious?" She shook her head in mock despair. "What a shrew you must think me."

When he didn't answer immediately she looked at him askance and found his attention focused elsewhere. Curious, she followed the direction of his stare. Shading her eyes against the glare of the sun, she made out the shapes of a dozen slender canoes heading toward the island. Each canoe was manned by a half dozen Indian braves.

"Who are they? What do they want?"

"British reinforcements. Ottawa, most likely," Luc ventured. "Your father should be pleased."

Something in his tone caught her attention. She glanced at him inquisitively. "Are you not pleased as well?"

"Of course," he amended hastily. "Their presence strengthens the British position."

Luc and Gillian arrived at the shore just as the first of the canoes were being dragged to the gravel beach. A group of villagers clustered to watch the event. Small boys brimming with bravado and energy darted about while their more timid sisters clung to their mothers' skirts. Gillian was tempted to remain a good distance from the activity but, emboldened with Luc as her escort, she edged closer.

One brave in particular captured her attention. Perhaps it was the deference others accorded him, but more likely it was his demeanor that set him apart. Tall, sturdy as an oak, with bold features and a bladelike nose, he shouldered a mantle of authority. Shell ornaments dangled from his pierced ears and tattoos covered his muscular forearms. His black hair was worn short with feathers twisted into the upright knot at his brow. He stood, arms folded across his chest, supervising the unloading of the canoes. Beside her she sensed Luc's body stiffen with tension.

"What is it?" she whispered. "Who is that man?"

"His name is Red Dog," Luc returned, his gaze fastened on the man in question.

"Do you know him?"

"Yes, unfortunately."

"Does he live here on the island?"

"No," Luc said with a shake of his head. "He's a war chief, a former lieutenant under Tecumseh's command."

"But no longer?"

"Tecumseh was killed last year in the Battle of the Thames."

As though sensing himself the object of scrutiny, Red Dog turned toward them. Recognition—and malice—glittered in his obsidian eyes as his gaze settled on Luc. He advanced toward them slowly. His rolling swagger had the unconscious grace of a predator stalking its prey. Gillian sidled closer to Luc, wanting his protection, willing to lend hers. Never before had she witnessed such a blatant display of raw power.

Red Dog halted before them. Gillian stood unmoving, scarcely breathing. Red Dog, his eyes alert and hooded like a hawk's, studied her briefly before moving on to Luc. Gillian wanted to recoil at the pure hatred she saw mirrored there.

"The Great Father has deemed our paths cross once more," Luc said, breaking the terse silence.

Red Dog grunted. "Soon the time will come to test our strength, our skill. Only one shall survive."

"I do not fear you, Red Dog."

"Then you are a fool." Red Dog spat derisively. Whirling away, he stalked up the path toward the fort.

Gillian stared after him with a mixture of relief and trepidation. "What have you done to turn that man into your enemy? Why does he hate you so?"

"It's none of your affair." The muscle in Luc's jaw bunched. "If you are wise, you will avoid Red Dog at all costs."

"But why? I have done nothing to gain his enmity."

Luc stared down at her, his expression stern, uncompromising. "Stay away from him, Gillian."

"You have no right to give me orders," she said with an obstinate shake of her head. "I deserve at least some explanation if you expect me to heed your advice."

"Do not treat my warning lightly. In Red Dog's eyes, any association with me makes him your enemy too. He is dangerous."

Remembering the hatred burning in the warrior's onyx gaze, Gillian could only ponder what might have precipitated the rift between the two. Shivering, she drew the shawl more tightly about her.

"Where are you off to?"

"I'm going for a walk."

"I'll go with you."

Gillian blew out an impatient breath. "I don't need a nursemaid. Nor do I want your company."

She left Luc staring after her, a disgruntled look on his face. For her first expedition, she chose a narrow dirt road winding along the water's edge that led eastward away from the village. A woman carrying a basket of eggs approached from the opposite direction. A small boy of three or four skipped at her heels. As she drew nearer, Gillian guessed the woman's age to be near that of her own. How nice it would be to have someone to talk with. Her spirits lifted at the prospect.

As the two women came abreast, Gillian smiled and prepared to exchange pleasantries. The woman, however, was of a different mind. Instead of a greeting, the woman gave her a blank stare as she swept past.

"But, Mama," the lad wailed, still staring at Gillian over his shoulder, "you didn't smile back at the angel lady."

"Come, Jacob." The woman grabbed her toddler's arm to hasten him along. "That woman is no angel. And she isn't a lady either."

Stunned speechless by the cruel remark, Gillian stared after them in disbelief. She had never set eyes on the woman before. What could she have possibly done to earn such vitriol?

Head bent in thought, she continued on her way. A short distance farther, she came upon an old woman, her gray hair covered with a kerchief, sweeping the stoop of a small stone cottage.

"Good day," Gillian called cheerfully.

The woman paused in her task to scowl at her, then went inside the cottage, letting the door slam shut behind her. Gillian shook her head, puzzled by the odd behavior of the islanders. What had she done to provoke such a cool reception? How could she have offended people she had never met? Their obvious lack of friendliness made her feel even more of an outsider.

Rounding a bend in the road, she found a sunny spot amid some boulders. A good place, she decided, to sit and contemplate her predicament. Lake Huron spread in front of her like a rumpled blue blanket. Waves lapped against the sand, the sound rhythmic, lulling. Puffy white clouds drifted lazily across an azure sky. Gulls with wings stretched wide glided overhead. Gillian's unruly thoughts were in variance to the peaceful setting that surrounded her. Though undeniably beautiful, it was far too remote, too isolated, for her taste.

She couldn't—wouldn't—stay in these cursed northwoods. Who could she persuade to take her away from this loathsome island? Luc du Pré couldn't be trusted. He had obviously pledged his loyalty to her father. And if she did find someone, what could she offer in exchange? She had little money to give as a bribe. Pensively, she toyed with the small ruby brooch she habitually wore pinned above her heart.

Her brain churned, trying to match problems with possible solutions. Once she managed to flee Mackinac Island, her father would be too busy, too preoccupied, to give pursuit. If she could reach another British stronghold, she would seek passage on one of the ships that plied the Great Lakes, then go on to England. Upon reaching London, she would throw herself on Aunt Phoebe's mercy. It would only be until she turned twenty-one, a little more than a year from now, at which time she would repay her aunt's generosity.

Suddenly, the fine hairs pricked along the nape of her neck. She tensed as she felt herself being watched. Tamping down the urge to bolt and run, Gillian turned her head and looked over her shoulder. Her questioning gaze encountered the solemn face and bright eyes of a young Indian girl. Relief left her weak, and feeling somewhat foolish.

"Hello," Gillian said with a tentative smile.

The child made no attempt to return the smile, but continued to regard her cautiously.

"Don't be afraid. I won't hurt you." Remembering the apple she had placed there earlier, Gillian reached into her pocket and held it out to the little girl. "Would you like this?"

When the girl made no attempt to claim it, Gillian placed it on a boulder an arm's length away. The child eyed the tempting offer in silence, then crept closer and snatched it with both hands before turning and scampering back into the woods.

"Wait, don't go . . ."

But the child had vanished.

With a sigh, Gillian climbed to her feet and returned to the fort. She felt like a leper. A pariah. Everyone she had encountered thus far had shunned her. First the woman with the little boy who had likened her to an angel. Next the old lady sweeping her stoop. Now this dark-eyed wood sprite.

After an afternoon spent in the bright sunlight, the high walls of the fort cast the parade ground in shadow. Not waiting for her eyes to adjust to the dim light, Gillian stepped across the threshold and collided with a figure standing just inside the open portal.

"Watch where you walk," a gruff voice reprimanded her.

Gillian blinked, then stared transfixed into Red Dog's hard black eyes. Her gaze dropped lower and settled on the collection of tattoos on his massive forearms. Viewed at close range, she noted that they depicted a mass of snarling dogs. "I-I'm sorry . . ." she mumbled, readjusting the shawl about her shoulders. The action drew his attention to the ruby brooch pinned to her gown.

He stared, transfixed by the pretty red stone.

A kernel of an idea took root. She raised her hand and lightly stroked the piece of jewelry. The blood-red ruby glittered, sending off a shower of sparks. "Do you like it? It once belonged to my grandmother."

Red Dog's face took on an avaricious expression. "It has fire, magic."

"The stone is called a ruby. It's very valuable." At the sound of brisk footsteps, Gillian glanced up to find Luc striding toward her, a scowl on his face.

"Your father is expecting you," he announced without ceremony.

"Now?" she asked, unable to mask her irritation.

"Now." Luc firmly took her elbow and steered her toward the officers' quarters.

She cast a glance over her shoulder. Red Dog stood exactly where she had left him, gazing after them. She hadn't mistaken the covetous gleam in his eyes at seeing the ruby brooch. He thought the stone magic. She smiled to herself at the notion. Yes, magic might be precisely what it might turn out to be. Grandmother's brooch might help her stage a disappearing act from this wretched place.

"What were you talking to Red Dog about?" Luc demanded as soon as they were out of earshot.

Gillian tugged her elbow free from his grasp. "I hardly think it's any of your business."

"Your father made you my business."

"I told you before, I'm too old for a governess. If you need something to take care of, find a pet."

He halted abruptly, positioning himself directly in front of her. A single glance at his face told her that she had tested his patience to its limit. Instinctively, she retreated a step.

"The captain doesn't seem to have much confidence in your ability to take care of yourself," he informed her coldly.

Her cheeks flamed at the insult. "I can take care of myself perfectly well with no help from you."

"Judging from the company you choose, I doubt that." Before she could frame a suitable rejoinder, he continued, "I warned you earlier. Red Dog is dangerous. Stay away from him."

"And if I don't?"

Tension stretched between them, a taut band about to snap. Gillian gradually became aware of the quiet surrounding them. Except for a few sentries on duty, all of the soldiers were in the mess hall for their evening meal. No one would rush to her aid if she called for help.

Reaching out one hand, Luc ran the back of his fingers along the fragile line of her jaw. Gillian froze, startled by the unexpected caress.

"You are a very beautiful woman," he murmured. "A desirable woman."

Nervously, Gillian moistened her lips with the tip of her

tongue. His touch was wreaking havoc on her determination to dislike him. She leaned toward him fractionally, unconsciously welcoming his touch.

Abruptly, his hand dropped from her cheek. His velvety voice hardened to granite. "I've seen Red Dog's leavings. You would no longer be pretty when he finished with you."

A chill swept over her at his words. With a woman's sixth sense, she knew he referred to a personal loss. Impulsively she placed a hand on his arm, wanting to ease his pain, erase the bleakness from his expression. "Who was this woman you speak of, Luc?"

He shook off her touch. "Red Dog does not hold life sacred. Guard yours with care."

Turning, he stalked away.

She watched him leave. Who was the girl, or the woman, who evoked such passion in the fierce voyageur? She admired—almost envied—the one who could fan smoldering emotions into a raging inferno. Whoever the woman was, Luc must have cared deeply.

And he still mourned her loss.

Chapter Six

When after several days of pouting and wallowing in self-pity her father showed no sign of relenting, Gillian decided it was time for a change of tactics. She woke one morning with a renewed sense of purpose. If she could demonstrate responsibility and sound judgment to his satisfaction, perhaps then he might be willing to reconsider. Well, she thought as she swung her legs out of bed, she would prove the model of decorum and responsibility. Slipping out of her nightdress, she quickly washed and dressed. She reminded herself that she was a soldier's daughter. All her life, she had been exposed to hearty doses of discipline and lectures on duty. If her plan succeeded, with a little planning, a bit of luck, and a concentrated effort on her part, she might reap untold rewards.

Gillian began her campaign with a vengeance. Immediately after breakfast, she knotted a strip of linen about her waist to protect her dress, fastened a kerchief over her hair, rolled up her sleeves, and set to work. She ran her dust cloth along the mantel, wrinkling her nose with distaste at the cloud of gray fuzz the cleaning rag had dislodged. She filled a basket with empty whiskey bottles she found stashed in cupboards and drawers. In her estimation, Private Bunton had done a poor job of maintaining her father's living quarters. As long as things were neat and tidy on the surface, her father might be willing to overlook cobwebs in the corners, but she insisted on higher standards.

The time passed quickly. Once the nooks and crannies were free of dust, she grabbed a broom and attacked the cobwebs, then diligently swept the floorboards and front stoop. That completed, she inspected the living quarters with a critical eye. Though spotless, the large room with its simple furnishings still seemed lacking. Perhaps rearranging the furniture would help. Contemplating the possible configurations, she opened a window, stuck out her hand, and vigorously shook the dust cloth.

"What the . . ." an angry voice demanded, then lapsed into coughing.

"I'm so sorry . . ." Her apology drifted into silence as Luc du Pré's angry face peered back at her. He looked so disgruntled, she stifled a giggle. "I didn't realize anyone was out there," she said.

"Well, you should have looked first," he grumbled.

She arched a brow. "What were you doing skulking outside my window, du Pré? Were you sent to spy on me?"

"I don't skulk," he growled. "Since it's past noon time, your father requested I bring your dinner from the mess hall."

"Oh," she replied. She had gotten so involved in her cleaning project, she had lost track of time. "Then you may bring it in, if you like."

Seconds later, Luc appeared on the threshold, holding a napkin-covered tin plate. He stood watching her in silence, a strange expression on his face.

Gillian proceeded to ignore him. Walking over to the faded damask settee, she pushed and shoved until it finally budged from its resting spot against one wall.

"Just what do you think you're doing?"

She paused, blew a wisp of hair from her eyes, and snapped, "Moving furniture, you big ox. What does it look like?"

He set the plate of food aside and elbowed her out of the way. "Where would you like it?"

"There," she said, pointing toward the center of the room. "Place it so that it faces the door."

He gave her a dubious look but did as she directed.

Tilting her head to one side, she rested a finger against her cheek and studied the effect. "I'm not sure. Move it just a little closer toward the window."

Wordlessly, Luc moved it to the left.

"No." She shook her head. "That doesn't look right either."

"I'd hate to play chess with someone who changes her mind as often as you," he grumbled. "Maybe if you turned the sofa so it faces the fireplace?"

"Better, much better." She nodded approvingly. Eager to see the results, she pulled one of the chairs into place at a right angle to the settee. Pleased at how it looked, she started for the second. Luc intercepted her and placed it so that both chairs faced each other from opposite ends of the sofa.

"Are we done yet?"

"Almost," she replied as she started to haul one of the benches from the trestle table.

"I'll do it," he muttered. "Where do you want it?"

"Behind the settee. Then"—she gave him a sheepish smile—"if you'd kindly move the desk to the corner near the door."

Once the final item was in place, she surveyed the results.

The quarters now appeared less regimented, homier. "Yes, definitely an improvement. This is a much cozier arrangement for conversation, don't you agree?"

Luc grunted. "No matter how nicely you arrange the furniture, I can't envision the captain engaged in cozy conversation."

An image flashed through her mind. A nearly forgotten memory of her mother and father, young and happy, lightly bantering on a settee while she played at their feet among her dolls. Had life once been so simple, that pleasurable? Since her mother's death, it seemed her father had forgotten how to smile. Had forgotten how to love his daughter. And had developed an inordinate fondness for rum and whiskey.

To disguise her lapse into nostalgia, she adopted a brisk tone. "You do good work, du Pré. Lucky for me you happened along when you did."

"And if I hadn't?"

She shrugged. "Then I would have managed without you."

"Somehow you didn't impress me as a housemaid."

"I'm not," she amended with a rueful laugh. "I'm just glad my friends in London can't see me now."

"And what do you suppose they'd think if they could?"

She smiled at him, warmed by the teasing glint in his dark eyes. "If they had found me sweeping and dusting, they'd swear I'd taken complete leave of my senses."

"Seeing you wearing an apron and kerchief, I thought perhaps you had."

Flushing at the reminder, she whipped the covering from her hair and smoothed back wayward tendrils. "Thank you very much for your assistance, and," she added "for bringing my lunch."

He made no move to leave. Instead, he took the kerchief from her hand and, catching her chin between thumb and forefinger, used it to dab at her cheek. "Hold still," he ordered when she started to squirm. "You look like an angel with a dirty face."

She couldn't have moved if she had tried. She stood mute, rooted to the floor. Eyes wide, she stared into his exotically handsome face. Whenever he was this close, inertia seemed to spread through her body, draining every thought from her head and sharpening her senses.

If she had a similar effect on him it wasn't evident as he stepped back and handed her the kerchief. "There; your face is clean."

She scrambled for a degree of equanimity—and failed.

He turned to leave but paused at the door. "Next time call me before you start moving heavy objects. You could hurt yourself."

Then he was gone.

Gillian stared at the closed door with a mixture of frustration and confusion. Luc du Pré was an enigma. Infuriating one moment, gentle and considerate the next.

Either way spelled trouble.

Lunch over, Gillian swept a final approving glance around the living quarters. Pride and a sense of accomplishment filled her. Her father had seen fit to arrange the furnishings around the perimeter of the room with military precision. Now the room seemed more welcoming. She hoped her father would approve of the new look. But, she rationalized, he spent so little time away, he would hardly notice the changes.

She smoothed the paisley shawl draped over the back of the settee for a bold splash of color. The room still needed a bit of brightness to relieve the drab. A braided rug on the pine floor would help. Perhaps a visit to one of the trading posts on Market Street would provide the item she sought.

She shrugged into her pelisse, tucked a small volume of poems into a pocket along with a handful of raisins, and stepped onto the porch. The afternoon was overcast, the sky a dull silver dome. Undaunted, she skirted the parade ground, passed through the entrance, which she had learned was called the south sally port, and started down the ramp.

In the field below the fort, a trio of soldiers assigned to garden detail attacked the hard soil with rakes and hoes in preparation for spring planting. As she drew nearer, the men slowed their work to track her progress. Something about the avid way they watched her made her uneasy. She tried to ignore the uncomfortable sensation.

The leader of the group, a corporal judging from his uniform, swaggered forward until he partially blocked her path. Wiping the sweat from his brow with a sleeve, he leaned against the shovel handle. "Where's a pretty girl like you off to this fine afternoon?" he asked with a cheeky grin.

"I beg your pardon," she returned coolly, stunned by the man's insolence.

"We heard the captain's daughter had come for a visit. My friends and I got to thinkin' you might be lonely, bein' so far from home and all."

"Please step out of my way, Private," she ordered, intentionally demoting him a level.

His cronies, who had wandered closer, hooted with laughter.

"No offense, miss. We just thought you might be in need of some male companionship to lighten the day."

Gillian observed the bold young corporal more closely. He was probably only a year or two older than she, good-looking, with a shock of light brown hair and an engaging grin.

"Name's Hunter," he offered as his hazel eyes wandered over her slender form.

"And huntin' is what Hunter does best," the red-haired, freckle-faced private volunteered.

"Just ask any o' them Indian maidens about Hunter," added the third. The young private, probably still in his teens, beamed Hunter a look of admiration. "They'll tell you he treats his women real good."

Hunter preened at the praise. "Never had no complaints."

"Well, Hunter, if you don't step aside this instant, you're about to hear your first."

"Hey, there's no need to get uppity." The red-haired private leaped to his comrade's defense. "He's just tryin' to be friendly."

"I choose my friends with care."

The men snickered.

Gillian's gaze swept over the three. Her initial unease increased. As the daughter of the ranking officer, she was accustomed to courtesy and respect from the men in his command. But this impudent trio offered neither.

Hunter leered at her over the shovel handle. "You told us you choose your friends with care. Is that how you select your lovers, too?"

Gillian's cheeks stung. "I don't know what you're talking about. Now let me pass this instant."

Hunter flashed a broad grin but didn't budge. "Just wanted to let you know I'd like to be next on the list to warm your sheets."

Gillian couldn't believe her ears. Where had these dolts gotten the notion she was a woman of loose morals? Only two people here on the island knew of her disastrous encounter with Jeremy Blackwood. Her father and . . .

Luc du Pré.

The loose-tongued bastard! He had wasted no time spreading the tale of her liaison. Furious with Luc—and inexplicably hurt by his actions—she shoved Hunter out of her way. "If I had a list, soldier," she said through gritted teeth, "I wouldn't waste good ink writing your name."

Hunter's cronies hooted with mirth at her sharp rejoinder. "You'll come around," Hunter called after her, undaunted. "I can outperform any man on this island, including the redskins. After London, you'll be bored in this backwater. You'll be wishing for someone like me to keep you entertained."

"Not in this lifetime, Private," she said, skirting around him, head high, cheeks burning.

Fury lengthened her stride. A cool northerly breeze fanned her heated face. She fought the impulse to find Luc and viciously rip him apart. Anger rendered her incoherent. She needed time to calm down. If she confronted the voyageur in her present state, she would only succeed in making a fool of herself. Tears of impotent rage stung her eyelids. She could never recall being this angry. She felt betrayed all over again. Du Pré was on the same level as Jeremy Blackwood.

Because of that rogue half-breed, every man in the fort would regard her as an easy mark for a romp between the sheets. No decent woman would befriend her. Small wonder everyone she had met thus far had avoided her as if she had the plague. Her reputation was in tatters, smeared beyond redemption.

And all because of Luc du Pré. She longed to hurl herself at him, pummel him senseless. But not even the satisfaction of seeing him brought to his knees, bruised and bloody, would undo the damage. Where men were concerned, she had no judgment at all. First Jeremy, and now Luc. She never would have believed a man who had been so considerate could also be so deceitful.

She paused when she reached the lakeshore to draw a steadying breath. She had intended to visit the trading post, but after the unpleasant confrontation with Corporal Hunter, she was no longer of a mind to shop. Once more she took the path that wound away from the village.

Needing to put distance between herself and the fort, she adopted a fast pace. Gradually her anger ebbed and her walk slowed. She glanced across choppy, slate-colored waters. Another island, appearing even more desolate than Mackinac, crouched low on the horizon. She felt like a hostage, a prisoner. Instead of a cell, her prison was a remote island, and instead of iron bars she was confined by a wide expanse of water. Cold and deep. Impossible to traverse unaided.

If only she could find a way to return to England. . . . If she should find a way off this cursed island, days would elapse before her father even noticed her disappearance. By then she would be far away. After a token effort, Father would give up the search. After all, he had more pressing matters to attend to than a runaway, recalcitrant daughter who possessed the morals of a dockside trollop.

Her steps slowed as she came upon a massive rock formation just ahead. She gazed at the structure in wonderment. Nature had carved the native limestone into a majestic arch that towered high above the water.

"It is called Arch Rock."

Gillian spun around to find the small Indian girl she had seen after her arrival on the island. The girl regarded her with a solemn expression.

"Grandfather say it's made by tears."

"Tears?" Gillian repeated thoughtfully. "Someone would have to shed a great many tears to create a hole of that magnitude."

The girl nodded gravely. "Grandfather say She-Who-Walks-in-the-Mist very beautiful—and very sad."

"Tell me about her," Gillian encouraged. She sat down on a large boulder, afraid any sudden movement on her part would send the sprite scampering off.

The little girl maintained a safe distance but didn't flee. "She-Who-Walks-in-the-Mist fell in love with handsome son of a sky spirit. Her father very angry. He beat her and tie her on that high rock."

Gillian's eyes followed the direction the child pointed toward. A shudder rippled through her at the image of a beautiful Indian maiden cruelly punished by an irate parent. "What happened to her?"

The girl perched on the edge of the boulder next to Gillian, ready to flee at the least provocation. "She-Who-Walks-in-the-Mist weep for her lover. Tears melt the stone and make the arch with her on top."

"How tragic," Gillian murmured, touched by the maiden's plight. "Did her lover ever come to rescue her?"

"Oh, yes." The girl gave Gillian a bright smile. "One night her brave come and carry She-Who-Walks-in-the-Mist to the land of the Sky People, where they live happy ever after."

"Thank you for sharing your lovely story."

When the little girl lapsed into silence, Gillian withdrew the small volume of poems from her pocket and opened the book. As waves lapped rhythmically against the rocky shore, she pretended to ignore her small companion.

"What is that?" the girl asked at last, her natural curiosity overcoming her reticence.

Gillian turned a page, purposely not looking up. "This book tells pretty stories, too. They're in a form called poetry."

"Poetry? What's poetry?"

Gillian pondered the question before answering. "Poetry

is like a song. Some poems tell a story, some express one's thoughts."

Inch by inch, the little girl edged closer, craning her neck for a better look at the words printed on the page. "Where you come from women read?"

"Not all women, but many learn how. Even some as young as yourself."

The girl digested this information for a moment in silence. "Grandfather say only men need be smart."

Gillian shook her head vigorously. "Women are smart, too. Sometimes smarter," she added in a conspiratorial whisper.

The comment drew a delighted burst of giggles. Gillian smiled, too, feeling her spirits lift at the sound. "What do they call you?"

"Aupetchi."

"Aupetchi," Gillian repeated thoughtfully. "That's such a pretty name. What does it mean?"

"It mean robin, like the bird."

Gillian smiled. Yes, she thought, the name Robin perfectly suited the small girl with the bright, inquisitive eyes and quick, birdlike manner.

Aupetchi didn't return her smile. Instead she studied Gillian gravely.

"What's troubling you, my little Robin?" Gillian probed gently.

"I, too, would like to learn words on paper. Would you teach Aupetchi to read?"

Closing her book, Gillian studied the girl with renewed interest. "Learning to read takes much time, much hard work."

"Aupetchi not care. I show Grandfather women are smart, too."

"Very well." Gillian nodded slowly. "In that case, I'd be

delighted to instruct you. We'll begin our lessons tomorrow."

"I meet you here tomorrow when the sun is high." Aupetchi scrambled from the rock, an eager smile transforming her serious little face. "I learn quick. You will see."

Gillian watched her climb among the rocks, then disappear into the thick woodland beyond. Getting to her feet, she brushed the dust from her pelisse, then headed toward the fort in a much calmer frame of mind than she had left. She welcomed the prospect of teaching the young Indian girl how to read. It would help fill the idle hours until she could formulate a plan to leave Mackinac once and for all.

As she came around a bend in the trail, she spotted Luc pulling his canoe onto the beach. He stowed the paddles, then fell into step beside her.

"You're looking pleased with yourself," he said by way of a greeting.

She ignored him, not trusting herself to speak, hoping he'd take the hint and go away.

"Enjoy your walk?"

She began the trek up the steep embankment. Out of the corner of her eye she saw one of the soldiers who had harassed her earlier nudge the other. Soon all three stopped toiling to watch her and Luc. No doubt they wondered if Luc du Pré had been selected as her next paramour.

"In another month, you'll find the island much more to your liking."

In another month, she fumed inwardly, *I hope never again to hear the name of this blasted backwater.* The muscles in her legs strained from her effort to reach the summit in record time. The sooner she was out of Luc du Pré's company, the better. It was all she could do to keep her temper under tight rein. After slandering what was left of her reputation, how dare he act as though nothing was amiss?

A frown drew Luc's brows together. "You're acting odd. Is something wrong?"

Gillian swept through the portal of the fort, then whirled to confront him. " 'Is something wrong?' " she mimicked. "You have some nerve." Not waiting for a response, she marched toward the Stone Quarters.

"What the devil . . . ?" Stunned by the vehemence in her tone, Luc observed the stiff set of her shoulders, her ramrod-straight back as she stalked away, then hurried after her, catching her just as she reached the porch.

"Are you going to tell me what's wrong, or do you want to play games?"

"Games!" Spark to tinder, temper ignited in her eyes, making them glow like hot blue flames. "You're a fine one to speak of games, du Pré."

What the devil had gotten into her? Luc wondered. He bounded onto the porch, took her by the shoulders, and turned her to face him. He stared down into her mutinous countenance. For a brief moment, he was tempted to crush her lips against his, to fan the fires of anger into burning passion. Ruthlessly, he quelled the impulse. She meant nothing to him, he reminded himself. She represented the British. The enemy.

"Are you going to tell me what's wrong, or must I use other means to find out?"

Not the least intimidated by his threat, she glared back at him. "I should have known you couldn't be trusted."

Frustrated, he resisted the impulse to shake her. "You're speaking in riddles."

"Did you think I wouldn't find out?" she asked, her low-pitched voice vibrating with fury.

A single possibility chilled him like a blast of Canadian wind. Had she learned his secret? Unconsciously, his grip tightened, his fingers biting into her flesh. "Find out what, Gillian?"

"Do you mistake me for a fool?" Gillian tore herself free from his grasp. "I despise you, du Pré. You're nothing but lying, traitorous scum. Your presence sickens me."

She disappeared inside with a resounding slam of the door. Luc stood on the porch, staring unseeingly at the closed door. *Lying, traitorous scum?* Scathing words from a proper English miss. Had she somehow stumbled upon the truth? Had she learned that he served the American cause, not the British? How could that be?

Agitated, he dragged a hand through his shoulder-length mane. Impossible. Or was it? Did she suspect he spied for the Americans, and not the British? No, it was impossible. Yet what else could she have been talking about?

Chapter Seven

"Do you think she knows?"

The question hung heavy in the dank air of Skull Cave. Luc had asked himself the same question numerous times since his conversation with Gillian that afternoon. "I can't imagine how she might have learned the truth."

"Yet the chit called you a traitor." Toad scratched his shaggy beard. "Why else would she say such a thing?"

Luc squatted on his haunches and stared out at the narrow slit of an opening at the star-speckled sky beyond. "I'm not privy to the workings of a woman's mind. Least of all Gillian Stafford's."

"Well, you'd better exert all your charm to find out what's going on in the lady's head. If not," Toad warned, "your usefulness will be eliminated."

"How do you propose I do that?"

"Bed her if you must. After they bare their bodies, women like nothing more than baring their souls."

The thought of bedding the prickly English rose would

present no hardship. Luc shifted his weight as desire surged through him. He wanted her. It was that simple, that elemental. He had felt the intense urge to make love to her the first time he set eyes on her. He doubted, however, that his passion would be reciprocated. When the time came to mate, Gillian Stafford would select an Englishman of her own station, someone like her cherished English lover, not a man of mixed blood such as himself.

Toad pulled out a small cloth sack and bit off a hunk of tobacco. "You'll have to act soon. It's only a matter of time before she confides her suspicions to her father. If they weren't estranged, she probably would have already told the old man."

"She couldn't possibly have guessed I side with the Americans."

"If she knows, she'll have to be silenced."

"Silenced?" Luc jerked his head around to peer into his contact's face.

Toad thoughtfully chewed his wad of tobacco. "Don't care how you go about it. Just make sure she doesn't talk."

Luc mulled over the directive in silence. He could never lift a finger against a woman, much less cause one grave bodily harm. Perhaps he could play on her desire to leave Mackinac. Buy her cooperation by offering his assistance. Damn her hide! He needed to be here at the fort, where he could report on British activity, not transporting the girl halfway across Canada.

"What other information do you have for me?"

Luc sighed, relieved that the subject had changed. "Red Dog arrived with a small party of men. Other war chiefs will soon follow. Red Dog is expected to lead their council."

Toad grunted. "He's well respected—and feared."

Luc knew that many feared the man. But he didn't number himself among them. Where Red Dog was concerned, he was merely biding his time, waiting for the day when they would meet face-to-face on the field of honor. Only one would walk away. A score would be settled. A debt paid.

"Have you learned about supplies?"

"Several bateaux are under construction at Nottawasaga Bay. Small cannons can be mounted in the bows of these vessels, which will furnish some protection against small raiding parties. I should know more the next time we meet."

Toad rose from his crouched position. "Your first order of business is to find out what the girl knows about your activities. Dispose of her if you must."

Luc remained in the cave for a long time after Toad had left. What had prompted Gillian to accuse him of being lying, traitorous scum? Reason told him that it was highly improbable that she knew he sympathized with the American cause. Unless . . . Could she have overheard his conversation with André Tousseau? But if she had, why had she waited so long before saying anything? All of his rendezvous with Toad took place late at night. Superstition prevented even the Indians from braving Skull Cave at such an hour. Tales abounded that the cave had been an ancient burial ground.

Gillian's attitude toward him had undergone a complete reversal between that morning, when he had helped her rearrange the furniture, and later that afternoon. But what, he frowned, could have caused the dramatic change?

"A dinner party! How delightful."

"Wear a pretty dress," Randolph Stafford counseled. "I'll be here for you promptly at six. Don't keep me waiting."

"Yes, Father." The minute her father left, Gillian raced

up the stairs, excited at the prospect of an evening spent socializing. The invitation to join Margaret and James Babcock at their home had come as a pleasant surprise. Her father had informed her that the couple were prosperous traders and well-respected citizens of Mackinac Island. Margaret loved to entertain and was considered the island's undisputed hostess.

Gillian spent the afternoon preparing for the event. She heated water and took a long, leisurely bath, using a bit of her precious lavender to perfume the water, then washed and dried her hair. Choosing which gown to wear took a great deal of consideration. She finally selected a rose-colored gown of lightweight wool batiste with a rounded neckline and high waistline and a velvet spencer in a darker shade of rose. After some debate, she pulled her hair into a simple but elegant French twist.

When her father appeared precisely at the appointed hour, he nodded his approval and offered his arm. Together they left the fort and made their way down Market Street toward a spacious, two-storied, gambrel-roofed home that stood somewhat apart from the others.

Margaret Babcock opened the door at the first knock. "Captain Stafford," she greeted them expansively. "We're so happy you were able to attend and bring your lovely daughter. I've been looking forward to meeting her."

"It was so kind of you to invite us, Mrs. Babcock," Gillian said, recovering from her initial surprise at finding her hostess possessing the blue-black hair and dusky skin of a native.

Margaret smiled. "I see from your expression that no one bothered to explain that I am a metis."

"Excuse my ignorance, Mrs. Babcock," Gillian murmured, "but I am unfamiliar with the term."

"No need to apologize. The word simply means that I am of mixed blood—as are many are on the island. My mother was Chippewa, my father a French trapper." She ushered them into a parlor where the another couple waited.

A tall, distinguished gentleman with a thick head of gray hair rose to greet them. He pumped Randolph Stafford's hand, then bowed low over Gillian's. "How fortunate you are, Randolph, to be reunited with your only kin. Daughters bring a special light to a father's eyes and a special warmth to his heart."

Gillian felt an instant liking for the man she assumed was their host. She cast a surreptitious glance at her father, hoping to see some sign that he shared James Babcock's sentiment. But his expression was carefully schooled. He had once held her in high esteem. Would he ever again?

"This is hardly time for a filial visit, James." Randolph removed his tall shako and handed it to a young serving girl.

Babcock gave a careless shrug. "If you're referring to rumors of an American attack, you worry for naught. The Americans don't stand a prayer against the Crown."

"Spoken like a loyal British subject," Randolph returned with a tight smile.

"Here, here," a male voice applauded.

Gillian peeked around her hosts to the other guests in the room beyond. She immediately recognized the woman as the one who had shunned her. Her young son, on the other hand, had been friendly as a pup, likening her to an angel and questioning his mother's animosity. The gentleman, a smallish man with a receding hairline, she assumed was her husband.

"May I present Henry and Judith Mayfield." Margaret smoothly made the introductions. "Henry was active in the fur trade until the war started."

"Once hostilities cease, this island will again be the hub of the fur trade," Henry Mayfield stated with the utmost confidence. "John Jacob Astor already has his sights set on expanding operations here."

Judith remained silent, eyeing Gillian with thinly veiled dislike. The petite brunette would have been pretty if not for her habitual petulant expression.

"Ah," Margaret exclaimed when a knock sounded on the door. "The last of my guests have arrived."

While she went to greet them, the serving girl returned with a tray of cordials, which she offered to each guest in turn. Gillian took a sip and her eyes met Luc's over the rim of her raised glass. The shock of seeing him caused her hand to tremble. She lowered the cordial glass slowly, careful not to spill its contents. He looked quite handsome, she thought resentfully. In deference to the occasion, he had abandoned his voyageur attire for more conventional clothing. Snug-fitting nankeen breeches molded his muscular thighs. A tobacco brown jacket, gold-striped waistcoat, and pristine white shirt and cravat completed his costume. His hair was drawn back and tied neatly at the nape of his neck with a narrow ribbon.

She had been so preoccupied cataloging every detail of Luc's appearance that at first she failed to notice his companion. Her eyes widened in surprise at finding Luc accompanied by a priest. Tall and wiry of stature with a wreath of snow-white hair, he approached her, his hands extended in greeting.

"I am Père Robichaud," he said in a voice thickly accented with French. "I have heard much about you, child. At last we meet."

Gillian forced a smile, inwardly wondering if rumors about her had reached the priest's ears as well. "The pleasure is mine, Father."

"Now that everyone is here, we can adjourn to the dining room. My cook has just told me that dinner is ready," Margaret Babcock said.

Gillian and her father followed their host and hostess while the others trailed behind. Tall tapers burned on either end of a table set with bone china and gleaming silver. Gillian gasped in appreciation at finding evidence of civility in the midst of a wilderness.

"Your home is truly charming, Mrs. Babcock."

In spite of a feeble effort at nonchalance, the woman looked inordinately pleased with the compliment. "Why, thank you, dear. Please, call me Margaret."

James and Margaret took their places at either end of the table. Gillian was seated with her father on one side, Luc on the other. Judith Mayfield sat opposite her, between her husband, Henry, and Père Robichaud. Gillian spread her napkin across her lap, all the while painfully conscious of Luc seated next to her. Her earlier enthusiasm for the dinner party plummeted. It was difficult to maintain a lighthearted spirit with Judith shooting daggers at her from across the table.

The light brush of Luc's elbow against hers didn't help ease Gillian's tension. Instead, it simmered close to the surface. She was sorely tempted to lash out at him anew for slandering her reputation but for her father's sake knew she must keep a civil tongue. Drawing in a calming breath, she pasted a bright smile on her face.

Margaret turned to Gillian. "I'm pleased you and Judith have finally been introduced. Since the two of you are close in age, I'm sure you'll find interests in common. It would be wonderful if you could become friends."

Judith shook her head in vigorous denial. "I fear that would be an impossibility. Young Jacob demands most of my time."

"And since I'm only here for a brief visit, there is little time for a friendship to develop," Gillian countered frostily.

The timely arrival of dinner saved her from further conversation. A plump, red-cheeked cook entered, straining to carry a heavy platter

"Ah, wild turkey." Père Robichaud rubbed his hands in anticipation. "A particular favorite of mine."

The cook set the platter in front of James Babcock, who stood and carved the bird with the precision of an army surgeon. The girl arrived and poured wine from a heavy pitcher. After Père Robichaud offered grace, dishes heaped with vegetables were brought from the kitchen and circulated among the guests.

"Would you care for potatoes?" Luc inquired in a polite voice.

Afraid her temper would flare and she might be tempted to dump a bowl over his head, Gillian refused to meet his eyes. "Yes, thank you," she replied, taking the potatoes from him, careful to avoid touching his long, tanned fingers.

"Carrots?"

Her mouth clamped tightly, she grabbed the vegetable dish without a word. She spooned a portion onto her plate, then passed it to her father, who regarded her quizzically before resuming his conversation with Henry Mayfield.

Père Robichaud accepted a serving of turkey, then rested his mild gaze on Gillian. "Is this your first opportunity, Miss Stafford, to meet some of the island's citizens?"

"Yes, it is, Father. And please, call me Gillian."

"The northwoods are a far cry from England. Are you having trouble adjusting to the change?" he inquired kindly.

Next to her, Luc paused, awaiting her reply.

"Some," she answered truthfully. "But I pray the conflict will soon be ended, and my stay here brief."

James Babcock held his glass high. "To a speedy resolution of the war."

Randolph Stafford followed suit. "God save the King."

Of one accord the guests raised their glasses in a salute to king and country. From the corner of her eye, Gillian noted that Luc hesitated before lifting his. For a fleeting moment, she had the impression he was reluctant to join in the toast, then dismissed the notion as fanciful. Her father trusted du Pré implicitly. She had no call to doubt his loyalty to the crown.

"Ah, Margaret," Henry Mayfield beamed jovially. "You make the best elderberry wine in the entire northwest."

"And Henry should know," Judith added. "He's quite the connoisseur of fine wine."

Gillian's gaze darted between the pair. Had she detected a note of discord? Or was she being fanciful yet again? As she watched, Henry drained his glass and signaled the servant girl for more.

Henry leered at Gillian over his wineglass. "My son must have seen you the other day when you were out walking. He hasn't stopped talking of you since."

"Indeed," Gillian replied, her fork poised in midair.

Randolph dabbed the corner of his mouth with a napkin. "What did the lad have to say about my daughter, Mayfield?"

"The boy likened her to an angel in a picture book." Henry Mayfield chuckled as though greatly amused by the notion. His wife snickered behind her napkin.

An uncomfortable silence descended over the table. Gillian kept her gaze fastened on the roll she was buttering. Everyone knew. Everyone thought her a slut.

Beside her Luc du Pré cleared his throat. "I thought much the same as your son, Mayfield, the first time I saw Miss Stafford. She rather resembles a certain illustration in one of your books, don't you agree, Père Robichaud?"

The clergyman's startled dark eyes flew from Luc to Gillian. "Ah, yes," he said, recovering from his surprise. "Yes, indeed. There definitely is a resemblance. If any of you care to drop by St. Anne's, I'll be happy to show you the book in question so you can decide the similarities for yourself."

Margaret Babcock urged everyone to help themselves to seconds and ordered her serving girl to refill the wineglasses as the conversation turned to events surrounding the expected arrival of more troops.

Gillian breathed a sigh of relief that the awkward moment had passed. Help had come from an unexpected source—Luc du Pré. Her initial burst of gratitude, however, quickly faded. No doubt a guilty conscience, rather than a noble nature, prompted the action. Unfortunately, his effort was too little, too late, to repair the blow to her reputation.

"It's my understanding, Captain, that the fort is being assigned a new commander. Is there any truth to the rumor?"

At James Babcock's question, Gillian sat up straighter, her problems temporarily forgotten. Was someone being sent as permanent replacement for her father? Did this mean he would leave Mackinac? Possibly even return to England?

"It never ceases to amaze me how quickly rumors abound." Randolph Stafford calmly pushed his plate aside and reached for his wineglass. "You've heard correctly, my friend."

Henry leaned forward, arms folded on the table in front of him, eager to learn all the details. "Well, man, who is he? When will he arrive? What do you know of him?"

"The new commander will be Lieutenant-Colonel Robert McDouall, a Scotsman and an eighteen-year veteran. He recently served as aide-de-camp of General Proctor."

"How soon will he arrive?" Luc asked.

Randolph drained his glass, then helped himself to

another. "In a matter of a few weeks. Mid-May at the latest."

"He'll bring reinforcements with him," Père Robichaud stated, lathering butter on a flaky dinner roll.

"And provisions." The trader in James Babcock rose to the fore.

Margaret voiced the question uppermost in Gillian's mind. "What about you, Captain? Will you remain on Mackinac Island, or will you be sent elsewhere?"

"Why, I'll remain here, of course," Randolph assured his hostess. "I'll do everything in my power to make McDouall's transition a smooth one. In the meantime, work on the new fortification will continue as scheduled."

Gillian watched, her mind a whirl, as the servants cleared the dinner dishes and served dessert. She merely toyed with the apple-cherry cobbler swimming in rich cream. For a brief moment, she had dared wish her father might be reassigned. Then she could leave this island for good. Her fragile hope had burst like a soap bubble. Her father, so it seemed, was to remain at this blasted outpost, and unless she could come up with an alternative plan, she would, too.

Gradually, she became aware of a tapping sound. She cast a sidelong glance in Luc's direction and found him restlessly drumming his fingers against the tabletop. Every line of his body seemed taut, tense. His finely chiseled cheekbones appeared more sharply sculpted, his jaw rigid. Sensing her interest, he turned his head slightly and their eyes locked. His eyes, nearly black in their intensity, bored into hers. Dark, mysterious, compelling. Gillian felt as though she was being sucked into a black vortex, helpless to resist its force.

"Well, Daughter, I hate to spoil your evening, but I still have work to do."

Gillian blinked and slowly turned toward her father.

Reality slipped back into place. She shook her head to rid it of Luc du Pré's strange effect upon her. He could send her senses reeling with a single look. Dangerous; the man was definitely dangerous. And not to be trusted, she reminded herself.

Shortly thereafter, the dinner guests bid their hosts good night and dispersed. As she and her father left the Babcocks', Gillian glimpsed Luc and his friend, Père Robichaud, heading down Market Street, their long strides in perfect rhythm.

News of her indiscretion must have spread to friends and acquaintances in London as well as to people here. The notion sickened her. Her reputation was sullied on both sides of the Atlantic. She and her father had nearly reached the fort before she found the courage to voice another concern. She cleared her throat to draw her father's attention. "Were my actions responsible for someone other than yourself being named commander?" she asked in a subdued tone.

He pinned her with an icy blue stare. "So, you're belatedly wondering how your scandalous behavior might have affected others?"

Shame and guilt engulfed her. At the time, she had been too infatuated, too self-centered, to view her actions through another's eyes. She had never paused to consider that her assignation with Jeremy might be discovered. Never dreamed he had lied to her. Never imagined that he was already wed.

Never, never, never. The word echoed through her head. "I realize how selfish I was not to consider how this might jeopardize your career." The admission came hard.

Her father gave her a long, speculative look. "Put your mind at rest, Gillian. The British higher command has more important factors to consider than a man's flighty daughter."

His words only marginally alleviated her fears. " 'If you can't control your offspring, how can you control your men?' " she quoted a phrase she had once overheard. "That's very much how many think."

"What's done is done." He walked briskly across the parade ground toward post headquarters. "In any event, McDouall is well qualified for the position. It's my duty to assist him in any way possible."

Gillian sighed as she watched him disappear into his office. She supposed she should feel grateful that her father didn't hold her responsible that his military career had failed to flourish. Yet she couldn't help but feel at least partially responsible. The breech between them yawned even wider. She wondered how different their relationship might have been if her mother were still alive. The father she remembered from childhood had been quick to smile and laugh, unafraid to show affection. He rarely drank. Circumstances had transformed Randolph Stafford into a cold, dispassionate man. A virtual stranger.

Knowing sleep would be impossible, Gillian decided to walk about the compound. The fort was virtually deserted. Reveille sounded at five o'clock, and, except for sentries posted in the blockhouses, most of the men retired early. The night breeze carried the ever present scent of evergreens. A crescent moon played hide and seek with flotillas of dark clouds. Dark and lonely, the night complemented her mood. She was doomed to remain on this blasted island indefinitely.

With no one to blame but herself.

The admission only added to her frustration. Her infatuation with Jeremy Blackwood had led to her downfall. At the time she fancied herself in love with the dashing infantry lieutenant. She gave a short, humorless laugh. How readily she swallowed his flattery, his protestations of undying devotion—his deceit. Countless times he whispered what a perfect wife she'd make. He failed to add, however, that he already had a "perfect" wife . . . in Sussex. Naive and gullible, she had never doubted his sincerity.

If not for her aunt's timely interruption at the inn outside London, Gillian would have let Jeremy make love to her. As it was, her virginity was still intact, though her reputation was in ruins. Nice girls simply didn't tryst with men—married or not. Society considered lovemaking without benefit of clergy shameful behavior. What a witless little fool she had been. Well, she would never again be so easily duped. Men weren't to be trusted.

Luc du Pré included. Gillian's mouth hardened at the thought of the rugged voyageur. Quick as a snake, he had spread tales of her dalliance with a married man. He had been privy to a private conversation between father and daughter and used that information as ammunition. Gossip about her resounded through the small island like the blast from a cannon. Soldiers made crude advances; decent women shunned her. Almost instantly, she had become ostracized. An outcast. All because of Luc du Pré's loose tongue.

Again she felt the sting of betrayal. Once more her judgment of men had been found lacking. In spite of frequent irritation at Luc's high-handed manner, she had believed he possessed a certain strength of character. That he was decent, honorable, not a gossipmonger.

Absently, head bent, she fingered the ruby brooch pinned to her velvet spencer. Lost in contemplation, she nearly collided with a figure lurking deep in the shadows near the entrance to the fort. She let out a startled gasp before recognizing the man.

"Red Dog." A slight tremor in her voice revealed her fright.

The Indian merely grunted an acknowledgment. He remained in the shadows, arms folded across his wide chest.

His black gaze gleamed like onyx in the meager light, hard and cold. The shell ornaments in his pierced ears swayed slightly.

Distinctly uneasy under his unblinking perusal, Gillian began to skirt past him when his words stopped her.

"Red Dog much admire your stone of fire."

She glanced down at the brooch, then back up, trying to gauge his expression. This wasn't the first time, she recalled, that he had admired the gift from her grandmother. "Thank you," she replied slowly. "It's my favorite piece of jewelry."

"We make trade."

Her eyes widened in surprise. "Trade? What do you mean?"

"I give you what you want. You give Red Dog fire stone."

"Exactly what do you have that I might want?" she asked cautiously.

"You not like it here," he stated with calm assurance.

She caught her lower lip between her teeth, her mind working feverishly. Was this the opportunity she had been praying for, nearly despaired of finding? Had her ticket to escape come in the shape of a surly Ottawa chieftain?

"I can take you far away," he said in reply to her unspoken questions.

"When?" The single word came out as a whisper.

"Meet at bluff west of village night of the new moon."

Red Dog turned and vanished into the darkness. Gillian, her step lighter than it had been in months, returned to the quarters she shared with her father. Her freedom for the price of a trinket. She had struck a worthy bargain. Soon, soon she would leave this place forever.

Stepping onto the porch, she looked across the parade grounds at the golden rectangle of light coming from post headquarters. Later, when she was far away, she would write her father and explain her actions. But by then there would be little he could do. He would scarcely notice her absence, much less miss her.

She opened the door and went inside. Granted, Red Dog intimidated her, made her a tad uneasy. Luc had described him as dangerous, but surely he had exaggerated. The Ottawa had no reason to cause her harm. At journey's end she would simply hand him the brooch. He would have his prize, and she hers.

Chapter Eight

The daily afternoon reading lessons with Aupetchi had become the brightest part of her day. Gillian smiled and hummed softly as she tucked a gift for her little friend into her embroidered silk reticule. Still smiling, she left the Stone Quarters and headed out of the fort. She passed through the arched entryway and into the sunlight. She paused on the top of the ramp to allow her eyes time to adjust.

A loud shout sounded from the village below, followed by a clamor of excited voices. Curious, she looked down to see Mackinac's inhabitants streaming from their homes and businesses and hurrying toward the shore. Had the Americans arrived? Her heart skipped a beat as she looked toward the lake.

She blinked, not trusting her own vision. Then, shielding her eyes against the sun's glare, she looked again. Several light frigates with billowed sails were making their way toward the island. Two dozen or more bateaux rode foam-crested waves on either side like so many baby ducklings surrounding their mother.

Almost of their own accord, her feet carried her down the ramp toward the gathered throng. Behind her, a bugler summoned the garrison with quick, impatient notes of his horn. The sound lingered in the spring air long after the call ended. Gillian found a vantage point somewhat apart from the rest. Tension sang in the air as the flotilla drew closer. The mood of the townspeople turned solemn. Their expressions reflected varying degrees of apprehension and anxiety. The crowd parted to make way for James Babcock, who arrived telescope in hand.

The tension infected Gillian, too. She watched with baited breath as the man raised the scope and trained it on the approaching vessels.

After a long moment, he let loose a jubilant shout. "They fly the Union Jack."

A roar of approval rang from those assembled. This outcry brought home to Gillian as nothing else had thus far that though thousands of miles from England, she stood firmly entrenched in a British stronghold. She released a sigh of relief, then smiled.

Next to her, a grizzled trapper scratched his jaw. "Thought fer sure the first arrivals this spring would be flyin' the stars and stripes."

"And be firin' their cannons," another added with a toothless grin.

"What's happening?" Gillian asked, still not certain of the significance of the event.

The trapper regarded her as he might an addled child. "The army's sent reinforcements."

"And by the looks of it, a large shipment of provisions." Gillian turned her head to find Margaret Babcock at her side. "The past winter was brutal. At times we had barely enough food to keep body and soul alive."

Unsure how to respond to the woman's comment, she kept silent. A twinge of guilt assailed her, knowing others had suffered while she lived in relative luxury, safe, warm, and well fed. Gillian's gaze swept the crowd, now immersed in a partylike gaiety, then rested on Luc's lean, muscular figure. Anger and a sense of betrayal surged through her at the mere sight of him. She had begun to warm toward the voyageur, even look forward to time spent in his company, until she realized his perfidy.

As though sensing himself watched, Luc cast a glance in her direction before returning to study the frigates riding low on the waves. If he had noticed her aloofness, it didn't seem to bother him. She was grateful that since the Babcocks' dinner, he had made no effort to approach her and initiate conversation. He seemed as eager to avoid her as she did him.

Margaret followed the direction of her stare. "Ah," she exclaimed softly. "I see by your expression that the handsome M'sieur du Pré holds no appeal for you."

"I despise him."

Margaret regarded her with a raised brow. "Do you dislike him because he is of mixed blood?"

"N-no," Gillian stammered, taken aback by the woman's blunt question. Initially she had viewed Luc in light of his heritage, but no longer. "No," she answered more firmly. "That has nothing to do with my feelings toward him."

"Good, I am glad to hear that." She gave an approving nod. "Marriages between whites and Indians are not unusual on Mackinac. Many times couples are married and several of their children baptized all on the same day."

Gillian stared at her companion, openmouthed, shocked by her candor.

Margaret merely chuckled at her expression and moved off to join her husband farther down the beach.

Once inside the snug harbor, the frigates lowered their

sails and dropped anchor. Men swarmed about the decks with the well-trained efficiency characteristic of the British Navy. As Gillian looked on, a small boat was rowed toward shore. All its occupants were resplendent in brilliant scarlet coats and tall, black, bucket-style shako hats. All the men, that is, except one, who was clad in bottle green. She was so intent on watching the scene unfold that she didn't notice Red Dog sidling closer.

"I see you wear the fire stone." The Ottawa's dark gaze greedily fastened on the ruby brooch pinned to the collar of her high-necked dress.

Gillian resisted the urge to retreat. Apprehension tickled her spine. Something about the man made her nervous. With a single look, he brought to mind tales of Indian brutality that circulated around London drawing rooms in hushed voices. Foolish, she knew; surely a product of an overactive imagination.

"Do you have a message for me, Red Dog?"

Though his wide mouth curled in a smile, not a trace of humor reached eyes as black as an abyss. "Tonight," he whispered. "When the moon is high."

She opened her mouth to question him further, but he was already moving away. *Tonight! Tonight, the wait was over; her fondest wish would be granted.* She had been ready for a week, her belongings stashed below her bed. Luc's warning about the man resounded through her head, but she stubbornly turned a deaf ear. Red Dog was a competent canoeist and that was all that mattered. They had entered into a simple agreement. After he completed his portion of their bargain, she would keep hers. Her freedom for the price of a trinket. A prize worthy of the cost.

"It's Colonel McDouall," James Babcock shouted. "The fort has a new commander."

No sooner had the announcement been made when the rat-a-tat-tat of drums sounded over the babble of voices.

Then, the sweet, high sound of a fife joined in, its notes lilting on the spring breeze. Heads swiveled in the direction of the fort. The entire garrison in crisply pressed uniforms and polished brass paraded through the sally port and down the rampart. Each man carried a rifle with a fixed bayonet slung across one shoulder. Their black stovepipe hats and bright red coats formed a vivid contrast against the stronghold's white limestone walls. Gillian spotted her father marching, head high, shoulders back. If relinquishing his command to another upset him, he didn't allow it to show.

She worked her way to the front of the crowd in time to observe McDouall as he climbed from the small craft and stepped ashore. He was a slender man of medium height. Russet-colored hair and long sideburns peeked from beneath his plumed shako. In deference to his former unit, he wore a uniform of bottle green with a crimson sash draped Scottish style over his right shoulder. A fur-trimmed dolman adorned with black velvet on the collar and cuffs was elegantly slung across his left. A silver whistle and chain hung from a black belt around his waist.

Randolph Stafford called his men to attention, then saluted smartly. "Captain Randolph Stafford of the Sixth Royal Veteran Battalion at your service."

The new commander returned the salute. "Lieutenant-Colonel Robert McDouall of the Glengarry Light Infantry Fencibles," he responded in a thick Scottish brogue.

"Welcome to Fort Mackinac. If you'll follow me, Colonel, I'll conduct you on a tour of your new command."

As she watched, her father led a contingent of officers from both regiments toward the fort. Gillian could not begin to guess his thoughts. Did he feel bitter? Angry? Or was he simply relieved to turn over the reins of leadership? She realized with a pang of regret how very little she knew about the man inside the soldier's uniform. When this senseless war ended, she vowed, she'd make him proud of her. Until then, however, she had to follow the dictates of her heart.

A steady stream of supplies was rowed ashore until the entire beach was littered with barrels, crates, and burlap sacks. A work crew was organized to transport the provisions to the fort, where they would be cataloged by the quartermaster, then placed in the storehouse. Every able-bodied man in the village lent an eager hand to the task, while the women formed small groups and talked among themselves.

Feeling every bit the outsider, Gillian turned and slowly made her way along the lakeshore. The arrival of additional troops and supplies reaffirmed the popular belief in an impending assault by the Americans. And England's equal determination to repel their attack. Judging from the large amount of provisions that had arrived, the British had no intention of surrendering this strategically located island to their enemy. How frightening it must be for innocent citizens to be caught between warring nations. She shuddered at the thought, chilled in spite of the warm spring sunshine. She was glad that when battle lines were drawn she would be far away.

As she rounded a bend in the trail, Arch Rock came into view. Gillian immediately spied Aupetchi perched on a boulder, eagerly waiting her arrival. The little girl's solemn face lit with one of her rare smiles when she saw her approach. At the sight of it, Gillian's mood lightened. Mindful of the small gift tucked into her reticule, she hastened her step.

Aupetchi scampered down from the rock to meet her. "I thought you forgot."

"Forget our lesson?" Gillian grinned down at her. "Never."

Once they were seated side by side on a sun-bleached

log that had washed ashore, Gillian picked up a stick and drew in the wet sand. "Today we will concentrate on the letter *B*. Now tell me what sound *B* makes."

Aupetchi promptly complied.

"Very good." Gillian beamed approval. "What are some words that begin with that letter?"

The little girl's brow puckered in concentration. "Bird, boat, big . . ."

". . . braid." Gillian gave the child's hair a playful tug.

"British," Aupetchi added with a pleased smile.

"Excellent. You learn very quickly. Soon you will be reading." *But she wouldn't be here to witness the proud moment.* The realization saddened her. Would anyone continue their lessons after she left? Probably not, she admitted with a stab of guilt.

"You all right?" Aupetchi tugged at her sleeve. "You sick?"

Gillian shook her head in vigorous denial, then cleared her throat and, reaching into her reticule, brought out the gift she had brought. "I have a small present for you."

Aupetchi warily examined the sheaf of papers that had been folded in half and bound with bright yellow ribbon. "What is this present you give me?"

"I have made you a primer."

The girl regarded her curiously. "A primer?"

"Yes, my little Robin." Gillian gave the little girl's shoulders an affectionate squeeze. "A book. Your very first reader. A simple test of your new skills."

The next hour passed quickly for both pupil and teacher. Heads bent, they had lapsed into a fit of giggles over a silly combination of rhyming words when startled by a familiar baritone.

"Am I interrupting a lesson in progress?"

Aupetchi jumped to her feet, the book clutched to her chest, her face wreathed in smiles. Not at all eager to confront Luc du Pré, Gillian rose slowly, brushing the wrinkles from her skirt. Her eyes swept his tall figure, taking in the moccasins muffling the sound of his footfalls. "Can't you make noise, du Pré, like everyone else?"

Luc ignored the question. "Isn't it time for school to be out for the day?" he asked, squatting on his haunches so he and the child were at eye level.

"Gillian made me a primer." Aupetchi extended her gift for his inspection. "She is teaching me to read."

"You . . . ?" He arched a brow. "Read?"

"And why not?" Gillian leaped to her little friend's defense. "She has a mind like a sponge and is willing and eager to learn."

"Gillian say women are smart as men," Aupetchi piped up. "Sometimes smarter."

"Is that right?" he drawled, straightening.

Gillian raised her chin a notch, ready with a scathing retort, only to find a teasing glint in the voyageur's chocolate-dark eyes. The unexpected discovery effectively silenced her.

"Perhaps, the pretty m'selle could teach even a stupid oaf like me?"

His deprecating description of himself was reminiscent of André Tousseau's baiting that evening on St. Joseph's Island. She had been fully prepared to see du Pré take umbrage at André's comment. Instead, to her amazement, he had returned the remark in kind. She had been amazed at their camaraderie. When he put forth the effort, Luc du Pré could ooze charm like any dandy at court. It could almost make her forget that he had destroyed her reputation. Almost . . .

"I thought, du Pré, you had no need to learn your letters."

His mouth curved attractively. "Isn't a person allowed a change of heart?"

"Not in your case," she snapped.

Not the least perturbed, he winked at Aupetchi. "Perhaps you'd share your primer?"

"Gillian say I learn quick. Maybe if I am good, you'll let me . . ." Her sentence cut off abruptly.

Puzzled, Gillian looked from one to the other, but both avoided meeting her eyes. How odd, she thought, frowning. It was as if an unspoken command had passed from man to child.

Luc cleared his throat. "Your grandfather has been searching for you, little one. He needs your help gathering firewood."

Aupetchi started to scamper off but stopped and turned back. "Tomorrow?" she asked, her eyes fixed hopefully on her teacher.

Gillian knew that in all likelihood she would never again see her eager pupil. Tomorrow, if all went according to plan, she would be miles from here on the long journey home. Aupetchi would be the only one on the island who would mourn her absence. Without turning her head, Gillian felt Luc's all too perceptive gaze fasten on her. Aupetchi waited patiently for her response.

"Tomorrow," Gillian repeated softly. At the lie, she felt a lump of remorse the size of a small fist rise in her throat. The girl ran off, disappearing around a bend in the trail.

"Are you all right?"

She blinked back moisture from her eyes. "Yes, thank you. I'm fine."

Luc hooked his thumbs in the sash about his waist. Tilting his head to one side, he studied her through narrowed eyes. "You had a strange look on your face just now as you watched Aupetchi leave."

"You're imagining things." She ducked her head and started to leave, but he fell into step next to her.

"Maybe you really are the angel young Jacob Mayfield claims."

She gave him a sharp look. "You're beginning to worry me, du Pré. I think perhaps you've spent too many hours in the sun."

He gave her a bemused glance, then sobered. "You've worked a minor miracle on Aupetchi. It's good to see her smile again. I thought I even heard the two of you giggling."

"She's a sweet child, and very bright."

Luc nodded. "Life hasn't been easy since she lost her mother last winter."

"My poor little Robin," Gillian murmured sympathetically. "I had no idea. She never once mentioned her mother's passing."

"I noticed a change in her recently, but until now I didn't know who was responsible for it." He stopped, angling his body so that the path was blocked. "Her grandfather has been deeply concerned. Your kindness is greatly appreciated."

As she stared into his handsome face, she felt a softening toward him. He had frightened her once, and still did. But for different reasons. With seemingly little effort, he exerted a strange effect upon her. A single glance could set her heart hammering, a smile turned her knees to jelly, and a touch . . . A touch sparked sensations best kept away from flame. To distance herself, she retreated a step, then quickly skirted around him.

"I noticed Red Dog sought you out down by the shore."

His words stopped her cold. Did he suspect the bargain she had struck with the Ottawa war chief? That she was planning to escape when the moon dangled high above the trees? She hid her panic behind hauteur. "What brought you here, du Pré? Were you spying on me?"

He snorted in disgust. "Don't flatter yourself, m'selle."

"Then can you explain what you're doing here?"

"My cabin is not far from Arch Rock."

"Oh . . ." She flushed with embarrassment. His logical explanation made her feel foolish.

"What did Red Dog want from you?"

His persistence irritated her. "I am free to speak to whomever I please. I am not accountable to you, my father, or anyone else."

"Well, maybe you should be." Impatiently, he dragged a hand through his hair. "How many times do I have to tell you to stay away from the man? He's evil, a menace to innocent young girls like yourself."

"Innocent!" she cried angrily. "What a strange choice of words to hear coming from your mouth. If you recall, du Pré, I am considered quite experienced in the ways of men. I repeat, I'm free to talk to anyone I choose, and that includes Red Dog."

He stepped closer. Fascinated, she watched angry red color creep across his sculpted cheekbones.

"Stay away from him," he growled. "I'm warning you for the last time."

Pure contrariness goaded her to challenge him. "Stop issuing orders. Red Dog has given me no cause to doubt him. In my opinion, he's as honorable as most men I've met, and more than others."

A muscle ticked in Luc's jaw as he fought to control his temper. "I don't want you hurt."

Pressing a hand to her breast, Gillian widened her eyes. "Surely, M'sieur du Pré, you don't harbor a certain fondness for me."

"This isn't a game, Gillian," he gritted from between clenched teeth. "You don't have any idea what a man like Red Dog is capable of."

"Then enlighten me." *Let him tell me*, she thought, *what caused the enmity between them*. Again she wo about the woman he had alluded to previously. Again she felt an unreasonable pang of jealousy.

Seconds ticked by with excruciating slowness. Luc scowled darkly as he waged an inner war. At last he spoke, breaking the heavy silence. "You'll just have to trust me. What I know about Red Dog isn't fit for delicate ears."

"Trust you?" She laughed bitterly. "That's the last thing I'd ever do."

She left Luc standing alone in the middle of the lakeside trail. Even with her back turned, she felt his angry stare follow her departure. He was furious with her. He had asked for her trust and she had laughed in his face. Revenge should be sweet, yet hers tasted like gall.

Barely noticing the bushes of dainty yellow flowers blanketing the craggy bluff, she trudged toward the village. Truth was, she didn't trust Red Dog completely, but if she was to leave Mackinac she had no other choice. She only wished she was half as confident as she tried to appear. But Luc's warning kept chiming through her mind. It wasn't so much what he said but what he refused to say that worried her most of all.

Chapter Nine

The moon shimmered like a pale gold medallion against black velvet. From his vantage point on a bluff west of the village, Luc shifted position. Although the hour was late, all his senses were fully alert. Over the years, and especially since the war began, he had learned to rely on his instincts. And right now they screamed a warning.

He glanced upward. The moon crept steadily along its arc until it was nearly overhead. Frowning, he returned his gaze to the shore below. Red Dog's canoe with its distinctive markings had been beached some distance from the others. Luc would have recognized it anywhere by the crude carving of a dog stained in red at one end, a bloody tomahawk at the other. He had observed Red Dog sidling up to Gillian that afternoon while supplies were being unloaded, seen him whisper in her ear, seen her nod of agreement, then watched as Red Dog ambled off with a satisfied smirk. The two had entered into a conspiracy of sorts, of that Luc was certain. Gillian Stafford, under a patina of sophistication, was as unsuspecting as a doe being lured into a hunter's trap.

His thoughts went back to their encounter at Arch Rock. He had been amazed at finding Gillian and Aupetchi together, their heads bent, one dark as a raven's wing, the other fair as summer wheat, giggling like schoolgirls. The sight had warmed his heart, and caused him to view Gillian Stafford in a new light. He tried to dismiss the captain's pretty daughter as shallow and selfish, too absorbed in her own problems to be concerned about others. Perhaps he had been too quick to judge. She had made her dislike of Indians no secret, yet she had befriended a small child of Ottawa parents. Aupetchi was clearly flourishing under the woman's attention.

Luc remembered seeing the little girl's sunny smile, a smile that had been absent since her mother passed away that winter. His spirits had lifted at the sight of her smile, the sound of her laughter. He owed Gillian for that unexpected gift. That in itself was worth the price of losing a night's sleep.

Gillian had told Aupetchi that women were as smart as men—sometimes even smarter. The observation obviously delighted the child. If his suspicions proved correct, he would debate that point. Certainly Gillian wasn't using her brain where Red Dog was concerned. Was her desire to leave Mackinac strong enough to defy logic? Common sense? Was it worth her life?

He blew out an impatient breath. Restless, edgy, he tried to find a more comfortable position from which to keep watch. By now, Toad would be halfway to Cheboygan, where he would relay the news of the arrival of British reinforcements. Luc hoped Toad would also relay his deeper concerns to the high command. He had tried to impress upon the man the need for swift, decisive action. The need to strike the stronghold at its weakest. Every day the Americans waited to launch their assault lessened their chance for success. England, it seemed, would stop at nothing in its bid to retain control of Mackinac Island. Today's events only served to reinforce Luc's theory. And this, Luc knew, was only the beginning. More troops were yet to arrive, along with hundreds of their Indian allies. That combined with the fort's almost impregnable location made the American's task a formidable one.

At first he thought he merely imagined movement. Rubbing his eyes, Luc strained to see through the darkness; then he tensed. A solitary figure approached along the trail leading from the village. As it drew nearer, he could discern a slender figure swathed in a dark cloak and lugging a cumbersome burden. Gillian! Even in the dead of night, he could recognize her. How quickly he had learned her walk. Not far behind, another figure stealthily crept along the path, careful to stay in the shadows afforded by bushes and shrubs. Luc instantly recognized Red Dog. Was Gillian aware that she was being followed? Or did she suspect someone close behind and not care?

Trying not to make a sound, Luc made his way down the steep bluff, closer to the water's edge. His instincts had been correct. Guided by the light of the full moon, the pair planned on leaving the island for parts unknown. Luc stationed himself at a spot not far from Red Dog's canoe, where he could see and hear what was said yet not be detected.

Gillian halted just shy of the canoe, an overstuffed valise hugged to her chest, and looked about. Every line of her body was taut as a bowstring. Pale moonlight limned delicate features etched with apprehension—and anticipation.

Red Dog waited until her back was turned to make his presence known. "You bring fire stone?" he demanded gruffly.

Even from a distance, Luc detected the urgency in the Ottawa's voice.

The valise slid to the ground. Gillian whirled around, one hand pressed to her throat. "You startled me." Her voice wavered.

Red Dog merely grunted. "You bring fire stone?"

"Yes," she replied, then cleared her throat. "I told you I would bring it with me."

"Give it to me." Red Dog held out his palm. "Now."

She shook her head with stubborn determination. "Not until after you complete your part of the bargain."

Glowering, Red Dog stepped closer until he was separated from her only by a hairsbreadth. His hand snaked out and latched onto her wrist. "I said now."

She twisted free and stepped back. "Not until you take me away from here."

Luc felt a grudging respect when Gillian held her ground, refusing to be intimidated.

"How do I know you'll take me away if I give it to you first?"

"You call Red Dog a liar?" he snarled.

Gillian swallowed audibly but held her ground. "That isn't what I meant. Grandmother's brooch is very precious. I want to make certain you'll keep our bargain."

Red Dog turned abruptly and started back the way he had come. He had taken only a half dozen steps before Gillian cried out, stopping him.

"Wait! Don't go." She fumbled frantically with an object pinned to the bodice of her dress, then held it out for him to see. The ruby gleamed dark as congealed blood in her outstretched palm. "Here, take it."

The last piece of the puzzle fell into place. Gillian was bartering her grandmother's jewelry in return for what she perceived as her freedom. Red Dog stood motionless, relishing his victory in this battle of wills. Luc took quick advantage of the moment by darting from his cover and sprinting toward Gillian.

"Luc . . ." Her jaw dropped with surprise.

Before she could divine his intent, he snatched the brooch from her hand. Raising his arm, he pitched it far into the lake, where in landed with soft *plink*.

Both Gillian and Red Dog stared at the inky water in stunned disbelief.

"What were you thinking?" Gillian whispered, shaking her head. "What gives you the right?"

Red Dog's fury couldn't be expressed in words. The malevolent glitter in his eyes mirrored his hatred. His expression contorted with rage, he lunged at Luc, hands curved, ready to curl around the neck of his enemy.

Luc brought up his knee, striking his foe in the groin. With a groan, Red Dog crumpled to the ground where he lay doubled over, holding himself.

Gillian stared at his writhing form in amazement. Everything had happened so quickly, so unexpectedly, she was at a loss for words.

Before she could recover her wits, Luc picked up her valise in one hand, took her elbow with the other, and half dragged her away. She cast a final glance over her shoulder. Red Dog lay rocking back and forth, his hands between his legs, moaning.

"How the hell did you manage to get past the sentries?" Luc asked through gritted teeth.

She had to practically run to match his long strides. "It's none of your bloody business."

"Tch, tch," he scolded, clucking his tongue. "Such language."

"Let go of me, you brute." She tried to jerk her arm from his grasp.

Luc's hold tightened. "Didn't I warn you to stay away from Red Dog?"

"Why should I listen to you? Red Dog has no reason to wish me harm."

"Don't you have a brain inside that head of yours? Any common sense at all?"

"Do you realize what you just did?"

"I realize exactly what I just did. You should be thanking me." Luc cast a sidelong glance at her. Her face was pale as the moonlight itself. Her voice sounded strangled by unshed tears. He felt himself softening toward her and hardened his resolve.

"You ruined everything. Everything . . ."

"You fail to comprehend that in all likelihood I saved your life."

"Impossible." She shook her head in denial. "Red Dog promised to take me away from here. Back to civilization."

"He'd take you away all right, much farther than you planned. Most likely to a cold, watery grave."

"Nonsense. You're exaggerating, only saying that to frighten me." In spite of her brave denial, Luc felt the shudder that rippled through her at his blunt description.

He stopped at the edge of the village. They stood glaring at each other, the silence broken only by the gentle lapping of waves upon the gravel beach. God, she was the most aggravating, the most infuriating woman he had ever had the misfortune to meet. He had never known anyone who could make him lose his temper so quickly.

In the moon's golden glow, the blond tendrils framing her face appeared spun silver. Emotion added depth and brilliance to her eyes, making them sparkle like twin sapphires. Luc found himself wondering how she would look with her hair flowing loose about her shoulders. Like an angel in a picture book?

"What do I have to say to make you understand?" he asked, dragging his hand through his shoulder-length hair. "Red Dog only wanted the jewel. Once he had the ruby, you'd become a hindrance. No one would ever know that you never made it beyond the straits. He'd weigh your body down with rocks. The waters are so deep, it would never surface."

What little color she had drained from her face. "No, stop it." She put her hands over her ears to shut out his words. "You're only saying that because you once had some disagreement over a woman."

The valise dropped to the ground. He wrapped his hands around her upper arms, his fingers tightening convulsively. He wanted to shake her until her teeth rattled. Drawing a ragged breath, he regained a semblance of control. "Come on," he urged tersely. "Let me get you back to the fort where you're safe."

She dug in her heels, refusing to budge. "Can't you get it through your thick head? I don't want to go back. I don't want to be there. I belong back in England."

"Stop behaving like a spoiled child!" A muscle ticked in his jaw. "Michigan is where you're at, and where you'll stay until this war is over. The sooner you accept this, the better off you'll be."

She tossed her head, the hood of her cloak falling to her shoulders. "Tell me, du Pré, in my situation would *you* sit meekly and do nothing to escape a situation you found intolerable?"

He watched emotions flit across her features. Anger, resentment, despair, frustration. "No," he answered truthfully, "but I hope I'd use better judgment than to trust such as Red Dog. Just how did you propose to get to England? Did he offer to row you across the Atlantic?"

"All Red Dog needed to do was take me someplace secure in British hands. From there, I could make arrangements for the remainder of the journey."

Luc regarded her with a raised brow. "The Americans retain firm command on Lake Erie, while the balance of power continually shifts back and forth on Lake Ontario. You conveniently forget you're caught in the middle of a war. That wonderful plan of yours would have placed you in grave danger.''

"You're so smug, so condescending," she snapped. "Stop treating me like a child."

"Then stop acting like one." No, she wasn't a child. It would be ludicrous to think of her as such. She was a woman—all woman. He shook his head to clear his unruly thoughts.

Not in the mood to fend off another of her vitriolic attacks, he picked up her bag and hurried her past a village deep in slumber. Off to their right, Indian allies had erected a handful of tents in an open field near the shore. From a distance, lights from scattered campfires resembled fireflies. Gillian's breath was becoming more labored. Luc couldn't tell if it was from anger or exertion as they climbed the street beyond the sleepy village.

They had nearly reached the cutoff to the fort when Gillian's foot caught in the hem of her cloak and she stumbled. Luc caught her before she fell and pulled her against him. Lips parted in surprise, she stared up at him. Her body molded his perfectly, gentle, graceful curves against hard planes and angles. Soft, yielding. His gut tightened in response. Fascinated, he watched her eyes darken to the smoky blue of a summer night. She started to speak, but before she could utter a syllable, he silenced her the only way he knew how.

Hard and demanding, his mouth descended over hers, effectively smothering an angry tirade. He meant it to be a simple kiss. A kiss borne of anger, frustration—and desire. But her lips were incredibly warm, undeniably sweet. The faint scent of lavender that hovered about her tugged at his senses. Suddenly Luc no longer wanted to conquer and plunder, but wanted the woman in his arms to surrender willingly. An inner voice prompted him to change tactics.

Slanting his mouth across hers, he gentled his touch. Coaxing, persuasive, savoring. His effort was rewarded seconds later when she leaned into him, tentatively returning the kiss. Her arms crept around his neck, her fingers burrowing into the long hair at the nape of his neck.

Gradually he deepened the kiss. His tongue probed the seam of her lips, seeking entry. Her lips parted, and his tongue slipped inside to tease hers in age-old love play. She shyly met his advances with those of her own. Wild and sweet. He marveled at a response that seemed as natural as a wildflower to May sunshine.

At a noisy rustling in the underbrush, Luc and Gillian quickly sprang apart, the mood broken. A raccoon emerged, stared at them with bright-eyed interest, then waddled off in search of food. The brief respite allowed sanity to return, bringing self-loathing in its wake. Luc cursed himself for a fool. God, what the hell was he doing? This woman was his sworn enemy. Needing to shatter the spell she wove so effortlessly, he chose his weapon and took aim.

"Just as I suspected," he drawled. "There's fire under all that frost. No wonder you earned your reputation." By her stricken expression, he knew his jibe had struck its mark.

Eyes wide with hurt, she stared at him. Then slowly she raised a hand that visibly trembled and wiped his taste from her kiss-swollen mouth. "I hate you, Luc du Pré," she said in a choked voice, then picked up her bag and ran toward the fort.

Luc made no attempt to follow but stood in the middle of the road and watched her retreat. At that moment, he hated himself. Using cruel words as ammunition, he had punished Gillian for his own weakness. Deliberately, callously inflicting pain. She had given him mindless pleasure, stirred his senses and, in return, he had wounded with deadly accuracy.

He raked his fingers through his hair. It couldn't be helped. In the long run, what he had just done would be for the best interests of both. This was war. They were enemies, as different from each other as two people could be. He couldn't afford to forget again.

Squinting through the darkness, Luc could barely make out Gillian's distant figure moving steadily toward the sally port. When would she finally stop rebelling against her fate? Why couldn't she be content to stay in Michigan? Why was she so insistent upon leaving? She reminded him of trapped animals he occasionally came across who chewed off their own legs in order to free themselves. He had tried everything short of the cold, hard truth to warn Gillian away from Red Dog. Running Fawn hadn't listened either when he had tried to tell her the man was dangerous, evil, the devil incarnate.

Sweat beaded his brow at the memory of Running Fawn's broken, battered body. He didn't want Gillian to suffer the same fate. But why should he expect her to believe his story when none of the British officials had? Someday, he vowed, Running Fawn would have her justice. Justice the British had denied her. He could never feel anything but loathing for any and all things British. And that included the British captain's beautiful daughter. His hatred for the British ran deep.

Nearly as deep as his hatred for Red Dog.

Luc turned in the direction of his cabin. From this night forward he would have to guard his back. Red Dog would not allow a blow like the one he had received tonight to go unpunished. Not only had Luc humiliated the Ottawa

war chief, he had robbed him of his magic "fire stone."
Red Dog was predictable. He would exact revenge.

Slowly. Painfully.

Luc du Pré complicated everything.

Gillian raced through the shadows afforded by the towering limestone walls. She sensed her progress being monitored by the sentry stationed in the west blockhouse but didn't care. The French brandy she had slipped the man earlier would ensure his silence. She cast an anxious glance at the barracks as she hastened past. Gillian breathed a sigh of relief at finding the long, two-story building dark and silent beneath the full moon.

Her prayers had gone unanswered. She had hoped never again to see the inside of Fort Mackinac. But that blasted du Pré had ruined everything. Everything. She blinked back tears of rage. If not for him, she would be far away by now, instead of returning to her father's quarters like a thief in the night. Raising her hand, she touched the bodice of her dress where her grandmother's brooch had recently been. She had lost both the heirloom and her chance to flee. Damn Luc du Pré!

Careful not to make any noise, she opened the door of the officer's quarters and slipped inside. The snick of the latch seemed uncommonly loud in her ears. She paused on the threshold, waiting for her eyes to adjust to the gloom.

"Gillian, is that you?"

She started at the sound of her father's voice. "Yes, Father, it's me. Forgive me if I've disturbed your sleep."

A narrow sliver of light peeked from beneath his bedroom door. "What are you doing up at this hour?"

"I know it's late, but I was unable to sleep." She barely

had time to stash her belongings behind the settee before
he appeared in the doorway, pulling a flannel dressing
gown over his nightshirt.

He frowned at finding her fully dressed. "It's after midnight. Where have you been?"

The sharp accusation in his tone stung. "I-I've been
walking."

"At this hour?"

"I didn't look at the time." She unfastened her cloak,
folded it, and laid it over the back of a chair. "I was restless
and thought some fresh air would help me relax."

"It isn't safe for a young woman to be out alone."

"What could be safer than a fort prepared for a siege?"
she countered.

"That isn't what I meant, as you very well know." His
frown deepened. "What will people think?"

"My reputation could hardly be in worse shape than it
is already," she said with a harsh laugh. "Let people think
what they will."

He jammed his hands into the pockets of his dressing
gown but made no move toward her. "I have no idea how
word got out; nevertheless, the damage has been done."

"Yes, I suppose so." Suddenly she felt unutterably weary,
defeated. "As you just reminded me, Father, the hour is
late. If you'll excuse me, I think I'll go upstairs to bed."

He cleared his throat. "Gillian . . . ?"

She paused on the second step, her hand on the rail.
She'd tiptoe down later to retrieve her belongings from
behind the settee. "Yes, Father?"

"If you're worried about the American attack, don't
be. We're well prepared to repel any invasion they might
launch. When we're finished with them, they'll regret they
ever wasted ammunition in their feeble attempt."

"Thank you for your reassurance. I'll rest easier knowing
we're safe."

"Gillian . . ."

She had mounted two more stairs when her father's voice called out for the second time. She waited, not speaking, puzzled by the tenuous note in his voice. Something was different about him tonight. He was being almost too nice. Then it dawned on her—he was sober.

"Never mind," he muttered. "Sleep well, child." Turning, he vanished into his room.

Gillian felt a crushing weight on her shoulders. As had happened many times since her mother's death, important things were left unsaid. Apologies, compliments, endearments, locked inside, condemned to eternal silence. How sad for them both. Her throat tightened with unshed tears. "Good night, Father," she whispered, knowing he couldn't hear her. "I love you."

She wished for a way to repair their relationship. His drinking had an adverse effect on his personality, made him meaner, more volatile. The chasm between them had widened until it yawned like a canyon. The fact saddened her. In spite of his seeming indifference, she loved him and yearned for his approval. Swallowing the lump in her throat, she climbed the stairs.

Once inside her attic room, she didn't bother lighting a lamp. She sat on the narrow cot, her head resting against the wall, waiting for her father to fall asleep so she could fetch her valise from its hiding place. The events of the night rose up to overwhelm her. A single tear slid down her cheek. As much as she detested this island, for the time being it seemed Fort Mackinac was destined to be her home. She had attempted to flee and failed miserably. Now she must try to make the best of the situation. Never had she felt so entirely out of place, an alien in a strange land. This vast, uncivilized country terrified her.

. . . and confused her.

Just as her feelings for Luc du Pré did. She traced a

fingertip over her bottom lip, teased by the memory of his kiss. The ruggedly handsome voyageur confounded her more than the northern territory itself. She should hate him, not wonder how it would feel to be lost in his arms. Why did she burn when he touched her? Melt when he kissed her? She despised herself for the sensations he evoked. What kind of woman was she? Perhaps she richly deserved public condemnation. She had chosen unwisely in responding to Jeremy Blackwood. She was determined not to repeat her mistake.

Rising from the bed, she walked to the window. Silvery moonbeams formed a fairylike span between the island and the mainland. She wished she could skip across the ephemeral bridge and leave her problems behind.

Chapter Ten

"Well, Daughter, congratulations on a job well done." Randolph Stafford stood in the center of the living quarters, noting the changes Gillian had made for the first time. "You've transformed this place."

Gillian swelled with pride under her father's rare praise. All the little touches she had added created a homier atmosphere. Multicolored rag rugs purchased from an elderly widow were scattered over the pine floorboards. A chipped pitcher filled with wildflowers sat on the corner cupboard. A length of cheerful green-and-white plaid muslin found in one of the trading posts formed a swag above the window. A shallow wood bowl filled with potpourri on the trestle table filled the room with the scent of dried apples, cloves, and cinnamon. A small collection of books, a basket of needlework, and a shawl draped over the back of the settee added a personal touch that had been lacking. The atmosphere no longer seemed austere but inviting.

"All this hard work deserves a reward."

"A reward?" Gillian's eyes lit with interest. Her father's generous words made her suspicious. Why was he suddenly being so nice? Perhaps, just perhaps, it was an attempt to repair their damaged relationship. "What sort of reward did you have in mind?"

"The colonel is sending me across the straits to Mill Creek. I need to make arrangements with John Campbell for a shipment of lumber. I thought you might care to accompany me."

"I'd love to."

"Good." He nodded approvingly. "I believe Campbell has a daughter near your age. I thought the companionship of another young lady might be a welcome diversion."

"When are we going?" She could scarcely contain her excitement.

"Be ready to leave promptly after the noon meal."

The minute her father left to return to headquarters, Gillian flew up the stairs and began searching for an appropriate dress to wear on her first visit off the island. Something not too plain, not too fancy. Fashionable but understated. She wanted to make a good impression on the mill owner's daughter. How wonderful it would be to find a friend to ease the loneliness. Thanks to Luc du Pré, tales about her liaison in England had severely curtailed any friendships she might have formed with other women on the island. Now she had to search elsewhere for female companionship. She held up the striped blue muslin then discarded it. The pink foulard quickly met a similar fate. After much indecision, she finally settled on a dress of lavender muslin sprigged with dainty yellow flowers and lace trimming the high neck and long sleeves.

As she tied the yellow satin bow of a straw bonnet with a wide brim and high crown beneath her chin, she stepped back to examine her reflection in the small beveled mirror. Pursing her lips, she studied her image. Her daily afternoon walks were taking their toll on her complexion. No longer an almost translucent ivory, her skin had taken on pale golden undertones from hours spent outdoors. The contrast made the hue of her eyes bluer, brighter. Though loathe to admit it, the new environment agreed with her. She looked glowingly healthy and fit.

She bent to pick up the warm woolen shawl she knew she'd need on the lake crossing. Her eyes rested on the fur throw at the foot of her cot. Unable to resist, she ran her hand over the thick pelts, delighting in their luxurious softness. She had considered Luc thoughtful and gallant for providing for her comfort during the long journey from St. Joseph's Island. Never had she guessed him a scandalmonger. She sighed and turned away. Where men were concerned she habitually exhibited poor judgment. Neither Jeremy Blackwood nor Luc du Pré were worthy of trust.

She was ready and waiting when her father returned. Taking his arm, she was aware of the many admiring glances that followed them as they left the fort. Others, she knew, were speculative, critical. She kept her head high, determined not to let anyone or anything put a damper on the afternoon excursion.

Her resolve was put to the test when she sighted Luc du Pré waiting for them on the beach. Gillian stared at him with dismay. They hadn't spoken since the night of her aborted escape—the night he had kissed her. Luc glanced up at their approach, his expression devoid of emotion. They might have been strangers instead two people who had shared a moment of passion.

"What are *you* doing here?" she asked, her voice sharp, accusing, knowing the answer to her question was blatantly obvious.

The corner of his mouth lifted in amusement. "What does it look like, m'selle?"

She turned to her father. "Isn't there anyone else who can take us?"

"Gillian!" Her father frowned at her, appalled by her outburst. "Where are your manners? I've never known you to be deliberately rude."

"It's of little consequence," Luc said. "I don't take offense easily."

Stafford ignored Luc's attempt to intercede. "Surely, Daughter, you can have no legitimate objection to du Pré. No one is more qualified to transport us across the straits. Now be polite and apologize for your behavior."

Seething under her father's censure, she avoided meeting Luc's eyes. "I'm sorry, m'sieur," she mumbled, insincerity in every syllable.

"Please overlook my daughter's lapse of manners." Stafford shook his head. "At times, her actions completely baffle me."

"Think nothing of it, Captain Stafford. Young women, so I've observed, are often guided by emotion rather than logic."

Gillian's hands clenched at her sides, the nails digging into her palms. She yearned to wipe the condescending smirk from the voyageur's handsome face. She had ample reasons to dislike him—all well justified. He was arrogant, condescending, deceitful, an opportunist. He had not only ruined her reputation but her chance to flee, then compounded his list of affronts by boldly kissing her. When she closed her eyes, she could still remember the sensations that cascaded through her under his masterful touch. Shameful, erotic, exciting.

Stafford flicked a speck a dust from his sleeve. "Let's get underway, shall we?"

An almost imperceptible signal passed between the two men. Luc swept Gillian off her feet in one smooth motion. Her arms automatically wrapped around his neck as he splashed into the water. The wide brim of her bonnet shielded her from seeing his entire face but put her eyes level with his mouth. Unbidden, unwanted, the memory of his kiss resurfaced. Her cheeks grew warm; her pulse accelerated. Until the moment his lips had taken command of hers, she hadn't realized a kiss could unleash such tumult. Certainly Jeremy's never had. While pleasurable, she had never felt as though she were drowning in a sea of pure bliss.

Luc deposited Gillian on the narrow seat in the front of the canoe. The craft rocked from side to side as her father climbed in behind her. Then Luc gave the canoe a gentle shove and quickly swung himself over the edge. Picking up a paddle, he sent the birch bark craft slicing through the foam-crested waves.

"The straits form the meeting place of two great lakes," Luc announced midway to their destination. "Lake Michigan is to our right, Lake Huron on the left."

Once again Gillian was awed by the vast wilderness. Lakes in the Michigan Territory seemed as enormous as oceans. Directly ahead, a dense green forest loomed larger with every stroke of Luc's paddle. Virgin tracts of timber stretched as far as the eye could see. This land, she reluctantly admitted, possessed a strange, primitive beauty. Untamed. Waiting to be conquered by hardy individuals unafraid of the challenge. Men like Luc du Pré. Or women such as Margaret Babcock. People who could carve out a life for themselves, strike a balance between comfort and hardship. She definitely didn't number among them. She needed to feel accepted by those around her, feel at ease in her surroundings, not constantly ostracized and intimidated. No, she sighed, she didn't belong here.

And never would.

The trip was completed in less than an hour's time. The instant the canoe scraped bottom, Luc leaped ashore and guided it to the pebbled beach. Placing his hands at Gillian's waist, he swung her to the ground, then lent a hand to assist her father from the craft.

The British captain rubbed his hands in satisfaction as he surveyed the area. "No shortage of lumber here, is there? Campbell should be able to supply our needs quite adequately."

Luc stowed the paddles under the seats. "Many acres of forest were already cleared when the fort was relocated some years back."

Gillian glanced at Luc curiously. Had she detected a subtle rebuke in his tone? she wondered.

"Well, there's much more where that came from. I doubt that we'll ever run out of trees to cut." Stafford shaded his eyes and looked back across the lake toward the island. "I'm expecting a bateaux to join us, along with a small contingent to help transport the lumber. More men were sent to purchase necessary items in the old village. They also have orders to rendezvous here."

"The sawmill is this way." Luc led them toward a well-trod trail leading away from the water's edge. Gillian and her father kept close behind.

"You mentioned an old village, Father. I didn't know there was another settlement close by."

"The original fort was located about six miles west of here. Upon assignment there in 1779, Major Patrick Sinclair deemed it wise to move the entire fort across the straits."

Gillian looked back over her shoulder at the expanse of water separating the island from the mainland. "However did they manage such a feat?"

"Buildings were dismantled one by one," Luc explained. "During the course of the next two winters, they were transported across the ice. St. Anne's Church was the first to be moved."

"The barracks, guardhouse, and storehouse are also the original buildings brought from Michilimackinac." Stafford swatted at a deer fly buzzing around his head, then continued. "The present site is much more desirable. In addition to a fine natural harbor, the island is more defensible in case of attack."

"Attack?" Gillian echoed. "Was the old fort ever under attack?"

"Many years ago," her father replied brusquely. "A renegade Indian by the name of Pontiac led a vicious massacre on troops stationed there."

Luc scowled. "Many consider Pontiac a great chieftain—and a fearless leader."

"Ridiculous," Stafford snapped. "The man was nothing more than a ruthless savage. It's common knowledge that Pontiac sided with the French against the English during the French and Indian Wars."

Gillian knew that in her father's estimation nothing was more despicable than being an enemy against the crown. Only death was considered fitting punishment for anyone found guilty of such a heinous offense. "Tell me more about the massacre," she asked, her interest piqued in spite of herself.

Luc launched into the story as they wound through the woods toward the sawmill. "It occurred while the English were celebrating the king's birthday. As part of the celebration, the Chippewa played a game of baggitway. The object was to throw a wooden ball toward a post located on opposite ends of the playing field. The teams employed various tactics in order to score a goal. As a result, vicious fights were routine among the participants."

Randolph Stafford picked up the tale. "The officers and enlisted men watched with keen interest, wagering on which team would win the contest. Suddenly, the ball was tossed over the wall of the fort. The players, pretending to be caught up in the spirit of the game, streamed through the open gate, stopping only long enough to grab weapons concealed beneath their women's blankets. Before the British realized what was happening the Indians turned on them."

"And the soldiers?" Gillian asked, already dreading the answer. "What happened to them?"

Luc held aside a low-hanging branch for Gillian and her father to pass under. "Most were killed outright. The rest were taken prisoner."

"What about the prisoners? Did they survive?"

"Some of them were also killed."

"Slaughtered like cattle." Stafford forged ahead.

Gillian looked to Luc for confirmation, but he avoided meeting her gaze. "The remainder of the prisoners were sold or traded among the tribes and eventually returned to the British at Montreal."

Randolph Stafford aimed an accusing look at Luc over his shoulder. "The entire time the French-Canadians at the fort did nothing to prevent the massacre. Absolutely nothing."

Refusing to rise to the bait, Luc merely shrugged. "They, too, would have forfeited their lives had they interfered."

Gillian shivered at the cold indifference in his voice. The sorry plight of the soldiers at old Fort Michilimackinac clouded her excitement at visiting the mainland. She couldn't dispel the certainty that those poor unfortunate men had suffered untold horrors before their ordeal finally ended. "And the Indian chieftain Pontiac—what happened to him?"

Stafford let out a harsh bark of laughter. "The bastard ultimately was forced to pledge fidelity to the British."

"He was murdered by a tribe of Illinois. Some say it was in retaliation for stabbing an Illinois chief in Detroit." Luc leveled a hard stare at the British captain. "Pontiac is considered a great hero among my mother's people, the Ottawa.''

No one spoke again until they reached a wooden footbridge that spanned a babbling creek. No sooner had they crossed onto the opposite side when a loud thumping sound commenced, followed by a shrill whine. The harsh noise made Gillian want to put her hands over her ears and grit her teeth.

"What is that horrid racket?''

"Campbell's water-powered saw.'' Her father cupped his hand around his mouth in order to be heard. "Clever fellow, Robert Campbell. He devised a way to produce sawn lumber twenty times faster than pit sawyers. Imagine, twenty times faster! His son, John, runs the place since his father passed away.''

A short distance farther the trail opened onto a wide clearing. The mill area teemed with activity. Great piles of felled trees were stacked nearby. The pungent scent of fresh-cut wood filled the air. The mill itself was a narrow structure on wooden stilts that straddled a creek. A long sluiceway connected it to a dam beyond. Acres of land had been cleared for crops. Cattle grazed contentedly in an adjoining field. A spacious frame house sat at a right angle to the mill, which Gillian assumed to be the home of the Campbell clan. Altogether, she concluded, Mill Creek appeared to be a prosperous and efficiently run operation.

A stocky man with auburn hair and a bushy beard hurried forward to greet them with a broad grin. "Ah, Captain Stafford, I was expecting you.''

"Campbell.'' Randolph pumped the Scotsman's hand. "Good to see you again. Your business seems to be thriving in spite of hard times.''

"This blasted war has wrecked havoc with the fur trade. Pity.'' Campbell shook his head in mock sorrow. Then, smiling once again, he turned his attention to Gillian, who stood slightly behind her father. "Who may I ask is this charming young lady?"

Stafford promptly performed the introductions. He made no attempt, however, to acknowledge Luc's presence.

Gillian shot Luc a surreptitious glance to see how he reacted to the slight. He was being treated more like a lowly servant rather than a valued ally. But if he was upset or angry, he kept his feelings well hidden.

"Gillian, I'm afraid, has chosen a rather inopportune time to visit the Michigan Territory."

"Yes, I quite agree. The timing is unfortunate," Campbell commiserated. "Matter of fact, I've sent my wife and daughter to stay with my wife's younger sister until the situation here is resolved. I don't want to risk their well-being."

Gillian's fragile hope of a friendship with Campbell's daughter burst like a bubble. She had discovered that it wasn't the shops or theaters she missed the most when she thought about London. It was the young women whose friendships she had taken for granted. Friends who shared the little, everyday events in life. If she were still in London, she wondered if they would continue to be her friends. After word spread about her escapade with Jeremy, she doubted any of them would associate with her.

"I'm sure you can find some way to entertain yourself, Daughter, while Mr. Campbell and I discuss business."

"There are a variety of scenic trails," John Campbell volunteered helpfully. "Most afford pretty views with wildflowers and the like. There's a beaver dam a little ways up the creek. You might even spot a deer or two."

"Don't worry about me, gentlemen. I'll meet you back here later."

As she turned to leave, Campbell gave her father a hearty slap on the back. "Heard you've been building a new fortification should the Americans attack."

"That's correct. But in order to complete it quickly, the army needs lumber. We're both reasonable men, Mr. Campbell. I think we should be able to come to terms."

"While we're talking business, maybe the army would also like to purchase some grain from my gristmill. I understand you have a lot of hungry mouths to feed with all the reinforcements sent your way."

Gillian gladly left the men to their negotiations. Without turning her head, she sensed Luc's intense gaze follow her as she chose a path running parallel to the creek and into the surrounding forest.

Setting aside her disappointment, she concentrated instead on enjoying the sunny spring afternoon. The scenery was enchanting. The woods were thick with red oak, pine, cedar, maple, and aspen. Here and there, she spotted dogwood in bloom. Wildflowers lifted delicate faces to the sun; trillium, lady's slippers, and glossy yellow ones she failed to identify. Continuing along the trail, she successfully located the beaver pond. Fascinated, she watched the sleek little animals construct a dam of logs, branches, rocks, and mud.

Slowly she started back toward the mill. Knowing there was no need to hurry, she sat down to rest beside the creek. The sound of water tumbling over its rocky bed had a soothing effect. Occasionally the peace and quiet was interrupted by the distant thump and whine from the mill. The sun seemed uncommonly warm, and she yawned. Taking off her bonnet, she leaned against a sturdy oak and promptly fell asleep.

Her dreams were happy at first, filled with a pastel kaleidoscope of changing shapes and colors. Then the colors darkened, deepened. Luc's face emerged through a swirling mist. The dark shade of his eyes was so intense, they looked almost black. But instead of frightening, they beckoned. Instead of coldness, they burned with passion.

She stirred restlessly, vaguely aware of wanting, longing for something just beyond her grasp.

The murmur of men's voices intruded into her dream world, and she opened her eyes. Disoriented from sleep, she stared up at three figures limned against the sunlight filtering through the overhead branches.

"The beautiful maid wakens and finds a handsome prince."

The man in the center raised a bottle to his lips and drank deeply. "Hunter certainly is a smooth-talking devil."

"Certainly is, Wilcox," the third man agreed, accepting the bottle and taking a swig.

Gillian raised herself up on one elbow. She recognized the men now. They were the same trio of soldiers who had accosted her shortly after arrival.

"A pretty girl shouldn't be wandering about the woods alone." Hunter gave her a slack-mouthed smile. "She could meet up with a savage redskin."

The men hooted with laughter at Hunter's remark. The red-haired man called Wilcox swiped at his streaming eyes with the back of his hand, then erupted in another fit of giggling. Gillian shook her head, disgusted at the men's antics.

"You men could land in the guardhouse for drunkenness." Feeling at a disadvantage, Gillian scrambled to her feet. "Surely you have duties to attend to."

"No one even knows we're here yet," Wilcox volunteered.

"Wilcox, Grayson, and I decided there was no need to hurry reporting in." Sauntering closer, Hunter reached behind her and tugged at the coil of hair that had become loosened from its pins while she slept. It fell across her shoulder like a heavy rope.

Angrily, Gillian batted his hand away. "Keep your hands to yourself, soldier."

Hunter was undeterred. "It's not very smart, wandering so far by yourself. With all the noise from the sawmill, you could scream your head off and no one would even hear."

The other two men closed in until they formed a loose ring, cutting off her escape. Gillian took a step backward but was brought up short against the trunk of the tree. Her initial irritation fled in the wake of fear. It wasn't Indian savages who worried her, but three drunken soldiers. Alcohol fogged logic and numbed the conscience. It also removed common sense.

"Kindly get out of my way and let me pass." In spite of her increasing nervousness, she forced herself to speak calmly.

Hunter raised the bottle and took a deep swallow. He leered at her. "What are you willing to grant in exchange for your freedom?"

"I'll forget this little incident ever happened." Gillian was proud of the fact that her voice didn't waver.

Grayson and Wilcox traded hopeful looks, but Hunter, the bolder of the three, wasn't satisfied. "I had something else in mind."

Reaching out, Hunter ran his hand along her jaw. "How about a little kiss for starters? I have it on good authority that you're good at it."

Gillian jerked away from his touch. Her head reeled from the sour smell of his breath. "I'd rather kiss a skunk, Private."

His eyes narrowed at the insult. "You're all hoity-toity," he sneered. "Well, I'm not fooled by your fancy airs. A friend of mine was on sentry duty the other night. He saw you kissing that half-breed. No telling what else you're giving away for free. Maybe you ought to give us a sample, too."

The men caught her as she tried to run.

"Not so fast."

Gillian could barely hear Grayson's slurred voice above the wild thundering of her heart. The whine of a saw sounded from a distance. She knew it would be futile to scream. No one would hear her above the mill's racket.

"You're not getting away this easily." Wilcox's face was flushed nearly as bright as his hair.

"Let go of me, you louts!" She tried to wrench free, but the men tightened their grip.

Hunter smirked and seemed to enjoy watching her struggle. "That's not a good way to behave when you need a favor. Why don't you ask us real nice?"

"You can go straight to hell," Gillian spat.

Instead of being enraged, the men laughed.

"Temper, temper." Hunter clucked his tongue reprovingly. "The lady has spirit. Maybe that's what appeals to the half-breed. What do you say, men, how about a little contest?"

Grayson scratched his jaw. "What sort of contest?"

"How about finding out which one of us is the best kisser? We'll let the lady be the judge."

"What's the prize?" Wilcox asked, clearly intrigued by the notion. "Contest's no good without one."

"Winner names his prize."

"She'll be my partner at the next garrison dance?"

Hunter gave a snort of disgust at Wilcox's naïveté. Grayson sniggered.

"She's no longer a virgin," Hunter sneered. "Why settle so cheaply?"

"After all, you're not asking for anything she hasn't given before."

The three hooted with laughter.

"You men must be crazy!" Aghast, Gillian looked at each of the two men who still held her firmly between them. "You'll be court-martialed. Thrown in the guardhouse—or worse."

Wilcox swallowed noisily and started to relax his hold.

"Don't be such a bloody coward, man," Grayson snapped.

Hunter lowered his voice and spoke in a more persuasive tone. "How long has it been since you've had a woman? Have you forgotten how good it feels?"

Wilcox's Adam's apple bobbed in his thin neck. "Yeah, I want to, but what's to stop her from telling the old man?"

"There are ways." Hunter took a long pull from the bottle, then wiped his mouth with the back of his hand. "Trust me, my friend, there are ways."

The blood congealed in Gillian's veins. She searched the faces of her captors, but her fragile hope of gaining her release withered and died.

"Stand back, men, while I demonstrate how it's done."

Gillian struggled against their hold to no avail. Hunter swaggered toward her. Grayson gave her a rough shove, and she stumbled forward. Hunter caught her about the waist and jerked her against him.

"C'mon, sweetheart, don't play coy."

Her stomach churned from the smell of whiskey and sweat. She turned her head sharply, and his lips missed her mouth and grazed her ear instead. Bracing both hands solidly against his red wool jacket, she pushed with all her might. "I told you to let go of me."

"You heard the lady. Release her. Now!"

Heads whipped in the direction of the softly spoken command. Luc! Gillian felt an overwhelming sense of gratitude as he stepped from the cover of trees, looking every bit as fierce as his Ottawa ancestors.

"Stupid half-breed," Hunter sneered. He relaxed his

hold slightly but didn't release her. "Can't you count? There are three of us and only one of you."

"I'd advise you to take your hand from the lady before I break it."

Though he didn't raise his voice, something in Luc's tone must have alerted the men that his was no idle threat. Even though they weren't directed at her, his words sent a chill down her spine.

"So that's how it is. She's your woman." Hunter pushed Gillian away as if suddenly discovering her diseased. "I wouldn't soil my hands on a woman who's been with a half-breed."

Fear fluttered along her nerve endings. Gillian's gaze flew to Luc. Feet firmly planted, arms crossed, he appeared deceptively relaxed. But she knew otherwise. She sensed the tension radiating from him like waves of heat. Never taking his eyes off the men, he reached out and, drawing her to his side, shifted his body so that he stood between her and danger.

"One of you against the three of us," Hunter taunted. "I think the half-breed needs to be taught a lesson, don't you, men?"

Grayson nodded enthusiastically. "Du Pré lacks the proper respect for the British uniform. He needs to be brought down a peg or two."

"Yeah," Wilcox parroted, eager to gain his colleagues' approval. "Let's teach him a lesson."

Three against one? Gillian felt ill. Luc didn't stand a chance. They'd beat him to a bloody pulp. "No harm's been done." She cleared her throat nervously. "If you leave now, I promise I won't mention this incident to my father."

"Bitch!" Hunter snarled contemptuously. "I'll teach you a lesson or two after I finish with the half-breed."

Bringing down the arm that held the whiskey bottle, Hunter smashed the glass against the trunk of a tree. Chunks of green glass glittered like emeralds in the long grass. Hunter clutched the bottle neck in one hand, its jagged points aimed at Luc's throat.

Chapter Eleven

Hunter grinned. "Now we'll separate the men from the boys."

"This is going to be good." Grayson rubbed his hands in glee. "I saw Hunter gouge a man once in a Bristol pub. He's quick as lightning."

Luc dropped his voice so only Gillian could hear. "As soon as I engage their attention, run to the mill where you'll be safe."

"Not so brave are you now, half-breed," Hunter taunted. He dropped into a crouch.

Luc stepped forward, away from Gillian, then he, too, crouched low, his gaze fixed on Hunter. Slowly the two men began circling the small clearing.

Hunter's cohorts cheered him on.

"After Hunter's worked his art, du Pré," Grayson boasted, "you'll be so ugly no woman's ever going to want to bed you."

"Yeah," Wilcox chortled. "Unless he wears a bag over his head."

Like dance partners, Luc and Hunter moved in carefully choreographed steps. First one way, then the other. Hunter's right hand was never still. He sketched small circles in the air with the broken glass.

Gillian edged away until her back was pressed against the rough bark of a tree. In spite of the problems Luc had caused her, deserting him was impossible. Her eyes fastened on the scene unfolding before her. She bit her lip to keep from crying out. She was vaguely aware of a heavy thumping but couldn't tell if it came from the saw-mill or from inside her own chest. She flinched at the high-pitched screech of metal against wood. Or was it tension rasping nerves already raw? She could no longer differentiate. Just as steel tore through lumber, violence ripped the gentleness from the spring afternoon.

Wilcox egged his friend on. "Give it to the bastard."

Hunter lunged forward, the sharp bottle edges aimed at Luc's face. Luc neatly feinted his thrust. Frustrated, Hunter lunged again, but alcohol had slowed his reflexes, making them awkward, clumsy. Almost lazily, Luc spun on the balls of his feet. Catching Hunter's wrist, he gave it a vicious twist. The crunch of breaking bone could be heard in the sudden stillness. Howling in pain, Hunter sank to the ground, clutching his injured arm against his chest.

Luc turned to the other two soldiers who watched in bug-eyed silence. "Who wants to be next?"

Grayson and Wilcox looked dubious.

"Did you see that? He tricked me," Hunter charged, his face pale, his eyes bright with malice. "Dirty Indian fighting. Don't let him get away with it!"

Grayson, not wanting to be labeled a coward, flew forward, balled up his fist, and let it fly. Luc dodged the blow, which glanced off his jaw and cut his lip. Joining in the fray, Wilcox leaped on Luc's back, clinging like a monkey to an organ grinder. Wilcox slid his arms around Luc's upper torso, pinning his arms at his sides. Before Luc could free himself, Grayson landed a solid punch just below the colorful sash around his waist.

Mobilized by Luc's grunt of pain, Gillian looked about for a weapon. She spotted a sturdy branch nearby. Careful not to draw attention to herself, she edged over and quickly picked it up. She was about to raise it and bring it crashing down on Grayson when Luc recovered from the blow.

Rearing back so Wilcox must either support his weight or crumple beneath it, Luc kicked both feet into Grayson's chest. The air left the soldier's lungs in a soft *whoosh* as he sagged to the ground. Thrown off balance, Wilcox's knees buckled. Whirling around, Luc plucked him up by the collar and tossed him on top of his two cronies.

Luc stood over the trio of redcoats. "Gentlemen—and I use that term lightly—are you ready to declare a truce? Or do you need further lessons?"

Wilcox struggled to rise from the heap. "No Indian savage is . . ."

Luc shoved him down, then, grabbing both him and Grayson by the hair, knocked their heads together with a resounding *clunk*. Dazed, they slumped back to the grass. "This discussion, I presume, is finished."

When no argument was forthcoming, Gillian came to stand beside him. She gazed down at the three soldiers sprawled at her feet. They no longer posed a threat of any kind. If not for Luc du Pré's timely intervention, the outcome would have been quite different. She refused to think what might have resulted if he hadn't happened along when he had.

Luc scowled down at the untidy group who were beginning to emerge from their drunken haze. "A final bit of advice," he warned in a voice threaded with steel. "If any of you so much as utters one inappropriate word to Miss Stafford, I'll tie your testicles in knots. Now get out of my sight before I'm tempted to do just that."

Amid a chorus of grunts and groans, the men scrambled to their feet. Wilcox half supported Grayson, who continued to wheeze from the blow to his chest. Before turning down the path to the mill, Hunter glared back at them.

"You'll be sorry, du Pré. When battle lines are drawn you'll find yourself on the wrong end of a musket."

Gillian breathed a sigh of relief as they staggered across the clearing, disappearing into a stand of aspen. Unthinkingly, she placed her hand on Luc's arm. "Do you think Corporal Hunter would actually shoot you?"

Luc gave a careless shrug. "Oh, he means it all right. Hunter would be happy to claim he found my body with a musket hole through the heart."

She regarded him with troubled eyes. First Red Dog, now Corporal Hunter. Once again her actions had placed him in jeopardy. "I'm sorry," she murmured. Feeble as it sounded, it was all she could think to say.

He glanced pointedly at her hand, which still rested on his arm. "I'm not looking for sympathy."

She quickly withdrew her touch. "I wasn't offering any," she snapped, irritated at him, at herself. It was a bald-faced lie and they both knew it.

"Prickly as ever, I see." His chocolate-dark eyes took in her disheveled appearance. "Are you all right?"

She felt self-conscious under his scrutiny. "I'm fine. Thank you."

His brows drew together in a frown. "If memory serves, I thought when the fight started I told you to run back to the mill?"

"I must have forgotten." She looked him square in the eye and dared him to call her a liar.

He motioned at the sturdy branch she still clutched. "And what, may I ask, were you planning to do with that?"

Feeling foolish, she tossed it aside. She tried for nonchalance. "For a moment, I feared the men would best you. I thought I might need to defend myself."

"Or, perhaps, defend me?"

She refused to meet his gaze. Luc du Pré had the uncanny ability to see more than she wanted to reveal.

"I don't think those men will cause any more trouble. Your father will see to it that they enjoy a lengthy stay in the guardhouse."

"I don't intend to tell Father."

"Why not?"

"My reputation's already in shambles. I don't need any more notoriety." She stooped to gather some of the pins that had fallen from her hair. "Besides, as you just said, they no longer pose a threat to me."

Luc shook his head in amazement. Gillian Stafford constantly surprised him. She had barely escaped a brutal assault, yet instead of succumbing to hysterics, she had been about to leap into battle. Beneath a cool, sometimes prickly exterior, she hid a surprising abundance of warmth and passion.

He watched her rearrange the long coil of wheat-colored hair into a smooth knot at the nape of her neck, her movements graceful, feminine. He was aware of how each time she raised her arms her bodice pulled taut across her breasts. Beneath the soft flowered fabric, the outline of her nipples was plainly visible. He ached to rub his thumbs over the tempting little buds, to tease them, to watch them swell and pout.

She glanced at him from under long lashes, then nervously ran the tip of her tongue across her bottom lip. "Is anything wrong?" she asked, her voice huskier than usual.

He cursed himself silently. Yes, he wanted to tell her,

there was something wrong. He shouldn't be entertaining thoughts like this about the daughter of an enemy. Yet he couldn't seem to control them. Whenever she was this close, his body turned traitor. More and more, he found himself imagining what it would be like to make love to her. To see her pale hair fanned across dark fur, her slender body naked and bathed in firelight. He grew hard at the thought.

"Hurry up, will you?" he said gruffly. "Your father will wonder what's keeping you." Why did thoughts of this particular woman haunt him night after night? They shared little in common. They were total opposites. Was he so shallow that he could be easily swayed by a pretty face and eyes as blue as a summer sky?

"You're bleeding."

Wayward thoughts were jerked back to the present. Absently, he touched the corner of his mouth. "It's nothing."

"But it is."

Before he could protest, she caught his hand and led him toward the creek. He looked on, bemused, while she fumbled in her reticule for a lacy handkerchief, then, kneeling down, moistened it in the water.

"Hold still," she ordered as she rose on tiptoe and dabbed at the tiny laceration.

"You don't have to . . ."

"Shh . . ." Gillian placed one hand along his jaw while she concentrated on the task. "Father will want to know what happened if he sees your face bloody. Besides, after coming to my rescue, it's the least I can do in return."

Was she really as cool and detached as she seemed? Luc wondered. Or did she feel it, too—this strong pull of physical attraction that drew him to her like a magnet.

He wrapped his fingers around her wrist and pulled her hand away. "That's good enough," he growled.

She opened her mouth as if to protest, then changed her mind.

Instead of releasing her wrist as he intended, he traced tiny circles on the soft inner surface with his thumb. He felt her pulse skip a beat, then race like a jackrabbit under his touch. She gave him a tentative smile, and he found himself smiling back.

"I haven't properly thanked you."

"Is that what you're feeling now? Gratitude?" His eyes probed hers, searching, searching. . . .

"Yes . . . no . . ." She shook her from head side to side. "I'm not sure what I'm feeling. You confuse me."

"You confuse me, too," he admitted, dragging a hand through his hair. He dropped her wrist, and stepped back, needing space between them. Needing a continent, an ocean, to separate them. Why the hell was he getting more and more involved with the pretty daughter of a British captain? They came from different worlds, were on opposing sides in a war. A future of any sort was impossible. She had made it clear that she hated his home. What was he supposed to do, offer to go with her to England?

"Damn you, Luc du Pré, must you complicate everything? Nothing is ever simple with you."

Gillian's anger acted as a tonic. He used it to create leverage between them. "If you had half a brain in that head of yours, you'd avoid encouraging men like Hunter."

"Encourage . . . ? Is that what you think?"

"It's lucky for you that your father asked me to keep an eye out for you. Trouble seems to follow you around." He bent down, picked up her bonnet, which lay near the base of the tree, and handed it to her.

She snatched it from him and jammed it on her head. "None of this would have happened if not for your high-handed ways."

Luc shook his head in amazement. Gillian Stafford had

to be the most infuriating woman he had ever met. "I fail to follow your logic."

"If you hadn't tossed my grandmother's brooch into the lake, I'd be far away by now. I'd no longer have to endure the unwanted advances of enlisted men—or your arrogant, condescending ways." She attempted to tie the satin ribbon of her bonnet into a tidy bow. Her agitation was so great, however, that the bow resembled a sorry attempt by a young child.

"Are you implying that I *owe* you protection?"

She gave a jerky nod. "Keeping an eye out for my well-being is penance for spoiling my clever plan to leave this place."

"Keeping an eye out for you will be my passport straight to heaven," Luc muttered under his breath as they headed back to the sawmill.

Neither spoke as they wound their way through the woods. They had no sooner stepped into the clearing when they were spotted by John Campbell and her father.

"Just in time for tea," John Campbell announced with a broad grin. "My wife baked her famous shortbread before she left. Wait 'til you try it."

Randolph Stafford took Gillian's elbow and steered her toward the Campbell homestead. "You missed the commotion, Daughter."

"Really?" she replied, glancing over her shoulder at Luc, who stood watching them from the edge of the clearing. He had rudely been excluded from the invitation for tea.

Stafford followed the direction of her gaze. "Du Pré," he called out, "prepare the canoe for departure within the hour. It's time we return to the island."

"Some of your father's men got into a scuffle with a group of French trappers." Campbell pulled out his pipe. "You should see the shape they're in."

"My boys said the trappers took exception to the British

uniform." Stafford guided Gillian around a stack of freshly cut timber. "I'm proud of the way they stood up for the Union Jack, even if it cost one of them a broken wrist. I'm rewarding their bravery with an extra measure of whiskey."

How ironic, Gillian mused, whiskey being the reward for drunken behavior.

Humming softly to herself, Gillian reached for the tin of shortbread John Campbell had insisted she take with her after visiting his mill the previous afternoon. The shortbread would be the perfect treat to accompany her tea. She had found the familiar ritual oddly comforting. She set the tin on the table next to the tea canister, then set out a single cup and a china teapot.

While she waited for the water to boil, she swept a critical glance around the living quarters. A sense of satisfaction welled up inside her. Yes, she definitely had a domestic flair. No one could have been more surprised than she at the discovery. Now she was turning her attention to acquiring cooking skills. Thus far, her attempts had been simple but tasty, with no major disasters. The time spent observing André Tousseau on St. Joseph's Island had served her well. The wiry Frenchman had been an excellent cook and hadn't seemed to mind her endless questions.

She added another log to the small fire in the hearth, smiling as she remembered the little voyageur's quick wit and humor. How strange that he and Luc du Pré were fast friends when they appeared such opposites. Insults had darted back and forth. But instead of fisticuffs, barbs ended in laughter and more good-natured banter.

A knock at the door ended her rumination. The timid knock was followed by another, firmer, more authoritative. Gillian smoothed her hair in place as she crossed what she referred to as the parlor. She wondered who could possibly be calling on her. Thus far, visitors had been nonexistent. Before opening the door, she cast a quick glance about to make sure everything was tidy. Apparently she and her father were alike in some respects. Randolph Stafford would be pleased to know that she had inherited his penchant for orderliness.

Gillian's mouth opened in surprise at finding Aupetchi on the narrow porch. "What brings you here, my little Robin?" she asked, recovering from her shock. "I've never known you to venture inside the fort."

Aupetchi beckoned to someone over her shoulder. "My grandfather want to meet you."

Gillian's gaze flew upward as an elderly man mounted the steps. A mane of snow-white hair framed a seamed brown face. A collection of colorful feathers dangled from an orange beaded band around his forehead. A copper pendant hung from a leather thong around his neck. Though his shoulders were bowed with age, he carried himself with dignity and pride.

Uncertain how to greet her visitor, Gillian gave him a tentative smile that he acknowledged with a solemn inclination of his head.

Aupetchi, however, did not suffer from a loss for words. She took charge, making introductions. "This is my grandfather, Wind Spirit. He is chief of our village."

"I wish to thank you for your kindness to my granddaughter." With this, he handed Gillian a small, cloth-wrapped package.

Gillian stared at the gift in amazement, then belatedly recovered and remembered her manners. "Please, come in."

When Wind Spirit hesitated, Aupetchi quickly intervened. "Please, Grandfather." Smiling sweetly, she tugged at his hand.

Wind Spirit's heart would have had to be made of stone

to resist the child's winsome appeal, Gillian thought. The glow in the old man's eyes spoke volumes of the affection he felt for the child. Knowing they shared this common bond helped ease Gillian's awkwardness. "I was just about to have tea. I'd be honored if you'd join me."

At Wind Spirit's nod of assent, Gillian stepped aside. Wind Spirit and Aupetchi entered the parlor and stood looking about with interest. Gillian realized that this must be their first visit to the home of a white man. She motioned them toward the settee while she chose an adjacent chair. Both of them perched on the edge as though ready to take flight.

"Go ahead, Gillian," Aupetchi urged. "Open your present."

It was obvious that the gift was bringing the child much pleasure. Gillian made a great show of examining it first, then held it up to her ear and listened while Aupetchi giggled at her antics. Finally, very slowly, she removed the cloth wrapper. Aupetchi bobbed left and right in her eagerness to get a peek.

"It's absolutely beautiful," Gillian breathed as she viewed the contents. She held up a small bag of doeskin as soft as silk that had been painstakingly and elaborately embroidered with beads.

"Do you like?"

"I love it. Thank you."

"It's like bag you carry—a r-ridicule."

"A reticule," she corrected with a smile. "I've never seen another quite like it. All my friends will envy me."

Aupetchi's smile stretched from ear to ear. "I asked my aunt to make it for you."

Gillian turned to Wind Spirit, who had observed their exchange in silence. "I'm afraid I don't understand what I did to deserve such a generous gift."

"It is the way of the Ottawa," Wind Spirit explained, his

voice grave, sonorous. "The exchange of gifts forever binds the giver and the receiver."

She spread her hands in a helpless gesture. "But I have nothing to give in return."

Wind Spirit smiled for the first time. "You have given us the greatest gift of all. You have put joy back in our little one's heart when we feared it gone forever."

"Aupetchi is very bright. Teaching her to read has also brought me pleasure."

"After her mother die, Aupetchi did not smile. We feared she had forgotten how. Now, because of you, she is happy again. Please accept gift to thank you."

Gillian stroked the soft leather bag. "I shall cherish this always, but not as much as I cherish our friendship."

"See, Grandfather," Aupetchi exclaimed. "I told you Gillian was friend of the Ottawa."

Wind Spirit put his arm around his granddaughter's shoulders and hugged her.

Gillian gazed at the pair, touched by their obvious devotion. They cared deeply for each other and were not ashamed to show their emotions. She admired—and envied—them. She wished she could express her own feelings that openly with her father.

Remembering the pot of water simmering on the hearth, she said, "Please, join me."

Wind Spirit started to rise. "We do not want to be a bother."

"I don't often have guests. It would mean a great deal to me if you would reconsider."

Aupetchi caught his sleeve. "Please, Grandfather."

"Very well." He acquiesced with a regal nod. "We will be happy to partake in ceremony of the tea."

The next hour passed enjoyably. After some prodding, Wind Spirit told Gillian more about the small band of Ottawa in which he was a civil chief. During the summer months, he said, women of the tribe planted corn, beans, squash, and pumpkins. What couldn't be eaten fresh was ground into meal or baked into bread. The men fished either alone or in groups. Then, during the winter, nearly the entire tribe left the village for months of trapping and hunting. Only the infirm and elderly remained behind. The fur pelts they obtained were bartered for European goods.

"Ottawa comes from word *adawe*, which in our language means 'to trade,' " Aupetchi informed Gillian proudly.

Gillian started at a knock on the door. Apologizing to her guests for the interruption, she hastened to answer it.

She found Luc du Pré on the doorstep. He looked as unhappy to see her as she was to see him. "Du Pré, what are you doing here?"

"Your father sent me to fetch a book he needs." He kept his tone impersonal, businesslike. "He told me exactly where to find it. If you don't mind, it should only take a minute."

"Very well." Stepping aside, she allowed him entry.

He paused just inside the door as he noted the changes she had made since his last visit. "Very nice," he murmured.

"Thank you." Her words came out sounding stiff, wooden. How ironic, she mused. What had taken her father weeks to notice, Luc had observed instantly. Bitterness twined with melancholy. Why did Randolph Stafford always compare unfavorably with others?

Luc stepped farther into the room and noticed Aupetchi and Wind Spirit for the first time. Puzzled, he glanced from the Ottawa chieftain's face to the crumb-filled plate on his lap, then back to his face. Aupetchi gazed back impishly.

"Chief," Luc greeted the man deferentially. "I didn't expect to find you here."

Wind Spirit lifted his cup in salutation. "And I did not expect to find you."

"We're having a tea party," Aupetchi giggled. "In her land, Gillian say they do it each day."

Not wanting her guests to think her ill-mannered, Gillian reluctantly gestured toward a vacant chair. "Would you care to join us, M'sieur du Pré?"

A smile tugged at the corner of Luc's mouth. "As much as I'd like to accept your gracious offer, I'm afraid I must decline." He bowed slightly.

Gillian flushed beneath the thinly veiled sarcasm. Blasted man. He was actually laughing at her. He knew perfectly well she didn't want him to stay . . . and why. "Well then, we won't detain you any longer. I know Father dislikes to be kept waiting."

"Don't neglect your guests on my account, m'selle. Your father gave me precise directions." He crossed the parlor toward the bedroom her father occupied.

Just as she was about to sit back down, she recalled that Luc couldn't read. There was no way he could distinguish one book from another in a row of identical-looking volumes. "Excuse me for a moment," she said as she popped back up. "I need to help M'sieur du Pré find a certain book. I had forgotten he doesn't know how to read."

She heard a stifled giggle from Aupetchi, along with a whispered admonition from her grandfather as she hurried across the room. Luc stood, his back turned away from her, scanning the titles on the bookshelf. Frozen in place, she watched him very deliberately select the appropriate volume.

"Luc du Pré!" she managed to find her voice. "You deliberately deceived me into thinking you illiterate."

He turned to her with a mocking smile that lent him devilish appeal. "You made assumptions, m'selle. I simply let them go uncorrected."

Aupetchi ran to Gillian's side. "The black robes taught Luc many things."

"Is that right?" she gritted between clenched teeth. She could cheerfully strangle him.

The little girl nodded vigorously, oblivious of the swirling undercurrents. "Luc very smart. He can read two languages. He speak three."

"Three?"

"French, English, and Ottawa." Aupetchi ticked them off on her fingers.

Luc strolled toward Gillian, the heavy volume casually balanced in one hand. "Actually, in addition to Ottawa, I'm fluent in several other Indian dialects."

As she felt her cheeks grow warm, Gillian silently cursed her fair skin tone, which betrayed every nuance of emotion. For weeks now, Luc had enjoyed himself at her expense. He had allowed her to think he was nothing but an ignorant backwoodsman, unschooled and unlettered. All the while laughing behind her back.

From the parlor, Wind Spirit chuckled good-naturedly. "Our friend Luc often finds humor in strange places."

Luc returned Gillian's withering stare with a boyish grin.

"Luc made me promise not to tell. He said it would be a fine joke." Aupetchi's smile faded as she gazed into Gillian's face. "Are you angry?"

Gillian studied the child's face, which had become pinched with worry. "No," she said slowly, dredging up a smile for her little friend's benefit. "I was merely unaware of M'sieur du Pré's strange brand of humor."

Wind Spirit drained the last of his tea, not seeming to mind that it had grown cold, and rose to his feet. "It is time for our visit to end. Next time, Miss Gillian, you come to our village."

"I'd like that very much." As she said the words, she realized she meant them.

Gillian placed her hand gently on Aupetchi's shoulder as she walked the girl and her grandfather to the door. She was conscious of Luc following close behind. She could hardly wait to tear him apart the minute her company left. On several occasions, Luc had listened to her extol the merits of an education. Politely declined her offer to tutor him. Then, secretly laughed at her. Just as he had the night she had foolishly mistaken André Tousseau's dog for a bear. Poor, innocent Scout. The dog didn't possess a vicious bone in his oversized body. His only fault was boundless energy and unabashed goodwill. In retrospect, however, she supposed the situation had appeared rather humorous. Recalling the incident with sudden clarity, she smothered a laugh.

"What is so funny, Gillian?" Aupetchi asked.

She playfully tweaked one of the girl's braids. "One day, little one, when you are sad, ask M'sieur du Pré to tell you about the black bear who turned into a dog. The story will make you laugh and forget your sorrow."

"I, too, would like to hear the story." Wind Spirit's black eyes shone with warmth and humor. "It is my hope you will come soon to our village."

"I will," Gillian promised. "And thank you again for the lovely gift."

Wind Spirit smiled and took Aupetchi's hand. "It is you who have given a gift without price."

Gillian watched them leave with a sense of regret. She ignored glances from a company of soldiers passing by on their way from drill who obviously wondered why the daughter of a British officer would entertain local Indians.

Behind her, Luc discreetly cleared his throat. "Are you certain, m'selle, that you want Aupetchi to hear the story of you and the bear?"

She turned to him with a shrug "It no longer matters."

"Wind Spirit is very grateful for the attention you've

shown his granddaughter. Aupetchi talks of you all the time."

"I've grown quite fond of her." Gillian watched Luc switch the leather-bound book from one hand to the other. She temporarily set aside her irritation with him to appease her curiosity. "Aupetchi's mother ... what happened to her?"

"She was fishing on the lake after a thaw. The ice broke. Though she was rescued, she caught a chill and died not long after. Aupetchi has been grieving ever since. Nothing seemed to help."

The child's plight brought tears to her eyes. "Losing a mother so young can be devastating."

"Everyone was worried." Luc's voice deepened. "Then you came along."

Gillian fought to resist the spell he wove so effortlessly. She felt herself warming toward him. It was becoming easier and easier to forget the reasons she disliked him. "You give me too much credit. Surely Aupetchi was beginning to emerge from mourning before I arrived."

"Perhaps, perhaps not." Luc's dark eyes never left her face. "Are you still angry with me for letting you think I couldn't read?"

He stood so close, it was hard for Gillian to think clearly. As always around him, she felt the strong pull of physical attraction. "Yes, of course I am," she replied, trying to summon a modicum of righteous indignation. "You were having fun at my expense."

"It isn't wise to make assumptions. Things are seldom as they seem."

"Apparently not."

He made no move to touch her, though she irrationally wished he would. Instead he watched her, an oddly intent expression on his handsome face. Anticipation trickled through her. The world around her seemed to fade into the background. Activity on the parade ground blurred. The bugler's notes turned mute.

"Gillian . . ." Luc began hesitantly.

She searched the face so close to hers. It no longer seemed arrogant, but uncertain. Patiently, she waited while he struggled for words.

"Sometimes I wish things could be different between us. I wish we could start over again."

"I do, too." She smiled, a bitter, sad smile. "But we both know that's impossible. Too much has happened."

Gillian turned and left him standing there. Inside, she leaned against the closed door. Unshed tears pricked her eyelids. *Blast you, Luc du Pré, I should hate you. I want to hate you.*

Why can't I?

Chapter Twelve

"Tell me everything that's happened since last time we met," Toad demanded.

Luc shifted his weight, trying to find a more comfortable position on the hard stone floor of the cave. "Robert Dickson arrived yesterday. He brought more than a hundred warriors from some of the western tribes along with him."

"As many as a hundred, eh?"

Luc nodded grimly. "Another hundred or so are expected within the week."

"Who the devil is this Dickson? Seems I heard the name before but can't quite place him. Refresh my memory."

"If you saw the man, you wouldn't likely forget him. He's a strapping Scotsman, a trapper who comes to Mackinac by way of Canada. Indians call him Mascotapah, the Redhaired Man."

"Confounded Scots," Toad growled. "First McDouall, now this Dickson fellow."

"It's rumored he exerts immense influence over the

Sioux, Winnebago, and Menominee tribes, partly because of his marriage to a Sioux woman. I suspect it's largely due to Dickson's forceful personality.''

Toad grunted. "The British will be hard pressed to feed all those empty mouths.''

"Against that many Indian allies, it's the Americans who will be hard pressed to recapture the island,'' Luc retorted. "And in answer to your comment, McDouall has appealed to General Gordon Drummond, the new commander in Upper Canada, for additional supplies to replace the rapidly dwindling stores.''

Toad reached into a shirt pocket, pulled out a pouch, and bit off a wad of tobacco. "What else have you heard?''

"Wind Spirit said plans are being made for a council of war chiefs from the various tribes. McDouall is going to address them personally.''

"Who do you think the chiefs will choose to speak for them?''

"It's too early to say. Red Dog's name has been mentioned.''

"Don't get discouraged, lad. The Americans still have a trick or two up their sleeves.''

Luc studied his contact with renewed interest. "What do you know that I don't?''

Toad's chuckle rattled in his chest like gravel. "There's activity afoot designed to upset the British strategy. They're going to be mighty unhappy to find Americans in the midst of territory they've occupied for half a century.''

"Where?''

"All in good time, lad.'' Toad chuckled again, then spit out a stream of tobacco juice. "All in good time.''

"You dole out information as though it were pearls,'' Luc grumbled. "I tell you everything, you tell me nothing.''

"If the enemy discovers you're an American spy, they

will torture you until you talk. I don't need to remind you of the Indian ways."

Luc was silent. The thought was not a pleasant one.

"One thing I can tell you, since it's now public knowledge. A man by the name of Andrew Jackson has just been promoted to major general. Many predict it's a name that'll be heard from again before this war ends." Toad scratched his thick beard. "By the way, lad, are you still keeping close tabs on the Stafford girl?"

Mention of Gillian Stafford immediately put Luc on the defensive. "What does that have to do with anything? She's of no use to us."

"Maybe, maybe." Toad shrugged. "She might be privy to more information than you think. Men often boast in front of a beautiful woman. She is a beauty, isn't she?"

"Yes," Luc admitted grudgingly. "She's a beauty."

"Turn on the charm, du Pré. Find out what she knows."

Luc stared at his moccasins. "I'm afraid the lady in question doesn't find me charming."

"Nonsense," Toad scoffed. "Other women do. Why should this one be different?"

But she *was* different. Gillian Stafford was unlike any woman he had ever met. He could easily dismiss other women from his thoughts, but not Gillian. She lingered in his mind like the haunting smell of roses in an English garden.

"Once the British get wind of the surprise the Americans have in store, there will be hell to pay. Keep your ears open and your eyes peeled. This war can't grind on much longer. Mark my word, lad, things'll come to a head before summer's over."

Luc remained in Skull Cave long after Toad's departure, his thoughts as black and gloomy as the inside of the cavern itself. He, too, sensed the situation building toward a climax. Both British and American efforts were gaining momentum.

He wished Gillian Stafford was tucked safe and sound in far-off England. He didn't like the notion of her caught in the middle of things. Impulsive, inexperienced, she had a knack for trouble. She had naively put her trust in Red Dog, then narrowly escaped rape by three drunken soldiers. Frowning, he wondered what had precipitated the incident at Mill Creek. Were the men merely drunk, and too long without a woman? Or had Gillian initiated a flirtation that had spun out of control?

Granted, he could understand their temptation. Gillian's sensuality was impossible to resist. Not for the first time, his thoughts strayed to her English lover. Did she still pine for him? What kind of man made a woman relinquish everything she valued? Respect, family, home, pride, virtue. The answer came swift and crystal clear: Only a man who had won her heart could demand such a price.

Rising to his feet, he brushed the dust from his pants, then left the cave. Outside the entrance, he stared up at the sky. Clouds rolled across the heavens, occasionally parting to reveal a smattering of stars. Perhaps, after the war ended, he'd take André's advice and find a suitable wife, settle down, raise a family. But, truth to tell, he wasn't willing to settle down with just any woman. He wanted someone special—someone who would be both companion and lover. Chances of finding such a treasure were slim. He might as well wish on a star in a distant galaxy.

June 5, King George III's birthday, dawned warm and sunny. Even the weather, so it seemed, cooperated for the grand celebration scheduled in his honor. How ironic, Gillian mused, that the king should be oblivious to all the fuss being made. Everyone knew England's monarch had

been declared mad and his son, the Prince Regent, ruled
in his stead.

The festivities would begin late that afternoon and continue well into the night. From the upper gun platform,
which provided a panoramic view of the town and harbor,
Gillian had watched the last of the bateaux arrive along
with a company of soldiers. Villagers scurried below like a
colony of ants. A steady procession of sailing craft brought
visitors from across the straits from as far away as Cheboygan. Following McDouall's address to the assembled chiefs,
everyone had been invited to the fort for food, drink, and
entertainment.

When the time came, Gillian donned a dress of blue-
and-white-striped bombazine that she had been saving for
a special occasion. Picking her straw bonnet off its peg,
she hurried out to join the crowd gathered near the shore.
She spotted Margaret and James Babcock, but before she
could join them, Judith Mayfield walked up and began
talking with them. Gillian contented herself with a shady
spot beneath a sugar maple.

The crowd grew quiet as the Indian chiefs, led by Red
Dog, filed out of the council house at the base of the bluff.
Tribal leaders magnificently adorned in beads and feathers
made a truly impressive sight. Even more impressive were
the faces of the men themselves. Stern, proud, primitive.
She chafed her upper arms to dispel a sudden chill. She
glanced upward expecting to see a cloud covering the sun,
but to her surprise the sky was clear.

A roll of drums reverberated from within the fort. All
eyes were drawn to the south sally port as the entire garrison proceeded to march down the ramp, colors flying.
Directly behind the standard bearer came the musicians.
The rat-a-tat-tat of snare drums mixed with the high, plaintive notes of tin flutes. The parade of scarlet jackets, white
pants, and tall, black shakos formed a brilliant splash

against the white limestone walls. An unexpected burst of patriotism caught Gillian unaware. Nostalgia swept over her, so powerfully she could have wept. Suddenly England, and everything English, seemed very dear. Home no longer seemed so far away.

Bagpipes wailed as McDouall, distinctive in the bottle green uniform of the Glengarry Light Infantry, stepped forward to address the assembled Indian chiefs, who sat in the middle of the clearing in a semicircle, their warriors close behind them. An expectant hush fell over the gathering.

"My children," McDouall cried, "do not be deceived by the artifice and cunning of the Americans. Are any of you so blind that you cannot see they will be satisfied only when the Indians have been destroyed root and branch? Your only hope of avoiding this terrible fate is by joining hand in hand with the king's warriors in driving the Big Knives from this island."

Gillian saw Red Dog nod his agreement.

"Happy are those warriors who rush into the fight," McDouall intoned. "Those warriors have justice upon their side. Go forth into combat for the tombs of your forefathers. Fight for those lands that ought now to afford shelter and sustenance to your wives and children."

Gillian's attention wavered beneath the Scotsman's rhetoric. She searched the crowd for familiar faces. She spotted Aupetchi among a small group of Ottawa. When the girl noticed her, she broke into a wide smile. Gillian waved, then raised her arm so Aupetchi could see the beautifully beaded reticule slung over her arm. The child tugged on the arm of the woman next to her and pointed at Gillian. The woman, upon seeing the handiwork, returned Gillian's tentative smile. Gillian's gaze fell on the knot of island tradespeople. They listened to McDouall with varying degrees of interest. Young Jacob Mayfield dozed in the grass at his parents' feet.

McDouall raised his voice dramatically. "The king has defeated his enemies in Europe and can now bring all of his great power to bear upon the United States. If the chiefs are loyal to Britain, English traders will soon be among you. Britain will look out for you in the peace settlement.

"The king will help you recover old boundaries. Great Britain will make peace only on the express condition that your interests shall be considered first, your just claims admitted, and no infringement of your rights permitted in future."

Wild cheering erupted from the Indian allies. Red Dog shook a clenched fist skyward and let out a war whoop that raised the fine hair along the nape of Gillian's neck. Her glance slid sideways and landed on Luc, who stood close by. Instead of seeming pleased with the response, he wore a dour expression. Was he disappointed that McDouall failed to mention rewarding all those who aided the British, not just the Indians? Surely Luc must know her father wouldn't allow Luc's loyalty to go unrecognized.

McDouall waited until quiet was restored. "On behalf of His Majesty, King George the Third, we thank you for demonstrating your loyalty by hurrying to defend Michilimackinac in this critical hour." McDouall's brogue thickened as he sought Shakespeareanlike eloquence. "You possess the warlike spirit of your forefathers. May the Great Spirit give you strength and courage in so good a cause and crown you with victory on the day of battle."

The speech finally over, the garrison marched back to the fort accompanied by beating drums and bleating bagpipes. The townsfolk and invited guests followed at a more leisurely pace. Gillian's ears still rang from the shrill war cries of hundreds of Indian warriors. McDouall had made

King George sound like an omnipotent god. How many of the colonel's promises would Britain honor? And how many were rhetoric? The man was a politician, as well as an orator. He had told his allies exactly what they wanted—and needed—to hear. But could he deliver what he promised? Would he? With a shake of her head, Gillian resolutely banished her skeptical thoughts.

Mouthwatering aromas of roasting meat filled the air. Long tables in front of the quartermaster's storehouse groaned with food. Platters heaped with sliced beef, pork, and smoked fish were placed, along with bowls of vegetables and baskets of bread. The women of the village had contributed to the feast with an appetizing display of cakes and pies. No one objected to the simple but hearty fare. The occasion provided a splendid opportunity to put worries of the pending American attack aside and enjoy one another's company.

After filling her plate, Gillian wandered about looking for a place to sit. Two soldiers, fresh-faced and eager to please, seeing her dilemma, jumped up and offered her a seat on a bench outside the barracks. She ate slowly, enjoying all the activity, the gaiety, going on around her.

"You shame us, du Pré," a man scolded.

At mention of Luc's name, Gillian's head snapped up. To her right, a group of voyageurs stood talking among themselves. Most shared certain characteristics. The men were short in stature, thick set, and heavily muscled through the arms and shoulders. Luc appeared a giant in comparison, standing nearly a head taller than most. The others, she noted, were clad in their Sunday best with colored sashes and ostrich feathers tucked into their beaver hats.

"Why you refuse to spend your coin on nice clothes?"

A nattily dressed man brushed the lapel of his merino jacket.

"You embarrass your friends, *mon ami*."

"Ah, Louis," Luc laughed. "Not everyone wants to strut around like a peacock."

"Why do you save money, du Pré? You have no woman to impress."

"Du Pré has no need to spend his money." Louis gave Luc's shoulder a friendly slap. "Women like the handsome bastard. He just snap his fingers, and they come."

"I, too, have seen du Pré work his magic." A swarthy-faced man wiggled dark, bushy brows suggestively. "Wives, daughters, grandmothers, no woman is immune."

"Enough, Claude," Luc pleaded. "Now it is you who embarrasses me."

Just then, Judith Mayfield strolled past. Gillian couldn't help but notice the sidelong glance she cast in Luc's direction. Luc seemed oblivious of the speculative look as he strolled off with his friends.

Gillian stabbed the slice of beef on her plate with unnecessary force. Judith Mayfield was a married woman. She had no call to look at Luc du Pré as if he was an item up for auction. And who were these women the voyageurs referred to? Daughters of fur traders? Trappers' wives? Ottawa maidens? She had never noticed Luc paying court to a slew of admirers. Did their knees grow weak, their pulses race, at his touch?

Irrationally irritated at the notion, she stared after his retreating back. Whether fashionably clad in snug-fitting nankin breeches and waistcoat as he had been at the Babcocks' or in the rugged attire of his trade, he was strikingly handsome. Watching him walk away, Gillian recalled a phrase she had once heard: Clothes didn't make the man, but rather, the man made the clothes. Luc du Pré was a shining example of that home truth.

Disgusted with herself, she set her plate aside. Whenever du Pré came near, her common sense melted into a soggy mass. Her righteous indignation vaporized. The man was a menace. A scandalmonger. A common gossip. She could forgive his arrogance, tolerate his patronizing ways, but she couldn't forget that he had willfully destroyed any chance she might have for a normal existence here on the island. Ostracism filled every day with a deep, abiding ache.

The music started as the sun went down. A sunburned man with sergeant's stripes sawed a bow across the strings of a fiddle. One of the voyageurs Gillian had seen with Luc enthusiastically squeezed a concertina while a spindly private made a simple flute warble sweeter than a lark. People gathered along a section of the parade ground that had been designated for dancing. As she edged closer, she discovered several couples already stepping to a lively country dance. Even the plain and homely girls quickly found themselves much sought after. She was surprised to see men, who, no doubt, were accustomed to a scarcity of partners, pair off. Her toe tapped restlessly in time to the music.

"May I have this dance?"

Gillian looked into the smiling face of a man she hadn't seen before.

"I can't believe my good fortune," the young man said as he led her toward the dancers. "My first day here, and I meet the prettiest girl on the island."

After the first set of dances, Gillian found herself in constant demand. Temporarily, at least, no one seemed to pay any heed to her tarnished reputation. For a while, she resolved to put past problems aside and relish the present.

"Mind if I cut in, Lieutenant?"

"Father," Gillian cried in delight. "I didn't know you liked to dance."

"There are a great many secrets a father keeps from a daughter," he replied as he bowed, then held out his hand. "However, I fear I might be a bit rusty."

"You acquit yourself admirably," she told him when they met for a promenade.

"There have been few occasions to practice. I confess, I'm less agile than I used to be."

"Still, you cut a dashing figure."

A small smile softened his expression. "Your mother used to think so."

"Do you think of her often?"

He cleared his throat. "Every day."

"I, too," she admitted softly.

Neither spoke again as they executed the dance steps, meeting, parting, rotating partners. Both seemed afraid to strain the tenuous bond.

When the dance ended, he bowed again. "Now, Daughter," he said ruefully, "if you will excuse me, I must review some items with the officer of the day."

"I'll walk with you to headquarters."

Gillian placed her hand in the crook of his arm, and together they strolled across the parade grounds, savoring a companionable silence.

After bidding her father good night, she sank down on a bench some distance from the dancing, content to watch the festivities from the fringes. Out of the corner of her eye, she saw Luc materialize out of the darkness. Wordlessly, he sat on the opposite end of the bench.

She waited for him to speak, but when he didn't, she finally broke the silence. "I haven't seen you dance tonight, du Pré."

He sipped from a tin cup he held in one hand. "Is that an invitation?"

Her eyes flew wide at the suggestion. "Of all the brash, conceited . . ."

"As testy as ever, I see." He chuckled, a deep, throaty sound that rumbled in his wide chest. "You never disappoint me."

"I was merely making an observation," she said primly, turning her attention back to the dancers. In truth, concentration was difficult when every fiber of her being seemed centered on the man at her side.

"I couldn't help but notice, you were never at a loss for partners."

So, he had noticed. The knowledge warmed her. Then, just as quickly, it annoyed her. Though he had been observing her from the sidelines, he hadn't once cut in. Hadn't requested a single dance. Not that she wanted him to, of course. She determined not to let her frustration show by changing the subject to a neutral one. "What did you think of McDouall's speech this afternoon? He was quite eloquent, don't you agree?"

"He's a pompous windbag." He raised his cup and took a swallow.

Gillian tipped her head to one side and studied him. Any softness about him seemed to have vanished. His features had taken on a certain cutting sharpness. Under her assessing gaze, his cheekbones appeared more finely chiseled, his jaw square and granite hard. Even his wonderful, wide mouth had an implacable set. Suddenly, there was a fierceness about him that frightened her.

"Why do you say that?" she asked warily.

"Because that's what he is. McDouall deliberately lied before the council of chiefs."

Gillian recalled her own skepticism earlier. Still, it was one thing for one Englishman to criticize another, and another matter entirely for an outsider to do the same. "Surely the king will generously reward his allies."

"England only wants what's best for England. It couldn't care less about the rights of the Indians." Bitterness laced each word. "Promises mean nothing to it."

"I thought you admired the British," she protested. "That you support their efforts."

"Are you questioning my loyalty?" he growled. "You once called me a traitor. Is that why?"

She gasped at the implication. "Of course not. Never once have I questioned your loyalty to the crown. Should I?"

Sighing deeply, he pinched the bridge of his nose between thumb and forefinger. "Let's forget this conversation ever took place, shall we?"

"If you like." She nodded uncertainly.

"I'd like very much." He raised his cup, then tipped it upside down, draining the contents on the ground. "Too much rum loosens my tongue."

"Mmm," she murmured. "I'll store that little tidbit away for future use." Grabbing his hand impulsively, she pulled him to his feet. "We're being far too serious. Tonight is much too pleasant to spoil it with talk of politics."

She half-pulled, half-dragged him toward the dancers.

"What do you think you're doing?" he asked, but she noticed he didn't resist.

"Just for a few hours, let's set hostilities aside. Let's pretend we've just met, and we're starting fresh." She shot an impish glance over her shoulder. "Come, du Pré. Dance with me."

Luc grinned back, no longer the fearsome, dark stranger but a flirtatious beau. The sight of that smile made her heart stutter.

The fiddle struck up the notes of a waltz, a new dance that had become popular in European ballrooms the previous year. Gillian loved nothing better than to be held in a pair of strong arms and twirled in graceful circles until her head spun.

"I don't suppose you know how to waltz?" she asked a shade wistfully.

Before Luc could answer, a soldier dipped into a low bow in front of Gillian.

"May I have this dance?"

Gillian sucked in her breath, staring in stunned disbelief at the trim, lithe figure clad in the uniform of an infantry lieutenant. The uniform was impeccably tailored. Every strand of the soldier's thick, wavy brown hair was neatly combed into place. Her head whirled dizzily as she absorbed the details. It couldn't be. It just couldn't be. . . .

But it was.

Jeremy Blackwood raised his head and smiled into her astonished face.

Chapter Thirteen

"Shall we demonstrate to these peasants how it's done in London?"

Numb with shock, Gillian allowed Jeremy Blackwood to lead her onto the makeshift dance floor. Wordlessly she placed one hand on his shoulder, the other lightly in his. The irresistible strains of the waltz flowed around her, over her, through her, captivating her. Jeremy smiled into her upturned face as they slowly circled the floor.

Dimly aware of his light, possessive touch at the small of her back, Gillian's thoughts spun backward. To a time when being held in Jeremy's arms seemed as precious as life itself. Under his tender nurturing, first love had blossomed. Love delicate and sweet as a wildflower.

And just as short-lived.

Still dazed by his unexpected appearance, she stared helplessly into the face she had once loved and thought never to see again. Jeremy smiled charmingly, clearly relishing his effect on her. He adroitly maneuvered her through the prescribed set of glides and swirls. Like a puppet responding to its puppeteer, Gillian followed his cues.

When the music ended, enthusiastic applause jolted her out of her trancelike state. For the first time she was fully aware that she and Jeremy were the only couple on the dance floor. Her cheeks burned with embarrassment. Jeremy, however, didn't appear the least discomfited at being the center of attention. If anything, he looked pleased by the adulation.

Gillian's attention fell on the one person who wasn't clapping. Arms folded across his chest, Luc stood exactly where she had left him. Guilt rushed over her. Finding Jeremy Blackwood standing before her had wiped all else from her mind. She had abandoned Luc on the sidelines without a thought while she literally waltzed into Jeremy's waiting arms. Even so, Luc had no cause to glower at her like that, his eyes dark, accusing, disapproving. She didn't owe him an explanation. She was free to dance with whomever she wished. Still ... an incessant voice that she couldn't silence wondered what it would be like to be held in Luc's arms. To be whirled around until she was giddy and breathless. To have him smile down at her as Jeremy had.

She doubted she'd ever find out. Luc, his expression shuttered, turned and walked away. A knot of irrational disappointment lodged in her chest.

"You're even more beautiful than I remember, darling." Jeremy's words brought her crashing back to the present as he led her from the floor. "Have you missed me as much as I've missed you?"

Gillian was spared a reply by Margaret and James Babcock, who approached them with a purposeful step.

Margaret, dressed in her Sunday finery, waved a fan

painted with an Oriental motif. "Goodness, watching the two of you twirl around certainly looked invigorating."

"On my last trip to Montreal," James continued, after the perfunctory introductions, "everywhere I went I heard about the new dance sweeping European ballrooms."

Gillian forced a smile. "I must warn you, many consider the waltz indecent."

"Some even call it vulgar," Jeremy added, dropping his voice to a conspiratorial level.

Margaret's fan snapped shut. "What sheer and utter nonsense!"

"My wife and I pride ourselves on the fact that we draw our own conclusions."

Margaret sniffed. "We don't base our judgments solely on other people's opinions."

Gillian looked more closely at the older woman. Did Margaret Babcock's words carry a double meaning? Was she referring to the gossip circulating about her tryst with an English officer? How would she react if she knew the man in question was standing here at her side? With shock? Outrage? Disbelief?

"Since you youngsters are no strangers to the waltz, we were wondering if perhaps some evening you might give us older folk a lesson or two."

"Absolutely, sir," Jeremy replied without a second's hesitation, then turned to Gillian. "But only if Miss Stafford consents to be my partner for the evening."

"Well, Gillian," Margaret prodded hopefully, "will you and Lieutenant Blackwood be gracious enough to show us the steps? Provided, of course, we can prevail upon the musicians to cooperate."

"Of course." What else could she say? It would seem churlish to refuse the simple request. "We'd be happy to teach you the waltz."

"Good!" James rubbed his hands together in anticipation. "Let's make it soon, shall we?"

The music started again. Sprightly notes from a tin whistle, crisp and light, flirted with the throaty wail of a bagpipe. A strapping red-haired man by the name of Dickson dressed in a traditional kilt leaped onto the dance floor. His feet fairly flew as he executed the intricate folk dance of his native Scotland. The people watching burst into loud cheers and yelled out encouragement.

Jeremy grasped Gillian's arm. "It's been so long," he whispered. "Let's get away from this crowd. There's so much we need to talk about."

Gillian resolutely extracted her arm. "On the contrary, there's very little left to say."

"Ah, my darling Gillian, I beg to differ with you."

Gillian cast a furtive glance around to see if anyone was eavesdropping on their exchange. Much to her relief, everyone's attention seemed occupied with the Scotsman's amazing agility.

"My feelings for you haven't changed. Hear me out," Jeremy pleaded. "You owe me . . . you owe *us* . . . at least that much."

"I owe you nothing," she snapped, her voice rising.

"Hush, darling." Now it was Jeremy's turn to sweep a surreptitious look about to make certain no one had overheard. "Please give me a chance to explain. Don't deprive me of a few priceless moments of your company."

"Very well," Gillian agreed against her better judgment. This time when he took her arm she didn't protest. Jeremy guided her toward the west blockhouse, the farthest point from the merriment. She tried to convince herself that she was going with him merely out of curiosity. It would be interesting to hear him defend his actions. As though, she scoffed, it was possible for a married man to defend his attempt to seduce an innocent girl. Being alone in his company would also serve to test her reaction—and her resistance—to him.

"I can tell you're still angry with me."

"Considering how you deliberately deceived me, I have every right to be angry."

"Of course you do, my sweet. What I did was inexcusable."

"What are you doing here, Jeremy?"

"What am I doing here?" He smiled at her condescendingly. "Darling, I'm a soldier. I go where I'm sent."

"Of all places, you had to be sent to Michigan?"

"Chalk it up to coincidence." He tucked her hand in the crook of his arm. "Now that Napoleon has been soundly defeated, all His Majesty's efforts are directed at winning a decisive victory over these Yankees."

"Father will be furious when he learns you're here on the island."

Jeremy laughed off her fear. "He may not approve, but there's not a bloody thing he can do about it. I take my orders from a higher command."

Gillian wasn't convinced. "Father has many well placed friends."

"Don't worry, darling." He patted her hand reassuringly. "He's only a captain. I intend to distinguish myself while here in the northern theater. Then, if all goes according to plan, I'll receive a promotion and share equal rank with your illustrious father. By the way, is he still drinking?"

Gillian would have stumbled had it not been for Jeremy holding her arm. "How did you know about his drinking?"

Jeremy shrugged. "It's common knowledge, darling. Why do you suppose he has remained the same rank for so long?"

He sounded so pompous, so self-righteous, it was starting

to grate on her nerves. Had he always been like this? she wondered. If so, why hadn't it bothered her before?

Jeremy stopped near the blockhouse but far enough away that their conversation couldn't be overheard. "Look at me, Gillian. Then tell me nothing's changed between us."

Gillian indulged the urge to study him carefully. It was easy to see how Jeremy Blackwood could capture a girl's fancy. Resplendent in a uniform especially tailored to fit his tall, slender frame, Jeremy appeared every bit as dashing as she remembered. Brass polished, boots buffed, light-brown hair brushed to a satiny sheen. Every detail perfect. Effortless charm, impeccable manners, flawless taste. Sophisticated and witty. He embodied everything she had once thought she desired in a mate.

He hadn't changed one iota. But she had. She no longer felt the same thrill of excitement at being in his company. Tonight, she could view him with detachment.

Jeremy placed his hands on her shoulders. "You're staring at me as though I was a stranger."

"It's been a long time, Jeremy. I never expected to see you again." Though she didn't pull away, neither did she step into his embrace.

He smiled, undaunted by her lack of response. "Fate has intervened on our behalf, darling. Have you forgotten what we once meant to each other?"

"No," she said, her voice husky. "I haven't forgotten."

Emboldened, Jeremy continued. "Darling, I've never stopped loving you. Seeing you tonight, holding you, brought back treasured memories."

Gillian searched Jeremy's blue-gray eyes. "Why didn't you try to contact me after Aunt Phoebe discovered us together at the inn?"

He gazed at her, the very picture of earnestness. "I sent countless messages trying to explain. If you didn't receive them, it's probably because your aunt intercepted and destroyed them.''

"What about your wife, Jeremy?'' Gillian asked, her voice suddenly choked with emotion. "Did you conveniently forget she existed?''

He ran a hand over his wavy locks, careful not to disturb a single strand, then sighed. "Penelope and I long ago agreed to go our separate ways. Sadly, ours was not a love match.''

"Then why, pray tell, did you marry her?''

He hung his head sheepishly, studying the ground. "Penelope tricked me into believing she was pregnant. I felt compelled to do the honorable thing and offer matrimony.''

"I see,'' Gillian said slowly. "And if I had become pregnant as a result of our liaison, what 'honorable' thing would you have offered me?''

Jeremy seemed momentarily taken aback but quickly recovered his composure. "Darling, you're forgetting I'm a gentleman as well as a soldier. Why, I'd offer you my protection. See that you were cared for during your confinement, then help locate a suitable family for the infant.''

From this night forth, Aunt Phoebe would forever be in her debt. She realized she had narrowly averted disaster. Jeremy Blackwood was nothing more than a charming scoundrel. She let out an unladylike snort of disgust. "Supporting two households is hardly an option on a lieutenant's wage.''

He gave her a confident smile. "My wife is wealthy. She gives me a generous allowance.''

Had Jeremy only married Penelope for her wealth? Gillian wondered, then was ashamed of herself for such a thought. But after the revelations she had just heard, anything was possible.

"Gillian, my sweet, at least give me a chance to explain.''

"Very well." She folded her arms across her chest, temper crackling along nerve endings. "Why didn't you tell me from the beginning that you were already married?"

"I was a selfish cad. Don't judge me too harshly." Reaching out, he ran his hands up and down her arms from elbow to shoulder. "I was desperately unhappy. Then I met you . . . and all that changed."

He could be very persuasive. Gillian felt her resolve waver for a fraction of a second, then harden as she deliberately recalled the heartache and humiliation she had suffered as a result of his perfidy. "And your wife?" she persisted. "Is she also desperately unhappy?"

"Forget Penelope, darling. We rarely see each other. We have absolutely nothing in common. Marrying her was the biggest mistake of my life."

And thinking she loved him had been the biggest mistake of hers.

Gillian shook her head in disgust. She was no longer the naive young girl she had been in England. He had said he loved her. She had interpreted that to mean he wanted to marry her. How stupid to have made that assumption. What a fool she had been.

"You should have been honest with me from the beginning. I no longer feel the same toward you."

"Gillian, surely you can't meant that. It's only injured pride that makes you lash out." Jeremy pulled her into his arms, but she turned her face, and the kiss intended for her mouth grazed her temple instead. "Don't be hasty. You professed to love me once. How can such tender feelings change so dramatically?"

She shoved free from his embrace. "It's over, Jeremy."

He looked so crestfallen than Gillian felt a stirring of sympathy. Perhaps he truly regretted what he had done. What a miserable existence it must be to be trapped in a marriage without love. After all, she admitted with painful honestly, Jeremy hadn't forced her to do anything unwillingly. She had gone with him of her own accord.

"Lieutenant Blackwood . . ." a voice called. "Is that you, sir?"

"State your business, Private," Jeremy snapped as a spindly soldier emerged from the shadows.

The private touched the tip of his shako. "Major McDouall sent me, sir. He's called an officers' meeting."

"*Now,* Private?" Jeremy asked, his irritation obvious.

"Yes, sir." The private bobbed his head to emphasize each word. "Major's just come from the Indian council. He's waiting at post headquarters to brief the officers."

Jeremy turned to Gillian. "I won't let this matter rest until you've given me a chance to make amends. We'll discuss it later."

She watched him disappear into the night with the private at his side, struggling to match his longer strides. Shaken by the unexpected encounter, she sank down on a bench partially concealed by bushes. She pressed her fingertips to her throbbing temples and rubbed. Confronting Jeremy after all these months had proved a strain. He couldn't accept the fact that her feelings had radically changed since their last meeting. Lies and deceit did not foster affection. Why was that concept so difficult for him to believe? She had surrendered her heart, her soul, and had been on the brink of surrendering that precious gift a woman can bestow only once in a lifetime. But Jeremy's deception had transformed something beautiful and special into a tawdry, ugly affair.

With a weary sigh, she tried to recall what had attracted her to him. In the beginning, he had seemed absolutely wonderful, attentive, witty, charming. When she was in his company, he made her feel beautiful and desirable, as if she was the only person in the world who mattered. She had foolishly believed every compliment sincere, every endearment heartfelt. Though she still found him handsome to look upon, she no longer found anything in his character to admire. His actions had revealed his true colors. He was nothing more than a cad. A coward. As far as she was concerned, further discussion was unnecessary.

She no longer felt like the same person she had been in London. She had become infinitely wiser, wary of men who hid true intentions behind false promises. When—if—she gave her heart again, it would be to a man worthy of trust.

Not eager to rejoin the celebration but reluctant to retire to her attic room, Gillian contented herself by observing the festivities from a distance. Torches ringed the dance floor where couples gaily jigged. Tipping back her head, she looked up at the sky. A million pinpricks of silver light were sprinkled across a bed of midnight-blue velvet. The moon hung suspended like half a broken locket. It was a beautiful night, a night for lovers.

As though proof of her theory, two figures strolled closer, arms entwined. The pair stopped near her bench, separated from her by the wide bush. Gillian decided to remain where she was rather than risk their mutual embarrassment by suddenly making her presence known.

"It's the truth. I swear it on my mother's grave," the soldier said.

"You say she actually slept with the man?"

"That's what people do when they go off to an inn."

Another giggle.

"Another kiss, and I'll tell you the best part."

The ensuing silence told Gillian that the girl had readily complied.

"Seems the gentlemen in question failed to inform the girl that he already had a wife."

Gillian froze. There could be no mistaking the fact they were talking about her.

"No . . ." the girl said in a shocked voice. "You mean she didn't know the man was married?"

"Swear on my mother's grave."

"No wonder no decent woman wants to associate with her."

"Imagine, the captain's daughter disgracing his good name. News like that would drive any man to drink."

"How do you know so much about her?"

Gillian strained to hear the answer to the girl's question.

"Oh, I've got my ways."

"C'mon, Johnny, tell me how you found out."

The man's voice sounded vaguely familiar. Gillian searched her memory to connect it to a name and face.

"I'm captain's orderly," he boasted. "I'm privy to all sorts of information."

Bunton? Private Johnny Bunton?

"I found a letter her aunt sent all crumpled in a ball near the fireplace," Bunton continued. "Way I figure, Captain must have been aiming to burn the bugger, but it missed its mark and fell into my hands instead."

"Bet he was fit to be tied."

"Never seen him lose his temper that bad," Bunton confessed. "The captain harbors a fondness for rum. Puts him in a foul mood, that it does. He was drinking pretty heavy for a while. Once he heard McDouall was on the way, he cut back. But he was pretty heavy into the sauce the night his daughter arrived. Couldn't help but overhear things."

"What sort of things?"

Gillian squeezed her eyes shut. Every detail of that meeting was permanently stamped in her brain.

Bunton lowered his voice. "He really tore into the girl. Called her a tramp."

"You don't say . . ."

"Almost felt sorry for her, I did."

"Her kind won't go long without a man to warm her sheets," the girl predicted knowingly. "Did you see the way she looked at the lieutenant she danced with?"

"Mmm-hmm," Bunton agreed. "I told you the tale would be worth a kiss or two. Time to pay the piper."

Gillian was forced to endure more giggling, punctuated by smacking sounds.

"What other gossip have you heard, Johnny?"

"Well, now, let me think . . ."

The voices trailed off as the pair moved out of earshot.

Gillian slowly rose to her feet. First Jeremy's reappearance into her life, now this. The evening was filled with one surprise after another. All the time she had blamed Luc for malicious gossip, Johnny Bunton, her father's orderly, had been responsible. Scalding hot shame burned through her, melting the core of ice that encased her emotions. At every turn she had berated Luc, cursed his loose tongue. Called him a traitor.

Driven by a fierce need to make amends, she picked up her skirt in both hands and raced across the parade ground. She had to find him, explain, and apologize. Then beg his forgiveness.

She had done Luc du Pré a grave injustice.

Chapter Fourteen

The celebration was still in full swing even though the hour was late. Gillian slowed as she approached a group of people gathered near the barracks. Her gaze swept the crowd, but she didn't see Luc's tall figure among them. She hesitated, biting her lower lip in indecision. She felt terrible. Remorse gnawed at her for the way she had treated him, the repeated insults. Her actions had been reprehensible. She envisioned his chocolate dark eyes, his stern, unsmiling mouth, his cool, remote expression. Begging his forgiveness would be a humbling experience, but her conscience wouldn't let her rest until she found him and apologized.

A chorus of male voices raised in song drew her closer to the crowd. Though the words were in French, the jaunty rhythm was clearly that of a sea chanty. She stood on tiptoe for a better look. A dozen or so voyageurs, Luc among them, occupied one end of the barracks porch. Some sat on upturned kegs, others perched on the rail, while the rest stood in various poses. Tenor and baritone blended in perfect harmony, causing the breath to catch in her throat.

When the sea chanty ended, the voyageurs began a ballad. Gillian wormed her way through the crowd until she stood near the front, where she had an unrestricted view of the singers. At an unspoken signal, Luc moved to the forefront, braced one leg on a porch rung, rested his arm across his knee, and casually leaned forward. Clearly at ease before an audience, he performed solo.

Gillian listened, enthralled by his deep, resonant baritone. Though she couldn't understand the words, the music spoke to her of love and longing. It started a vague, nameless yearning deep inside her. A hunger for something just beyond her grasp. She knew with absolute certainty that until she found that elusive link, her soul would not be complete.

All of the voyageurs joined in the chorus. The song ended amid enthusiastic applause. Luc acknowledged the ovation with a smile, then stepped back. The audience begged for more, and the men quickly obliged. She kept her gaze fixed on him, willing him to glance her way. She fidgeted restlessly, thinking he'd never notice her, but just when she was about to give up hope, he spotted her out of the corner of his eye.

Her expression must have conveyed a sense of urgency. Luc frowned slightly but left his fellow voyageurs and sprang off the porch to join her. "You look worried. Is anything wrong?"

"Yes. No . . ." She wrung her hands nervously. Now that he towered above her, she fumbled for words. "I-I need to talk to you."

"All right."

"There's something I have to tell you. . . ." Her voice trailed off.

"Spit it out, Gillian. You've never been bashful."

Their hushed tones drew irritated glances from those nearby, who were trying to listen to the music.

"Not here. I need to speak with you privately." She made a small, desperate motion with her hand. "Walk me home. We can talk on the way."

With a curt nod, he fell into step next to her.

Tension tightened around her chest. Why must it always be so difficult to own up to mistakes? she wondered bleakly. So hard to swallow one's pride and suffer humility? To hide her attack of nerves, she grabbed the first topic to enter her mind. "I should mention how much I enjoyed the singing. You have a beautiful voice."

"It's adequate." He shrugged off her praise. "Voyageurs often sing while paddling. The rhythm helps keep time with the canoe's paddles."

"You didn't hum a single note on the canoe trip from St. Joseph's Island. Next time I'll insist upon music."

He regarded her with a raised brow. "You didn't seek me out to talk about singing. Does this by any chance have to do with the lieutenant you danced with?"

"Jeremy?" After Johnny Bunton's startling revelation, she had completely forgotten about Jeremy Blackwood.

"On a first-name basis already? The man must have made quite an impression." There was nothing melodious about Luc's baritone now; it was hard, cold, cutting.

"We knew each other in England," she admitted. She kept her gaze on the distant silhouette of the blockhouse at the far edge of the fort. "This only has to do with him indirectly. It's primarily a matter between you and me."

He didn't press for further details, and she was grateful.

Upon reaching the Stone Quarters, she climbed the steps to the porch, turning to face him from the uppermost tread, which put them on eye level. She drew a shaky breath, then released it. "I've done you a grave disservice and must beg your forgiveness."

"You're not making sense, *chèrie*." The velvet was back in his voice. "Why do you feel this need to apologize?"

Gillian's knees weakened at the endearment. She almost lost her nerve. "I called you a traitor," she said, her voice barely audible. "More precisely, lying, traitorous scum."

"Yes," he agreed amiably. "Those were your exact words. And now something has happened to change your opinion of me?"

She swallowed and gave a small nod.

"You no longer consider me 'lying, traitorous scum'?"

Gillian could have sworn she detected a hint of laughter humming through his seriousness. "No," she admitted, shaking her head. "Not after tonight."

He came up the steps so that she had to tilt her head to look at him. The porch seemed to shrink in size. Suddenly it seemed much smaller than it had been a moment before. Minuscule, actually. Everything, everyone, but the two of them faded into a blurry backdrop.

Raising his hand, he lightly skimmed the backs of his fingers along the delicate angle of her jaw. "Tell me what happened tonight that changed your opinion."

"Don't, please . . ." Nerve endings skittered beneath his touch, electrified. "I can't think when you touch me."

He seemed to eat up her face with his eyes. With maddening slowness he withdrew his hand.

Gillian released a shuddering breath. God help her, but she wanted him to touch her. Wanted him. In a very elemental way. The knowledge terrified her. A single touch from him had a more devastating effect than all Jeremy Blackwood's sweet kisses and tender caresses combined. Luc made her forget her resolve to avoid romantic entanglements. The thought almost made her laugh aloud. There was nothing remotely romantic about her relationship with Luc du Pré. The attraction she felt was purely physical, the result of some strange chemistry between them. In all other respects, they were poles apart. They shared little in common. Yet logic seemed to flee when he stood this close.

Needing as much space as possible to separate them, she deliberately retreated until her back pressed against the door frame. "I blamed you for being a gossip. I'm sorry, Luc."

Luc gave her an incredulous look. "Me? A gossip?"

She nodded miserably. "I made an assumption. All this time, I was convinced you were the one who told everyone about my past. I believed it was because of you that none of the women would associate with me. I blamed you because Corporal Hunter and his friends made lewd offers and advances."

"How did you come by such a crazy notion?"

"It wasn't crazy," she flared. "I had good reason to suspect you."

He folded his arms across his chest. And waited.

"Who else could have spread the tale?" she asked, feeling more than a bit defensive. "After all, you were the most logical person to suspect. You were the only one present the night I arrived. You heard Father read Aunt Phoebe's letter. Heard him call me a . . ." Her voice broke.

Luc moved forward but stopped when she held up a hand to forestall him. "What made you realize you were mistaken?"

"After Jeremy and I talked tonight, I needed time to think. I was still sitting on a bench when a couple approached. They didn't see me on the other side of a bush. I couldn't help but overhear their conversation. Private Bunton boasted of finding my aunt's letter."

"Bunton!" Luc swore savagely. "Wait until I get hold of the slimy little weasel."

Gillian was inexplicably touched. Once again Luc was willing to do battle for her. But she had caused enough bloodshed already. "Leave it be, Luc. The harm's been done. Once spoken, words can't be recalled. Besides, I don't need friends easily swayed by rumor."

"You truly amaze me." Luc dragged an impatient hand through his hair. "I can't believe you thought me the sort who engaged in idle gossip. No wonder you held me in such low esteem."

"It was an honest mistake, Luc, and I'm sorry." She eyed him uncertainly, trying to gauge his mood. "I was lonely and, on many occasions, lashed out at you. I don't like being ostracized."

"Is it so important what others think?"

"Of course it is."

An expression disturbingly like disappointment flickered across his features, then vanished so quickly she wondered if she had imagined it. A shadow perhaps? The night playing tricks with her vision? Somehow she couldn't shake the sensation that she had plunged headlong into a baited trap.

"Are you angry with me?" she ventured.

"No." His mouth curved in a self-deprecatory smile. "I don't think I'm capable of staying angry at you for long."

Warmed by his response, she returned the smile. "I'm sorry I misjudged you. I wish there was some way I could make it up to you."

His voice deepened to a throaty purr. "Well . . . maybe there is a way."

She nervously moistened her lower lip with the tip of her tongue as he edged closer. The action drew his attention to her mouth. Her heart tripped faster than the roll off a drummer's sticks. He took another step closer, his lithe stalk that of a jungle cat confident of its prey. Gillian would have retreated but for the doorjamb pressing against her spine.

"Gillian . . ." he sighed her name.

She stood motionless, scarcely daring to breathe. He closed the narrow gap between them, then reached out and lightly placed his fingertips along either side of her jaw, gently raising her face to his. His eyes held hers captive while he lowered his mouth to hers.

"As retribution, I demand a kiss . . . a single kiss," he murmured, his lips hovering over hers.

"A kiss . . . ?"

Torture. Paradise. A request impossible to resist.

Resting her hands against his hard-muscled chest, Gillian rose on tiptoe. Her eyelids drifted shut. Her lips parted of their own accord. She brushed her mouth against his, softly, tentatively, once, twice, then again. His lips were firm yet yielding, mobile, and hungry for the taste of hers.

Placing his hands at her waist, Luc drew her closer and deepened the kiss. His mouth slanted over hers. She needed no further encouragement to twine her arms around his neck. His tongue eased into her mouth, the rough tip sliding over the satiny inner surface of hers, hot, teasing, enticing. A single kiss wasn't enough. Could never be enough. She pressed against him, eager to meld her body against his powerful frame, wanting more, needing more.

"Gillian! Is that you, girl?"

Guiltily, they sprang apart. At the sound of Randolph Stafford's irate voice, the misty spell Luc had managed to weave splintered. A world filled with jagged edges and discordant sounds snapped into focus. Gillian drew a ragged breath, striving to regain a measure of composure.

"You were looking for me?" she asked, proud that her voice didn't quaver as her father stormed up the steps.

Ignoring Luc, he turned the full force of his fury on his

daughter. "When were you planning to tell me your lover is here at Fort Mackinac? Or didn't you intend to tell me? Did you foolishly think I wouldn't find out?"

Gillian stared at her father in dismay. "I only learned that he was here tonight myself."

Stafford glowered at her, clearly unhappy with her explanation. "Imagine my surprise when I found Lieutenant Jeremy Blackwood listed on the roster of newly arrived troops."

"I was just as surprised as you."

Her father had been drinking; she could smell it on his breath. As usual, alcohol had made his temper unpredictable.

"I'm warning you, girl." He grasped her arm and ushered her inside. "There'd better not be any funny business between the two of you or you'll regret it."

The door slammed shut.

Luc had heard enough. More than enough, actually. He left the Stone Quarters behind and headed across the parade grounds and out of the fort. He didn't even pause when he heard someone call his name. *Lieutenant Jeremy Blackwood!* So Gillian's lover finally had a name. No doubt the man in question was the wavy-haired devil who had claimed her for a waltz. Gillian's face had taken on a rapt expression as she gazed at her dance partner. Jealousy ripped into him with sharp talons.

Only minutes ago Gillian had stared at him with the same rapt look, practically inviting his kiss. Was this all a game to her? Was she using him to even the score with Blackwood? Did she intend to use him as a pawn to make Blackwood grovel? Some women wouldn't hesitate to use any means at their disposal.

Yet her response to his touch seemed so spontaneous, so guileless. How could anyone who looked that sweet and innocent have devious intent? Gillian, innocent? Not any longer. Thanks to that scoundrel Blackwood, she was schooled in womanly ways. She had surrendered her innocence to a pasty-face redcoat. The thought of her with Blackwood made him seethe with anger.

He turned up the path leading to his cabin. The breeze from the lake helped cool his temper. What should it matter who Gillian Stafford chose as a lover? She could have one or a dozen. It was no concern of his. She was British to the core—his enemy. He picked a stone from the path and hurled it into the trees. Regardless of how many times he reminded himself, he forgot everything when he gazed into her beautiful face. A face like an angel.

God, what had come over him? She was like a sickness, a disease. Was there no cure? he wondered bleakly. He had never been the sort to lust after a woman, never suffered the lovesickness that afflicted many of his fellow voyageurs. Before meeting the English beauty, his life had been simple, uncomplicated. Now he was preoccupied with odd longings. In the past, whenever he and some woman had shared an attraction, they had joined their bodies to satisfy a mutual urge. Then, physical needs assuaged, he'd walked away without a thought. Perhaps making love to Gillian Stafford would rid him of this constant craving. Once lust was appeased, he would be cured. His life would return to being simple, uncomplicated.

Regardless of how pleasant the thought of making love to Gillian was, he needed to put her from his mind and concentrate instead on the task at hand: to gather as much information as possible from the British and pass it along through Toad to the Americans. He stopped short, groaning aloud. He was no better than that loose-tongued bastard, Bunton. He, too, had divulged Gillian's secret. A fact that until now he had ignored. What a convenient memory! He had wasted no time telling Toad the reason Gillian had been banished from her home. Toad could have spread the rumors as easily as Bunton.

I don't like being ostracized. He remembered her words, the wistfulness in her voice, the fleeting sadness on her face.

He should have been the one begging forgiveness—not her.

"What were you thinking!" Randolph Stafford railed.

Gillian spread her hands in a hopeless gesture. "It's been nearly a week since we celebrated the king's birthday. I hoped they would forget."

"This extremely awkward situation is entirely your fault." Hands clasped behind him, Randolph Stafford paced the width of his quarters. "You should never have agreed to teach the Babcocks that blasted dance."

"What else could I have done? It would have been churlish to refuse."

The truth of her statement momentarily silenced his tirade.

"Perhaps I can claim to be indisposed."

"They'll only postpone it until you're well again. No," he said, shaking his head, "I fear a refusal of any sort is quite out of the question."

"But, Father, how can you insist I attend?"

"Even during the American occupation of the fort, the Babcocks remained loyal British supporters. I don't want to appear disrespectful."

Gillian traced the pattern on the worn damask settee with a fingertip. "I know how you feel about Jeremy. I'm certain he's been invited as well."

He dismissed her concern with an impatient shrug. "I've given this invitation a great deal of thought. Except for me, no one knows the name of the chap who dishonored you."

She flushed at the blatant reminder. "Luc knows. He couldn't help but hear you."

Stafford snorted derisively. "Luc du Pré is a voyageur, a half-breed, a man of little consequence. He's smart enough to keep his mouth shut about what he overhears. If not, he knows the consequences."

Gillian shivered at the cold, unfeeling tone. This was a side of her father—the military side—she rarely witnessed. He would show an enemy no mercy.

"The soirée begins promptly at eight on Friday evening. I trust you'll comport yourself with the dignity befitting my position and not disgrace me further."

At his admonition, resentment flared within her. She dropped her gaze to hide her reaction. Did he think she would flagrantly offer herself to a man who already had a wife? Did he think she had so little pride, so little self-respect? And so few morals? Perhaps that was precisely what he thought. Hadn't he already labeled her a slut?

Interpreting her silence as consent, he stopped pacing, picked up his shako, and strode toward the door. "Make sure you're ready. I don't want to keep them waiting."

Gillian rested her head back against the settee and closed her eyes. At one time, the prospect of an entire evening in Jeremy Blackwood's company would have sent her into a tizzy of anticipation. He was witty, charming, sophisticated. She had felt special to be singled out as his partner. But ever since her aunt had interrupted their tryst with the shocking revelation of a wife in Sussex, her estimation of him had plummeted. In the intervening months, her emotions had run the gamut from disbelief, outrage, betrayal, until finally all she felt was disgust. She loathed herself for being a poor judge of a man's true character. She had fancied herself in love, had been willing to surrender her virtue. Jeremy, in return, had merely toyed with her tender feelings. He wanted her body with no regard for her heart. He planned to use then discard her as efficiently as yesterday's uniform.

Sighing, she rose from the settee and went to stand by the window. Troops crisscrossed the parade ground to the barked commands of a drill sergeant. She wished she could command her emotions as easily. Mistakes, she had once read, were such only if one didn't learn from them. Well, she didn't plan to repeat her folly. Never again would she be so easily gulled.

As the dreaded hour approached, it was Gillian's turn to pace. The lavender foulard swished about her ankles with each agitated step. The evening stretched ahead interminably. It would require all her acting skills to smile, be polite and gracious, while maintaining a distance without offending her hosts.

She glanced at the small enameled clock. It was unlike her father to be late. Tension knotted the muscles at the back of her neck. She could only pray Jeremy wouldn't disclose by word or action that they had known each other in England. Such a revelation would surely lead to speculation on their past relationship.

Lost in gloomy reverie, she started at a knock on the door. Strange, she thought as she hurried to answer it, Father never knocked.

"Luc . . ." she gasped as she swung the door wide.

"Your father sends his regrets," he announced without preamble. His scowl indicated his displeasure. "Colonel McDouall called a meeting of his staff."

"Oh, I see." Before she could rejoice at her last-minute reprieve, Luc pricked her bubble of optimism.

"Your father prevailed upon me to be your escort."

"Oh ..." It would have been difficult to waltz with Jeremy under her father's watchfulness, but, somehow it would be worse under Luc's. Especially considering their last meeting. Her cheeks burned, remembering his kiss.

"Are you ready?"

Wordlessly, she picked up a lightweight shawl from the back of a chair and went with him. Side by side, they left the fort and walked down the ramp. Neither spoke until they turned up Market Street.

Gillian cleared her throat and voiced the concern uppermost in her mind. "After Father's outburst last we met, I'm sure you're aware that Lieutenant Blackwood is the man with whom I was once ... involved."

"Who you are *involved* with is no concern of mine."

His curt reply cut her to the quick. "I mentioned Jeremy's name only because he will be present tonight." She tried to keep the hurt from seeping into her voice. "The Babcocks expressed an interest in learning how to waltz. They asked Jeremy and me to teach them."

His jaw clenched. "Your father explained the situation. He's concerned that your behavior might reflect poorly on him."

"I'm in need of neither chaperon, nursemaid, nor spy. I was simply going to prevail upon your sense of discretion. It wouldn't do for anyone on the island to know Jeremy and I were once ... *involved.*"

"The burden of discretion lies with you, m'selle."

"From the grim expression on your face, it appears *I* am the burden. You don't seem eager for an evening in my company."

"I've little interest in frivolous social events. There are more pressing matters that draw my attention."

Gillian slanted him a look. "And just where does your interest lay?"

"Military matters interest me," he admitted grudgingly.

"And that's why you spend much of your time in my father's company?"

"I've been able to learn a great deal from him."

"The war can't continue forever. What then, Luc? Will you return to the life of a voyageur? Or do you want more?"

Taciturn or not, the man intrigued her. Until just now, she hadn't realized how little she knew about him. Granted, she had made observations and deductions, reached certain conclusions, but there were many more things she didn't know. Such as what subjects interested him. Did he have any family? Dear God ... She stopped dead in the middle of the road. What if, like Jeremy Blackwood, he had a wife stashed in some backwoods village?

She was dimly aware that Luc had stopped walking also and was frowning down at her. "Are you married?" she blurted out.

He stared at her as though she had taken leave of her senses.

Gillian gave in to the childish urge to stamp her foot. "Damn you, Luc du Pré, answer my question. Are you or aren't you married?"

Now it was her turn to be surprised as Luc tossed back his head and laughed. The sound of the rich, hearty laughter was infectious. Her lips twitched with the urge to join him. As much as she loved seeing him smile, she found that she loved the sound of his laughter even more.

Gradually his merriment subsided. "No, *chérie*. I am not married, nor have I ever been married. Now, does that satisfy your curiosity?"

Gillian smiled with pure feminine satisfaction. She was still smiling moments later when Margaret Babcock opened her front door.

Chapter Fifteen

Mrs. Babcock ushered them into the parlor. In preparation for the evening's event, rugs had been rolled up and removed, furniture pushed against the walls. Two fiddlers, one in a soldier's uniform, the other wearing trapper's garb, tuned their instruments in a corner. The squawk of a bow and the plucking of strings punctuated talk and laughter. Much to Gillian's dismay, she discovered that the Mayfields had also been invited. Judith treated her to a disapproving glare, then presented her back.

Jeremy, resplendent in his impeccably tailored uniform and shiny brass, greeted Gillian with a warm smile. Ignoring Luc, he bowed low over Gillian's hand. "You're looking especially lovely tonight, Miss Stafford."

Gillian, aware that others observed the exchange with varying degrees of interest, shifted uncomfortably under his flattery. She couldn't stop worrying that someone might suspect the true nature of their relationship.

Margaret Babcock beamed at her guests. "I hoped an

evening devoted to music and dance would help dispel the gloom. All everyone talks of anymore is the possibility of an American attack. Tonight should provide a welcome diversion."

"Here, here," James echoed approval of his wife's plan. "After seeing Miss Stafford and Lieutenant Blackwood waltz, it's been the only subject my wife has talked about." Henry Mayfield ran a hand over his thinning hair.

Judith gave Jeremy a coy smile. "I must confess, Lieutenant, we're most eager to learn."

"Unfortunately, M'sieur du Pré has no partner." Margaret shook her head sadly. "Most of the wives and unmarried daughters have gone elsewhere until the conflict is resolved."

"It's unlikely they will return," James added somberly.

"And why do you say that?" Gillian asked.

"In order to answer your question, Miss Stafford, you'll need to know what happened two years ago." Henry Mayfield assumed the role of historian. "The British waged a surprise attack against the Americans, who previously occupied the fort. The commander, a young man by the name of Lieutenant Porter Hanks, surrendered the fort without a single shot fired."

"A cowardly act," Jeremy sneered.

"Some argue the reverse," Luc contradicted.

"Really!" Jeremy made no attempt to hide his scorn. "How else can you describe such a decision?"

"In Hank's defense," Luc pointed out in a mild tone, "no one had bothered to inform him that war had been declared. The Americans were outnumbered at least ten to one. Hanks was advised that should he resist, the entire garrison would be massacred."

"Given the circumstances, young Hanks made a prudent choice," James agreed. "Regarding Miss Stafford's original question concerning the scarcity of eligible females, American citizens were given a month in which to pledge an oath of allegiance to the British or leave the island. Some refused and left for outposts held by the United States in either Detroit or Chicago."

At a subtle hand signal from Margaret, a serving girl entered bearing a tray of cups filled with mulled wine. The scent of cloves and cinnamon spiced the air.

Judith took a dainty sip. "Many citizens, however, such as ourselves, proved to be staunchly loyal to the British."

Puzzled, Gillian shook her head. "I don't understand how a British landing could go undetected."

James helped himself to a serving of wine. "The enemy was well informed of the single flaw. The fort is only vulnerable at one point—the high ground to its rear."

"Not to fear." Jeremy intercepted Gillian's look of alarm. "The construction of Fort George on that very site is nearly complete. Mackinac will be impregnable against attack. The Americans, when—and if—they arrive, will be soundly defeated."

"Enough talk of war," Margaret scolded. "Tonight we will learn the new dance sweeping Europe."

Liberal servings of mulled wine helped induce an atmosphere of gaiety and reduce inhibitions. When the fiddlers played the first notes of a waltz, everyone was eager to begin.

Jeremy offered his arm to Gillian. "Shall we proceed with the lesson?"

Pasting on a smile, she followed him to the center of the room. She placed a hand on his shoulder and tried not to stiffen when he placed his at her waist.

"Allow us to demonstrate."

His movements graceful and fluid, Jeremy whirled her about the room as the others looked on. Gillian tried to concentrate on the music and dance steps, not Luc's frown of disapproval.

"Relax, darling," Jeremy murmured. "You look tense. You don't want these nice people to think something's wrong, do you?"

Drawing a deep breath, Gillian willed tense muscles to relax.

"Ah, much better," Jeremy said, his voice low and molasses smooth. "Did I tell you how lovely you look tonight? But then, you're never less than perfect."

"Flattery will not gain you a prize, Jeremy."

He pretended to pout. "You wound me."

"How odd," she murmured as they whirled about the parlor. "I always thought it impossible to wound someone without a heart."

"Tsk, tsk," Jeremy clucked, undeterred. "Sarcasm doesn't become you. Unless you're careful, it will rob your beauty."

"What sage advice from the thief who tried to steal my virtue."

Gillian felt keen satisfaction when Jeremy's usually effortless glide nearly faltered. He made no further attempt at conversation during the course of their dance.

Their small audience clapped appreciatively. As Jeremy grinned and bowed, Gillian felt Luc's eyes bore into her. She deliberately avoided meeting his gaze but couldn't help but wonder what he was thinking. He knew about her relationship with Jeremy Blackwood. Did he think she enjoyed or encouraged Jeremy's attention? Did it bother him to see her in the arms of another? Or perhaps he didn't care.

"Lieutenant," Margaret stepped forward, "perhaps you'll be my partner.

James Babcock offered Gillian an arm. "And Miss Stafford shall be mine."

Judith and Henry, not wanting to be left out, joined them while Jeremy patiently cajoled Margaret to follow his lead. Step, step, glide, circle. Over and over he repeated the pattern until Margaret gained confidence.

James, his brow creased in concentration, gamely followed suit. He grinned broadly when Gillian praised his efforts. Henry Mayfield's attempts were less successful, his movement wooden and clumsy. Watching him from the corner of her eye, Gillian felt a stirring of sympathy. The poor man definitely lacked grace. He reddened in embarrassment each time his wife loudly complained that he tromped on her slippers. Luc watched the activity from a chair on the sidelines, his thoughts carefully masked.

When the dancers finally paused to give the musicians a much-needed rest, Margaret served her guests small iced cakes and more of the delicious mulled wine.

"I hope we're not imposing on your free time, Lieutenant." Margaret delicately dabbed at a fine bead of moisture at her temples. "You must find this all a bit tiring after long hours of drill and target practice."

"Not in the least, madame. During the season in London, parties often lasted until three or four in the morning." Jeremy selected a cake, then turned to Gillian. "Isn't that right, Miss Stafford?"

"Quite true, Lieutenant, but my habits have changed since arriving in Michigan. I fear I could no longer continue such late hours."

"Unfortunately, there's little to do in this wilderness that requires late hours." Then, afraid he might have offended his hostess, Jeremy added hastily, "That's why, dear lady, your invitation was greeted with such delight."

A quiet knock halted further discussion.

A servant quickly answered the door, then stood aside.

"Père Robichaud." Margaret greeted the newly arrived guest with fondness.

"Did you mention you were serving chocolate cake tonight, Margaret?" The Jesuit's dark eyes twinkled with humor.

"You have a bigger sweet tooth than any two-year-old," Margaret scolded laughingly.

Père Robichaud smiled, unabashed, as he helped himself to one of the cakes.

"Father may occasionally refuse dinner invitations, but never do I remember him refusing dessert," James informed the others.

Gillian watched in amusement as the tall, thin priest devoured every last crumb, then looked longingly at the half-filled tray of treats, clearly tempted to take a second. Meanwhile, Judith engaged Jeremy in a discussion of London fashion, hanging on to his every word. While Margaret excused herself to attend to refreshments, the men huddled together, talking about the completion of Fort George. Gillian stood somewhat apart from both groups, feeling the outsider.

She stared resentfully at Luc du Pré's back. He wasn't doing anything to make this blasted evening any easier, she fumed. He hadn't spoken to her since they arrived. It was as if he had forgotten her existence. Did he think she liked being thrown together with Jeremy Blackwood?

"Are you enjoying yourself this evening, m'selle?" the clergyman inquired.

"Umm . . . yes, Father." The instant the words were out of her mouth she could have bitten her tongue. Not only had she lied, but she had lied to a man of the cloth. "Actually, no, I'm not," she admitted.

Père Robichaud chuckled. "I thought as much from your expression. My young friend, Luc, seems to share your sentiment. He confessed his distaste for this dancing lesson."

Gillian took a small sip of wine. "Mrs. Babcock is convinced it provides a welcome distraction from talk of war."

Père Robichaud's head bobbed in agreement. "Margaret's right. It's good people can forget even for a single evening that soon their homes will be under siege."

"I'm surprised to find you here, Father. The waltz has created a great deal of controversy. I thought you might disapprove."

He shook his head sadly. "I find it ironic that some consider a dance sinful when people kill each other in the name of commerce."

Gillian found herself warming toward the priest. He seemed both tolerant and sensible, two characteristics she admired. She had mistakenly assumed he would be stern and judgmental, but instead he seemed kind and open-minded. She could understand why Luc chose him as a friend. At the sound of Luc's resonant baritone, her attention strayed in his direction.

Père Robichaud was quick to note her distraction. "My former pupil seems quite taken with you."

Her face flushed, Gillian quickly turned back to the priest, who seemed to be watching her in elfin delight. "Really?"

"Really," Père Robichaud insisted. "Luc speaks of you often. The Indian child, Aupetchi, he said, blossomed under your gracious tutelage."

"Aupetchi brings me joy as well. In addition to being my student, she has become my friend. Her grandfather, Wind Spirit, has also shown me much kindness."

"Ah, yes." Père Robichaud succumbed to temptation and helped himself to another cake. "Wind Spirit has earned my highest regard."

The Babcocks' serving girl interrupted the men's conversation with a message for Henry Mayfield. After listening intently, Henry nodded and turned to his host. "As much as I regret it, I must attend to business matters."

"Now . . . ?" Judith wailed plaintively.

"I'm sorry, my dear, but McDouall just authorized funds for gifts for the newly arrived Indian allies. They demand payment in whiskey. He fears they'll grow impatient waiting."

"But it isn't fair." Judith pouted. "Why must a horde of savages ruin our evening?"

"If I may make a suggestion," Margaret offered, tactfully ignoring the woman's thoughtless remark, "Henry, why not allow your wife to remain for one final lesson? When the dancing is finished, James will escort her home."

After a glance at his wife's hopeful expression, Henry agreed with alacrity.

No sooner had the door closed behind her husband than Judith wondered out loud, "With my husband gone, what will we do about partners?"

"No problem." Margaret leveled a look at Luc. "M'sieur du Pré has spent the entire evening lazing in a chair while we cavorted. It's time for him to participate in the fun."

"No, no, not me," Luc protested. He turned to Pére Robichaud for assistance. "Father, perhaps you'd like to take a turn about the floor."

"And miss the opportunity to sample another sweet? Oh, no, *mon ami.* You are the one with a quick mind . . . and nimble feet."

"Good," Margaret exclaimed in satisfaction. "It's settled, then."

James stepped forward and with a courtly bow claimed his wife for a dance partner. Gillian felt moved at the sight of Margaret's answering smile. Even after years together, it was plain to see the affection the couple shared.

"Lieutenant Blackwood," Judith cried, intercepting Jeremy before he could approach Gillian, "I'm afraid I haven't quite mastered the steps. My husband, I fear, lacks your grace on the dance floor."

Jeremy quickly concealed chagrin beneath charm. "Then, dear lady, it will give me great pleasure to show you."

"Wonderful," Margaret applauded. "That leaves Luc and Gillian as partners."

At a nod from Margaret, the two fiddlers struck up a waltz and the dance began.

Setting her cup aside, Gillian caught Luc's eye. "I recall that you do not care for dancing. I have no objection to sitting this one out."

"No, m'selle," Père Robichaud disagreed heartily. "Luc was my best pupil. He learns quickly, as you are about to find out."

Gillian raised a brow. "Show me how quickly you learn, m'sieur. I dare you," she added with an impertinent grin.

"Never could resist a dare." His mouth curled in amusement. He placed his hand at the small of her back. "Like this, m'selle?"

"Like that, m'sieur." Gillian rested her hand in his callused palm. She tried to ignore the pleasant tingle that raced up her arm. And the heat along her spine where his hand touched her waist.

Luc smiled down at her. "Aren't you worried that I'll crush your toes and ruin your slippers?"

She slanted him a smile in return. "I'm willing to risk being crippled."

Luc's steps effortlessly matched the rhythm. They circled the room in flawless precision, their movements smooth and flowing. He moved with such ease that Gillian immediately became suspicious.

"Who taught you to waltz, du Pré? And don't fib," she cautioned, "or I'll report you to your priest."

"His name is Gustave, and he boasts the bushiest beard in all Upper Canada."

Gillian's steps nearly faltered. "Surely you jest."

Luc laughed softly at her incredulity. "I exist among a merry band of men who love nothing better than to dance and sing. Women partners are scarce, so we make do. You haven't lived until you've seen André Tousseau perform a minuet. He even dons a wig."

She laughed out loud at the mental picture he had created. From the short time she had spent on St. Joseph's Island, Gillian knew the little Frenchman was incorrigible. He possessed a lively sense of humor and a wicked sense of the absurd. She could easily picture him mincing about in a lady's wig, prancing and bowing, his black eyes alight with deviltry.

Her laughter faded, but a dreamy smile remained. She surrendered to a sense of sheer and utter contentment at being held in Luc's arms while he whirled her in slow, lazy circles. She felt as though she were floating on air, weightless as dandelions gone to seed.

When the last notes faded, she joined with the others to applaud the musicians' able efforts.

Margaret fanned her flushed face. "James and I wish to thank you for sharing a most delightful evening with us."

James echoed her sentiments, then turned serious. "If rumors are true, it may be some time before we'll share another quite like it."

"Keep the faith, my children," Père Robichaud counseled. "Pray the enmity between great nations will soon be ended."

Jeremy stood straight and tall. "And England will emerge victorious."

Heads bobbed in agreement. A ripple of voices concurred.

While the musicians packed away their instruments and drifted off, guests bid their hosts farewell.

Jeremy approached Gillian, a determined gleam in his blue-gray eyes. "Since we both have the same destination, Miss Stafford, I'd be happy to see you safely home. There's no need for du Pré to make the long trek."

"That's very considerate, Lieutenant . . ."

Luc interrupted before Gillian could lodge a protest. "Captain Stafford gave me explicit orders that I should be his daughter's escort this evening. I gave him my word."

"Nonsense." Jeremy's upper lip curled in derision. "Are you placing your value above that of an officer in His Majesty's service?"

"I'm sure Luc meant no personal affront, Lieutenant," Père Robichaud said in an attempt to disarm the hostility.

James cleared his throat uneasily. "I find it commendable of Luc to honor the captain's request in spite of any inconvenience."

Jeremy's jaw jutted at an obstinate angle. "But it's poor judgment to choose some backwoodsman over an officer."

Gillian accepted her shawl from the servant who watched the scene with avid interest. "Since Father entrusted my safekeeping to M'sieur du Pré, I have no choice but to trust his judgment." She draped the light wrap over her shoulders and, with an air of finality, placed her hand in the crook of Luc's arm.

Père Robichaud sighed with approval. "No one could be more trustworthy than Luc to escort his daughter."

A red flush crept upward from the collar of Jeremy's jacket. "Excuse me, Father, but are you implying that I'm not?"

The priest regarded the soldier with mild reproach. "Why, Lieutenant, your trustworthiness has never been questioned!"

James Babcock smothered an exaggerated yawn behind

his hand. Margaret took her cue from him. "I fear my poor husband needs his rest. Could we prevail upon you, Lieutenant Blackwood, to walk Mrs. Mayfield home?"

At the request, Judith's expression underwent a transformation from sulky to joyful. "Oh, Lieutenant," she gushed, clutching his sleeve, "with all these savages overrunning the island, I'd feel so much safer with a brave soldier like yourself."

Jeremy conceded defeat with a tight-lipped smile. With a stiff bow to the Babcocks and a parting glare at the others, he left with Judith Mayfield hanging on to his arm and chattering like a magpie. If the woman only knew the truth about the man she seemed so fascinated by, Gillian thought. But she could hardly fault Judith. She, too, had once reacted much the same. It wasn't until later that she had learned the truth. Jeremy was a polished red apple with a rotten core.

Luc bid his friends a terse good night, then strode off, with Gillian hurrying to keep pace. She could sense the tension humming through him like the plucked string of a fiddle. Without a moon to guide her feet over the uneven dirt road, she nearly stumbled. "Luc, please, slow down."

Wordlessly, he accommodated her request.

She stole a sidelong glance at his profile. Remote and hard, his features could have been carved in granite. His heavy silence was beginning to wear on her nerves. When they turned toward the fort and he still hadn't spoken, she broke the silence.

"You seem angry. Have I said or done anything to offend you?"

He glanced down coldly. "Did it please you to have two grown men fighting for the privilege of escorting you home?"

Stunned by his outburst, she stared at him in disbelief. "I never wanted . . ."

He cut her off. "Didn't you?"

"No, of course not," she denied hotly.

He looked unconvinced. "You brought Blackwood to his knees. Another minute and he would have groveled at your feet."

His accusation sent her reeling. "That was never my intent."

"Wasn't it?" he sneered. "Did you see his face when you chose me over him?"

Dazed, she could only shake her head.

"If you were using me to settle an old score, you succeeded. Tell me," he gritted, not slackening his pace, "does revenge taste sweet?"

"I . . ." Her voice trailed off. Tears pricked the back of her eyelids, and she blinked furiously to keep them from falling. Damned if she'd let Luc see that his charges had hurt. In the past she had taken his support for granted, assumed he'd be her staunch defender, her protector, her advocate. But he had ruthlessly abdicated his responsibilities. His low opinion of her rivaled Judith Mayfield's.

She brought her chin up a notch. In that instant she decided not to dignify his erroneous assumptions with a reply. Drawing her tattered pride about her like an invisible cloak, she uttered not a single word in her own defense.

Not as they walked up the steep ramp to the fort.

Not when they entered south sally port.

Not upon reaching the officer's Stone Quarters.

As the door slammed shut behind her, she muttered that it would be a cold day in hell before she'd beg forgiveness for an offense she didn't commit.

Chapter Sixteen

Gray clouds draped the sky like dingy bed linen. The air was heavy, sullen. For days, villagers spoke of rain; for weeks, soldiers talked of battle. Not a drop fell, not a rifle fired. The constant tension frayed Gillian's nerves wire thin and fragile.

Restless, she tossed her book aside and paced the length of the parlor. A vague discontent plagued her. The fault lay with Luc du Pré. Quick as a minnow, resentment wriggled through her. Luc was to blame for her ill-tempered disposition. She fumed every time she remembered him accusing her of trying to make Jeremy jealous. They hadn't spoken since. She picked a pretty piece of driftwood from the desk, absently rubbed its smooth surface, then set it down. Why would Luc think such a thing? Couldn't he see that she detested Jeremy? How could he believe she could melt in his arms one night, then throw herself at another? The last question hurt most of all. Did he think her so flighty, so lacking in character? Couldn't he sense that he was the one she cared about?

Horrified, she stopped short. The realization drove the breath from her lungs. She felt hot, then cold. *Luc du Pré? The man she cared about?* When had that happened? How? But the answers to those questions weren't important. She knew with absolute certainty that Luc mattered to her, mattered very much. The realization terrified her. How could she hope for a future with a man so totally wrong for her?

They were complete opposites. Shared nothing in common.

Came from different worlds.

The parlor walls seemed to shrink around her, hemming her in, trapping her. Needing to escape a problem she didn't know how to solve, Gillian fled. With no conscious destination in mind, she left the fort with a purposeful stride. Habit carried her along the lakeshore path toward her customary meeting place with Aupetchi.

Instead of soothing, the crash of waves against the gravel-strewn shore added to her growing disquiet. Seagulls screeched as they skimmed the water's surface, then dove for fish. Their raucous cries grated on nerves already stretched close to breaking.

As she neared Arch Rock, the young girl bolted around a bend in the path and hurtled toward her. Gillian's smile of welcome faded at seeing worry etched on the small face.

"Aupetchi, what's wrong?" Gillian picked up her skirt and ran to greet her. "Is it your grandfather?"

Aupetchi struggled to catch her breath. "No," she gasped.

"Then what is it, child?" Concerned, Gillian stooped to study her little friend more closely. The girl's honey-bronze skin seemed a shade paler than usual, her dark eyes wide and anxious.

"No, not Grandfather. This."

Aupetchi raised her hand, and for the first time, Gillian noticed the white envelope she clutched. Her pulse quickened as she took it from the girl. She immediately recognized the bold, familiar script.

"Where did you find this?" Her tongue shaped the question with reluctance.

Aupetchi pointed to a nearby rock. "I come to our meeting place hoping you'd be there. This waiting instead."

The message was from Jeremy. But how could he have known where to leave it? Had he been spying on her, cataloging her habits? The notion left her uneasy. Her gaze swept the high bluff and surrounding forest, half expecting to see a vivid scarlet jacket emerge from among the evergreens. However, except for branches swaying in the wind, there was no movement. She and Aupetchi were alone.

The girl tugged on her skirt. "Is the paper bad?"

Gillian tried to summon a reassuring smile. "Don't worry, little one. It's merely a message from a former friend."

"This someone . . ." Aupetchi said, clearly perplexed, "he no longer your friend?"

"No," Gillian replied, clearing her throat. "Not any longer." Resolutely, she broke the sealing wax and withdrew the single sheet of parchment. A small gasp of dismay escaped as she read, then reread, the missive.

I have privileged information concerning your father's career. He is in serious danger of court-martial. Only you can prevent this grave humiliation. If you care about him,

*come at once. I will be waiting at the cabin by the crooked
tamarack.*

Once again, Aupetchi tugged her skirt. "You all right,
Gillian? Are you sick?"

The child's voice rang hollow, as though coming from
a great distance away. An avalanche of thoughts, questions,
and emotions tumbled through Gillian's mind. Court-
martial? What kind of trouble had her father gotten himself
into? What could she possibly do to prevent it? The military,
she knew, meant everything to Randolph Stafford. The
disgrace of a court-martial would surely kill him. In spite
of their past differences and harsh words, she owed him
her loyalty. She would do what she could to help him.

"I'm sorry I bring you paper that make you sad."

Gillian rested her hands gently on the girl's shoulders
and bent down until they were at eye level. "I need to
meet someone at a cabin near a bent tamarack tree. Do
you know of such a place?"

Aupetchi swallowed, then nodded hesitantly.

"Will you take me there? It's very important," she added,
when the child still seemed reluctant.

"I take you," Aupetchi said, her small face solemn. "Follow me."

Aupetchi turned in the direction from which she had
just come, and after a short distance, veered away from
the lakeshore trail up a narrow path running diagonally
toward the top of the bluff. Gillian scrambled after, using
bushes and trees as handholds. Once or twice her feet lost
purchase on the loose stone, but she righted herself and
gamely followed. Nimble as a mountain goat, Aupetchi
seemed to suffer no such problems.

At the summit, Gillian paused. A stiff breeze had kicked
up from the north, rifling the leaves overhead and whip-
ping the waves below into white-crested froth. A glance at

the sky revealed lowering clouds. Rain that had dawdled for days now seemed anxious to debut.

"This way." Aupetchi beckoned.

Gillian hastened after her. The ground dipped to form a shallow basin. In its center sat a cabin of rough-hewn timber roofed with cedar shingles nestled amid a copse of maple, beech, locust, and pine. A tamarack tree, bent nearly double by the elements, stood sentinel near the front door.

"If you want, I stay?" Aupetchi offered.

Gillian felt Aupetchi's hand creep into hers and gave it a reassuring squeeze. She realized she didn't relish the prospect of being alone with Jeremy. "Yes, I'd like you to stay."

Jeremy approached through the trees at the far side of the small clearing. He scowled when he saw that Gillian wasn't alone. "Send the child away or I'll leave and your father can bid his career good-bye."

Aupetchi looked at Gillian for direction, her dark eyes wide with concern.

Gillian silently debated what to do, then acquiesced to his demand. "Go, Aupetchi. Don't worry about me. I'll be fine."

After a backward glance that conveyed uncertainty, Aupetchi ran off.

Jeremy smiled the smile of the victorious. "It took you long enough, darling. I was beginning to wonder if the Indian brat had delivered my note."

Gillian stiffened at the disparaging remark directed at the child. "Please don't refer to my friend in that manner."

"Friend?" he snorted contemptuously. "How pathetic. Not only do you claim a child as a friend but a red-skinned one at that."

"If you continue to hurl insults, I'll leave."

"Very well," he acquiesced, strolling closer. "Let's not waste precious time arguing."

"Why did you lure me here?"

"Gillian, darling." He held out his arms. "Is this any way to greet a lover after a lengthy separation?"

She neatly sidestepped him. "You're not my lover. In fact, you never were in the carnal sense of the word, regardless of what people think."

Indeed, she wondered how she had ever been infatuated with this man. Once she had been willing, even eager, to surrender everything—her heart, her soul, her innocence. In return, he had betrayed her trust, broken her heart. If not for her aunt's timely intervention, she would have even more regrets.

Undeterred by his cool reception, Jeremy continued, "You have no idea of the subterfuge to which I had to resort in order to meet you without your father glaring daggers."

Furious, she waved the note beneath his nose. "Tell me what trouble my father is in and how I can help him."

Jeremy splayed his hand against his chest. "Your coldness is an arrow straight to my heart."

"I believe you missed your calling, Jeremy. You should have been on the stage."

"You've turned cynical. I remember you as soft, sweet. Trusting." He reached out and stroked her cheek. "Prove to me this wilderness hasn't changed you. Made you hard and unfeeling."

She jerked away from his touch. Raising her voice to be heard above the wind rattling through the trees, she brandished the crumpled note. "This is the only reason I'm here."

He took a step closer so that mere inches separated her heaving chest from the red wool of his uniform jacket. "The captain is in serious trouble with his superiors."

Nervously, Gillian tucked a strand of hair behind her ear. Concern washed away all traces of anger. "What sort of trouble?"

Jeremy gave her a sympathetic smile. "Seems your father suffers from a severe drinking problem."

This wasn't the shattering announcement she had feared. Gillian wasn't sure whether to feel relief or alarm. "Father's fondness for spirits has hardly been a secret."

"True," Jeremy conceded, "but it's reached a point where McDouall questions your father's ability. He considers him unreliable to carry out certain responsibilities. He fears that under the influence of alcohol his judgment is unsound, his orders irrational. A court-martial will relieve him of duty."

"Father has been much better since my arrival. He hardly drinks at all," she protested, her mouth dry with fear. But even as she boldly made the statement, she knew it was a lie. Her father had been drinking heavily the night of King George's birthday celebration. She had smelled the whiskey on his breath as he hustled her inside after learning of Jeremy's presence at Mackinac. "He's making every effort to curb his drinking."

Jeremy watched her closely, not fooled by her denial. "I thought it only fair to warn you how his superiors view him. Perhaps you can talk sense to him."

"If you have nothing more of importance to impart . . ."

She moved to step around him, but he reacted swiftly to block her retreat. "Gillian, darling, you're trying my patience."

"And you're trying mine," she retorted. "You tricked me into meeting you. Father's habits are hardly a new concern. He's imbibed heavily ever since Mother's death years ago."

"Can you find it in your heart to forgive me? I'm a

desperate man!" He caught her arm. "I was willing to use any ruse that might bring us together. Not long ago you would have rushed into my arms, overjoyed at the sight of me."

She stared into the handsome face of a man whom she once thought she loved and felt nothing but disgust. "And once upon a time I was an ignorant, naive girl who made the grave mistake of trusting a scoundrel only interested in seduction."

Jeremy's brow wrinkled with irritation, then smoothed. "We've had no time to be alone, to remember what we meant to each other. I don't know who this cabin belongs to, but it's not being used. Let's finish what we started in that little inn outside London."

Gillian's eyes widened at the blatant proposal. "Surely you aren't suggesting . . . ?"

Jeremy shrugged, his eyes fastened on her hopefully. "Except for your little red-skinned friend, no one knows about our rendezvous. Neither of us will be missed for hours."

"You expect me to act as though nothing happened?" she asked in patent disbelief.

"You professed to love me. If your aunt and her friend hadn't interrupted when they did . . ."

Gillian hung her head, shamed by the memory. It had taken seeing him again to make her realize she had thought herself in love with a man who did not exist. She had loved the image he projected—not the man himself. She had never really known Jeremy Blackwood at all.

"Come, darling," he wheedled. "Prove your feelings haven't changed."

His hold tightened, but she wasn't alarmed. Jeremy fancied himself too much of a gentleman to ever harm a woman. "Prove it, Jeremy? How?"

"Allow me to kiss you. Then if you deny my kiss evokes

any feelings, I'll go away and promise never to bother you again."

Gillian stared into his smug, self-confident face. A single kiss was a small price to pay to be free of his demands. "All right," she agreed slowly.

"I knew you couldn't resist." Smiling, he lowered his mouth to hers.

Gillian didn't draw away as he pulled her closer. She placed her hands against his chest, neither repelling nor welcoming his advances. His lips claimed hers, but her body remained untouched by desire. A wonderful sense of liberation enveloped her. She felt nothing. She was free of him. Closing her eyes, she waited for the kiss to end.

Determined to elicit a response, he ground his mouth against hers.

Suddenly, they were forcefully, violently separated. Luc stood behind Jeremy, a fistful of Jeremy's jacket bunched in his hand, while Jeremy sputtered in the stranglehold. Luc had plucked Jeremy away from Gillian as easily as a gardener might pick a slug off a rose.

Gillian's eyes flew wide. She recoiled at the expression on Luc's face. Black eyes burning with rage, he looked every inch the fierce Ottawa warrior, ready to do battle.

"What the bloody hell . . . ?" Jeremy swore.

Luc gave Jeremy a vicious shake, then set him on his feet. "Stay away from her, Blackwood—if you value your scalp."

Jeremy ran his index finger along the collar of his jacket and struggled for composure. "That's no way to address an officer in His Majesty's service," he blustered. "I'll see you banished from this post for your insolence."

"Tell the lady the real reason you want to seduce her," Luc growled. "Is it because you love her—or because you hate her father?"

"Jeremy, what is he talking about?" Gillian demanded.

Jeremy glared at Luc through narrowed eyes. "He's probably indulged in too much firewater. Everyone knows redskins have a low tolerance."

The muscle in Luc's jaw bunched ominously, the only visible sign he struggled to control his temper. "Are you afraid to tell the lady that your interest is prompted by revenge? That dishonoring her is your means to get even with her father for refusing your promotion?"

Confused, Gillian looked from one man to the other. "Is that true, Jeremy?"

He shot her an impatient glance. "Are you going to take the word of a savage?"

"Luc has never lied to me," she replied evenly. "You have."

A dull red stained Jeremy's patrician features. "Indians," he spat, "by their very nature, are a bunch of lying bastards."

Luc's hands balled into fists. "Get out of here, Blackwood, before I tear you apart with my bare hands."

Jeremy straightened his shoulders, then made a vain attempt to smooth his wind-rumpled hair. "Very well. Come, Gillian. I'll escort you back to the fort."

"No." She shook her head in vigorous denial. "I'm not going anywhere with you—ever."

"You're actually siding with an ignorant half-breed." Jeremy eyed her in disbelief. "Choosing him over one of your own countrymen?"

"Run, Blackwood," Luc purred, steel under velvet. "Run while you still can."

Apparently deeming it unwise to press the issue, Jeremy did just that. He disappeared over a ridge as fat drops of rain began to fall. Thunder cracked and lightning zigzagged across a storm-darkened sky. The clouds opened and spilled their icy contents, thoroughly dousing everything below in a matter of seconds.

Luc put his arm around Gillian and, head bent, ran toward shelter. Above their heads, branches slashed back and forth in frenzied movements. Even through her clothing, Gillian felt needle-sharp pellets of rain sting her flesh. From the woods came the grinding tear of splitting wood, followed by a crash that shook the ground beneath her feet. The small clearing seemed a mile wide as they made a mad dash through the storm.

Luc used his body to shield hers as best he could. Upon reaching the cabin, he lifted a latch and they stumbled inside. After shouldering the door closed, he crossed the room, knelt before the stone fireplace, and began adding wood from a pile stacked by the hearth.

Gillian stood dripping wet and shivering just inside the doorway, allowing her eyes time to adjust to the dimness. Soft, murky shadows veiled the cabin's interior. Skinny fingers of light poked through cracks in the shutters. Rubbing her arms to erase the chill, Gillian looked around curiously. Even by her standards, the one-room cabin appeared surprisingly clean and tidy. A comfortable-looking chair was pulled before the hearth. A trestle table and large bed comprised the rest of the furnishings. The most arresting article was a giant bearskin rug spread over the well-scrubbed pine floorboards. Fascinated, Gillian stared at the gaping mouth, the yellow-spiked teeth, the deadly claws. She remembered her fright on St. Joseph's Island when she had believed herself stalked by a fearsome beast. Her fear had been justified. The animal was every bit as ferocious as she imagined. Had Luc killed this creature? And at what cost? She shuddered at the thought.

Luc waited until assured the tinder would catch, then glanced across the room to the spot where Gillian stood. Rage at finding her in the arms of Jeremy Blackwood still hadn't abated. He wanted to throttle the son of a bitch. To tear him apart, make him suffer. The force of his hatred was overpowering and primitive, defying logic and mocking civilization.

Water streamed down Gillian's face, puddled at her feet. The wind had loosened the pins in her hair, and the usually neat coil straggled down her back. The thin fabric of her dress clung to enticing curves and rounded breasts. Her nipples formed hard pebbles beneath the damp cloth. He felt his manhood swell against his deerskin breeches.

"You're looking at me strangely. Are you angry with me?" She caught her lower lip to keep her teeth from chattering.

Angry at her, at himself, Luc tossed another log onto the fire. "Get out of your wet things."

"T-take off my clothes?"

"Would you rather catch your death of cold?" he snapped. "There's a blanket on the bed. Use it to cover yourself."

Still she hesitated.

He let out his breath in an impatient hiss. "I'll keep my back turned."

A fresh bout of shivering overtook her. "All right," she agreed with obvious reluctance. "Since you promise not to look."

He tried to block out the sound of her movements. At the sodden plop of fabric against wood, he grit his teeth. The image of her slender, lithe form and full breasts cavorted through his mind with devilish glee. He received only the tiniest glimmer of relief at hearing her strip the blanket from the bed and cover herself.

He didn't look up as she padded toward him.

"I'll hang my things here by the fire to dry."

He rose from his haunches, braced one hand against the mantel, and stared broodingly into the leaping flames. "Why did you let the bastard kiss you? Haven't you learned your lesson? Have you forgotten he's married?"

She came to stand next to him. "It was a test of sorts."

"A test?" He turned his head sharply. She stood close, hands outstretched toward the heat, the blanket tied around her, leaving her shoulders bare—vulnerable. His throat felt so tight, he could barely speak. Damn her! The witch had cast a spell on him. "A strange sort of test, if you ask my opinion."

"Perhaps." She smiled slightly and shrugged a slender shoulder.

Irrationally, Luc hoped the small gesture wouldn't dislodge the blanket. And was disappointed when it didn't.

"I needed to prove, once and for all, that Jeremy no longer has any effect on me."

"Did he?"

"None." Her smile widened. "Absolutely none at all."

Her answer wasn't enough to satisfy him. He needed to wipe the memory of another man's kiss from her memory. Needed to brand her his exclusively. Needed to possess. Need swiftly changed to hunger—hunger that had to be appeased regardless of cost. His self-control was being sorely tried.

"There's no need to glower." Reaching up, she smoothed the frown between his brows. "It was merely a kiss."

At her touch, his control snapped. "Merely a kiss?" he asked, dragging her against him.

Before she could reply, his mouth swooped down and feasted on hers. Feasted, devoured, fed a raging hunger. God, her lips were sweet. He could never drink his fill. Ravenous, he probed the seam of her lips and slid his tongue into her mouth. Gillian's arms slipped around his neck, and she leaned into him. He curved a hand around the back of head, holding her captive while he plundered her bounty. His tongue swept over the sharp ridges of her teeth, the slick, wet lining of her mouth. A muffled groan of pleasure escaped when her small tongue, tentative but eager, touched his.

Abruptly, he withdrew. Grasping her shoulders, he held her at arm's length. Lightning flashed, its eerie glow seeping through closed shutters, followed by a loud crash of thunder. "And mine, Gillian—was it merely a kiss?"

She gazed up at him, blue eyes heavy-lidded and smoky with passion. "Magic," she murmured. "Your kisses are magic."

Goaded by an unrelenting desire for total possession, he needed to make her forget that Jeremy Blackwood had been the first man to claim her. His gaze never wavered as it locked with hers. "I want you."

Chapter Seventeen

"I want you, too," Gillian sighed.

All the events in her life seemed to have led to this moment. There was no right or wrong, no yesterday or tomorrow. Only the present, with this man who had stolen her heart.

Triumph arced in his dark gaze, replaced by passion. One by one, Luc removed the remaining pins from her hair and let them drop to the floor. When her damp tresses tumbled down her back, he drew his fingers through them slowly until her hair was spread over her shoulders like a mantle. Cupping his hands on either side of her face, he tipped it up to his and brushed a kiss across her mouth. "You belong to no other."

The rapid drumming of rain on the roof echoed the beating of her heart. Just as he proclaimed her to be his, she knew in the depths of her soul that he was hers. She watched as he peeled his wet shirt over his head and tossed it aside. The wide expanse of burnished flesh was stretched taut over steely muscle. Unable to resist, she drew her hand over the powerful expanse. It felt smooth, warm, like polished teak. "You're beautiful," she murmured. "Like a sculpture."

He swept her up in his arms and carried her toward the bed. Excitement bubbled through her veins at the thought of the intimacy they were about to share. She studied the face so near her own. Desire sharpened his features, making them appear even more exquisitely sculpted. Square, determined jaw, generous, mobile mouth, autocratic nose, and those wonderful deep brown eyes that could melt her heart with a glance. Until Luc, she had never suspected a woman could lust after a man, but she had been mistaken. She wanted him, just as he wanted her.

Gently, almost reverently, he placed her on the mattress. The bed ropes squeaked as his weight joined hers. He reached out to loosen the knot that secured the blanket in place. A rosy blush tinted her cheekbones. Overcome by an unexpected bout of shyness, she placed her hands on top of his, stopping him.

His hooded gaze locked with hers. Capturing her hand, he turned it over and brushed a kiss across the sensitive flesh along her inner wrist. "Have you changed your mind, *chérie?*"

Her pulse jerked spasmodically in response to his touch. Speech impossible, she moved her head back and forth.

"Don't be afraid," he whispered in a voice like raw silk. "I'd never hurt you."

She forced herself to remain motionless while he unfastened the blanket she had tied around her, spread it open, then leisurely perused her naked body. His eyes were hot, searing; her flesh burned beneath his look. Instinctively she sought to shield her nakedness. A slight movement of his head signaled his displeasure, and she ceased her attempt.

Luc stood, quickly shed the rest of his clothing, then stretched out beside her, claiming her mouth for a languorous, drugging kiss. Gillian's mind emptied. She pressed closer, seeking to mold her soft, feminine curves against hard, masculine planes. She felt the thrill of pure exhilaration at his low groan of arousal.

Before she had time to savor his reaction, his hands swept down over her body from hairline to hip. The callused pads of his fingertips created an erotic contrast against the unblemished texture of her skin. His lips left her mouth to travel downward, trailing light, teasing kisses along the line of her jaw, the column of her throat. She shivered with delight.

"Cold," he murmured, continuing his delicious brand of torture.

She gasped as he found the sensitive spot behind her ear. "Cold? How can I be when your touch heats my blood?"

He smiled, pleased by her response. "Soon, very soon, I'll make you burn."

She sucked in her breath when he cupped her breast. Before she could recover from her surprise, he rubbed the pad of his thumb across her nipple. Instantly it became pebble hard, eager and throbbing for more. Dipping his head, he drew it into his mouth and flicked his tongue over the taut peak. Pleasure speared through her, its tip sharp, almost painful. Threading her fingers through his hair, she arched her spine, silently entreating him for more.

How naive she had been. She had assumed lovemaking consisted of a series of kisses, followed by an elemental coupling of two bodies. She never suspected it involved this fevered play of hands and mouth, touching, tasting, bombarding the senses until nothing else mattered, nothing else existed.

The last remnants of coherent thought fled as Luc's

interest strayed lower. His mouth trailed moist, nibbling kisses down her abdomen, then lower still. She quivered beneath his touch. A clap of thunder from the raging storm muffled her unintelligible cry of desire. Her body surged, restless, seeking. She clutched the bedding, relaxed, then clutched again. Liquid pooled, hot and heavy, between her legs.

"Good," he murmured thickly. "I want you as hungry for me as I am for you." Shifting position, he angled his body against hers, pinning her against the mattress. Using a knee, he nudged her thighs apart. He reclaimed her mouth, his agile tongue dueling with hers in a series of thrusts and parries.

Diverted by his clever tactics, Gillian was unprepared when his hand slid between her legs and his fingers unerringly found the core of her femininity. Startled, she surged against him as he nimbly caressed the most intimate part of her. A maelstrom of sensation rioted within her. He eased one finger inside her. She stopped breathing. Her entire body drew taut as a bowstring. Then his hand moved, and her body began to undulate in mindless concert. Her breathing resumed, ragged, uneven. Drowning in a sea of uncharted sensations, she couldn't think, could only feel.

Racked by a nameless yearning, Gillian clung to him, dimly aware that a soul-shattering discovery awaited just beyond her grasp. Anticipation tiptoed along her nerve fibers, the intensity building, building, building with each persistent caress. Trapped in passion's thrall, Gillian gazed into Luc's face and saw desire mirrored in dark pools.

"Luc . . ." she cried as a sensation so intense it bordered on pain convulsed her body. Swift as a comet, she felt herself hurtle heavenward, then shatter into a billion tiny bursts of light. Then, filled with joy and wonder, she began a slow descent back to earth, carried on a gentle current of air.

"Now, *chèrie,* you will be mine." Luc positioned himself between her legs and entered with one smooth thrust.

Pain, sharp and agonizing, ripped through her, shredding the silken cocoon of contentment. She sank her teeth into her lower lip until she tasted blood. Luc stilled, staring down at her in shock and confusion as comprehension dawned. As the discomfort gradually subsided, she was aware of a fullness, a pressure, filling her. She moved slightly to ease the ache between her thighs.

Grasping her hips firmly, Luc thrust again, then finding a rhythm, repeated the motion until she began to move with him. Her eyes widened as pleasure flickered, then rekindled. Smoldering embers erupted into flame, burning hot and bright. She wrapped her legs around him and held on.

Luc threw back his head as a primal groan tore from his throat. With a convulsive shudder, he emptied himself into her.

Spent, he collapsed at her side. Tenderly, he smoothed damp tendrils from her brow. "I was your first. Why didn't you tell me?"

She summoned a tremulous smile. "No one believed I was still innocent. Were you any different?"

He wiped the smudge of blood from her lower lip, then brushed a kiss as soft as butterfly wings across the tiny cut. "I would have believed you."

Her chest constricted at his simple affirmation of faith. Not trusting herself to speak, she nestled closer, resting her head on his shoulder, an arm across his chest. Rain pattered softly on the roof overhead. She could feel the steady beat of Luc's heart beneath her hand. Gillian had never experienced such a profound sense of peace or belonging. Closing her eyes, she offered up a small prayer of thanksgiving, then promptly fell sound asleep in his embrace.

Luc pulled the blanket over them and stared at the ceiling. He was filled with wonder at the priceless gift Gillian had bestowed upon him. And equally humbled and guilt-ridden. His needs had been selfish, greedy, her response selfless, generous. Seeing her in the arms of that damn redcoat triggered a raging jealousy. *Jealousy*, of all things. Fellow voyageurs would howl with laughter at the thought of Luc du Pré brought to his knees by a woman. He was reputed to be impervious to women's wiles, protected by an invisible shield. It was common knowledge that he never, ever, lost his head over a pretty face.

Never, ever, lost his heart.

Absently Luc smoothed Gillian's tousled hair. Soft, silky, amber tendrils. The texture fascinated him. Unable to resist, he caught a long strand and slowly wound it around and around his fingers, then brought it to his lips. The sweet, delicate fragrance of lavender teased his senses. Gillian sighed in her sleep, her breath a warm whisper across his flesh. Desire stirred anew, and he struggled to hold it at bay. His sole intent had been to erase memories of any others who might have touched her, to stake his claim.

Somehow she had neatly turned the tables.

Damn, what had he done? She was the enemy. What made this woman different from all others? Why this fierce need to protect, defend? Possess?

The cabin door flew open on its hinges and crashed against the wall. With a start, the couple on the bed awoke, their limbs still entwined.

"Father . . ." Gillian gasped in dismay.

"So it is true," Randolph Stafford thundered.

Jeremy stood behind him, gloating. "Told you that you'd find them together, sir."

Gillian hugged the blanket to her chin and wished this was all a bad dream.

"I didn't want to believe it when Blackwood first came to me." Stafford wrapped his hand around the hilt of his sword. "If I hadn't seen this with my own eyes . . ."

Luc slid out of bed, scooped his pants from the floor, and stepped into them. "Don't blame Gillian, sir. I assume full responsibility."

"I trusted you," Stafford said, pointing an accusing finger. "And you betrayed me by bedding my daughter."

"Father, neither Luc nor I deliberately tried to . . ."

"Silence!" Tight-lipped, his fair complexion suffused with color, Stafford glared at his daughter with malevolence. "There is no excuse whatsoever for your conduct. You have disgraced my good name for the last time. You're nothing but a whoring slut."

Luc sent his fist smashing against the older man's jaw. Randolph Stafford went down like a felled tree. Gillian scrambled from the bed, the blanket once again draped around her. She knelt at her father's side to help, but he shook off her attempt.

"Now you've done it, du Pré," Jeremy crowed. "If you were a soldier, you'd face a firing squad for striking an officer."

"No one speaks to Gillian in that manner—not even her father," Luc growled, his hands bunched into fists at his side.

Rubbing his injured jaw, Stafford slowly climbed to his feet. Gillian, shaken by the sudden violence, rose and stood silently at Luc's side.

"You greatly disappoint me, Gillian," Jeremy sneered. "I never would have guessed your standards were so low that you'd give yourself to an ignorant savage."

Gillian raised her head proudly. "Quite the contrary," she informed him, "where men are concerned my standards are extremely high, which is why I prefer Luc's company to yours."

Furious, Jeremy started to raise his hand, but one look at Luc's face gave him pause to reconsider. "You and your half-breed deserve each other," he muttered.

"Enough!" Stafford roared. He stood straight and tall, his shoulders back, and turned his attention on Luc who stared back with no sign of fear. "While I don't have the authority to have you shot, I do have enough influence to see that you leave Mackinac Island and never return. Unless, of course ..."

Seconds marched by with slow, military precision.

Luc broke the taut silence. "Unless what, sir?"

"Unless you do the honorable thing and marry her," Stafford said in a cold, clipped voice, ignoring Gillian's gasp of disbelief. "Take my daughter off my hands once and for all. From here on, it'll be your job to keep her in line, not mine."

Color leeched from Gillian's face. A whirring sound filled her head. "Father, you surely can't mean that."

Icy blue eyes flicked over her briefly. "I can and I do."

Upon hearing those words uttered with such finality, a chill seeped into the marrow of her bones. She clutched the blanket tighter until her knuckles gleamed white. She had never been so profoundly humiliated—or so hurt. Auctioned like a slave on the block. Forced on a man reluctant to claim her. And by her own father of all people.

"Bravo, sir." Jeremy beamed his approval. "Excellent! No decent man will have her after word gets out that she's slept with an Indian."

"Surely such measures are unnecessary." Gillian's voice sounded unnaturally high. "When I turn twenty-one I'll be financially independent and won't need a husband's support."

"Until then, Daughter, how do you propose to manage?

If you expect me to provide for you after this little escapade, you're sadly mistaken. I wash my hands of you."

Neither man wanted her, Gillian thought dully. The truth was painfully evident. Luc's silence betrayed his obvious reluctance to wed.

Stafford impatiently tapped his fingers against his thigh. "Well, du Pré, what's your decision?"

"How soon is the wedding to take place?"

"Tonight at the latest."

When she reflected back later, Gillian had little recollection of what happened in the intervening hours. Vaguely she recalled donning clothes that were still damp, leaving the cabin, and returning to the fort accompanied by her father. Jeremy hung around to witness her ordeal and seemed to be thoroughly enjoying himself at her expense.

Her father had insisted the ceremony take place before witnesses and be duly notarized. He wanted to make certain that no questions would arise regarding the legality of the marriage. Luc had prevailed upon his friend Père Robichaud to perform the rite, scheduled to take place at St. Anne's Church.

Now the actual time was at hand.

A flute trilled high and sweet. The notes of "Greensleeves," her favorite tune, floated through the church. Someone, Gillian mused, her father probably, had prevailed on one of the soldiers from the fort to provide music for the occasion. She found the small gesture oddly touching. And surprising in light of the harsh words spoken earlier.

Randolph Stafford presented his arm. "It's time, Daughter. Let's not keep the priest waiting."

His slightly slurred speech revealed that he had indulged in liquor since they had parted ways. She wondered if he had resorted to alcohol because he was saddened by the prospect of losing a daughter. Or rejoicing. With a sigh, she placed her right hand in the crook of his arm. In her left, she carried a fragrant bouquet of pink flowers—Wrinkled Roses, as they were called—that grew wild and sweet along the island's limestone-gravel beaches.

St. Anne's modest interior glowed with candlelight. Six tall tapers, three on either side of a carved wooden crucifix, stood on a cloth-draped altar. Margaret and James Babcock, the only guests, occupied a pew near the front of the church.

By tomorrow morning everyone on the island would know she had been found in bed with Luc du Pré. That he had been forced to marry her or leave his home. It would be difficult to look people in the eye. It was even more difficult to meet Luc's piercing gaze. What had seemed so right, so beautiful, just this afternoon had taken on a tawdry cast.

Numbly, she allowed her father to escort her down the aisle. Père Robichaud, his black cassock covered by a white surplice, waited at the foot of the altar, a worn leather missal opened to the appropriate page. She kept her eyes downcast but felt a telltale warmth stain her cheeks.

When they reached the altar her father stepped aside, and Luc came forward. She hazarded a sidelong glance. Her breath caught at the sight of him. Rather than his usual voyageur garb, he had elected to dress in the European manner, in thigh-molding breeches, a waistcoat of fine wool, and an immaculate white linen shirt and cravat. Tall, strong, and handsome, he was a bridegroom any woman would be proud of—and she was no exception.

As the priest began to read centuries-old marriage vows, a strange calm descended. Fears vanished, replaced by confidence. She not only admired Luc but respected him as well. He was decent and honest, traits she valued. She more than just cared about him, she acknowledged. Somehow, in spite of their many differences, she had fallen in love. With the admission came joy. A joy so great she felt illuminated from within.

Père Robichaud cleared his throat, then began.

". . . is not to be entered into unadvisedly or lightly; but reverently, discreetly, advisedly, soberly, and in the fear of God. Wilt thou, Gillian Elizabeth Stafford . . ."

Gillian repeated her vows, her voice soft, her response clear and unwavering.

Then it was Luc's turn.

"Wilt thou, Luc Matthieu du Pré, forsaking all others . . ."

Luc promised to love and to cherish in a deep, resonant voice.

"Now place your ring on the bride's finger," the priest instructed.

Reaching into a pocket of his waistcoat, Luc produced a plain gold ring, then slid it onto the third finger of her left hand.

A band tightened around Gillian's chest at the enormity of the act. The cleric's words sang in her mind, in her heart. *'Til death do us part.* A glance at Luc's expression revealed it equally somber. She wished she could read his thoughts at that precise moment. Did he share her newfound joy, her awe and wonder? Or did he feel trapped in a marriage not of his choosing? The notion undermined her fragile optimism.

Père Robichaud smiled benignly. "You may kiss the bride."

Gillian shyly raised her face to Luc's. His mouth twisted in a wry smile, one that didn't reach his eyes, before claiming her lips for a kiss that was disappointingly brief.

As they turned as newlyweds to accept congratulations, doubts purposely set aside, returned to plague her. Was Luc deeply unhappy? Angry or resentful? An inner voice refused to be hushed. Just because a man wanted to share a woman's bed didn't mean he wanted to share her life.

She detected the sour smell of alcohol on her father's breath when he bent to give her a perfunctory peck on the cheek. "Best wishes, Daughter."

Margaret Babcock, more effusive in her congratulations, hugged Luc, then Gillian. "I'm so happy for you. I knew it was a match the first time I saw you together."

James smiled warmly as he shook hands with Luc, then kissed the bride.

"I've taken the liberty of preparing refreshments." Margaret linked her arm through her husband's. "I absolutely insist we return to my house, where we can properly toast the newlyweds."

Gillian looked at Luc for his reaction. As though sensing her uncertainty, he picked up her hand, tucked it into the crook of his arm, and gave it a reassuring squeeze. "My wife," he said, choosing the words with care, "and I would be honored."

Gillian released an unsteady sigh. *Wife; he had called her wife.* A simple word, but never had any sounded as sweet.

"We have some chocolate cake at home, Father," Margaret cajoled, shamelessly preying on the priest's weakness.

"Well, I could never refuse a wedding party, or," he chuckled, "chocolate cake."

James turned to Randolph Stafford, who had maintained a distance from the little group. "Captain, I've been saving a bottle of brandy for such a special occasion. What do you say we break it open?"

Stafford gave a diffident shrug. "It isn't every day a man marries off his only daughter."

The Babcock home was a five-minute walk from St. Anne's. Everything was in readiness the moment they entered.

The Babcocks' serving girl offered Gillian and Margaret

each a glass of wine while the men talked among themselves, enjoying James's aged French brandy.

"I haven't had the opportunity to tell you what a beautiful bride you make. That pale blue dress suits you perfectly."

"Thank you, Margaret." Gillian took a sip of wine. "Like your husband and his brandy, I was saving it for a special occasion."

"And your hair looks especially pretty pulled high at the crown and left to fall down your back A simple but clever arrangement."

Gillian had dressed with Luc in mind, desperately wanting to please him.

"Did you like the music and flowers, dear?"

Gillian's attention drifted to the tall man in the corner who was now her husband, and Margaret had to repeat the question.

"What . . . ? Oh, yes, they were lovely. I must remember to thank Father for his thoughtfulness."

Margaret looked at her bemused, then shook her head. "No, dear, it isn't your father who deserves your thanks, but your husband."

She nearly dropped her wineglass. "Luc . . . ?"

"He insisted no wedding would be complete without them. In fact, the roses were his idea. Nothing else would do, I'm afraid."

"I had no idea."

Margaret chuckled. "James and I have been married for over twenty-five years, and at times men still baffle me."

Gillian took another sip of wine as she glanced across the room and met Luc's impenetrable dark gaze. He baffled her now. Would he continue to after twenty-five years together? she wondered. Somehow she suspected he would.

When Margaret excused herself, Gillian sought out Père

Robichaud. The gangly priest seemed entirely too quiet all evening, his smile strained. She couldn't help but worry that he was displeased with the union.

Though she didn't know the man well, she decided on a direct approach. "Father, forgive me if I'm mistaken, but you don't seem happy about my marriage."

"I've known Luc all his life." He pursed his lips and studied the carpet, avoiding her eyes. "I couldn't be fonder of him than if he were my own son."

"You doubt I am a suitable wife for him?" She couldn't keep the hurt from creeping into her voice.

"Do not be offended by what I am about to say, child." Worry crinkled his brow. "You and Luc are attracted to what is on the outside but do not truly know each other on the inside. I fear your differences may create problems."

"I see." Gillian traced the rim of her glass with an index finger. "Then why did you agree to marry us, Father?"

He smiled apologetically. "Because Luc was determined to marry you, whether or not I performed the ceremony."

She was growing more and more confused. She had sensed Luc's hesitation to wed, only to discover that he had insisted there be flowers and music at the church. He had overridden the objections of a priest rather than accept a civil ceremony performed by a notary. The good father was right; she knew very little about her new husband.

"I hope what I've said hasn't made you unhappy. I thought it best to be honest."

"Now I'll be truthful," Gillian said, squaring her shoulders and forcing a smile. "I love Luc. I give you my word that I'll be a good wife to him and will never give him cause to regret marrying me."

"It's time we drink a toast." James Babcock held up his hands for attention. He waited until the serving girl refilled all the glasses, then raised his glass high.

Luc crossed the room to quietly stand at Gillian's side, close but not touching.

"To the newlyweds, M'sieur and Madame du Pré," James declared. "May they share a long, fruitful life."

His glass poised in midair, Père Robichaud regarded the young couple somberly. "May God bless their union with love and grant them happiness."

Randolph Stafford remained conspicuously silent, scowling into his glass, then drained the contents in a single swallow.

Soon after the toasts were made and cake served, Stafford bid his hosts a terse good night. After thanking the Babcocks, Luc and Gillian left shortly afterward, drawing knowing looks from Margaret and James.

Dark clouds, remnants from the afternoon's storm, trailed listlessly across a murky sky. A pale halo of light surrounded the half moon, lending an eerie glow. Stars usually diamond bright appeared lackluster. Gillian and Luc walked side by side in awkward silence.

They continued along Fort Street, past the ramp leading into the fort itself. "I have no idea where your home is," Gillian confessed, breaking the uncomfortable silence.

"I bet to differ, madame, but you know my home quite well."

She heard the amusement in his voice, could imagine the way his lips curved. "It is you who are mistaken, m'sieur. You've never once mentioned where you live."

"Only this afternoon my humble abode withstood a storm on the outside and witnessed another from within."

Then it dawned on her. "The cabin is yours!"

He took her arm when the path grew narrow and steep. "That's why I didn't worry about the owner intruding."

Suddenly it all made sense, but there were still a few unanswered questions troubling her. "Did you happen to accidentally come across Jeremy and me on your way home?''

"Not quite.'' There was a cutting edge to his voice.

"How did you know where to find us?''

"Aupetchi,'' he said with a small shrug. "She came looking for me. Said she didn't like the man you were with and was worried about you.''

So, Gillian thought, her little Robin was responsible for the events that followed. Knowing how fond Aupetchi was of Luc, she suspected the child would be delighted to learn she and Luc were wed.

Luc cut up a trail between the fort and the redoubt. "I thought you despised Blackwood. Why did you agree to meet him?''

Gillian hated to admit how gullible she had been. She stalled for time but finally launched into an explanation. "Aupetchi found a note addressed to me. It was from Jeremy. He claimed he knew a secret that could destroy Father's career.''

"And did he?''

"He told me Father's drinking could lead to a court-martial. That Colonel McDouall had serious reservations about his ability to command.''

"The captain's drinking is hardly a secret. It was a long, hard winter. Things got out of hand.''

"It isn't easy for him to abstain, but he's been making an effort. Except tonight,'' she amended.

Neither spoke again until they reached the cabin. At the door, Luc paused and looked down at her. "I meant what I told your father earlier—about taking full responsibility.''

Gillian scuffed the ground with the toe of her shoe. "And I had no control over what happened?''

"I took unfair advantage.''

Suddenly she felt a surge of anger. "How noble of you to accept all the blame. As I recall, you didn't exactly force me to make love to you. What happened this afternoon was as much my doing as it was yours."

His jaw jutted stubbornly. "Men are more experienced in such matters. I should have given more thought to the consequences."

"Men!" She tossed her hands in the air. "Should I thank you for making the supreme sacrifice by offering marriage?"

"Is that what you think?" he said through gritted teeth.

"I don't *know* what to think." She blinked rapidly to hold back tears. "If you didn't want me, why not just say so?"

"Not want you?" He hauled her against him so abruptly that her feet left the ground. "How can you even think such a thing? I ache from wanting you. I want you so badly I can't think straight. I've wanted you from the moment I saw you high on a bluff scared witless by an imaginary bear."

His lips crushed hers, annihilating any lingering doubts she might have had. She clung to his shoulders, her need as fierce as his. He ravaged her mouth, alternately demanding and pleading for surrender. Then a subtle change occurred. The kiss gentled, became coaxing and cajoling. Gillian's senses reeled under the skillful assault. Her world spun like a child's wooden top, leaving her dizzy, light-headed.

The kiss ended as abruptly as it had begun. Dazed, she stared into the face of a savage warrior, his eyes burning black coals.

"I've never wanted another as I want you," he said, his usually velvety tones gruff with emotion. He kissed her again, a sweet, lingering kiss.

Then, reaching behind her, Luc opened the cabin door and nudged her inside. "Off to bed, *chèrie.* I'll join you shortly."

Choosing her prettiest nightdress from the trunk that had been delivered while they were at the church, Gillian undressed quickly, slipped into bed, and waited. When Luc failed to appear, she went outdoors to investigate. But there was no sign of him, no answer when she called his name.

Returning to bed, she curled on her side and, her cheeks wet with tears, finally fell asleep.

Alone.

Chapter Eighteen

"You what!" Toad's loud voice reverberated off the walls of Skull Cave.

"You heard me," Luc muttered. "Gillian Stafford and I were married this evening."

"Where were your brains, lad? In your britches?"

"Her father gave me no choice. It was marry her or leave the island. Besides, it was the honorable thing to do."

Toad smacked his palm against his forehead. "I can't believe what I'm hearing. The girl's been around a time or two. Bedding the captain's daughter isn't like bedding a virgin."

Luc kept his eyes focused on the dim light at the mouth of the cave and didn't utter a word.

"What about that chap back in England? You don't mean to tell me . . ." Toad gaped at the younger man in amazement.

"I was the first—the only," Luc admitted.

Toad swore softly. "Don't know whether to laugh or cry. A fine predicament you've got yourself into."

"It's no concern of yours," Luc snapped. "My being married to Stafford's daughter won't interfere with a thing."

"What do you take me for, a fool?" Toad hunkered next to Luc on the uneven floor. "Heed my word of caution, lad. If you don't watch out, you'll have lace curtains fluttering in the window and diapers flapping in the breeze."

"We didn't come here to discuss my personal life."

Toad blew out a long breath, then reached into a pocket, withdrew his tobacco pouch, and bit off a chunk. "What else have you got to tell me?"

"The Indians are becoming increasingly restless. They're impatient for action."

"Can't say I blame them," Toad sniffed. "I feel the same way myself."

Luc ignored Toad's comment. "Some of the younger officers are also complaining about the wait. Given a choice, they'd sail down Lake Huron and meet the Americans on the way up."

Toad let out a snort of derision. "A hare-brained idea if there ever was one."

Luc nodded agreement. "McDouall's canny enough to know that anything the British could assemble wouldn't stand a chance against American naval power."

"What's McDouall's plan?"

"He's content to sit tight and wait for the Americans to make the first move."

"Smart man, McDouall." Toad chewed thoughtfully. "What other information do you have for me?"

"The fort's filled to bursting with a large number of Indians from the northwestern tribes, mostly Sioux and Winnebago. Men and supplies are ready and waiting. All that's lacking is the enemy."

"Tell me about the lookouts."

"Half the garrison is posted along the ramparts at night to guard against a surprise attack."

Toad rubbed a hand over his bearded jaw, the rasp loud in the ensuing silence. "Take care no one sees you coming and going. This is no time to arouse suspicion."

"I take precautions. Make sure you do the same."

Toad stood, shuffled toward the opening of the cave, then peeked out. Satisfied all was safe, he turned back to Luc. "Time is coming, lad, when you'll have to make a choice. The girl you married—or your country. Can't have both."

Toad's anger had been justifiable. Long after he disappeared into the night, Luc remained lost in thought. He had allowed passion to obliterate logic. His actions that afternoon had been impulsive, thoughtless. Reprehensible. He had taken unfair advantage of Gillian. Now he had to deal with the consequences. Toad's words echoed in the stillness.

You'll have to make a choice.

Luc raked his fingers through his hair. The warning came too late. He had already made his choices. Two years ago, at the outbreak of the war, he had pledged his loyalty to the Americans. Long-standing hatred and distrust of the British had made the decision easy. Then, this afternoon, he had chosen to wed Gillian.

Can't have both.

God help him, as impossible as it sounded, he wanted both. He'd fight for his country. Sacrifice his life, if necessary. He had accepted that from the start. What astounded him was the realization that he'd fight just as fiercely to keep Gillian by his side.

But his bride was British to the core. When time for choices arrived, Gillian's loyalties would face the ultimate test. Was it fair to ask her to choose between him and her homeland? Thus far, they shared mutual passion. Perhaps the kindest thing would be to prevent a deeper attachment from developing. To maintain a distance.

Luc walked to the cave's entrance. More than anything, he didn't want to cause her undue pain. She was sweet, innocent, and deserved better. He hoped she didn't harbor feelings for him that he wasn't prepared to reciprocate. Hoped she didn't confuse physical need with something far more complicated.

Heaving a sigh, Luc left Skull Cave and ducked into a cover of trees. Slowly, he wended his way home. The thought of Gillian, soft and warm, snuggled in his bed, sent desire coursing anew. What harm could there be if they took pleasure in each other? an insidious voice whispered. Enough, he sternly admonished the voice. He needed a cool, rational head. Needed a tight rein on base urges, needed to establish boundaries.

At the cabin, Luc eased open the door and slipped inside. His attention was immediately drawn to the figure on the bed. Moonlight stole through the partially opened shutters, bathing Gillian's sleeping form in its lambent glow. Her long blond hair spilled over the pillow, framing her delicate features like a skein of spun gold. Unable to resist, Luc reached out and brushed a strand from her cheek. His fingertips came away damp with her tears. His chest constricted. In spite of his lofty intentions, he had hurt her. Undressing, he eased into bed; then, careful not to waken her, he gathered her into his arms and feathered a kiss across her temple.

"Forgive me, *chèrie,*" he whispered.

Outside the cabin, birds warbled a cheerful medley. Gillian stared glumly at the ceiling, wishing she shared their optimism. Try as she might, she couldn't understand why someone who claimed to want her so badly now ignored her completely. Since their wedding a week ago, Luc hadn't touched her. Absently she traced her lower lip. She tingled all over whenever she remembered how he had kissed her the night of their wedding. A kiss fueled by desire. And flavored with desperation.

Every night he returned long after she had fallen asleep, then slipped silently into bed. In the sleep-drugged hours of darkness, their bodies would seek the warmth and solace of the other's. Dawn would find them with limbs entangled, her head resting against his broad shoulder, or his bronzed form spoon-fashion around hers. Why couldn't there be the same intimacy during waking hours? Why did Luc deny them both unspeakable pleasure?

Even his absence teased her senses. She could still see the imprint of his head on the pillow, smell his unique scent of pine and musk. Her hand trailed lightly over the bed linen where his warmth seemed to linger. Somehow, she vowed, she'd find a way to burst through this barrier he had erected between them.

Luc du Pré was proud, independent. No doubt being forced to marry had gone against his grain. He was the sort to take the initiative for such a momentous decision, but circumstances had intervened. Given time, Luc would eventually admit they were well suited. Granted, there were differences, but none insurmountable. Once this blasted war ended they could forge a life for themselves. Whether here or in England, it no longer mattered.

As long as they were together . . .

She rose from bed, washed quickly, then pulled her hair into a loose knot on top of her head, leaving wispy tendrils at her temples and nape. She chose a pale lemon muslin dress sprigged with tiny violet flowers, the bright color a deliberate contradiction of her mood. Flinging open the shutters, she invited the bright July sunlight to banish the shadows. While enjoying a light breakfast, she planned her day. It was far better to be busy, she concluded, than to sit around brooding. She hadn't seen Aupetchi during the preceding week, not since her fateful meeting with Jeremy Blackwood. Perhaps it was time for her long-postponed visit to the Ottawa village. But first, she decided, she'd drop by the Babcocks' trading post and purchase Luc something to commemorate their marriage.

Her teacup poised in midair, she recalled Wind Spirit's words the day he and Aupetchi had given her the exquisitely beaded reticule. *"It is the way of the Ottawa,"* Wind Spirit had explained. *"The exchange of gifts forever binds the giver and the receiver."* The idea of being bound to Luc appealed to her—now and forever.

Gillian turned up the trail leading toward the Ottawa village. A perfect summer afternoon, she mused. She had been skeptical when André Tousseau had extolled Mackinac Island's beauty. But even so, his description hadn't done the island justice. No single jewel sufficed in comparison. Rather, it resembled an entire jewelry box spilling over with precious gems in various hues. The sky, an aquamarine canopy, stretched over the emerald green woodland. Through the trees, she caught occasional glimpses of Lake Huron. Sunlight shimmered on sapphire waters like a sprinkling of diamonds. A profusion of wildflowers in shades of amethyst, topaz, and pearl peeked out here and there like unexpected treasures.

Her reticule bumped lightly against her side with each step, its weight a reminder of the gift inside. She was pleased with her choice. At James Babcock's recommendation, she had purchased a hunting knife as a gift for Luc. James had proudly touted the knife's merits, claiming it perfectly balanced, the blade razor sharp, its steel forged by one of Spain's master craftsmen. Though she knew little of such items, Gillian had to admit it was a handsome piece, with its carved ivory handle and sheath of hand-tooled leather. She could hardly wait to see Luc's expression when she gave it to him.

The trees thinned to form a sunny, daisy-strewn meadow. In the center of the meadow stood a dozen or so bark-covered longhouses large enough to house several families. On either side and to the rear, plots of land had been cleared for gardens, where carefully tended plants flourished in tidy rows. She spotted Aupetchi among a small group of women emptying baskets of blackberries onto a finely woven rush mat.

Glancing up from her task, Aupetchi noticed Gillian for the first time. Her face lit in a lively smile as she ran to greet her. "I am happy to see you."

Gillian gave the girl's thick braid a playful tug. "And I to see you."

"Grandfather heard red jackets say you and Luc married. Is it true?"

"Yes, little Robin, it is true."

"Luc make you happy?"

Did Luc make her happy? Gillian carefully weighed the question. Luc du Pré—her husband, she amended—was a complex man. Strong, fiercely protective, sometimes arrogant, Luc was also capable of kindness and tenderness. "Yes," she admitted with a slow smile. "Luc makes me happy." That wasn't quite true, she realized. He made her more than happy; he made her feel complete. Whole.

"That is good." Aupetchi caught her hand and urged her toward the largest of the birch bark structures. "I worried you might be mad at Aupetchi."

"Why would I be angry at you? You're my friend."

"I thought maybe you mad because I tell Luc of your meeting with the redcoat."

Comprehension dawned as Gillian stared into the small, serious face regarding her so intently. "So that's why you've been avoiding me. Of course I'm not angry. You were only trying to protect me," Gillian said, giving the girl's hand a reassuring squeeze.

"I did not like the way the redcoat talk to you. Luc, I think, not like him either."

That was an understatement if there ever was one, Gillian mused, but she kept her opinion to herself. As they crossed the clearing, she was aware of covert glances cast her way by the women in the village. While not hostile, none appeared exactly warm or friendly. Men were conspicuously absent, except for a few of the more elderly. She recalled a previous conversation with Aupetchi. Summers, the child had explained, Ottawa men left their villages to hunt, fish, and trade.

Someone must have alerted Wind Spirit of her arrival. Arms folded across his chest, he stepped out of the center longhouse to formally welcome her. "You honor us with your presence."

"Thank you for your kind words." Gillian gestured at the villagers. "It seems not everyone shares your sentiment."

"Pay them no mind. Come, sit by my fire."

Wind Spirit led the way, with Gillian and Aupetchi following. Wind Spirit took his place on a low bench before the longhouse that served as his dwelling, then motioned for Gillian to join him. Aupetchi perched next to her grandfather. "It is not you, but your people that mine distrust. I have assured them that you are different. Your motives are pure. You wish us no harm."

"I'm afraid I don't understand," Gillian said, puzzled. "I thought the Ottawa were allies with the British."

"The Ottawa have learned to depend on gifts from the red jackets, but there is still much ill will between your people and mine."

A tall woman wearing a simple deerskin shift appeared with a wooden dish containing fresh berries and coarsely textured bread. She served the chief first, then Gillian.

"Enjoy food my daughter has prepared," Wind Spirit urged kindly.

Gillian accepted the offering from the woman with a tentative smile. "Are you responsible for this?" she asked, resting her hand on the reticule Aupetchi had given her. "The workmanship is beautiful."

The woman nodded and, flattered by the compliment, returned the smile before turning and leaving them to talk.

Unable to dismiss the chief's earlier comments, Gillian's curiosity goaded her for more detail. "Wind Spirit, you mentioned many Ottawa do not like the British. Why is this?"

"Ottawa have little reason to trust the red jackets."

"Why? What have they done to make you feel this way?"

"Troubles between our people go back many years." Wind Spirit grew reflective. "During what is called French and Indian Wars, Ottawa fought with the French against the British. When French lose and go home, my people suffer. The British refuse them many needed supplies."

Aupetchi leaned forward and grasped her grandfather's sleeve. "Tell her about the blankets," she urged.

"What about the blankets?" Gillian asked, dreading the answer but wanting to learn the truth. The small piece of bread she had just eaten felt heavy as a brick in her stomach.

Caught in the rays of the afternoon sun, the copper amulet around Wind Spirit's neck glowed like a live coal. "The British send Lord Jeffrey Amhurst. He hate the Ottawa and want them dead. Amhurst ordered blankets used by the white men with smallpox delivered to villages. At first, my people happy to receive gifts, but soon many take sick and die. Entire villages wiped out by white man's sickness."

Closing her eyes, Gillian shuddered. A cruel, heartless, calculated act of vengeance. The idea of deliberately infecting innocent people was too horrible to comprehend. If the story was true—and she had no reason to suspect otherwise—the Ottawa's dislike of the British was understandable.

Luc's mother had been Ottawa. Knowing how her people suffered under British rule, she could understand how Luc might resent them. Still, Luc worked closely with British forces. He served as a valuable ally, a liaison of sorts between the military and various Indian tribes.

"Through your husband, you now part of Ottawa family," Wind Spirit told her gravely. "Do not blame yourself for deeds of others."

Gillian managed a feeble smile of gratitude, then rose. "I must leave now. Thank you for your hospitality."

Wind Spirit and Aupetchi accompanied her to the point where grassy meadow joined woodland. "You and Luc are good people." The chief's seamed face creased in a benevolent smile. "My wish is that you walk together in happiness. That your union will bear fruit."

Her cheeks warmed at Wind Spirit's implication. Until now she had refused to consider the consequences of their lovemaking. The thought of a child, however, instead of being burdensome, brought a flood of anticipation. She'd welcome a son cast in his father's image, handsome and strong. Her need to see Luc, no matter how briefly, prompted her toward the fort rather than returning to the cabin.

The instant she stepped foot inside the sturdy limestone walls, she sensed a difference. The air hummed with tension. Soldiers scurried back and forth with a sense of purpose. Sergeants barked commands that privates hastened to obey. Most of the activity, she noted, seemed to center on post headquarters.

Warily, she approached a cluster of enlisted men conversing in terse tones near the barracks. "What's happened?" she asked. "Have the Americans been sighted?"

"No, ma'am." A baby-faced private vigorously wagged his head. "Couple men just arrived with news that the Americans are at Prairie du Chien."

"Prairie du Chien?" she repeated thoughtfully. "I don't believe I've ever heard of the place. Is it nearby?"

"No need to be frightened, ma'am. It's a trading post along the Mississippi River, a long ways from here."

A noisy contingent of traders and voyageurs marched across the parade grounds, banged on the door at headquarters, and were summarily admitted. As she continued to observe the goings-on, she saw Luc lead a contingent of Indian warriors, Red Dog among them, through the south sally port. Their bodies were streaked with gaudily colored greasepaint, their hair decorated with feathers. Their raucous shrieks sent shivers down her spine. They, too, headed directly for McDouall's office.

Red Dog glanced her way. His eyes narrowed into slits when he found her watching him. She took an involuntary step backward at the malicious evil reflected in his jet black glare. A thin smile of satisfaction curled his mouth at seeing her retreat. His hatred for Luc had apparently transferred to her as well.

You have no idea what a man like Red Dog is capable of.

Luc's long-ago warning sounded in her head. She intended to keep a safe distance from the fierce Ottawa chieftain. She didn't want firsthand knowledge of his capabilities.

Tidbits of conversation floated around her.

"We'll show the bloody bastards."

"Can McDouall spare the men?"

"Can't afford to wait. Got to act fast."

Determined not to leave until she had learned precisely what was going on, Gillian moved closer to the building that served as post headquarters. Hopefully she could have a private word with Luc, or perhaps her father, and learn the answers to her questions.

As luck would have it, she didn't have long to wait before Luc came out and crossed the narrow porch in long strides.

"Luc," she called out, hurrying toward him.

Surprise yielded to annoyance upon seeing her. "Gillian, what the devil are you doing here?"

His brusque manner stung, but ignoring the hurt, she met his gaze squarely. "I'm not budging until someone explains what's happening."

"This isn't a good time."

"It's as good a time as any," she fired back.

Muttering under his breath, Luc gripped her elbow and steered her around the corner of the building that afforded a small degree of privacy. "Emotions are running high. The situation here is volatile. Anything could happen."

Gillian jerked free from his grasp and whirled to confront him. "I'm not leaving, Luc du Pré, until I know what's going on. What is the significance of the Americans in some faraway place?"

"Prairie du Chien." He blew out an impatient breath. "The Americans are in the heart of an area the British have dominated for a half century."

"What does that have to do with us?"

"The Sioux and Winnebago who are already here now want to return home and defend their families from the Americans. British traders are equally perturbed at having the enemy intrude on their livelihood."

"What do you think will happen?"

"Pressure is being applied to McDouall to send a raiding party. He's giving it careful consideration."

She moistened her lower lip with the tip of her tongue. "D-does that mean . . . ?" she faltered, then voiced her fear. "If that happens, will you go with them?"

He braced an arm against the building alongside her head and grinned wolfishly. "Would you miss me?"

Her first impulse was to launch a vehement denial and erase the arrogant smirk from his handsome face. She hesitated a moment, then answered with painful honesty. "Yes," she said, her voice barely audible. "I'd miss you very much."

His smile vanished in a heartbeat. His dark eyes probed the depths of hers. Then he kissed her, a hard, possessive kiss that wiped all thought from her mind.

"Go," he said hoarsely, dragging his lips from hers. "It isn't safe for you here."

"All right," she agreed reluctantly. "I'll wait up for you."

She cast a final glance over her shoulder as she left the fort, but Luc had already disappeared. She'd wait—all night, if necessary.

But she doubted he'd be there to notice.

Chapter Nineteen

The hour of midnight had come and gone. Gillian tossed and turned. For the thousandth time, she wondered where Luc spent his evenings. Drinking or gambling? Reminiscing with his voyageur friends? Wherever, it evidently held greater appeal than she did.

Initially she had tried to convince herself that duties at the fort occupied all his waking hours. But activities there had quieted. A week ago, amid a loud volley of cannon fire, a fleet of bateaux and canoes started the long voyage to Prairie du Chien. Much to her relief, Jeremy Blackwood, as well as Grayson and Wilcox, two of the soldiers who had accosted her at Mill Creek, were part of the entourage.

Rolling onto her side, she punched her pillow and willed her tense body to relax. Suddenly, she froze. In the distance, she heard a faint crackling noise. Had the Americans begun their attack? she wondered in alarm. Kicking aside the covers, she scrambled out of bed and threw open the door of the cabin.

She stood transfixed on the threshold, totally unprepared for the sight that greeted her. Shimmering curtains of brilliant color, red, green, and violet, danced across the night sky in a dazzling display of pyrotechnics. The lights bowed and swayed like ghostly dancers in a heavenly ballroom.

"Beautiful . . ." she breathed, unaware she had spoken aloud. "Absolutely beautiful."

"I've always thought so, too."

Gillian started at the sound of Luc's voice coming from the darkness beyond. Stepping outside, she waited for her eyes to adjust, then was able to distinguish his figure standing near a stand of white birch. She walked toward him, her thin batiste nightdress a mere whisper in the tall grass. Side by side, they admired nature's amazing light show. Colors spread, faded, then burst anew. The spectacular sight was unlike anything she had ever witnessed.

"How incredible," she said in an awe-filled voice.

Luc glanced down at her. God, she was the one who was incredible. The sight of her quite simply stole his breath away. The sky forgotten, Luc feasted on the vision at his side. The sheer fabric of her nightdress draped her body like gauze, alternately hinting at and revealing the full breasts, small waist, and trim hips beneath. Her pale hair streamed like moonbeams down her back and around her shoulders, framing her delicate features. Her blue eyes were alight with wonder, wide and round as a child's on Christmas morn. She looked like an angel. His angel.

"I could watch 'til dawn."

Luc grinned at her enthusiasm. "If you plan to be here all night, I have the perfect solution."

Bemused, she watched him disappear into the cabin only to return moments later with a blanket tucked under one arm. He spread the blanket over the grass; then, lowering himself to the ground, he patted the spot next to him. He smiled in approval when she joined him without hesitation.

He positioned himself flat on his back, one arm folded behind his head, and gazed up at the sky. Gillian did the same. For a while they watched the shifting patterns in companionable silence.

"The northern lights never fail to impress me."

"What do you suppose causes them?" Gillian mused.

"All the forces of nature—sun, wind, and fire—conspire to grant us poor mortals a special gift."

"I never expected to actually see them, but I've read about them." Her hand crept into his, their fingers entwined. "In the Middle Ages, people believed the lights came from heavenly warriors. Soldiers who gave their lives for king and country. As a reward for their bravery, they were allowed to battle in the sky forever."

He raised her hand and brushed a kiss across the knuckles. "Another tale has it that the lights are torches used by spirits to guide the dead across a narrow bridge that spans an enormous abyss to their heavenly home."

Luc was also familiar with yet a third tale, a theory he didn't wish to impart. Many people, he knew, were convinced that the northern lights were an omen. Warnings of illness, plague, and death. The red lights were particularly meaningful. Red signaled the outbreak of war.

As they stared at the sky, a single star, far brighter than the rest, streaked across the heavens.

"A shooting star!" Gillian turned onto her side and rested her hand on his chest. "Did you see it? Did you make a wish?"

Reaching out, he threaded his fingers through her hair and then let the strands drift lazily about her shoulders. "Yes," he murmured. "I made my wish." He had wished for the impossible. Wished there was no need for secrets between them. That they could be lovers, not enemies. Impossible wishes. Impossible dreams.

Keeping his gaze fastened on hers, he curved his hand around the back of her head and gently forced her mouth to meet his. Gillian's lips parted, soft, yielding. He leisurely feasted on the honeyed offering. A craving consumed him. A single taste created a voracious need for more. Luc teased her tongue with his, engaging it in ancient love play.

"Sweet," he murmured, trailing kisses along her jaw, her throat. "Sweeter than wild berries."

He slipped his hand beneath the hem of her nightgown and felt her quiver when he touched her. Her flesh felt firm, satiny. His hand strayed higher, to the gentle swell of her hip, then slid to cup the mound of her femininity. She moaned softly and arched her pelvis against his palm, encouraging his exploration.

The thin layer of cloth separating them formed too great a barrier. "I want to feel you, all of you," he said. Impatiently, he tugged off her gown, tossed it aside, then divested himself of his own clothing.

Stretching out beside her, he reached for her again, but she placed a hand on his chest and forestalled the attempt. "Let me touch you."

Blood pounded through his veins at the softly spoken request. He didn't think he could withstand having her touch him. Doubted he could contain the blazing hot passion. He steeled himself to endure the exquisite torture.

"I want to learn your body as you learned mine," she whispered shyly.

He bit back a groan as she began her sensual assault. Her mouth trailed heated kisses across his chest, then paused to delicately flick the flat, male nipple with the tip of her tongue. His hands bunched into fists at his sides. He wanted to flip her onto her back and thrust deep inside until he found surcease.

Her exploration faltered as she encountered a trio of raised stripes along his left flank. "Scars?" she asked, her voice low. "What happened?"

He traced her spine with a fingertip and watched her eyes become heavy lidded with pleasure. "A reminder of my waltz with a bear."

She buried her face in the crook of his neck. "You could have been killed."

"Instead, the bear became my manitou, a spirit to lend me strength in time of danger."

With nibbling kisses and nimble hands, Gillian continued her thorough survey. His manhood hardened and throbbed, testing his control to the breaking point.

"The bear would have been kinder. You're the one who's killing me—in slow, painful degrees." Before she could object, he rolled her onto her back, pinning her beneath him. Silky tresses formed a fan of spun gold across the blanket. She gazed at him solemnly, her mouth red and swollen from his kisses.

"My turn." His mouth closed over a nipple and sucked gently. Then he turned his attention to her other breast, laving it with the same tender devotion.

She purred low in her throat, and he exulted at the sound of her arousal.

Luc slid his hand between her thighs and found her moist and ready. He lightly brushed the pad of his thumb over the tiny bud of her arousal until she writhed frantically beneath him. Every abandoned movement, every ragged breath, told him she was eager, impatient. As desperate for him as he was for her.

"Luc . . ." she begged. "Please, I can't wait."

And neither could he.

Positioning himself between her legs, he entered her. Snug and hot, she convulsed around him like a tight glove.

He threw back his head and let out a primal groan. God! This was so perfect, so right.

She wrapped her legs around his waist, and together they rode out the storm. She climaxed first, crying out his name. His hips pumped furiously, then he emptied his seed and, spent, collapsed on top of her.

Later, they lay content in each other's embrace while they watched nature's light show. A kaleidoscope of hues twinkled and shimmied against a dark sky. Changing from green to violet and finally to red.

Red. The color of war.

"The hour is late," Luc said abruptly. Rising, he scooped Gillian into his arms, blanket and all, and carried her inside the cabin. He kicked the door shut behind him, blocking out the ominous reminder.

Gillian reached up and traced the frown line between his brows. "I would hate to be the enemy of such a fierce warrior."

Enemy . . . ? Luc's frown deepened at her innocent choice of words. Little did she know that she *was* the enemy. Remember Running Fawn, he admonished. Remember your sister. He had once placed his faith in British justice, and they had betrayed that trust. He despised them for it. Conspired against them. Against all things British.

"Luc . . . ?"

He shook his head in a futile attempt to dispel black thoughts. After lowering Gillian onto the bed, he smoothed back her tangled hair, then gently cupped her face between his hands and gazed into trusting blue eyes the color of a summer sky. No, this woman wasn't the enemy, he acknowledged ruefully; she was his lover, his wife.

His very life.

Admitting the depths of his feelings left him shaken to the core. He lightly stroked her delicate cheekbone with the pad of his thumb. "Gillian," he said, his voice unusually gruff. "I would cut out my heart rather than intentionally cause you pain. It's important you believe this—no matter what happens."

"Luc, you're frightening me."

"Remember my words, *mon coeur*."

"I promise. Now remember mine." Placing her fingertips against his lips to forestall a reply, she smiled up at him. "I love you, Luc du Pré."

Stunned speechless, words eluded him. Seconds crept by. She had bestowed a priceless gift, All he felt was guilt. Guilt—and sadness. Once battle lines were drawn, any tender feelings she held for him would be irrevocably severed. The outcome was inevitable. She would hate him then as passionately as she claimed to love him now.

The silence was telling. He reached for her but, as though sensing his reluctance to return the sentiment, she evaded him, springing out of bed on the opposite side.

"Gillian, don't . . ."

"I almost forgot." She forced a smile as she retrieved a small package from the trunk at the foot of the bed and offered it to him.

"For me . . . ?" He stared at the polished walnut case she held. "What is it?"

"A wedding present."

"But I have nothing to give in return."

"What you've given me can't be put into words or contained in a box. Now open it," she said.

Accepting her gift, Luc lifted the lid, took out the knife, and held it up for inspection. After removing the knife from its leather sheath, he ran a fingertip along the blade, testing its sharpness. Satisfied, he balanced the carved hilt across one hand, enjoying its solid weight against his palm. It was beautifully crafted. Practical, yet handsome.

"Well . . . ?" she asked, searching his face for a reaction.

"I don't know quite what to say."

"Then don't say anything." She walked into his out-stretched arms. "Show me what you feel."

And he did.

Gillian inhaled the heady scent of the rose she had found on her pillow that morning. Luc, she thought with a dreamy smile. Though not one for flowery declarations of devotion, Luc showed his affection in a myriad of small ways. Several days ago, following their lovemaking under the northern lights, she had found a nosegay of forget-me-nots. Now, she fingered the velvety rose petal. Soon, she was certain, he would voice the words she longed to hear.

The unmistakable sound of horses' hooves drew her attention. Rushing outside, she saw Luc emerge from the surrounding woodland mounted on a dark bay with a white muzzle and stockings. Gillian felt her heart flutter at the mere sight of him, tall and impressive in the saddle.

He reined to a halt. "I borrowed one of the army's horses for the afternoon. Would you care to come for a ride?"

He flashed a smile, engagingly boyish, and she melted. "I'd love to," she replied, returning his smile. "But unfortunately I left my riding habit in England. I have nothing to wear."

He withdrew a parcel from his saddlebag and tossed it to her. "Consider your problem solved. Now hurry and change."

He looked so pleased with himself that she laughed out loud as she hugged the package to her chest.

"You're wasting time, madame. Your mighty steed, one of His Majesty's finest, grows impatient."

Gillian laughed again. The "mighty steed" to which he referred grazed placidly on a patch of sweet clover, giving no indication of being the least anxious to budge from the spot. Nevertheless, exhilarated at the prospect of an afternoon in Luc's company, she hastened inside and tore open the paper-wrapped parcel. Bemused, she held up a pair of doeskin breeches and a loose-fitting linen shirt. Not exactly what a proper English gentlewoman would wear on a ride through the park. But then, she grinned, she was no longer in England.

Minutes later she came out attired in her new garments with her hair tied neatly at the nape with a narrow blue ribbon. Luc's dark eyes smoldered with approval—along with another emotion she quickly recognized. Then, she was besieged with sudden doubt. "What if someone sees us? Such dress is considered scandalous."

"No need to worry." Leaning down, he offered a hand and swung her into the saddle with ease. "Except for sentries on duty, McDouall assembled the entire garrison for one of his long-winded speeches. If anyone dares a comment, they'll have to answer to me."

Luc urged the horse along a little-used trail leading in the direction opposite the fort. Sunlight filtered through the leaves, dappling the ground in shades of amber and jade. Birds sang in the branches while chipmunks and squirrels darted through the underbrush. Gillian turned her face upward and felt the warm kiss of the sun. Life was good. She realized that she was the happiest she'd ever been. Gloriously happy.

England was nothing more than a fading memory. The past. This land represented the future. There was freedom here, opportunity, less rigidity and more diversity, challenge, and adventure. If anyone had told her upon her arrival that she would adopt this wilderness as her home, she would have thought them mad.

The horse carefully picked its way down an incline, then stepped into an open field choked with daisies, wild strawberries, and campions. Clumps of hazelnut and hawthorn flourished. Scattered about were runt-sized apple trees. A pile of charred timber attested to former inhabitants.

"Who lived here?"

"An Irish couple farmed this site years ago. After their cabin burned, they left Mackinac for good, claiming they were tired of its harsh winters."

Gillian was surprised to see a well-tended two-story log house and various outbuildings. Corn and wheat thrived in fields cleared for planting. "Who does the farm belong to?" she wondered out loud.

"Michael Dousman. A prominent trader here on the island."

"Ah, yes," Gillian said. She recalled having once been introduced by Margaret Babcock. The man's assessing dark gaze had made her uncomfortable.

Luc made a sweeping circle of the field before continuing on. The trail descended in a series of thickly wooded hills, then traversed marshland rioting with cattails and smelling of mint. "Dousman is considered a traitor by his fellow Americans."

Gillian's curiosity was instantly piqued. "Why? What did he do?"

"In the summer of 1812, the American commandant commissioned Dousman, a captain in the Michigan militia, to visit St. Joseph's Island. He was to report back on British activities. On his way, he was captured by a British flotilla. He was sworn to secrecy and set ashore with directions to warn the villagers of the impending attack but not alert the garrison."

"I should think the villagers would be grateful for his efforts."

"The British were also quite grateful. Dousman's holdings have increased substantially of late, including some of the fields we just passed through."

Gillian thought she detected a note of censure in his voice. "You don't approve of his decision to aid the British?"

Luc shrugged. "A man must follow the dictates of his conscience, or he's not a man."

Pausing at the top of a small rise, the lake was plainly visible through the trees. Luc pointed toward the shoreline. "That's the spot where the British landed two years ago."

Though the site was picturesque, Gillian couldn't understand Luc's absorption. She was about to question his interest when he turned the horse away. They followed a path along the rim of a bluff that afforded stunning vistas of the lake below. Eventually they had gone full circle, and their cabin came into view.

Gillian had enjoyed the outing immensely and was reluctant for their time together to end. She wondered if Luc shared her feelings but, as usual, had no idea what thoughts went through his head.

She accepted the hand he offered and slid to the ground. He swung down behind her; then, to her surprise, he hooked an arm around her waist and pulled her against him. Startled, she stared into eyes so dark she could see herself reflected in them. Before she could draw a breath, his lips crushed hers. She clung to him so tightly, her nails dug into his shoulders. It was a kiss filled with longing and desperation, tinged with . . . ? Fear? It seemed to plumb the depths of her soul, demanding answers to unasked questions. Finally, he drew away, leaving her shaken and unaccountably anxious.

Her hand trembled as she touched his cheek. "Luc, please, tell me . . ."

The cabin door burst open and André Tousseau tumbled out. The little voyageur stopped dead in his tracks at catching them in an embrace. His initial surprise rapidly transformed into jubilation. "You big ox," he scolded, bounding toward them as quickly as his short legs would allow. His ever-present red knit cap bounced with each step. "You finally took an old man's advice."

Scout scampered out of the woods, barking excitedly, causing the bay to prance skittishly. Luc quieted the horse with a stern command, then tossed the reins over a low-hanging branch.

"André, you devil, what brings you here?" Luc asked, his hand firmly at Gillian's waist.

Quick to note the familiarity, André grinned ear to ear. "Aren't you the sly one? I told you months ago that you and the beautiful m'selle would make a perfect pair."

"She is no longer m'selle, but madame. Gillian is my wife."

André's smile faltered. "You're married?"

Gillian looked from one to the other, puzzled by the undercurrents she sensed rippling beneath the exchange.

"Then allow me to kiss the bride," André said, recovering from his surprise. He caught Gillian in a bear hug and gave her a resounding kiss.

Gillian returned the hug, then studied the little voyageur, her eyes dark with concern. "I hope you don't disapprove of Luc's choice."

"*Non, non.* The news merely caught me off guard." He spread his hands in a helpless gesture. "When I saw female belongings, I assumed Luc and a lady friend had formed romantic ties. I had no idea the female was m'selle. Last time, you two did not like each other."

Gillian smiled at the memory. She had despised Luc and his self-confidence nearly as much as she hated the encompassing wilderness. "Many things have changed since then."

"So I see." André gave Luc's arm a playful punch. "Now you like each other plenty."

His arm around Gillian, Luc started toward the cabin

with André bustling alongside. "You still haven't answered my question, André. What brings you so far from home?"

"St. Joseph's Island is a lonely place. I felt the need for companionship, but"—he gave Gillian a broad wink—"I see *mon ami* prefers the companionship of another."

"You'll at least join us for dinner."

"*Oui*, m'selle—madame," he corrected himself. "In your absence I have made myself useful. Dinner is almost ready."

"Then we are in for a treat." Gillian gave Scout a friendly pat. "My cooking skills are improving, but they'll never be a match for yours."

"While I am here I will teach you a few tricks. Soon you will be almost as good as André."

Luc nodded toward the bay, which contentedly munched grass. "Perhaps after dinner you would return the horse to the stable for me. While there, you can inquire about lodging."

"Good idea, *mon ami*, and it will save me the walk."

The hours passed quickly. Dinner turned into a festive affair, with much laughter and good-natured bantering. André was a skilled storyteller with a wicked sense of humor. Remembering André's fondness for a pipe after the evening meal, Gillian suggested the men go outside to talk and smoke while she tidied up. Her offer was accepted with alacrity.

"I can't believe you married the daughter of British captain," André said as soon as they were out of earshot.

Luc shrugged diffidently. "I thought you liked Gillian."

"I like her very much, but she's . . ."

". . . British?"

"Exactly. Where was your brain, *mon ami*? In your breeches?"

Luc flinched at the choice of words that closely mimicked Toad's. "Considering the circumstances, it was the only honorable course."

André's eyes rounded. "M'selle is pregnant?"

"No," Luc denied quickly. "At least, not to my knowledge."

André let out a low whistle as another possibility dawned. "Long as I've known you, I've never seen you lose your head over a woman."

"Who's to say I've lost my head?"

"You can't fool me." André gave a snort of disgust. "I know you too well. What do you suppose will happen once she learns you spy for the Americans?"

"Probably try to forget she ever knew me," Luc retorted, his voice bleak.

"Your lady has a temper. She won't be happy until your scalp is hoisted up the flagpole and flying alongside the Union Jack."

Luc knew his friend spoke the truth. From the very beginning, he had represented himself as something he wasn't. Gillian would be furious when she learned about his deception, and her feelings would be justified.

They were quiet for some time. Then André broke the terse silence. "The Americans will be here shortly. I do not understand their reasoning, but instead of attacking Mackinac, they first went to St. Joseph's Island. They didn't stop to question loyalty before torching everything in sight—my cabin included. Any day now, they'll turn their attention here."

"I'm sorry for your loss." Luc squeezed André's shoulder. "Now I must beg a great favor of you."

"You have only to ask."

"When the time comes, see to Gillian's safety."

"What about you? Who will guard your back?"

"Promise, André. I want her out of danger. Once the attack is imminent, see that Gillian goes to the fort immediately. The blockhouses should provide protection from heavy shelling from American guns."

For once all trace of humor was wiped from the little voyageur's wizened face. "You have my word, *mon ami*."

A handshake sealed their bargain.

Chapter Twenty

A heavy pounding on the cabin door woke the pair inside from a sound sleep.

"Who . . . ?" Gillian dragged a handful of hair out of her eyes.

"Wake up! Wake up!" Though André Tousseau's voice was muffled by the thick wood, his urgency was unmistakable.

Instantly alert, Luc sprang out of bed and, unmindful of his nudity, answered the door. "What is it?"

"The Americans," André huffed, breathless from running. "The American fleet has been sighted."

"Where?"

André wiped the perspiration from his brow. "They're anchored off the eastern end of Round Island."

"Wait here, *mon ami.*"

Luc closed the door firmly and turned to reassure Gillian. But there was no need. She had already pulled on her clothes and was racing about, stuffing belongings into a cloth bag. Luc dressed quickly, then took her arm and led her outside to where André waited.

"Go with André. He'll take you to the fort, where it's safe."

She dug in her heels. "What about you? Aren't you coming with us?"

The men exchanged anxious looks above her head. "There are some things I must do first."

André took her arm and tugged gently. "Come, m'selle."

Gillian shook her head stubbornly. "I want to stay with my husband."

A look akin to pain crossed Luc's features. "You must go before any firing begins."

André stepped forward with renewed determination. "Luc must see to the safety of his friends. He has responsibilities, obligations."

Gillian thought of the small Ottawa village, of Wind Spirit and Aupetchi, and was immediately contrite. She turned to Luc. "Forgive me for being selfish. If you send them to me, I'll see that they receive protection."

André could barely contain his impatience. "Hurry, m'selle."

Grimly clutching her bag, she crossed the small clearing with André at her side. At the point where the trail bisected the woods, she paused and looked back. Luc's tall figure stood silhouetted against a backdrop of dark pines. Remote. Solitary. Her heart wrenched at the sight.

Dropping her belongings, she ran back. Luc caught her in a tight embrace, pulling her against his chest and lifting her off her feet. He crushed her lips against his, the kiss passionate and all too brief, then set her from him.

Gillian felt a stirring of panic. Her instincts screamed that something was terribly amiss. "Luc, I'm frightened."

"No need to worry, *mon coeur.*" He cupped her cheek in one hand and smiled into her eyes. "As long as I have breath in my body, I will never let anything bad happen to you."

"I love you," she whispered.

"Then leave now, and let me do what I must."

Emotion clogged her throat, making speech impossible. Turning her face, she pressed a kiss into the palm. Through a mist of tears, she turned away and, this time, didn't look back.

Gillian and André joined the procession of villagers streaming up the ramp into the fort. The men, women, and children, their arms laden with valued possessions, were an unusually silent bunch. Stepping through the south sally port, she found a much different atmosphere. The fort was a beehive of activity. Buglers signaled orders in a rapid flurry of musical notes. Officers snapped commands that enlisted men scurried to obey. She caught a glimpse of her father as he conferred with Colonel McDouall at the edge of the parade ground. Indian allies in gaudy war paint and feathers congregated around their leaders or talked excitedly in tight groups.

Gillian pushed her way toward the gun platform. From there she had a commanding view of the lake. Across the harbor, five schooners bobbed in the blue waters off Round Island, a small, uninhabited island to the south. What were the Americans waiting for? she wondered. Why didn't they attack? If they planned a war of nerves, their campaign was succeeding. Tension in the fort was almost palpable.

While a group of soldiers angled cannons to gain optimum advantage, André tugged at her sleeve. "This way, m'selle."

Gillian followed without argument as he led the way toward the west blockhouse. The trio of blockhouses with their three-foot-thick limestone walls and overhanging second story were built to withstand small arms and artillery fire as well as to return fire through strategically placed ports. The three stalwart structures would provide protection against a frontal assault or, if the fort itself was breached, serve as a final refuge. Gillian joined the villagers who were being herded inside like a flock of sheep.

"You will be safe here, m'selle." André scuffed the ground with the toe of his boot and refused to meet her eyes.

She cast a pleading look at the little man. All traces of his customary ebullience had vanished. "How soon do you think Luc will join us?"

"Do not worry," he said, but his tone lacked conviction. Turning away, he vanished into the crowd.

Gillian lingered outside the blockhouse, hoping Luc would appear. Judith Mayfield and her young son, Jacob, rushed past just as the first cannon roared. The little boy held his hands over his ears and screamed in terror. His fear was communicated to several other children nearby who burst into tears and buried their faces in their mothers' skirts.

The fort rapidly filled to overflowing. Noise and confusion reigned. Gillian involuntarily took a step backward when a string of frightened horses was led past, their high-pitched whinnies grating nerves already raw. A young lad of twelve struggled to control them and keep them from rearing. When there was still no sign of Luc, she ducked inside the blockhouse to wait.

Over the next several hours, cannon fire echoed throughout the fort. The acrid scent of gunpowder wafted on the August breeze. Gillian's ears rang from the repeated firings. Then a profound silence descended.

Finally the quiet was shattered by a cheer that could have been heard clear into Canada. Unable to withstand the suspense another second, Gillian abandoned the blockhouse in search of an explanation.

She stopped a private hurrying past. "What happened? Why did the shooting stop?"

The private grinned, revealing a row of crooked yellow teeth in a grimy face. "The Americans didn't like their taste of British cannon. They're retreating."

Retreating? Picking up her skirts, she ran toward the Stone Quarters, where she would be able to see for herself. Knees weak with relief, she leaned against the side of the building to watch. The American fleet, sails billowing, moved away from Round Island toward Bois Blanc Island, farther to the south and well out of range of British guns.

Gillian remained where she was for an indefinite period of time, her gaze searching the throng for Luc's tall figure. She couldn't quite shake the unfounded notion that he was in grave danger.

In the distance, the American fleet regrouped and dropped anchor. Shading her eyes against the sun's glare, she saw a small boat lowered over the side of one of schooners. The craft steadily headed back once again for Round Island. A troop of soldiers, muskets in hand, raced by her toward the gun platforms. She caught some of their comments as they hurried past.

"They think to set up a gun position."

"The bloody bastards."

"We'll show 'em."

The thick walls of the fort reverberated with a string of high-pitched war whoops as Indian allies, led by Red Dog, raced after the soldiers. They ignored the ramp leading from the fort, instead rushing pell-mell down the rocky embankment toward the beach. Leaping into canoes, they paddled furiously toward the small group of Americans landing on Round Island. At a crisp command from Colonel McDouall, a contingent of soldiers hastened to follow suit.

Tension coiled in the pit of Gillian's stomach. Rooted

to the spot, she observed the drama being enacted. One of the Americans apparently noticed the rapidly approaching Indians and warned the others. Shots were exchanged, but no one seemed to be injured. The American soldiers frantically scrambled back into their small dinghy. All but one managed to avoid capture. Red Dog knocked the hapless man senseless, then hauled the inert body into his canoe.

When the party of Indians reached Mackinac Island once again, the prisoner was dragged to the shore, where they proceeded to viciously pummel and kick the hapless American soldier. Gillian bit down on a knuckle to keep from screaming in protest. Mercifully, a strong guard of British soldiers arrived in time to rescue the man from a brutal end. She pitied any poor soul who fell victim to the pent-up rage of their Indian allies.

By sunset the entire village below was deserted. Gillian sought out Margaret Babcock, and together the two women converted Gillian's attic loft into a dormitory of sorts for women and children. The thick walls of the officers' Stone Quarters would provide ample fortification in the unlikelihood of a nighttime attack. Gillian lay on her cot, unable to sleep, and stared at the exposed beams. The entire day had passed without a single word from Luc. Even André had disappeared. She no longer knew what to think.

The next morning dawned with more gunfire. Civilians huddled in the blockhouses while American ships and British cannons traded fire. Père Robichaud circulated among the villagers, offering comfort and encouragement.

Gillian caught his attention and drew him aside. "Father, have you seen Luc?" she whispered urgently.

The priest patted her shoulder sympathetically but avoided meeting her eyes. "Your husband is very resourceful. He would not want you to worry."

But worry consumed her. She could not rid herself of the notion that something was wrong. Dreadfully wrong.

The sun shone high overhead when an exuberant cheer swelled from the ranks of the soldiers. A ruddy-faced sergeant, his uniform blackened with gunpowder, stuck his head into the blockhouse. "Rest easy. The American guns can't be elevated high enough to pose a threat."

"Good thing, too." James Babcock wearily rubbed the bearded stubble on his jaw. "They could have inflicted serious damage."

"The fort's as formidable as Gibraltar," the sergeant boasted.

"Except for the high ground to the rear," James reminded the man.

"Fort George should see to our rear if the enemy attempts a landing."

Minutes crawled into hours. For the remainder of the day, time crept at a snail's pace. Finally, long fingers of twilight snuffed the light from the sky and drowned the island in purple shadows. People milled about, discussing rumors, debating tactics, stating opinions, making predictions. The endless rise and fall of voices irritated Gillian as much as the buzz of a mosquito.

Campfires dotted the parade ground. Soon the odor of roasting food permeated the twilight. Gillian wrapped a cloak about her shoulders to ward off the damp chill. She wove through the crowd, her gaze restlessly searching for one particular face but didn't find it.

The second night passed much as the first. Fitful periods of sleep alternated with bouts of wakefulness. Asleep or awake, images of Luc taunted, haunted. Where was he? What was he doing? Why? Again and again, these unanswered questions hummed through her brain like fragments of jarring melody.

Gillian woke to pearly gray light seeping through cracks

in the wooden shutters. Quiet so as not to disturb the women and children, who were still sleeping, she dressed quickly and went downstairs. The quarters she had once shared with her father looked as spartan as it had upon her arrival at Mackinac. All the small changes she had made had been eradicated. It was as though she had never lived there at all.

Absently she smoothed a hand over the worn settee. Her nerves felt threadbare, her eyes gritty. Luc had no right to subject her to such torment. It was inconsiderate of him to leave her to worry and wonder. Was he so busy he couldn't send word? Couldn't he extend the simple courtesy of informing his wife of his whereabouts? The more she thought about it, the angrier she became. She carefully nursed the steadily mounting fury. Welcomed its burning heat. Anything was preferable to the anxiety that threatened to paralyze her.

"Miss Stafford . . . ?" The question, muffled by the stout wooden door, was followed by a sharp knock.

Hurrying to open the door, Gillian found a young soldier standing on the porch. "I'm Mrs. Du Pré," she corrected. In spite of her resolve to the contrary, her heart leaped with hope. "You have a message from my husband?"

"No, ma'am," he said, his tone curt. "Captain Stafford wants to see you."

"Father?" Her mind spun with possibilities. "Why would he send for me?"

"Officers don't confide in enlisted men, ma'am. Captain said you're to come at once."

Plucking her cloak from a peg near the door, she hurried after the soldier. A ghostly blanket of fog covered the island. Only dim shapes of buildings were visible through the thick mist. Gillian pulled up her hood and clutched her cloak tighter to ward off the chill and dampness.

Even at such an early hour, post headquarters was filled

with men. The conversation dwindled and died the moment she entered. She stood statue-still inside the threshold. Quickly surveying her surroundings, she read varying degrees of hostility and suspicion in the men's expressions. Instinctively, Gillian squared her shoulders, lifted her chin, and braced for an attack.

Randolph Stafford made his way toward her.

"You sent for me, Father?" Gillian tried to act calmer than she felt.

"There are some things we must discuss—in private." Taking her elbow, he guided her through the gauntlet of watchful men and into a small office at the rear, then closed the door behind them.

"What is all this about? Does it have to do with Luc?"

He took a seat behind the desk but didn't invite her to sit in the chair reserved for visitors. "When did you last see your husband?"

She frowned, puzzled by the question, and even more by his tone. "Why, two days ago, when the American fleet was first sighted."

"And you've had no word from him since?"

"No, none." Her composure wavered. "Has anyone news of him? Is he all right? Has he been injured?"

"Calm yourself, Daughter. No need to become hysterical." Stafford folded his hands on the desktop and regarded her dispassionately. "Don't you find it strange that with the Americans on our doorstep, your husband is nowhere to be found?"

She moistened her lower lip with the tip of her tongue. "I'm sure there's a plausible explanation."

"Think about it." He leaned forward slightly, his blue eyes cool, assessing. "The time has come to take sides, to test loyalties, and Luc du Pré's nowhere to be found."

"Then, there has to be a good reason," she asserted stubbornly.

"Ah, there's a reason all right, but not a good one."

"What are you trying to tell me?"

"Quite simply, Daughter, if your husband is not with us, then he must be against us."

Gillian's mind rebelled at her father's words. It couldn't possibly be true. Luc was as loyal as she to the British. Just because he wasn't at the fort didn't mean he was the enemy. There could be dozens of reasons for his absence. Maybe he had been wounded in the cursory shelling. Perhaps he was with his Ottawa friends. "I don't believe any of this," she murmured with growing uncertainty.

"On several occasions, Red Dog has reported seeing du Pré roaming about the island late at night, long after everyone else was asleep."

"Red Dog and Luc hate each other," she defended hotly. "They're bitter enemies. Surely you don't believe anything he tells you." Unable to stand still, she paced the width of the small room.

Her father spared her a pitying glance. "Even you must admit your husband's activities seem suspicious. Though we have no concrete proof, we are forced to draw certain conclusions."

"Conclusions?" she repeated, her voice rising. "What sort of conclusions?"

"That your husband may be a spy for the Americans."

Gillian stopped pacing to stare at her father in stunned disbelief. "Luc? A spy?" Suddenly she felt as though she was suffocating and couldn't breathe. The room spun, tilted, then slowly righted itself. Tiny beads of perspiration dotted her brow.

Stafford pushed to his feet and came around the desk. Digging his fingers into her shoulders, he gave her a hard shake. "Get a grip, girl. This is no time for the vapors."

"That can't be. Luc wouldn't . . ." She looked into her

father's stern face, silently pleading with him to recant his harsh verdict.

"Accept it, Gillian." Stafford's voice gentled. "Luc du Pré is a spy. He was only using you."

Was her father speaking the truth? she wondered dully. All this time, had Luc only been *using* her, taking what she offered, never loving her? But if he wasn't a spy, how could the frequent late-night escapades be explained? If he wasn't a spy, why wasn't he in a British stronghold, helping stave off an enemy attack?

Unless he was the enemy.

The thought staggered her.

"Du Pré was privy to all the information here at headquarters," her father continued. "He passed it along to the Americans the first chance he got. Well, the bloody bastard had better guard his back. Red Dog would like nothing better than to personally strip the flesh from his hide."

She turned away as a wave of nausea washed over her. *Strip his flesh?* She recalled the Indian's brutal treatment of the American captive. In Red Dog's hands, Luc would be subjected to cruel and inhumane treatment. A shudder raced through her at the thought.

"I'm sorry, Gillian. I can see this has come as a shock." Stafford clumsily patted her shoulder. "I blame myself for this mess. I never should have insisted you marry the half-breed."

Her father's words seemed to be coming from a great distance away. Her control was about to shatter. If she didn't leave headquarters—and soon—she would embarrass them both. She paused at the door, one hand on the knob, and dragged in a ragged breath. As she fled the small office, she was aware of the curious stares that followed her departure.

All this time, Luc had lied to her, deceived her.
Betrayed her.

In a daze, she crossed the parade ground, heading for
the Stone Quarters, seeking shelter, escape. Luc's defec-
tion left her numb. Wounded her so deeply, pain couldn't
penetrate.

The bad weather remained constant. Gillian's mood,
however, did not. She alternated between fits of rage and
bouts of depression. She was plagued by a burgeoning
sense of betrayal. And with it came the pain. At times the
agony was so acute, she nearly doubled over. She felt as
though her heart had been ripped from her chest while
still beating. Everything she and Luc shared had been a
lie.

Head bent in thought, she wandered aimlessly around
the perimeter of the fort. As difficult as it was, she had
finally come to the realization that Luc had never truly
cared for her. Oh, he had desired her, but that was all.
While she had fallen in love, his emotions had remained
unaffected.

She berated herself for a fool. Where men were concerned she showed an appalling lack of judgment. First
with Jeremy Blackwood, now Luc du Pre. She had considered Luc decent, honorable. A man of character.

But where Jeremy had humiliated and embarrassed her,
Luc had broken her heart. Scalding hot tears streamed
down her cheeks. She paused alongside the barracks and
impatiently wiped them away.

A woman's voice came out of the fog. "Imagine, Luc
du Pré a spy."

"I don't care what anyone says, I feel sorry for the poor
girl."

Gillian recognized the voice of the first woman as belonging to Judith Mayfield. She remained where she was, hidden from view in the dense fog. Countless times in the past week she had blundered into conversations that terminated in uncomfortable silence. Intercepted pitying glances. Everyone, it seemed, knew that Luc was a traitor.

"No wonder du Pré was quick to marry her. He didn't want to antagonize her father by refusing."

The women moved off. Her father *had* threatened to banish Luc from the island unless he married her. A fact she had conveniently chosen to overlook. But she would delude herself no longer. Luc had only consented to wed in order to stay in her father's good graces.

Gathering her tattered pride about her like an invisible cloak, Gillian dried her tears. In the past week she had shed enough to last a lifetime. But no more. Luc du Pré didn't deserve the tears. Wasn't worth the pain. It was time to view him for what he was: a conniving, traitorous bastard. If he was captured, Red Dog would have to wait in line. She wanted to be the first to flay his hide.

Chapter Twenty-one

Nine days after the American fleet was first sighted, the weather cleared. As the August sun burned off the last vestiges of fog, it became apparent that the schooners were no longer anchored off Bois Blanc Island. Tension of a different sort infected the inhabitants of the fort. Every man, woman, and child knew the long wait was finally over. Speculation concerning the intentions of the American fleet ended with the distant sound of cannon fire.

Gillian hugged her arms about her waist and watched the preparations for battle from the top step of the Stone Quarters. At a snapped command, buglers raised their horns and summoned the garrison to assemble. Soldiers armed with flintlock muskets and fixed bayonets ran to join their battalions and fall into line. Several hundred Indians, fearsome in greasepaint and feathers, poured into the fort. McDouall, resplendent in the bottle green of the Glengarry Light Infantry, marched onto the parade ground and addressed his troops.

The colonel raised his voice to be heard above the volleys of artillery. "Sources have informed me that the American fleet has anchored three hundred yards off British Landing on the western end of the island. We have a choice: either meet the enemy halfway or wait for them to strike." He paused dramatically. "The Royal Artillery shall greet the intruders on the field of honor."

A wild cheer went up from those assembled, causing a prickling sensation at the nape of her neck. Gillian's mouth went dry with fear. The siege was about to begin.

McDouall directed a handful of Canadian militia to guard Fort Mackinac and the newly completed redoubt, Fort George. Then, amid a roll of drums, he marched from the fort with the lion's share of troops and nearly twice as many Indian warriors.

The civilians clustered in the blockhouses for protection. Even the children fell silent. Unable to remain idle, Gillian volunteered to assist the soldiers manning the guns on the second story. After recovering from their initial surprise, they accepted her offer.

"Could use an extra hand." A grizzled sergeant wiped his grimy hands on his cotton trousers. "Keep the fire blazing in the hearth. When I give the order, unload the shot."

A buck-toothed private nodded agreement. "If them bloody bastards get within our sights, we'll give 'em a taste o' lead."

Volley after volley of cannon fire exploded in the distance. Gillian tried to concentrate on the task at hand and keep her mind blank. Sweat trickled down her temples as she fed scraps of wood into the flames.

After a while the cannons ceased firing. An ominous silence descended.

Gillian gnawed her lower lip, then asked of no one in particular, "Do you suppose the battle is over?"

The sergeant grunted. "It ain't over until the Union Jack comes down."

Just when her nerves were about to snap, the quiet ended with the popping of musket fire. Her imagination ran rampant. She wanted to put her hands over her ears to block the sound. Instead she followed the sergeant's directions and carefully placed balls of shot in the blazing hearth with long tongs.

"If the bastards gets near, we'll drive 'em back with hot lead."

Gillian did as she was told, and tried to ignore her fears. She didn't want to think about Luc, didn't want to think about battle or bloodshed, but couldn't seem to help it. She wondered if at this very moment Luc was firing on those he pretended to befriend. Was his hatred for the British so intense that he wanted them dead? So great he'd use her, then casually discard her? Had the clues to his real feelings been there all along, and she too blind to see them?

After what seemed an eternity, only occasional musket fire could be heard. But mostly it was quiet. Quiet—and tense. The period that followed was the most difficult by far. Gillian feared she'd go mad from uncertainty when the unmistakably jaunty notes of fife and drum drifted across the island.

"McDouall's returning!" a sentry shouted from his lookout. "Praise God, we won."

"We beat the bloody buggers." The grizzly sergeant gave the young private a hearty whack between the shoulder blades, then danced a jig.

Gillian joined the others rushing from the blockhouses to view McDouall's triumphant return. The troops poured into the fort, flag flying. Robert McDouall proudly led his battalion, bloodied, disheveled, but remarkably intact, back from battle. Stretcher bearers brought up the rear and delivered the injured to the post hospital, located in a dilapidated storehouse. Gillian spotted her father in the swarm of red jackets, relieved to find him unscathed.

An unruly mass of Indians stormed into the fort, shouting and brandishing clubs and tomahawks. In their wake, they paraded two unfortunate captives, their hands bound behind their backs. Both had been stripped naked, their faces barely recognizable. Gillian watched with a growing sense of unease as they drew nearer.

Red Dog brutally jerked the short length of rope circling the neck of one of the prisoners and laughed when the man stumbled, then righted himself. The second man wasn't as fortunate. One of the braves purposely tripped him, sending him sprawling to the ground. Before he could struggle to his feet, others were quick to land kicks and blows on the poor man. A halfhearted command from one of the soldiers halted their sport. The barely conscious hostage was then hoisted into the air and carried aloft like a prized trophy.

As she observed with growing horror, Red Dog turned and singled her out with a glance. Sly, gloating, malicious, his look chilled her to the marrow. Again, he tugged on the rope he held, again his captive stumbled, nearly fell. This time, however, Gillian recognized his prisoner.

Luc.

She pressed a hand against her mouth to stifle a cry. All the blood seemed to drain from her head, leaving her faint and nauseated. Cold perspiration drenched her skin. She had wanted to see Luc suffer. Now it appeared she was about to get her wish. But the thought brought no pleasure, no comfort. Retreating from the crowd, she heaved the contents of her stomach behind a bush.

The spasms finally over, she dragged air into her lungs. Using the hem of her skirt, she wiped her face. Unable to witness any more of the victory celebration, she sought sanctuary in the quarters she once shared with her father.

She threw herself across the cot in the loft, trying to sort through thoughts, feelings, and reactions. She hated Luc du Pré with every fiber of her being. He was a traitor who deserved whatever harsh punishment was meted out to him. As an enemy, he wasn't entitled to pity. Or consideration and kindness. But overriding all was the memory of Luc's battered face. Stripped naked, bound and beaten, he had refused to tumble at Red Dog's feet, defiant even in defeat, proud even in captivity.

In spite of herself, she felt a stirring of sympathy. Sympathy for a spy? A traitor? Surely she must be mad. True, she hated Luc, but she didn't want him dead. Suddenly, it seemed imperative to learn his fate. Rising from the cot, she cast a quick look in the silvered glass on the wall. She barely recognized the image that stared back with untidy strands of hair hanging about a wan face, her clothing rumpled and soiled.

She took the time to wash, change clothes, and smooth her hair into a neat chignon at the base of her neck. Feeling more presentable, she hurried across the parade ground to post headquarters.

The door was ajar, and she entered without knocking. She paused on the threshold, seeking her father's figure from among the several dozen men gathered. A whiskey bottle and glasses on the desktops attested to the fact that she had interrupted a victory party. Everyone seemed in high spirits, recounting tales of the day's battle. Gradually, as the men became aware of her standing just inside the door, a hush fell over the room.

Alerted to her presence, Randolph Stafford separated himself from a group of infantry officers. Taking her elbow, he drew her aside. "What brings you here, Daughter? Can't you see I have duties to attend to?"

Gillian detected the smell of alcohol on her father's breath and knew he had already imbibed heavily. Knowing her father's moods at such times tended to be volatile, she came straight to the point. "I came to see what is going to happen to Luc."

"What do you care?" he sneered. "The man is a bloody traitor."

"Traitor or not, he is my husband," she reminded him. "I have a right to know his fate."

"Before today we had only Red Dog's suspicions. We might have gone easier on your half-breed, but no longer. The circumstances have changed."

"What happened to make you feel differently?" She struggled to keep her voice calm in spite of her mounting anxiety.

Colonel McDouall strolled over to join in their discussion. "Your husband, Mrs. du Pré, proved himself a dangerous adversary."

"He's far more clever than we anticipated." Stafford rocked back on his heels. "His brazen plan nearly succeeded."

Perplexed, Gillian shook her head. "What plan?"

"Du Pré's handwriting has been verified." McDouall produced a folded sheet of paper from an inner pocket and waved it at her. "Your husband sent a false report claiming American warships had landed troops between my forces and the fort itself. I withdrew in order to meet the threat. Most of our Indian allies came along as well, expecting to ambush the Americans. Fortunately, Red Dog and his men refused to leave their position. The Indians attacked the Americans, killing their leader, Major Holmes."

"It was during this skirmish that most of the American casualties occurred," Stafford interjected. "And the one in which your husband was captured."

McDouall continued the account. "With their commanding officer dead, the Americans were thrown into chaos. They found themselves outflanked and had little choice but to withdraw and return to their ships."

Gillian's mind whirled with various possibilities. Luc faced serious consequences. Would he be forced to face a firing squad? Sentenced to rot in an English prison? "What will Luc's punishment be?"

"Death is too good for the traitor." There was no hesitation on McDouall's part.

Careful to keep her face expressionless, Gillian surreptitiously wiped her moist palms on her skirt. "Then what do you intend to do?"

Neither McDouall nor her father met her gaze.

Stafford cleared his throat. "Red Dog has requested that your husband be turned over to his braves for punishment."

She forced herself to think over the buzzing in her head. "And have you made your decision, Colonel?"

"The request merits consideration," McDouall answered gruffly.

"But the two men hate each other." She couldn't contain the outburst. "I have witnessed how the Indians treat their captives. Red Dog will be merciless."

McDouall shrugged diffidently. "Red Dog deserves to be handsomely rewarded for his loyalty. The prisoner will simply disappear while in custody."

"Do you call this British justice?" she cried, outraged at the plan.

"Enough, Daughter!" Randolph Stafford's face reddened. "You have already taken up too much of the colonel's valuable time."

She turned to leave when McDouall's voice stopped her. "We hold you in no way responsible for your husband's actions. Although some initially questioned your loyalty, your conduct while the fort was under siege was commendable."

After murmuring an appropriate response, Gillian left headquarters in a daze. It had never occurred to her that she, too, might be suspected of betraying her country. That someone might be assigned to watch, then report on her activities. Volunteering at the blockhouse, however, had erased any such doubts. Now she was merely regarded as a loyal British subject who had the misfortune to marry a turncoat.

On McDouall's orders, the quartermaster had distributed barrels of rum and whiskey among the Indian allies. As darkness lowered, the sounds from outside increased, becoming more and more primitive. Gillian didn't bother to light a lamp, but remained huddled in a corner of the settee. She tried to convince herself that Luc deserved the fate reserved for him. He had not only betrayed England, but betrayed her trust. He knew the risks, had gambled, and lost.

But did he deserve the type of punishment Red Dog intended? an inner voice persisted. Did anyone? She had no doubt Red Dog was capable of extreme cruelty. Not even an animal should be subjected to such treatment.

Tears pricked her eyelids as she recalled Luc's words after making love beneath the northern lights. *I would cut out my heart rather than intentionally cause you pain. Believe me.* Though she hadn't understood, she hadn't doubted his sincerity.

His parting remark the morning the American fleet had been sighted returned to haunt her. *As long as I have breath in my body, I will never let anything bad happen to you.* Could she do any less for him?

Driven by a confusing blend of love and hate, she suddenly needed to go to him and see him one last time. At any moment, he could be turned over to Red Dog and his warriors; then it would be too late. Springing into action, she crossed the room. She reached for her cloak just as a knock sounded on the door, and froze.

"M'selle, open please," André Tousseau pleaded. "We know you are in there."

With a sigh of resignation, Gillian eased the door open a crack and found André and Père Robichaud on the doorstep. Both men were clothed in dark woolen capes with the hoods pulled low over their faces.

"Please, we need to speak with you," the priest said in low, urgent tones.

Gillian opened the door and admitted the men. "Allow me to light a lamp."

"*Non*, m'selle." André reached out a hand to stop her. "It is better this way."

Gillian studied the pair with a worried frown. "What brings you gentlemen here?"

"We have come to beg your help on Luc's behalf."

"I'm afraid there is nothing I can do." She shook her head sadly. "McDouall plans to turn him over to Red Dog in payment for his loyalty."

Père Robichaud took her hand and held it firmly in his. "I realize that Luc deceived you, but do you hate him so much you wish him dead?"

"No, of course not, but . . ."

She tried to pull away but the priest held fast. "You can't imagine how brutal the Indians can be. Some warriors have already brought souvenirs from the battlefield, grisly souvenirs, while McDouall and the rest turn a blind eye. Luc's death will be a slow, painful one. He'll be tortured, his body mutilated."

A shudder rippled through her. "How can I help?"

"I knew you wouldn't let us down." André beamed in

approval. "I have seen the way my friend looks at you, and you at him. It is easy to see you love each other."

But there was little time to debate the voyageur's belief. Père Robichaud quickly sketched a plan to gain Luc's freedom.

Shunning the light from bonfires that dotted the parade ground, two dark-cloaked figures slipped through the shadows. The weight of André's pistol rested reassuringly against her hip. Tightly clutching the drugged wine, Gillian offered a quick prayer that the desperate scheme would work. Surely the guards wouldn't refuse a prisoner a final visit from his confessor—or his irate wife.

Père Robichaud opened the door of the guardhouse, then stepped aside. "I'm here to administer last rites," he announced to the startled guards.

Gillian brushed past him. "And I'm here to give the lying bastard a piece of my mind."

The two soldiers serving as guards seemed startled by their unexpected visitors.

"Luc du Pré deliberately misled me," she declared heatedly. "Because of him, my own *father* questioned my loyalty."

"Remember, child, forgiveness is a virtue," Père Robichaud chided.

"Forgive him for making a fool of me? Never! I want the opportunity to tell du Pré how much I despise him."

The soldiers nodded their solemn approval at her tirade.

Gillian plunked the jug of Malaga wine on the small table. "It's hardly fair everyone else is celebrating while you're denied even a victory toast. I thought you men deserved a reward all your own."

The younger of the two eyed the bottle with interest but

reluctantly pushed it aside. "Drinking's not allowed while on duty, ma'am."

Père Robichaud smiled benevolently. "Surely the good Lord will not take you to task for a drink or two after a day on the battlefield."

"Well ..." The corporal licked his lips. "Maybe just one."

"Now if you'll kindly open the cell. ..." The priest motioned toward the locked door with a heavy iron grate covering a small window. "The prisoner should be allowed the privacy in which to confess his sins before meeting his Maker."

"You'll have to wait your turn, Father." Gillian swept past the priest and stood hands on hips by the locked door. "I intend to give the bastard a proper tongue lashing first."

The two soldiers exchanged wary glances; then the corporal slowly reached for a ring of keys and unlocked the cell door. From the corner of her eye, she saw the younger soldier uncork the bottle, then raise it to his lips. Slowly she released a pent-up breath.

Gillian stormed into the cell, Père Robichaud close at her heels. She stopped, horrified at the sight that greeted her. Luc lay curled on his side on a bed of filthy straw, naked, his wrists bound behind his back. Ugly, angry-looking bruises and welts covered his entire body.

At the sound of their entrance, he lifted his head and gazed up at her. Gillian bit her lower lip to keep it from trembling. His long hair was matted with dried blood. His face—his wonderful, handsome face—was hideously distorted from numerous blows, one eye discolored and swollen shut. Against all reason, she wanted to go to him, cradle his head against her breast, and whisper words of love and comfort. As though shamed by his injuries, he dropped his head to the straw and turned his face to the wall.

Père Robichaud briskly cleared his throat and shot her a warning glance. Gillian pulled herself together, knowing that if Luc's life was to be saved they had to act quickly.

Adopting a loud, strident tone, she began to berate him. "Don't think you fool me for an instant. I know you're only pretending to be asleep."

Père Robichaud knelt at Luc's side and whispered in his ear, "Luc, my son, can you hear me?"

Luc slowly raised his head and tried to focus the one eye that wasn't swollen shut.

Steeling herself for what had to be done, Gillian threw herself into the role she had agreed to play. "If you expect sympathy from me, Luc du Pré, you're sorely mistaken. I trusted you, and you betrayed that trust. You betrayed England."

Père Robichaud sliced the bonds at Luc's wrists with a pocket knife and silently urged him to his feet.

"You bloody turncoat." Gillian kept her back to the door to block the guard's view. "All these months, you only used me to get into Father's good graces. I hate you for what you did. You deserve everything you have coming. Red Dog and his men can't wait to get their hands on you."

Luc tensed at the mention of the name of his bitter enemy, then with a grimace of pain straightened. His eyes met hers across the space of a dim cell. A myriad of emotions, raw and turbulent, surged and sought to break free.

"And those nights I waited for you." Her voice caught, broke. Suddenly she was no longer playacting. "Now I know where you were. You risked everything—and lost."

Père Robichaud quickly divested himself of his cloak, black cassock, and moccasins and handed them to Luc. Luc started to demur, but Gillian interrupted.

"Fool," she spat. "Tonight you can be a martyr as well as a spy?"

Raising his voice, the Jesuit loudly recited a prayer of absolution. Luc drew on the priest's garments, his movements uncharacteristically slow and clumsy. Gillian fought the impulse to help but remained at her station. She darted a quick look out the small barred window. The guards were happily enjoying the wine, their voices becoming noisier, their words beginning to slur.

"Hurry," she mouthed.

Père Robichaud offered Luc a length of rope along with a linen handkerchief, and when Luc appeared reluctant to accept, shoved them into his hands.

"Forgive me," Luc murmured to his friend and mentor as he bound the priest hand and foot, then used the cloth as a gag.

Gillian handed Luc the pistol André had given her, then subjected him to a moment's intense scrutiny. Père Robichaud and he were nearly the same height. The robes would disguise the fact that Luc was the more muscular of the two. As a precaution, she tugged the hood of the cloak lower over Luc's face before nodding approval.

She drew a deep breath to steady her nerves. Once they made it past the guards, Luc would be well on the way to freedom. Their charade mustn't fail now. "Prepare to meet your Maker, du Pré," her voice rang out for the benefit of the guards. "I rue the day I ever set eyes on you, but I'll be a widow before dawn and will dance on your grave."

Turning on her heel, she sailed out of the cell, not daring to see if Luc followed. The guards grinned and raised their glasses in a salute as she swept past. "You ripped the bloody bastard a good one, girl."

"Would've done your old man proud," the other chimed in, then drained his glass and reached for the bottle.

Outside the guardhouse, Gillian forced herself to maintain a slow, sedate pace when her nerves screamed to pick up her skirts and run. Luc, his head bowed, managed to match her steps. But she knew him well enough to sense how difficult it was for him. Soldiers still on duty carried out their assignments, while others, too excited after the day's events to sleep, stood about in small groups. Neither spoke until they exited the south sally port and were on the road leading toward the village.

She glanced up at the sky where a quarter moon dangled amid a spattering of stars. "Wind Spirit has a canoe waiting at the foot of Market Street."

"What about you?"

"We'll part once we reach the shore. If I'm questioned, I'll claim you took the gun I had brought along for protection and, after overcoming the poor priest, you forced me along as hostage."

A hair-raising scream came from the direction of the Indian camp at the base of the hill. The cry turned her blood to ice.

"Poor bastard," Luc muttered.

Gillian stared at him, her heart pounding heavily against her ribs. "Was that an animal?"

Luc refused to speak, but in so doing answered her question. There had been two captives paraded through the fort, Luc and another. Unconsciously she pulled her cloak tighter. The fate of the "poor bastard," as Luc referred to the American, could easily have been his.

"Halt!" An authoritative voice rang out.

Gillian and Luc stood rooted to the spot. The canoe—his ticket to freedom—rested yards away on the gravel beach. Three men—infantry privates judging from their uniforms—appeared from around a bend in the road at the eastern end of town.

"Who goes there? Show your faces."

Swallowing bitter defeat, Gillian lowered the hood of her

cloak. Moonlight glinting on her pale blond hair quickly revealed her identity.

"Why, it's the captain's daughter," one of the men exclaimed.

"Didn't she marry that half-breed turned traitor?" another asked.

"Somethin' funny's goin' on." The third raised his musket, instantly suspicious, and addressed Gillian, "What brings you here this late—and with a priest?"

Before Gillian could speak, she felt the muzzle of a gun jammed into her ribs.

"Another step, gentlemen," Luc warned softly, "and the lady will have a hole in her side as big as your fist."

"You're bluffing."

"A desperate man has little to lose." Luc locked an arm around Gillian's waist and slowly forced her to accompany him toward the canoe. "I'm taking her with me, so don't get any foolish notions. The captain wouldn't be happy to learn his only daughter was killed by English shot."

Gillian struggled to break his hold. This wasn't part of the script. "You've gone mad, du Pré. Let go of me!" she demanded indignantly. "I've no intention of going anywhere with you."

"I'm in no mood for arguments. Get in the canoe— now!"

"You lying, traitorous scum. If you think for one minute . . ."

That was her last coherent thought as the butt of a pistol crashed against her skull.

Chapter Twenty-two

Gillian slowly became aware of lying on something hard and uncomfortable. Aware of a dull, persistent throbbing in her skull. Images shifted through her mind like broken bits of colored glass. Luc's battered body. Père Robichaud, dark and solemn. A cold, dank cell shrouded in shadow. The keen blade of terror, the bitter taste of defeat. A blinding instant of pain, then plunging into a black abyss. Had it all been a dream?

She stirred restlessly, then moaned as the slight movement caused the hammers inside her head to pound more ferociously.

"Lie still," a familiar voice urged. "Go back to sleep."

It hadn't been a dream after all. The soft-spoken command was accompanied by the steady splash of an oar. Details flooded back. She and Luc had been discovered just as he was about to make his escape. And Luc had made good his threat to take her hostage. Opening her eyes, she stared into a star-strewn sky.

"You hit me." Her tongue felt thick.

"I'm sorry, *mon coeur*," he murmured. "There was no other way."

"You hit me," she repeated in disbelief.

"If those soldiers suspected you were helping me escape, you'd also be found guilty of treason. I had to convince them you were coming with me against your will."

Gillian mulled over his words. Her mind was fuzzy, making it difficult to think logically above the ache in her head. "I didn't want to go," she said in a dull voice. "I hate you."

"I know." Regret laced his rich baritone. "But the price for helping a prisoner escape is much too costly. You'd be considered a traitor. Perhaps even executed. I couldn't take the chance."

Gillian released a sound that was part sigh, part sob.

"Try to rest. Your head will hurt less in the morning."

Keeping her eyes open required more effort than she was capable of so she closed them. "Where are you taking me?"

"As far from Mackinac Island as we can travel before daybreak."

Gillian slid into the comforting embrace of Morpheus.

Hours later, Gillian woke as the canoe bobbed on the waves. Then, after a muffled groan from Luc, it crawled forward. She opened her eyes and winced at the bright sunlight streaming into her face.

Luc sprang over the side and dragged the canoe to a narrow crescent of sand.

Feeling disoriented, Gillian raised up on one elbow and looked about. It appeared they were in a narrow cove flanked by a thick forest of evergreens. No traces of civilization were evident. "Where are we?"

"This is part of the Michigan Territory," Luc explained. "We ought to be safe enough here for the time being."

The weariness in Luc's voice prompted Gillian to regard him more closely. When he turned to assist her from the canoe, she was shocked by what she saw. Luc's face was drawn with fatigue, his features sharply chiseled. The black priest's robes robbed his skin of any remaining color and washed it with gray. One eye was dark purple, the lid swollen shut. Usually nimble and graceful, his movements seemed stiff and sluggish. It was plain to see that their flight from the island had sapped his last reserves of energy. She marveled at the sheer determination that had gotten them this far.

"I can manage." Before he could assist her, Gillian rose and leaped ashore, managing to do it without getting her slippers wet.

He stood watching her, a strange expression on his face. "I don't want your pity," he said at last.

"I never said I pitied you," she denied, but the hot flush in her cheeks betrayed her lie. "You like to think yourself invincible. That you don't need anyone. But all of us need help at some point. It's not weakness, just human necessity, and even you, Luc du Pré, are human."

He let out a long sigh. "You saved my life. I'm not ungrateful."

"Hmph," she sniffed. "Knocking me senseless is an odd way of showing your gratitude."

"You know I'd never willingly hurt you."

The rough sincerity resonating in his voice threatened the underpinnings of her composure. "I know nothing of the sort. In fact, I don't know you at all."

Instead of arguing, he simply inclined his head. "I deserved that. I can't expect you to understand."

Without further ado, he turned back to the canoe. Gillian wanted to rail at him, challenge him to at least attempt an explanation. She wasn't dense. Or unfeeling. She wanted to know why he hated the British enough to risk his life. Ask why he had lied to her, deceived her. But did it really matter? she wondered bitterly. Would learning his motives alleviate the pain of betrayal? Could she ever trust him again?

After removing the bundle of supplies, Luc dragged the canoe farther ashore and hid it beneath some bushes. "I was once with a group of voyageurs who took refuge here from a storm. There are several small inland lakes nearby with good fishing."

Gillian sorted through the items Wind Spirit, and perhaps André, had provided. Clothing, foodstuffs, flint, fishing line, hunting knife. Their friends, it seemed, had thought of everything. Finding a blanket, she spread it over a bed of pine needles. "Rest. I'll keep watch."

Luc opened his mouth to protest, but her implacable expression must have told him that debate would be useless. With some difficulty, he lowered himself to the ground, rolled onto his side, and instantly dropped into a sound slumber. Gillian sank down next to him and leaned back against a tree trunk. The simple fact that Luc had obeyed her without argument confirmed her suspicion that he had reached the limit of his endurance. The beating from Red Dog's warriors had been brutal, but not nearly as brutal as the ultimate fate they had planned for him.

Gillian plucked the remaining pins from her hair. Red Dog had been furious at losing the ruby brooch, his "fire stone." He would be even more furious at learning that Luc had thwarted his plans yet again. What lengths would he go to seek revenge? Would he follow them? She shivered. Even on a warm August day, the thought chilled her.

Surrounded by such pristine beauty, it was difficult to imagine war and hatred existed a short distance away. A honey bee buzzed nearby as it collected pollen from a wildflower. Gray squirrels scampered on overhead branches. Lively little chipmunks darted among the dead leaves on the forest floor. Peaceful, serene, a lovely summer day. But Gillian knew the day was far from perfect. Back on Mackinac Island, Père Robichaud was probably being interrogated by the authorities. She fervently hoped the cleric's account would be believable. While the British congratulated themselves on victory, the Americans licked their wounds and plotted retaliation.

Gillian combed her fingers through her hair in an attempt to untangle the snarls. She didn't belong in this country. She had no future in this strange new land she had begun to regard as home. How ironic, she mused. Upon her arrival, she never would have believed it possible. But, for a short time, she had actually experienced happiness, contentment. Dreamed of a home and family with Luc at the center of that dream. All that had ended with his betrayal. There was nothing left for her here. This fledgling country held too many painful memories. She'd forever associate it with a place of heartache. It was impossible to separate the two. At the first opportunity, she'd return to England.

Then, she, too, dozed. When she woke hours later, she found Luc still in the same position. The steady rise and fall of his chest were his only movements. Her stomach rumbled with hunger, a reminder that she had not eaten since the day before. Getting to her feet, she left Luc to sleep and went in search of food. She hadn't gone far when she came upon a patch of blackberries. After greedily consuming a handful of the sun-sweetened fruit, she filled her handkerchief with more for later. Curious about the small inland lakes Luc had mentioned, she decided to explore her surroundings. She had gone only a short distance farther when the trees thinned to form a ring around an oval pool of shimmering sapphire.

The temptation too strong to resist, she quickly stripped off her wrinkled gown and petticoat, then slipped out of her shoes. Leaving on her chemise and drawers for modesty's sake, she waded into the little lake. She was delighted to discover the bottom sandy, and the water almost warm compared with the colder temperature of the larger lakes.

She dove beneath the waves, then splashed to the surface. Though not a strong swimmer, she was skilled enough to stay afloat. After paddling about until pleasantly fatigued, she flipped onto her back and drifted lazily. The sky was an unbroken sheet of blue unmarred by even a single cloud. She let her mind empty.

Luc watched Gillian from the cover of trees. He had experienced a moment of pure panic when he had awakened from a deep sleep and found her missing. He had barely felt the aches and pains in his battered body as he had rushed in frantic pursuit. Only now, after finding her safe, did his heart rate return to normal. Idly floating on the small lake's smooth surface, she resembled a water nymph with her hair streaming around her like coils of aged gold. Her eyes were closed, her expression serene, pure.

The need to protect surged through him. Along with the need to protect, a realization of another sort struck him with the force of a physical blow. *He loved her.* Now that it was too late, now that the damage had been done, he realized what he should have known all along. The fierce urge to protect, to guard and keep safe, stemmed from the deepest emotion of all—love.

Gillian had thought herself in love with him once. After everything that had happened in the last ten days, he wondered if she might still harbor tender feelings for him. Or had they all been transformed into loathing?

As he stepped forward, the slight rustle of snapping twigs alerted her of his presence. She floundered for an instant before her feet found purchase on the sandy bottom. Shaking the water from her eyes, she stared at him, her expression a mixture of fright and dismay.

Luc approached slowly, the priest's cassock swishing about his feet with each painful step. No longer proud and confident, but dirty and disheveled, beaten until he could scarcely move, he knew he must resemble a specter from a nightmare. He brushed matted hair out of his face, wincing as the movement tugged at a laceration on his scalp.

Gillian waded toward him, the water swirling around her slender hips and thighs. She eyed him warily.

With her hair slicked back, her features looked even more delicate and finely wrought. The wet batiste was transparent. The sodden undergarments molded each lush swell, every gentle curve, revealing, enticing, taunting. In spite of his injuries, the mere sight of her heated his blood.

"How long have you been standing there?"

"Not long." Even to his own ears, his voice sounded strangely hoarse.

Gillian made no maidenly attempt to cover herself. They knew each other much too intimately for false modesty. "You look like hell," she said without preamble.

"That's not surprising." A corner of his mouth quirked at her blatant assessment. She didn't mince words. "I feel like the devil."

There was no answering humor in her cool, blue gaze as she walked past him.

"I was worried when I woke up and you weren't there."

She scooped up her dress and petticoat. "I'm perfectly capable of taking care of myself."

"And me as well," he added ruefully. The small lake in front of him issued an invitation he couldn't resist. He was eager to wash the prison stench from his body, to feel clean again, whole rather than broken. Maybe then he would feel more capable of battling through the wall she had erected around her heart.

He began to untie the cord knotted at the waist of the Jesuit's robes.

"What are you doing?" she asked, though the answer was perfectly obvious.

"I need to bathe." As he started to remove the black wool garment, he bit back a groan at a sudden stab of pain. He suspected several ribs were cracked, if not broken, by repeated blows from Red Dog's band.

Tossing her things aside, she went to him.

"I'm not an invalid," he gritted as he continued to struggle with the cumbersome garment.

"Shut up, du Pré," she snapped. Her manner business-like, she eased the robe over his hips and torso, then drew it over his shoulders.

Although his pride suffered, Luc submitted meekly.

"There wasn't time last night to assess your injuries."

Luc forced himself to endure her inspection. He knew he wasn't a pretty sight, his body a patchwork of bruises, cuts, and scrapes. He sucked in a breath as her fingers gently probed a particularly tender area along his rib cage. "Red Dog's men aren't known for restraint."

"I have little medical experience, but I think a rib or two may be broken."

"Broken ribs are a small price to pay. If not for you, I would be dead."

"Your friends insisted I help." Gillian avoided his gaze. "After you bathe, I'll bind your ribs."

He caught her arm as she turned away. "Gillian . . ."

"Take your hands off me," she flared.

He released her at once. "I'm sorry . . ." he said, stumbling for words to right the wrong, to close the distance.

"Don't touch me—ever." She blinked back tears. "I hate you, Luc du Pré."

"Let me try to make amends." He took a step closer, but she retreated.

Her eyes burned like twin blue flames, scorching him with the heat of her emotion. "I hate you for what you did to me," she said, her voice low, choked. "I hate you even more for what you did to us."

Picking up her garments, she hugged them to her chest, then turned and fled through the woods.

Luc stared after her, his expression grim. He would willingly defend her honor, gladly sacrifice his life or slay a dragon. Yet he, her staunch defender, was the one who had hurt her the most. She had withdrawn from him completely, erecting a shield around her emotions. She had become remote, a stranger. Even though it was no more than he deserved, the reality was painful.

Gillian meant every word she had said. She did hate him. But most of all, she hated the fact that she loved him more than ever. How could that be? She wanted to cry out in frustration. Was it because she had nearly lost him? Because he touched a special place in her heart? She searched in vain for a logical explanation. In spite of her soul-searching, however, she finally admitted that, flaws and all, she loved Luc du Pré more than she imagined possible.

. . . the man who had crushed her dreams of a future.

By the time Luc returned to the spot where they were camped, she was calmer. She had donned the deerskin breeches Luc had given her, which she found in the bundle of supplies. One of his shirts, the sleeves rolled to her elbows, completed the outfit she found more suitable for a trek through the wilderness.

Hearing Luc return, she glanced up from where she sat cross-legged on the ground. He wore the priest's robe wrapped around his hips like a loin cloth.

He held up a trout. "I brought dinner."

"And I made bandages." She held up long strips of cloth torn from her petticoat.

Not giving him a chance to argue, she rose to her feet, took the fish from his hand, and set it on the ground. Planting herself directly in front of him, she steeled herself against the sight of garish purple bruises. Resisted the impulse to lightly trace the trio of scars left by his "waltz" with the bear. Hardening her resolve, she wound the cotton strips tautly around his rib cage, then split and tied the ends. "Better?" she asked.

He shifted his weight tentatively, then nodded his approval. "Much."

He reached out to smooth a tendril of hair that had fallen across her brow, but she glared a warning and stepped away. "I'll gather firewood while you clean the fish."

Later, as they finished their meal, the fading rays of the sun painted the sky and lake in iridescent hues of rose and mauve and gilt. The beauty was so breathtaking, it brought an ache to Gillian's chest. She cast a surreptitious glance at Luc and wondered if he, too, was affected by the glorious display.

The heavy silence between them was becoming increasingly uncomfortable. Finally Gillian could stand the tension no longer. "What do you suppose happened to Père Robichaud? Do you think the soldiers believed his story that you overpowered him?"

Luc looked out across the water. "He's a priest. People won't suspect him of lying. They'll assume he's telling the truth."

Gillian absently ate the last of the berries. She sincerely

hoped Luc was right. She had grown fond of the Jesuit and didn't want to see him suffer for his role in Luc's escape.

"Why did you agree to help, Gillian?" Luc asked, his voice gruff. "Surely after what I'd done, you wanted revenge."

"I did at first, but . . ."

He speared her with a dark look when her voice faltered. "But, what?"

She raised her eyes to meet his. "No one deserved the type of punishment planned for you—not even a mangy dog," she finished in a rush.

He had no response for her brutal honesty. Gingerly climbing to his feet, he smothered the small fire with handfuls of sand.

Gillian never took her gaze from him. Finally she could stand it no longer, and the question uppermost in her mind burst into the open. "Why did you do it, Luc?"

"Do what?" He sifted more sand over a fire already snuffed out.

"I don't understand why you hate the British so much you'd sacrifice your life opposing them."

He gave a diffident shrug. "I have my reasons."

But Gillian wasn't about to let him wriggle off the hook so easily. "It has to do with a woman, doesn't it?"

"Yes," he admitted after a lengthy pause.

She had asked the question, so Gillian knew she had no right being disappointed with the answer. It was, after all, what she had suspected all along. Nevertheless, it pained her to hear him admit it. She selfishly wanted to be the only woman in Luc's life, the only one he cared about. "Who is she?"

"My reasons have nothing to do with you."

"I'm British. Do you hate me as well?"

He looked at her in astonishment. "Why should I hate you? You're my wife."

"I'm your wife only because you had no other choice," she said, making no attempt to mask her bitterness. "It was either marry me or leave the island. And leaving the island would have meant the end of your treachery."

His shoulders sagged with weariness and defeat. "How can I prove I'm sorry for the distress I caused you?"

Springing to her feet, she crossed to him. "Help me return to England. I don't belong here—I never did."

Luc's dark eyes bore into hers, seeming to plumb the very depths of her soul. "Very well," he agreed at last. "If that's your wish, I'll take you to a British stronghold. From there you will be able to make arrangements for passage to England. Are you certain that's what you want?"

"Absolutely."

Later that evening, long after Gillian had fallen asleep, Luc lay on his back and watched the moon climb higher in the sky. Gillian had made her feelings quite clear. She wanted to return to England, and he had promised to grant her wish. She had risked her life to save his. This would repay the debt.

This was the most sensible solution—the only solution. Toad had once mentioned that Fort Niagara, located at the eastern tip of Lake Erie, was secure in British hands. Once Gillian was safely delivered there, he would be free to return to his duties in Michigan. His skills were still valuable. Although his usefulness on Mackinac Island had ceased, Washington wanted to be kept apprised of British activity in the area. He should feel relieved that the matter was resolved.

Not bereft.

Gillian had asked him if he hated her because she was British. After everything they had shared, how could the notion even cross her mind? He thought back to their first meeting. At the onset, he had been prepared to dislike her. He had regarded the daughter of a British captain with mild contempt. She had effortlessly disarmed him, insinuating her way past his defenses. Almost immediately he had begun to regard her less and less as English and more and more as a woman.

Unfortunately, circumstances placed them on opposing sides of a war. Hatred for the British had festered in him since his youth. The outbreak of hostilities between England and the United States offered a perfect venue to avenge the injustice done his sister.

As always the thought of Running Fawn prompted thoughts of Red Dog. The man would be furious that Luc had cheated death. The feud between them would not be settled until one or the other lay dead. But before an old score was settled, he had to make certain Gillian was safe. If Red Dog suspected even for a moment that Luc loved her, her life would be in danger. Luc fingered the knife at his side and vowed to remain vigilant.

Chapter Twenty-three

"The river St. Clair," Luc announced. As skillfully as a tailor threading a needle, he guided the canoe from Lake Huron into the narrow eye of the river.

Gillian looked about with interest. Just ahead, the noon sun danced across a mile-wide blue ribbon, causing the water to sparkle and shimmer. The countryside itself was remarkably flat. A small settlement of crudely built structures surrounded by verdant woodland occupied one shore. On the opposite bank, a light breeze rippled tall grasses that stretched toward a distant forest.

"The Territory of Michigan is to our right, Canada to the left." Then all Luc's attention was required to control the canoe through a series of eddies that tossed the small craft about like a cork.

Gillian clutched the seat with both hands. Turning her head, she observed a large Indian encampment on the Michigan side. A group of women cleaning fish on the sandy shore paused to watch their passage through the rapids. Finally the strong current caught hold and the canoe shot forward. Releasing a sigh, she willed tense muscles to relax.

For nearly a week, they had traveled long hours each day, stopping only to eat and make camp at night. She had gradually grown accustomed to sitting motionless for long periods of time. Though her body had adjusted to the inactivity, her mind hadn't. She missed sharing, discovering all the tiny details that made an individual unique. She found herself with too much time to think. To remember. Memories refused to be kept at bay. Tender, sweet memories filled with sadness and longing. A remembered touch, a kiss, a smile. Moments when their eyes had met, and her heart stuttered.

But if days were painful, nights were sheer torture. Circumstances had reduced them to virtual strangers. And it tore at her heart. She felt besieged with confusion. She had told Luc not to touch her, to stay away. She knew she should be grateful that he honored her request, not feel this nagging emptiness. Luc du Pré was an enigma. She both loved and hated the man who had deceived her— and gave her joy.

Gillian purposely emptied her mind of disturbing thoughts and concentrated on the passing scenery. Here and there she caught sight of settlers' dwellings and fields cleared for planting. A cow bell tinkled in the afternoon quiet, and once she heard the laughter of children. Some miles farther, she gasped in awe on spotting an immense herd of wild horses frolicking on the Canadian shore. Luc, too, it seemed, shared her appreciation. He ceased paddling and let the canoe glide with the current.

The sun was lowering in the sky when Luc veered from the river into a narrow channel on the Canadian side. Cries of ducks and geese filled the marshland with their incessant chatter. Otter and muskrat swam among the reeds. Indian canoes cruised past them, their bottoms filled with flapping fish. Some of the men traded greetings with Luc, which he returned in their native tongue. Others regarded them warily. As they rounded a bend in the channel, an Indian village came into view. Brightly decorated wigwams were spread across a wide, flat area. The women of the tribe were busily preparing the evening meal in blackened pots suspended from tripods over cooking fires. Gillian's stomach rumbled at the tantalizing odor of roasting meat wafting through the air.

To her surprise, Luc steered the canoe toward a strip of pebbly beach. "The Anishnabeg, more commonly referred to as the Ojibway, along with the Ottawa and Potawatomi, are People of the Three Fires," he explained. "They will welcome us with food and shelter."

"We're spending the night here?"

"No need to be afraid. They're a friendly people."

"I'm not frightened," she denied hastily. "It's only that until now you've avoided stopping at any of their villages."

"There are reasons." Luc leaped into the water and pulled the canoe ashore. Placing his hands at Gillian's waist, he lifted her to the shore.

She tucked a strand of hair that had escaped her braid behind one ear. His deliberate evasiveness irritated her. "Perhaps you'd care to divulge why you suddenly feel the need to socialize."

Ignoring her sarcasm, he pulled out their bundle of supplies. "No-Tin, their chief, and my mother were cousins. We will be safe here, and I have questions that need to be answered."

"What sort of questions?" Gillian asked, falling into step with him as he headed for the village.

He gave her a long, considering look, then shook his head in resignation. "I want to find out if the Ojibway have news of the war. They will know if Detroit is still in

American hands. More importantly, they'll know whether or not Fort Niagara is under the control of the British."

Her pulse quickened. "And if it is?"

He lengthened his stride. "Then Fort Niagara is our final destination. From there, you can secure passage to England."

"England . . ." Returning there had been her fondest wish since arriving in this wilderness, but somewhere along the way the notion had lost its appeal. She wanted to flee this strange new country, and yet she yearned to stay.

Her expression must have revealed her conflicting emotions because his gaze sharpened. "That is what you wanted, isn't it?"

"Yes, of course," she replied with more spirit. "That's exactly what I want."

Luc's assessment of their reception in the Ojibway village had been correct. Upon their arrival, he and Gillian were greeted by No-Tin himself and made welcome. After a meal of rabbit cooked over an open spit and corn roasted in the husks, Luc was invited to join the men who sat around a campfire smoking their pipes. From time to time, he glanced over at Gillian, who remained somewhat apart from the women of the village. He noticed her watching a small boy of about two years of age. The bright-eyed toddler, in turn, seemed fascinated by her wheat-colored braid, which hung over one shoulder.

"Your woman like babies," No-Tin commented, following the direction of Luc's gaze. "That is good. Anishnabeg believe children are a sacred gift to their people."

Luc remembered Gillian's affection for Aupetchi, and the hours she had spent teaching the girl to read. "Yes," he acknowledged with pride. "My woman has a good heart."

No-Tin nodded sagely. "A good heart is important when choosing a mate."

Luc had hardly chosen Gillian as much as she had chosen him. There had been an instant attraction between them at their first meeting. An attraction too powerful to resist. It had led to the inevitable coupling. Now they were bound together with invisible ties—body and soul. Even with an ocean separating them, she would remain in his heart.

As the hour grew late, people drifted away from their campfires and toward their wigwams. Again Luc's gaze rested on Gillian. The toddler had climbed into her lap and fallen asleep, his head pillowed on her breast. She absently stroked the boy's dark hair, her expression soft, vulnerable. A knot tightened inside his chest. It was clear to see that she loved children—regardless of the color of their skin—and, someday, would make a wonderful mother. If only things could have been different. . . .

While Luc watched, a woman whom he assumed to be the boy's mother took the sleeping child from Gillian's arms and motioned for Gillian to follow. She cast a dubious glance in his direction. At his nod of encouragement, she trailed the woman to a wigwam set somewhat apart from the others at the rear of the village. Ducking her head, she disappeared through the narrow opening.

Soon only Luc and No-Tin remained at the campfire. The fire had burned down to a bed of glowing orange. No-Tin poked at the coals with a stick. Sparks spiraled skyward, and flames leaped to life.

The Ojibway chieftain regarded Luc through hooded eyes. "Tell me what brings you here."

Luc inhaled a deep breath, then, while No-Tin listened gravely and smoked in silence, plunged into an explanation of the events leading to this moment.

"They will hunt you down," No-Tin stated when Luc finished his account.

"I know."

"You can travel faster without the woman."

Luc drew on his pipe, then slowly exhaled. "I am prepared to take my chances."

"You must move swiftly." No-Tin stared into the flames. "Red Dog is much feared. The girl's father thinks you have stolen his daughter. He will send Red Dog to find and kill you."

"Gillian is my wife. I cannot abandon her. In saving my life, she made Red Dog her enemy as well."

"Your woman's bravery is equal to her beauty."

Luc silently agreed. Gillian was a constant source of surprise—and delight. Tenacious as a wildflower and sweet as a rose, his delicate English bloom possessed a core of solid steel. She had repeatedly demonstrated inner strength, determination, courage, and passion befitting an Ottawa warrior.

"Your enemies may already have reached Detroit," No-Tin said, his frown deepening. "When you are not there, they will search here."

"Will you help us?"

"I cannot refuse the son of Lo-Tah, your mother." No-Tin rose to his feet. "I will come for you. Be ready to leave before the village wakes."

Luc waited until the fire died down a final time. He had pushed himself—and Gillian—to the limit, but he knew Red Dog couldn't be far behind. The man must have been furious to discover his prey had escaped his snare. And Randolph Stafford must have been livid as well. Even though the two were estranged, Gillian's father would be compelled to go through the motions of locating his kidnapped daughter. What better way than to assign the task to a trusted Indian ally? While the British would not condone any harm befalling Gillian, Red Dog would not suffer from any such restraint. Unless Luc delivered her safely into British hands at Fort Niagara, she could easily suffer the same fate as Running Fawn. A muscle in his jaw bunched at the memory. He vowed to protect her as he had been unable to do for his sister.

Finally Luc stood, knocked the ashes from the bowl of his pipe, then slowly made his way across the village to the place Gillian slept.

He found her in the throes of a nightmare. Meager light filtered through the flap of the tent, bathing her in liquid silver. Freed from its braid, her unbound hair streamed around her like a river of molten gold. Even in sleep, her delicate features were finely etched with tension. She restlessly turned from side to side, her chemise twisting about her thighs. His initial burst of desire was rapidly doused at her small cry of distress.

Bending over her, he gently nudged her shoulder. "Gillian, *chérie*, wake up."

"Run, run," she murmured, thrashing about. "They're coming."

He placed both hands on her shoulders and shook her more firmly. "Gillian, it's all right. Everything's all right."

Her eyes snapped open, fastened on his face. Disoriented, she stared up at him, eyes wide, fear and confusion flickering in their expressive depths. She blinked once, twice, as comprehension slowly dawned. "I . . . I had a horrible dream."

He eased down beside her and smoothed the tangled hair away from her face. In the dim light, her skin looked pale as marble. "Tell me about it."

She moistened her lower lip with the tip of her tongue. A shudder tore through her. "The dogs were so close."

Throwing caution to the wind, he gathered her in his arms and held her tight. "There's no need to be frightened. I'm here to protect you."

She wound her arms around his neck and buried her

face in the side of his neck. Another shudder raced through her, and she clung tighter. "We were being chased," she whispered, her voice choked.

Luc, his hand raised to stroke her hair, froze in the act. Had Gillian surmised the danger they were in? Had she guessed Red Dog would be in close pursuit? Luc had tried to be careful and not alarm her. Had his constant watchfulness alerted her of trouble? Or had she noticed something out of the ordinary?

She burrowed into his embrace. "In my dream we were being chased by a pack of mad dogs. It was so vivid, I could see their yellow fangs and the saliva dripping from their mouths."

Her breasts were flattened against his chest. Luc felt the rapid beat of her heart through the thin lawn of her chemise. He absently stroked her silky golden hair. "That's all it was, *chèrie*, a bad dream."

"It seemed so real." She let out a long, ragged sigh. "As the dogs drew nearer, I could see their faces clearly. They weren't those of animals, but Indians in war paint. Just like the ones who captured you at Mackinac."

His hands roamed up and down her spine, wordlessly comforting, reassuring. He wished with all his heart that he could promise she'd always be safe. But he couldn't. After everything that had transpired, he at least owed her honesty. "I'll do my best to deliver you into British hands. Once at Fort Niagara, you'll be safe."

"We ran, ran as fast as we could, but they kept getting closer and closer," she said, still caught up in the horror.

"Hush, *mon coeur*. Go back to sleep," he urged. He felt her head move in agreement. Determined to keep her nightmares at bay, he continued to hold her. Her body fit his as perfectly as a key to a lock. Gradually, he felt her heart rate slow and her body grow more pliant.

When he thought her asleep, he brushed a kiss across

her temple. Closing his eyes, he savored the sweet sensation of holding her again. Never would he smell lavender without thinking of her. Even after a week of travel, the elusive scent seemed to cling to her. It had taken nearly losing her to realize the true depths of his feelings. Soon now their paths would divide, and they would return to their individual worlds. In all likelihood they would never see each other again. He suspected her father would arrange to have their brief marriage dissolved. Sadness washed over him at the thought.

"Forgive me, *mon coeur*, if I deceived you," he said softly, his voice thick with regret. "Whatever you may think, believe me when I say you are my heart, my soul ... my life."

"I want to believe you," Gillian murmured drowsily. She tilted her head as though trying to read his expression in the darkness. "But I don't know if I can trust you."

Instinctively, his hold tightened. "Try, Gillian," he begged. "Just for tonight, try to forget, try to forgive."

"I—I don't ..."

He cut off her protest. "I need you."

Her breath hitched in her throat. She gazed into his face, her eyes seeming to plumb the recesses of his very being. Satisfied with what she found, she gave him a tremulous smile. "I need you, too."

He plunged his fingers through her hair, cradling the back of her head against his broad palm. Holding her a willing captive, he bent his head to hers. His mouth hungrily devoured hers in a kiss that left them both breathless. To his amazement, she opened to him, her need as greedy and fierce as his.

Dragging his mouth from hers, he spread eager kisses down her throat He paused at the junction of neck and shoulder and playfully nipped the tender flesh. She gasped first with surprise, then again as the flick of his tongue soothed the sting.

"Luc ..." She rubbed against him suggestively. "Make me forget everything ... everything but tonight."

"My pleasure, m'selle." He cupped her breast with one hand, his thumb rubbing her nipple until it furled into a tight bud. Ducking his head, he drew the other into his mouth, suckling until it, too, stood erect.

"Yes," she moaned softly. "Yes ..." She threaded her fingers through his hair and held his head to her breast. Her body began to move beneath him, signaling her burgeoning desire.

Luc drew back to regard Gillian through passion-clouded eyes. She lay sprawled beneath him in wanton disarray, her eyes heavy-lidded with passion, her lips rosy, swollen from his kisses. Her slender limbs were exposed to his gaze. Her breasts were rounded and full. Rosy nipples and dusky aureoles were plainly visible beneath the thin lawn. Tempting, tantalizing beyond reason.

But he wanted her naked. With an impatient growl, he stripped the chemise from her body, forcing himself to use care when he longed to shred it in his haste. He skimmed his hand down her creamy flesh, reveling in the smooth, satiny texture of her skin. He exulted when she quivered beneath his touch.

Gillian fumbled with the fastenings of his clothing, pulling and tugging in her eagerness. Once they were discarded, she lovingly caressed the hard, muscled planes of his chest. She paused when her hands encountered the bandage around his midriff, a reminder of his brutal beating. Her brow knit in concern. "Are you sure ... ?"

He silenced her with a deep, mind-numbing kiss, then grasped her hips and urged her pelvis against his. He rotated his hips slightly, grinding his engorged male shaft against her. "See what you do to me, *chèrie*," he rasped. "Does this answer your question?"

She laughed, her voice a low, throaty, feminine purr of satisfaction. She trailed her hand over his flat abdomen, then tentatively curled her fingers around his arousal and stroked its length. His breath hissed between his teeth as he battled for control.

He didn't know if he could stand it much longer. Lust and longing surged through him, threatening to overwhelm him. He pressed fevered kisses over her breasts and abdomen, nibbling, teasing, until she moaned in helpless pleasure. His long fingers brushed across the nest of amber curls at the apex of her thighs before separating the dewy petals of her femininity to discover the pearl within. She was hot, wet, ready.

She arched her hips in silent offering. With almost devilish glee, he teased and tormented the sensitive nub until she tossed her head from side to side and writhed in helpless abandon.

"Luc . . ." she pleaded brokenly. "Love me."

His heart thundering with desire, he entered her with a strong thrust. Paradise. He had discovered paradise in the guise of her moist, satin vault. He began to move, slowly at first, then with escalating urgency. Gillian wrapped her arms around his waist and held fast. Together, they moved to a rhythm as ancient as mankind itself. She climaxed, swiftly, violently, crying out his name. His own stunning release followed seconds later. With a mighty shudder, he emptied his seed.

He remained inside her until his breathing became less labored, then withdrew, relieving her of his weight. He stretched out beside her and drew her into an embrace. After pressing a light kiss to the top of her hair, he tucked her head beneath his chin and simply held her.

"Remember me, *mon coeur,*" he whispered hoarsely. "Remember us."

Neither spoke again, but were content to lie in each other's arms until morning. Their lovemaking had been bittersweet. Both knew time was running out.

Chapter Twenty-four

It was still dark when No-Tin awakened them. Luc signaled Gillian to be quiet as they quickly dressed and gathered their belongings. Sensing his urgency, Gillian didn't even take the time to braid her hair.

No-Tin waited just outside their wigwam. He held a finger to his lips for silence, then, after a sweeping glance over the slumbering village, motioned for them to follow. Their footsteps made tracks in the dewy grass as the three followed a trail leading away from the village to a corral holding a dozen or so sturdy Indian ponies. At No-Tin's low whistle, a pair of brown-and-white-spotted ponies trotted obediently to the edge of the enclosure.

For the first time, Gillian noted that No-Tin carried rope halters. He handed one to Luc, and the men efficiently slipped them over the ponies' heads. When the task was accomplished, No-Tin eyed Gillian dubiously. "No saddle. Must ride bareback."

"She can ride," Luc assured him.

No-Tin grunted, still not convinced. "Follow trail through the swamp. It take you to Lake Erie. There you leave ponies, take canoe."

Luc clasped the older man's shoulder. "Thank you, No-Tin. I am in your debt."

"No need for thanks. You are family," the chieftain replied gruffly. "Go now, before village wakes."

Luc lifted Gillian onto one of the ponies and handed her the reins. "Thank you, No-Tin," Gillian quietly echoed Luc's words of gratitude.

Luc mounted the other pony and urged it forward. "By cutting across Ontario at its narrowest point, we avoid Detroit," he explained over his shoulder. "The fewer people who see us, the safer our journey."

Grateful once again for the deerskin breeches she wore, Gillian pressed her knees against the sides of the spotted pony and held on. The eastern sky soon began to lighten from charcoal to pewter to silver. Then sunrise painted the early morning sky with brilliant streaks of rose and magenta until the entire world seemed encompassed in a radiant glow.

Their progress was slowed by the terrain. The path meandered through marshland and a thinly wooded area. Gillian was relieved when at last a small settlement came into view along the edge of a winding river. After being jostled for hours, she was stiff and sore. The fact that she hadn't eaten since the night before added to her discomfort.

Luc slowed and waited for her to come alongside. "This is Chatham. We'll stop here long enough to water and rest the ponies. And," he said, guessing she was about to protest, "there's a small alehouse where we can get something to eat."

The alehouse was run by a buxom woman with frizzy red-gold hair who introduced herself as Maude Stackhouse. Except for being dark and smelling of stale tobacco and ale, the place itself seemed clean enough. After wolfing down a plate of stewed beef, Luc left Gillian to consume her meal at a more leisurely pace while he made some inquiries. She felt the woman's scrutiny even without looking up.

"Gets lonely around here these days," Maude tossed out conversationally. "I'll be glad when the war's over. It's bad for business."

"Yes, I rather suppose it is." Gillian broke off a piece of bread.

"A year ago this town was overflowin' with folks. Lot of English here then, lot of redskins, too. The Battle of the Thames took place not far from here." She folded her arms and rested them on the stout beam that served as a counter. "Mebbe you heard of it."

"It sounds vaguely familiar." Then, not wanting to sound rude or ignorant, Gillian added, "I was still in England last year."

"Those Kentuckians," Maude reminisced with a broad grin that revealed a missing front tooth. "They was a wild bunch. Killed the Injun chief Tecumseh and took strips of his hide home to their sweethearts. Some bragged they was gonna use it fer razor strops."

The food Gillian had just eaten threatened to come back up. Savagery, it seemed, wasn't restricted by the color of one's skin. Americans, British, and Indians alike were capable of atrocities.

Maude, unaware of the effect of her words on her guest, continued. "The British general—Proctor was his name— sat with his wife and kid at that very table where you're sitting. A gentleman he was, real polite and all. Ever heard of 'im?"

Gillian pushed her plate aside. "I may have heard my father mention his name on occasion."

"You don't say?" Maude leaned forward with renewed interest. "Your father's a soldier, eh?"

Gillian had scarcely given her father any thought for over a week. Now she wondered if her sudden disappearance had caused him distress. Or had he merely attributed it to further irresponsibility on her part? "He's captain in the Sixth Royal Veteran Battalion assigned to Fort Mackinac."

Maude nodded knowingly. "I took you for quality, even dressed as you are in men's breeches. A body can always tell quality."

Gillian smoothed her hair self-consciously. She seriously doubted she resembled quality of any sort with her sunburned skin and wildly tangled hair.

"Where you headin' fer?"

"Fort Niagara." Gillian cast a longing glance at the door, hoping Luc would appear and save her from this woman's inquisition, but there was no sign of him.

The woman's curiosity was unflagging. "Once you get to Niagara, then what?"

Gillian toyed with the food on her plate. "I'm not sure," she admitted slowly. "I suppose I'll eventually return to London."

Maude picked up a rag and wiped the counter. "If you don't mind my sayin', I couldn't help but wonder what a proper English miss was doing with a half-breed."

Gillian's head came up with a snap. Anger made her eyes diamond bright. "That *half-breed,*" she announced in measured tones, "happens to be my husband."

Maude discovered a spot on the counter that required extra attention. "Sorry," she muttered. "With that long hair of his and those dark eyes, I jest assumed he was part Injun."

"He is," Luc informed her from the doorway. His broad shoulders blocked most of the light. With the sun behind him limning his tall, muscular form, he made a daunting sight. "I'm part Ottawa—and proud of it."

Maude Stackhouse gaped at him, then swallowed noisily. "I'll get them provisions you asked fer."

The woman returned minutes later with a small parcel of food. Luc paid for it with one of the precious coins Wind Spirit, or perhaps André, had thoughtfully included among their supplies. Then he and Gillian left the alehouse without a backward glance.

Luc's long strides ate up the dusty track that ran through the center of town. Gillian hurried alongside. The ponies waited for them near a crude log bridge that spanned the river.

After adding the parcel of food to the rest of their things, Luc placed his hands at Gillian's waist, about to lift her onto the pony. Instead she rested her hand on his cheek, which still bore fading bruises. "I'm sorry you had to over-hear the woman's thoughtless remark. It was ignorant and uncalled for."

"She didn't say anything I haven't heard countless times."

"But she called you a half-breed. It was meant as an insult."

"I *am* a half-breed." He wrapped his fingers around her wrist, his thumb absently stroking the sensitive flesh along the inner surface. "Half-breed, metis, mixed blood, whatever the term, it means the same."

Gillian tried to ignore the way her pulse leaped at his touch. "Doesn't that bother you?"

His mouth curved into a hard smile. "The English have called me those names since birth. The French, on the other hand, are more tolerant."

"Still . . ." she persisted, "that doesn't give anyone the right to make derogatory remarks."

With his other hand, he imprisoned her chin between

thumb and forefinger and tipped her face upward so she couldn't look away. "And what about you, *chèrie?* At one time, you were quick to label me 'savage' and 'half-breed.' "

"I, too, was ignorant. I'm sorry."

"What about now, Gillian; do you still think of me that way?"

The timbre of his voice, smooth yet rough, reminded her of black velvet. "No," she whispered, drowning in his dark, mesmerizing gaze. "Now I think of you only as Luc." *The man I love,* she added silently.

Satisfied with her response, he brushed her lips softly, gently with his. The kiss ended much too quickly as far as Gillian was concerned.

Luc helped her onto the pony, then mounted his and led the way across the narrow bridge. "I was told the trail winds through some swamp but eventually ends at the Lake Erie shore."

The swampland seemed to stretch for miles and miles. Gillian pitied the poor ponies, forced to constantly seek firmer footing. By the time they reached the cover of woods, the afternoon had turned cloudy. Blustery winds whipped the branches to and fro. Gillian couldn't help but notice how Luc kept glancing back over his shoulder. From time to time, she saw his hand rest on the handle of the knife strapped to his side. His tension transferred itself to her. She, too, started to look over her shoulder, not sure what she expected to pop out of the bushes.

"Luc, what's wrong?" she finally demanded, unable to stand the suspense any longer. "Do you think someone is following us?"

"It doesn't hurt to be careful," he replied in a noncommittal tone. "According to people in Chatham, there were several recent skirmishes in this region. The British won one, the Americans the other. There may still be troops nearby."

Gillian took a moment to consider what he had just told her. "Should we meet the Americans, you can claim to be an American with an English wife. If we encounter the British, I'll inform them that I'm English and you're escorting me to a British stronghold at my father's request. No reason anyone should question our stories."

In spite of her brave words, Gillian couldn't quite squelch a flutter of nervousness. Should a British detachment discover Luc's identity and the role he had played on Mackinac, his life would be forfeit. He was taking an enormous chance by escorting her into the heart of British-held territory. She should have insisted he leave her behind. But he had promised to take her to Fort Niagara. She knew him well enough to realize that once he had given his word, he wouldn't go back on it. His loyalty—even when misplaced—was absolute.

It was late afternoon when they emerged from the shelter of trees. Ahead of them lay the northern shoreline of Lake Erie. Luc frowned at the wide expanse of choppy gray waters crested with white. "Erie is shallower than the others. It'll be too difficult to traverse in this wind. Hopefully the wind will die down overnight, and we can continue in the morning."

Not waiting for Luc's help, Gillian slid from the pony's back. The solid ground felt good beneath her feet. The sky and water appeared a solid canvas the dull gray of gunmetal. The shoreline with its pebbly beach reminded her of Mackinac. A long strand of hair blew across her face, and she tucked it behind her ear only to have it come loose seconds later.

"What about the horses?" She patted her pony's smooth flank and was rewarded when it nuzzled her shoulder.

Luc took the reins from her and looped them over a

low-hanging branch. "I'll let them graze. Some of No-Tin's braves are due this way. They'll see that they're returned. In the meantime, we'll spend the night here."

"I'll gather firewood," Gillian offered.

"No!" The sharpness in his voice halted her in her tracks. "There will be no fire tonight."

Apprehension raced along her nerve endings. "Why not?"

"Trust me. Just do as I say."

With a toss of her head, Gillian advanced toward him, hands on hips. "Stop treating me like a child, Luc du Pré. Don't expect me to travel another mile unless you tell why you're acting like this."

He blew out an impatient breath. "There's nothing for you to worry about."

She fought the urge to stamp her foot in frustration. "Don't think I haven't noticed how you've been acting. You've been watchful ever since yesterday, when we came to the St. Clair River. It's gotten worse since we left Chatham."

He gazed up at the sky, studied the lake, and finally looked at her. "This region is more heavily populated. Already there have been many witnesses to our passing. There are few half-breeds traveling with blond, blue-eyed women. If someone was hunting us, we'd make an easy target."

"So you think someone is following us?"

He raked a hand through his hair. "I'm not sure," he admitted reluctantly. "It's possible."

A number of possibilities tumbled through Gillian's mind. "Father . . . ? Surely he doesn't think you'd harm me."

"Think about it, Gillian. His soldiers saw me knock you senseless, take you against your will. It was an act of a desperate man."

"I'm certain that in his heart, Father knows you'll protect me."

He moved closer to be heard above the wind. "How would it look to McDouall and the others if Captain Randolph Stafford made no effort to locate his daughter? It would seem peculiar, to say the least."

She gnawed her lower lip while she thought about what he had just said. Not only was Luc considered a traitor and a spy, but a kidnapper as well. She fervently hoped the garrison on Mackinac Island would be too preoccupied with the Americans to concern themselves with her whereabouts.

"Wait here," he said. "I want to scout around and see if I can find the canoe No-Tin told me about."

Luc left before Gillian could ask more questions. Truth be told, he was more concerned about Red Dog finding them than he was about the entire British Army. Red Dog would be relentless in his quest for vengeance. Years in the making, the time for a confrontation was nearly at hand. He could feel it in the tightness in his gut. It had been leading up to this moment ever since the day he had found his sister's broken body with Red Dog's amulet clenched in her fist.

But first he needed to remove Gillian from danger. Red Dog had no respect for women, no respect for life. By choosing Luc as her husband, Gillian had made him her enemy as well. Red Dog had a legion of followers, any of whom would feel privileged to divulge having seen Luc. Even the braves in No-Tin's village.

The trip across Ontario had taken longer than he had anticipated. Now the weather delayed them further. He could only hope tomorrow would dawn fair, the wind calm.

Fog rolled in off the lake as he returned to the spot where he had left Gillian with the ponies. They ate a meal of smoked fish, cheese, and bread purchased earlier that day at the Chatham alehouse. Afterward Luc fashioned a lean-to from saplings at the edge of the woods, then spread the blanket over a bed of pine boughs.

"Try to get some rest. We have a long day ahead of us tomorrow."

"What about you?" Gillian challenged. "Aren't you going to rest?"

"Later. First I want to take another look around, make certain we don't have any unexpected visitors."

"I'll go with you," she offered, scrambling to her feet.

"No. I can move faster without you getting in the way." Reaching into their supplies, he removed the pistol André had given Gillian the night she helped him escape from the guard house. "Here. Take this."

She stared at it dumbly as he thrust it into her hand.

"Do you know how to use it?"

"No," she returned, her voice faint. She eyed the weapon with fear and loathing. "I've never fired one before. I'm not sure I could."

"Just point and fire, but not too soon. Make sure your target is close, then aim at his chest and pull the trigger. Take time to make your first shot count. You won't get a second chance."

Gillian peered up at him, her face a pale oval in the swirling mist, her eyes wide with worry. "Why do I need a gun?"

"Just a precaution." He smiled, hoping to reassure her.

"I don't think I could actually kill anyone."

"You could if your life hung in the balance." Seeing her stricken look, he tried to lighten the moment. "Never can tell when you might see a bear. But before you shoot, *chérie*, be certain it really is a bear—not a shaggy black dog."

The reminder of her panicked flight from André's dog, Scout, drew a reluctant smile.

Gillian watched Luc disappear into the misty woods. She heard twigs crackle and snap, then the sound faded. Silence descended thick as the dense fog. She eased down onto the blanket, the pistol heavy in her lap. Everything Luc had told her made sense. They needed to be careful, take precautions. But he was still holding something back. She knew him much better than he thought. He wasn't worried about her father; he was worried about Red Dog.

Her father might put up a token effort to find her, but that would be all. She doubted he ever wanted to see her again. From the beginning, she had made no secret of her feelings for Luc. Her father was smart enough to guess that she had probably helped him escape. In Randolph Stafford's eyes, she, too, was a traitor, a turncoat. Once again she had disgraced his good name. It saddened her to think the chasm between them had widened even more.

Red Dog was another matter entirely. Remembering her nightmare of being chased by a pack of howling dogs the previous night caused her to shudder. The dog's faces had borne an uncanny resemblance to the Ottawa chieftain. A chill seeped into her bones. Red Dog's eyes had glittered with hatred at losing his "fire stone." Those same eyes had sparkled with malevolence and triumph the day he had paraded Luc, naked and beaten, back to the fort as a trophy of war. A trophy she had stolen.

Gillian pulled the blanket around her shoulders to ward off the chill. She needed Luc to hold her. Needed to rest her head against his chest and feel the strong beat of his heart. All day she had waited for some mention of what had transpired the night before. It was as if nothing had happened. *Just for tonight,* he had whispered. Was that all the time allotted?

The sound of wind hissing through the pines grated on her nerves. Behind her, she heard the rustle of small animals scurrying through fallen leaves along the woodland floor—the noise similar to that of stealthy footsteps. She glanced over her shoulder but couldn't distinguish any suspicious shapes through the ghostly blur. She started at the sudden screech of a gull. Waves lapped against the shore, the rhythm as regular as the ticking of a clock. Another reminder that her time with Luc was running out.

She set the pistol next to her, drew up her knees, then put her arms around them and began to rock. Luc would be back soon, she told herself, and her imagining would seem silly.

A slight noise coming from the direction in which Luc had disappeared drew her attention. Her breath caught in her throat at seeing Red Dog materialize from the swirling mist, a vision of evil, his bold features carved with victory and hatred.

Belatedly Gillian groped for the gun at her side. Red Dog, however, anticipated her move. He brought his forearm across her windpipe, cutting off any outcry. He used his other arm to wrench the firearm from her grasp. In an action reminiscent of Luc's treatment of his precious fire stone, he hurled the pistol into the lake, where it landed with a muffled splash.

She tugged on his arm around her neck, but his hold tightened. Breathing was increasingly difficult. She tried to suck in air and brought his laughter instead.

"Your lover has stolen my treasure." His hot breath fanned her cheek. "Now I steal his."

Slowly he increased the pressure. Gillian's world dimmed. Pinpricks of light danced against her closed eyelids, then everything turned black.

Chapter Twenty-five

Gillian woke in slow, painful degrees as she was ruthlessly bounced and jostled. She opened her mouth to register a groggy protest, but a thick cloth covered her mouth, preventing an outcry. Still disoriented, she tried to squirm, seeking a more comfortable position, and found she couldn't move.

Panic threatened to overcome her. Frantically, she fought against the bonds securing her wrists and ankles, pulling and tugging at the cords to no avail. An agonized groan of frustration and fear ripped from her throat, the sound muffled by the gag. She turned her head from side to side, but her hair fell over her face, obscuring her vision as effectively as a blindfold.

Droplets of water stung her face. Their coldness helped restore a measure of sanity. Closing her eyes, she drew in a steadying breath and with sheer force of will pushed down encroaching hysteria. Gradually her heart rate slowed, and her brain began to function. She tried to think, to concentrate and remember.

Where was she? What had happened? Where was Luc? *Think*, Gillian, *think*, she repeated over and over in her mind. It came back to her slowly. Red Dog emerging from the fog. His arm pressing against her throat. The world turning gray, then black.

Her ribs ached from the constant jostling. Gillian realized the fiend had tied her hand and foot and slung her over the back of one of the ponies. The splash of water told her that they were traveling at a rapid pace along the water's edge. The canny Ottawa was being careful not to leave a trail, making it harder for Luc to find her. But even in the midst of this horrible nightmare, there was one thing of which she could be certain: If Luc was still alive—and she prayed he was—he would come after her. And Red Dog knew it, too.

What had the madman said just before she had lost consciousness? Something about stealing Luc's treasure. Red Dog was a man of great cunning and pride. He would derive no pleasure, no satisfaction, from robbing a dead man. No, Luc couldn't be dead. Red Dog wanted to gloat over his trophy. Wanted to boast about his cleverness. The thought lent her hope that Luc would soon find them and would rescue her.

After a while even thinking got to be too much of an effort. Gillian simply rested her head against the pony's flank and tried to endure. She had no concept of how far they traveled or in which direction. Finally, when she thought the miserable journey would never end, the pace slowed, then stopped. She heard rather than saw Red Dog dismount, followed the crunch of footsteps on the gravelly beach. Then his moccasins appeared directly beneath her head.

Red Dog grabbed her by the hair and yanked her head

back so that he could see her face. "Did you enjoy your ride?"

He threw back his head and laughed. Gillian inwardly cringed at the evil, demented sound. Her heart hammering with renewed fear, she saw him produce a knife. Instead of using it on her as she feared, he sliced the rope beneath the pony's belly that had been used to tie her arms and legs. She slid to the ground like a sack of meal.

"Come." Red Dog hauled her to her feet. When her legs refused to support her weight, he dragged her unceremoniously in his wake and deposited her next to a large boulder.

Gillian shook the hair from her eyes and looked around. The bright sunlight caused her to squint and brought tears to her eyes. Blinking them back, she saw they were on a long narrow spit of sand that poked into the lake like an arthritic finger. From this vantage point, they could see anyone approach within miles. The only access to the mainland was by a skinny neck of sand.

"We will wait for your man to come for you. And then I will kill him."

The words were said with such cold-blooded calculation that Gillian couldn't suppress a shiver of fear. Red Dog saw it and laughed, pleased at her reaction.

Bending down, Red Dog pulled her into a sitting position and propped her against the boulder. Next he examined the cords at her feet and wrists. He grunted, satisfied with his handiwork and the knowledge that she couldn't wriggle free.

"Before he dies, I want to tell him what I have planned for you." Smiling broadly, Red Dog covered her breast with his large hand and squeezed.

The pain was excruciating. Gillian's breath hitched, and she moaned deep in her throat. She pressed against the rock in a vain attempt to escape the hurtful pressure.

"Good," Red Dog said in approval. "You fear me. I see it in your eyes." Slowly he released his hold.

Gillian's chest rose and fell in rapid succession. From behind the gag came strangled, sobbing noises.

Assured of his power, Red Dog squatted on his haunches in front of her. "Running Fawn, du Pré's sister, was afraid of me, too, before she died."

Running Fawn was Luc's sister? And Red Dog had killed her?

"But no one could prove anything." Red Dog chuckled, a laugh without humor that was more chilling than a threat. "Du Pré tried to tell the redcoats, but they chose not to believe him. Redcoats believed me instead. They need me," he boasted. "I am powerful. I have many warriors under my command. Warriors who will fight for the redcoats against the long knives."

Gillian's eyes widened in surprise at Red Dog's revelation. Her mind struggled to grasp the full meaning of his words. No wonder Luc hated the man with such vehemence. Red Dog had murdered his sister and lived to brag about it. Luc had turned to the British for justice, and they had ignored his plea. Dear Lord, no wonder he harbored such deep, abiding resentment for all things British.

"I have waited many moons for this day," Red Dog continued, unaware of the inner turmoil his words had created. "My manitou, my spirit, appeared to me in a dream and tell me the time has come."

Tired of baiting her, he sprang to his feet. Gillian wearily leaned her head against the rock and watched as he proceeded to take out an evil-looking knife with a curved blade. Next he added a tomahawk and a smaller knife to his arsenal. He then methodically set about sharpening his weapons. Did Luc stand a chance against all this? she wondered. The only weapon in his possession was the hunting knife she had given him as a wedding gift. Would that be enough to fend off this monster?

As the sun reached its zenith, her discomfort grew. The hot rays seared her skin, but worse by far was the raging thirst. Her tongue seemed twice its normal size, sticking to the roof of her mouth like a wad of cotton. Her head pounded and her eyes felt gritty from lack of sleep. Tired as she was, she wanted to be awake and alert when Luc arrived. Finally the effort was too much, and she succumbed to the need for rest.

When she woke from a fitful slumber, Red Dog was arranging piles of driftwood around them in a large circle. As though sensing her interest, he looked up and grinned. His task completed, he came over and crouched directly in front of her.

Gillian flinched when he reached out and roughly jerked the gag from her mouth. Out of habit, she dragged her tongue over her lower lip, which was dry and cracked. She felt pathetically, irrationally, grateful for the small freedom he had granted. But her gratitude was short-lived.

"Go ahead," he urged softly. "Scream if you can. No one will hear you."

If she had been able, she would have spit in his face. She glared at him instead.

"I like to hear a woman scream." Red Dog seemed amused by Gillian's feeble display of bravado. "Running Fawn screamed—as she fell from the cliff. Screamed all the way to the bottom."

The man was a monster, inhumane. He deserved Luc's hatred, and hers as well.

He brought his face closer to hers, so close she could see herself reflected in shiny onyx. "You want water?"

At the notion of having her raging thirst slaked, Gillian set all else aside. She nodded eagerly.

He rose and came back moments later with an army-issue canteen. He took a long swallow, letting the precious water dribble down his chin and onto his chest while she looked on helplessly. "If you want water, let me hear you beg."

Her mouth worked soundlessly. If he wanted her to beg, then pride be damned, she would. No price was too high.

"I don't hear you," he singsonged.

"Please ..." Gillian scarcely recognized the hoarse croak as being her own voice. "Please," she tried again.

Red Dog grabbed a fistful of her hair, forcing her head back, and smiled into her face. With cruel deliberation, he poured a stream of water over her upturned face, laughing when she greedily licked the precious droplets from her lips. Then he released her with enough force so that her head banged against the boulder. Gillian closed her eyes against the pain exploding inside her skull.

After a while the headache abated, but her thirst raged on. The few drops of water only whet her desire for more, just as Red Dog knew it would. Toward nightfall, he allowed her to relieve herself. When she was once again secure and propped against the boulder, he enjoyed a meal of dried meat and berries. Each time he caught her watching him, he made noisy, smacking sounds. "Hungry?" he taunted.

Gillian turned her head away, unwilling to participate in any more of his sick games. She shifted position, drawing up her knees and resting her forehead against them. There was nothing to do now but wait.

As darkness fell, Red Dog began to prepare for battle. Though she didn't watch, she heard him splashing about as he bathed in the lake, then return to shore. Later, curiosity prompted her to cast a sidelong glance in his direction. His face was a hideous mask striped with red, white, and black war paint. He was naked except for a breechclout. A large tattoo on his chest depicted a howling dog. As she watched, he slipped the smaller of the knives into his calf-high moccasins. His expression filled with malice, he ran the pad of his thumb along the blade of his tomahawk. When his thumb came away bloody, he smiled with grim satisfaction and licked the pad clean.

Red Dog then proceeded to light each of the small piles of wood until the two of them were encircled in leaping orange flames. Gillian dully wondered if hell could be much different, for the devil himself was surely personified in the form of an Ottawa warrior.

Tension mounted with each passing hour. Still there was no sign of Luc. Red Dog eventually grew impatient waiting for his enemy to appear. He pulled a bottle from his pack, took a long swallow, then wiped his mouth with the back of his hand.

He stood in the center of the ring of fire, his tomahawk raised high above his head. "Coward!" he screamed. "Step out into the open. Show me the color of your blood. Will it run yellow when I cut out your heart?"

But neither insults nor taunts produced results. Frustrated, he returned to the whiskey bottle time and again for comfort.

The long night passed slowly. Whenever the fires burned low, Red Dog replenished them with more wood. Gillian's eyelids, heavily weighted with fatigue, drooped shut. Then, shortly before dawn, she was awakened by a loud, blood-curdling cry that raised the fine hairs along the back of her neck and the gooseflesh on her arms.

Her heart pounding in her ears, she peered over her shoulder. She barely recognized the warrior who had leaped through the flames into the center of the ring. Luc, his face garishly painted, looked every inch the fierce Ottawa warrior. Like Red Dog, he, too, was naked except for a breechclout around his hips. Long feathers trailed from his hair. His bare chest gleamed like polished copper in the firelight. He spared Gillian only a cursory glance, then focused all his attention on his adversary.

Red Dog stood facing his opponent, braced for battle, his fingers curling around the handle of his tomahawk. "So," he sneered, "finally you have come for your woman."

"Was there any doubt?" Luc balanced lightly on the balls of his feet, the hunting knife poised and ready in his right hand.

"The spirits have ordained this moment. Before the sun sets on this day, I will feast on your heart."

"I would do likewise, Red Dog, but your heart is rotted with evil. It's unfit even for swine."

Gillian watched with bated breath as the two men dropped into a crouch and began circling each other. Red Dog was heavily muscled and easily outweighed Luc. Luc, on the other hand, was younger, more agile. If the alcohol had any effect on Red Dog, it wasn't readily apparent. Unless, perhaps, it made him meaner and even more aggressive.

Arm extended, slashing sideways, Red Dog moved first. The tomahawk whistled through the air, narrowly missing its target as Luc darted sideways.

Luc's dark gaze was locked on Red Dog. "Admit the truth, you lying scum. I want to hear you admit that you killed Running Fawn."

"It was her own fault. Your sister should never have fought me. She should have felt honored to give herself to a great warrior. Running Fawn was nothing more than a silly girl. A child." He spat on the ground to show his disdain.

"She was barely fifteen." Luc lunged, but Red Dog brought down his weapon at the last second, making a long gash on Luc's upper arm.

Gillian bit her lower lip to keep from crying out. She watched in horror as blood flowed from the wound and trickled down his arm.

Luc's only reaction was to grip his knife tighter.

"You stole my fire stone," Red Dog growled. "Now I take something you value. I will use your woman as I used your sister."

This time Luc didn't let the man's words provoke him into doing something rash. Instead he moved marginally closer, careful to keep out of striking range of Red Dog's tomahawk.

Red Dog held his ground. "Your head will decorate the pole outside my lodge." Then, tired of words, Red Dog hurtled forward, his weapon aimed at Luc's chest.

Gillian watched, a scream trapped in her throat, as Luc dodged out of the blade's path. The momentum caused Red Dog to lose his balance and sprawl headlong.

Before he could recover from his fall, Luc stepped on his wrist, exerting pressure until Red Dog's grip went limp. At the same time he released the tomahawk, Red Dog twisted his body. Using his free hand, he caught Luc's ankle and tugged. Luc went down. The impact of the fall caused the knife, which was slippery with blood, to fly out of his hand.

Red Dog hurled himself on top of his opponent. Both men rolled on the ground, their bodies locked in mortal combat. Red Dog drove repeated blows into Luc's side, where broken ribs were newly mending. Hearing his muffled cries of pain, Gillian felt them as though her own.

Luc somehow managed to wedge his feet between himself and Red Dog. With a mighty thrust, he sent Red Dog sailing through the air to land flat on his back. The men sprang to their feet and once more faced each other. Both Luc's knife and Red Dog's tomahawk lay just out of reach.

Gillian desperately wished she could do something to be of help but realized her silence would be her greatest contribution. Any distraction, no matter how slight, could prove deadly.

A sly smile curved Red Dog's mouth as he pulled his

second weapon from the sheath at his side. The curved metal glinted blood red in the flickering ring of fire. His smile widening, he teased and tested Luc's agility with a series of feints and thrusts. Graceful as a dancer, Luc darted and dodged side to side to avoid the bite of the blade.

Red Dog pounced, knife raised, but Luc neatly side-stepped. Luc wrapped his arm around Red Dog's throat and grabbed the arm holding the weapon and squeezed until it dropped to the ground. "Now the fight is even," he growled.

As Red Dog drew his leg higher, Gillian remember the second smaller knife, she had seen him slip into his moccasin.

"Luc," she cried out, her voice no more than a scratchy whisper of sound. "He's got another knife."

Her warning came too late. Red Dog jabbed downward, driving the thin blade into Luc's thigh. His leg buckled, and Luc crumpled to the ground. Red Dog snatched the larger blade from the ground and stood over him gloating, already victorious. "Prepare to die," he snarled.

Gillian pressed tighter against the boulder in an unconscious effort to make herself invisible. And then she felt it. The smooth, hard handle of the tomahawk against her ankle.

What happened next seemed a blur. As Red Dog raised the knife to strike, she kicked out with her feet, sending the tomahawk spinning into Luc's outstretched hand. Not having time to take aim, Luc let the tomahawk fly. The blade clutched tightly, Red Dog fell on top of Luc's prostrate form. Neither man moved.

A sob ripped through, a hoarse, gasping sound of despair. Her eyes swam with tears, obscuring her vision. She closed her eyes to block the sight of the inert forms of the two combatants. Another sob wracked her body. The sheer force of it scraped her raw throat.

"Hush, *mon coeur*, don't cry."

Was it really Luc's voice she heard? Or merely a vicious trick of her imagination? She blinked furiously. Luc's beloved face filled her vision—and provoked more tears.

He gathered her in his arms and cradled her head against his shoulder while gently stroking her tangled hair. "It's over," he whispered. "You're safe."

She gazed at him at first in disbelief, then with dawning joy. "I was so afraid . . ."

"Hush . . ." He brushed a kiss across her mouth to forestall the words. After freeing her wrists and ankles, he took her in his arms. He continued to hold her tightly, as though needing the feel of her nestled safe in his embrace.

Dawn eased over the horizon, heralding a new day, a new beginning. "I love you, Gillian du Pré," he whispered against her ear. "More than words can ever express."

Content, Gillian lay curled on her side, her head on Luc's shoulder, her hand on his chest. Luc's aim had been true. If she lived to be a hundred she would never forget the sight of the tomahawk protruding from Red Dog's chest.

Before they left this place, Luc would bury the body, but for now they had earned this time of rest. After slaking her thirst, she and Luc had left the narrow, sandy point. They had bathed in the lake, anxious to rid their bodies of Red Dog's contamination. Afterward, Gillian had donned the dress she had worn the night she rescued Luc from the guardhouse on Mackinac Island. Her shirt had been used to bind Luc's wounds. She was grateful they didn't appear more serious. A canopy of cedar formed a perfect shelter.

"I didn't know until last night that Running Fawn was your sister." Gillian tenderly caressed his chest, reassured by the strong thud of his heart beneath her hand. "I always suspected a woman was responsible for the enmity between you and Red Dog but never knew why."

Luc let out a long sigh. "Running Fawn was fifteen and I was twelve when Red Dog forced himself on her. I found her body, broken and battered, on the rocks beneath the east bluff. She clutched an amulet in her hand, one I had seen around Red Dog's neck. I wanted to kill him with my bare hands, but I was still a boy, and he was the tribe's war chief."

"So you elected to go to the authorities for help," Gillian supplied softly.

"Yes," he replied bitterly. "The commandant at the fort laughed in my face, then had me thrown out."

"And you vowed to avenge your sister's death—and have hated the British ever since."

"I hated them for laughing at me, but even more for failing to grant Running Fawn the justice she deserved."

Gillian was quiet while she contemplated a young boy mourning the loss of his sister and powerless to avenge the crime. "I finally understand your hatred for the British," she spoke at last. "But I can't change who or what I am."

"No, you can't." Luc caught her hand and pressed a kiss into the palm. "No more than I can change who or what I am. But just as you stopped thinking of me as a half-breed or savage, I have stopped thinking of you as English. To me you are simply Gillian. The woman I love."

Gillian's heart felt ready to burst from sheer happiness. She drifted into a deep sleep, secure in the knowledge that no matter how uncertain the future, they would face it together.

* * *

"Well, well, what have we here? Beauty asleep in the arms of a savage?" A strange male voice intruded into her sleep-fogged brain.

Luc and Gillian opened their eyes to find themselves surrounded by British soldiers with muskets drawn.

The leader, a sergeant by the chevrons on his uniform, roughly nudged Luc's injured leg with his booted foot. "Who are you, savage? Identify yourself."

Next to her, Gillian felt Luc's body tense. She had mistakenly assumed the worst nightmare was over, only to discover another was just beginning. If these men guessed Luc's identity, he would be executed as a spy.

"He is called Red Dog." Thinking quickly, she rose to her feet, managing to appear regal in spite of her disheveled appearance. "My father is Captain Randolph Stafford of the Sixth Royal Veteran Battalion assigned to Fort Mackinac."

"Sergeant John Waters," the man said by way of introduction. "Will you kindly explain, Miss Stafford, what you're doing this far from northern Michigan?" He waited a beat before adding, "While you're at, who is the dead man with a hatchet through his heart?"

Luc slowly got to his feet, his injured thigh making his movements awkward. He opened his mouth to speak, but Gillian abruptly cut him off.

"The man you're referring to is known as Luc du Pré. He's a traitor to the British cause. He used me as a hostage to escape the island. My father sent Red Dog, a trusted ally, to see to my safe return into British hands. A fight ensued, and du Pré was killed."

Sergeant Waters and his men withdrew to discuss this among themselves. Gillian's eyes met Luc's, silently pleading with him to understand. By robbing him of his identity, she was giving him back his life. Luc looked unhappy with the situation but slowly nodded in agreement.

The men returned, their decision made. "There's no further need of the savage." Waters gave Luc a dismissive glance, then addressed Gillian. "We're en route to Fort Niagara. You're to accompany us. Gather your things and be ready to move out in five minutes."

A lump the size of a fist was lodged in her throat. "If you gentlemen would grant a moment of privacy, I'd like to thank my friend for saving my life."

While the soldiers attended to their mounts, she turned to Luc. Instead of a long, drawn-out farewell, their parting was destined to resemble an amputation, swift and excruciatingly painful. "I had to say what I did to protect you. I couldn't bear the thought of you in front of a firing squad."

"Your quick thinking saved my life—again." Luc's eyes roamed over her face as though committing her features to memory.

"What will you do now? Where will you go?" The thought of being separated from him made her want to weep.

He lifted one shoulder in a diffident shrug. "Report to the commander at Detroit and request a new assignment. The Americans still need my efforts on their behalf."

"But . . ."

"Shh, *mon coeur*," he murmured. "You'll soon realize it's for the best. We come from different worlds. Return to England, that's what you've wanted from the start, forget about me. Forget about us."

"Time to go, miss," Sergeant Waters announced in a loud voice.

Aware of the keen interest of the soldiers observing their leave-taking, she resisted the urge to throw herself into his arms and beg him not to leave her. Instead, she raised on tiptoe and kissed his cheek. "Forget you?" She forced herself to smile, though her heart was breaking. "Never. Remember I love you, and love is the most powerful force of all."

Then she turned and left.

Chapter Twenty-six

One day bled into the next. One week blurred into two. A month crawled past. Summer waned into autumn. Then winter, stark and cold, was upon them. Just when Gillian nearly despaired the war would never end, peace was declared.

Gillian had left Fort Niagara weeks earlier on the advice of an Englishwoman with American ties. The woman had counseled that Gillian might have the best chance of locating her husband through the War Department in Washington, D.C. Gillian had made the arduous trip, determined to learn Luc's whereabouts. Unfortunately, thus far, she had been unsuccessful. Her luck, however, seemed to take an upward turn when she chanced to befriend Mary Barton in the lobby of the Georgetown hotel where she was staying. Mary's husband, Richard, acted as an aide to James Monroe, the secretary of war. Promising introductions to influential officials, Mary had enticed Gillian to accompany her to the gala celebrating the ratification of the Treaty of Ghent.

"Damage to the White House was quite extensive. Even though repairs are well underway, it will take some time before it can be occupied." Mary chattered on, ignoring Gillian's pensive mood. "Dolley Madison herself carried a portrait of George Washington out of the White House just before the British arrived to burn the city. The British, it's rumored, dined on the very dinner meant for the president—and while it was still warm."

"I see the destruction wherever I go." Gillian smoothed the fur of her muff. Even though it was considered an act of war, she couldn't look at the devastation done to the nation's capitol without feeling a twinge of guilt at her countrymen's deeds.

"As bad as it was, it could have been much worse had it not been for a thunderstorm that doused the flames." Mary gave her auburn curls a final pat as the carriage turned onto New York Avenue. "The tornado the following day also added to the damage."

The entire city seemed to be in a festive mood, Gillian noted, except for her. Church bells rang from every belfry. Lights blazed in the windows of every building, illuminating the city in a soft golden glow. Schools had been closed for the day, and even the legislature adjourned to celebrate the occasion. Her spirits would be much lighter if she could only arrange a meeting with Mr. Monroe. Mary had assured her that he would be present, and that she would prevail upon her husband for an introduction.

"Here, we are," Mary announced cheerily. "The Octagon House or, as some are calling it, the temporary White House."

Gillian studied the odd-shaped townhouse with interest,

and decided to reserve judgment on the unusual style of architecture.

A servant helped the women alight from the carriage. They joined a long procession of elegantly clad guests filing up the steps. "The Madisons are merely renting this place until their new home is completed," Mary explained in a low voice. "It belongs to John Tayloe, a wealthy friend of the president."

"It's quite . . . interesting," Gillian whispered back.

Mary waved at friends who smiled in return. "It was designed as a winter home by the same architect who created the plans for the Capitol building."

After handing their wraps to a servant, Mary looped her arm through Gillian's. "Everyone of any importance will be here tonight. Meet as many people as you can," she advised. "You never know who might be able to advance your cause."

Not long after their arrival, Mary spotted a group comprised of wives of various government officials. Gillian promised she would join them shortly but first wanted to see more of the uniquely designed structure.

A white-jacketed servant appeared with a silver tray. "Punch, madame?"

"Thank you," Gillian murmured, gratefully taking a cup of the chilled beverage.

She wandered about aimlessly. The large reception area was rapidly becoming thronged with people. Men were handsomely attired, many of them wearing army or naval uniforms, their chests gleaming with medals. All the women looked stylish in their best velvets and silks.

The room seemed to become increasingly warm from the press of bodies and the blazing chandeliers. A dull ache had begun behind her eyes, and she longed to get away from the crowd if just for a few minutes. She spied a partially open door and eased inside. The room served as a small study or library. A fire burned in the hearth, but otherwise the room seemed dimly lit and blessedly deserted. Unable to resist its appeal, she slipped inside and closed the door.

Gillian sank down into one of the two wing-backed chairs facing the fireplace, leaned her head back, and closed her eyes. As was her habit of late, she rested one hand protectively on her burgeoning stomach. She felt a soft bump against her palm as the child stirred within her. She smiled. *"It is the way of the Ottawa,"* Wind Spirit had once explained. *"The exchange of gifts forever binds the giver and receiver."* Luc's child, the greatest gift of all. But a child, she knew from experience, needed two parents. And she needed Luc as well.

Thank goodness for her grandmother's trust. It provided the means to keep her and their child in comfort while she searched for him. Her father's letter to his sister in London had reported her marriage to Luc, thus meeting the terms of the trust to her solicitor's satisfaction. The first funds had arrived shortly before Christmas and had been used to finance her trip. If no one in Washington could tell her where Luc might be found, she would move on to Detroit. Then, if inquiries in Detroit failed to elicit any information, she would return to Mackinac Island. She simply refused to entertain the notion that he hadn't survived the war. She'd find him, and when she did, she'd convince him that they should never again be apart. In spite of their different backgrounds, she'd convince him that they were perfectly suited

On the far side of the crowded room, a man turned to his companion. "What did I tell you, lad? Is it or is it not quite the celebration?"

Luc barely heard Toad's question above the heavy

pounding of his heart. His attention had been diverted by a woman with sleek blond hair the color of summer wheat. For an instant, he imagined it was Gillian. Then, just as quickly, he dismissed the notion as fanciful.

"You all right, du Pré?" Toad's bushy brows drew together in concern. "You look as though someone just stepped on your mother's grave."

Luc lifted a glass of champagne from the tray of a passing waiter, annoyed to find his hand unsteady. "I saw someone across the room who reminded me of my wife."

Toad, also known as Tobias Albert Dillworth, helped himself to a glass of champagne as well. "Give it up, lad. She's across the ocean by now. Probably at one of them fancy balls, or maybe at the opera," he added with a comical grimace.

"Yes, probably," Luc replied absently, but he continued to search for the elusive fair-haired woman who had sent his pulse racing.

"Are you sure you won't reconsider and return to Mackinac with me?"

Luc shook his head. "My mind is made up. I'm booking passage for England as soon as possible."

"The fur trade will flourish now that the war's ended." Toad patted his breast pocket, searching for the ever-present pouch of tobacco, then remembered that Luc had convinced him to leave it behind.

"The only reason I'm here tonight is because I agreed to help you petition President Madison for the return of your lands on Mackinac that were confiscated at the outbreak of the war. As soon as that matter is resolved, I plan to sail for England."

"Mark my word, lad, a lot of men are going to make their fortunes on Mackinac Island. Stay, and you could be one of them."

"Sorry, *mon ami*, as tempting as the prospect sounds,

the only beaver I'll be purchasing will be from a London shopkeeper."

"I'm sure the president will want to reward you, too, for services rendered during time of war. On more than one occasion, it nearly cost your life."

Luc knew there was only one reward that would satisfy him—Gillian. God, how he missed her, every second of every day. His life was empty without her. He was prepared to live in England if necessary. If that's where she was happiest, he'd learn to be happy there, too.

As Toad sipped champagne, a broad smile crept across his face. "Would you look at the two of us? None of my friends would recognize me without a scruffy beard. Took coming to the White House to get me to shave and you to get a decent haircut. Yet, here we are, strutting around like a pair of peacocks."

Luc grinned. His feelings mirrored Toad's. He wasn't accustomed to such finery, but the evening called for extraordinary measures. In anticipation of his impending voyage, Luc had reluctantly conceded to fashion. He had submitted his shoulder-length tresses to a barber's scissors and now sported short, cropped locks. He didn't know if it was the new haircut or the breeches and stylish tailcoat that were responsible for the admiring female glances. But there was only one female he was interested in, and she was a continent away.

Toad craned his neck, trying to identify some of the dignitaries. "Isn't that the president's wife, Dolley?" he asked pointing to a plump, matronly woman with sparkling eyes and an animated smile.

Luc followed the direction in which Toad pointed, but instead of seeing Mrs. Madison he saw shining golden hair. The woman's head was bent in conversation so he was unable to see her face. Once again he felt a jolt of longing, a longing so strong he had to confront the woman. Only seeing her closely at hand, knowing she bore absolutely no resemblance to Gillian, would put an end to this madness.

"Excuse me," he mumbled. He left a befuddled-looking Toad and threaded his way through the crowd. When he reached the other side of the room, the woman had vanished. He searched the crowd for another sight of her, but she was nowhere to be found. He knew he should return to Toad and apologize for leaving him so abruptly. He should, but he didn't.

Whoever the woman was, she couldn't have disappeared into thin air. Frowning, he looked around. As a result of the building's unique design, a series of smaller rooms opened directly off the larger reception area. One by one, Luc methodically began to check each one.

Telling himself this was insanity, promising himself he'd stop this nonsense, he opened the door of a cozy study. He was about to close it quietly when he noticed a slight movement in one of the wing-backed chairs. A silky blond head moved against the back. His chest ached with longing for the woman he had let walk out of his life, but not out of his heart. Foolish as it seemed, even seeing a stranger with Gillian's hair color made her seem just a bit closer, eased the longing just a fraction.

He stepped across the threshold, then stood in indecision. The person in the chair failed to stir. He debated whether he should retreat before she became aware of his presence. But that would be the cowardly course of action. No, he had wanted to see the woman face-to-face—satisfy this absurd compulsion. Taking matters firmly in hand, he loudly cleared his throat.

The woman in the chair slowly rose to her feet and turned to face him.

The floor seemed to drop out from under him. He couldn't speak, couldn't think. He could only stare in mute disbelief. Was he dreaming? Had he died and gone to heaven? Or, against all odds, had he really found Gillian, his own personal angel? His eyes couldn't leave her face. Impossible as it seemed, she was even more beautiful than he remembered.

"Were you searching for someone, sir?"

When she rested her hand on her rounded abdomen, he received an even greater shock. Gillian was pregnant with his child. Joy swept through him—a joy so intense that it brought the sting of tears to his eyes.

Gillian found the man's silence unnerving. His lean, broad-shouldered figure was backlit from the reception room beyond, his face swathed in shadows. He wore his dark hair short and his clothing fashionable. She had met few people since arriving in Washington. This man was a stranger, yet something about him seemed hauntingly familiar.

Canting her head to one side, she studied him quizzically. "Sir, have we met?"

"As a matter of fact, we have." The man stepped into the room and closed the door behind him, shutting out the bright lights and chatter. "You had an odd effect on my breathing the first time I saw you—and still do."

Gillian clutched the wing-backed chair. She shook her head to dispel her confusion. The low-pitched voice perfectly imitated Luc's rich baritone. Even the man's lithe movements aped her husband's casual grace. She had difficulty, however, reconciling this stylishly clad guest at a Washington reception with the man she had married.

"Gillian, *mon coeur* . . ." He stepped closer.

Gillian remained rooted to the floor. Her mind stubbornly refused to accept the obvious, that after all the lonely days, they were together at last. Then her resistance crumbled into dust, and with a choked sob, she flew into his waiting arms.

At the first touch of his mouth on hers, an intoxicating

bliss bubbled through her veins. She was flooded with a happiness that defied a poet's skill to describe. She returned his ardent kiss, her need mirroring his own.

When at last they drew apart their eyes feasted on the other. Her hand trembled as she traced his beloved features with her fingertips, his high, chiseled cheekbones, firm, molded lips, and strong jaw. He caught her hand and pressed a fervent kiss to the rapidly beating pulse at the base of her wrist.

"I feared I'd never see you again," she confessed.

"I vowed not to rest until I found you," he admitted.

"I didn't recognize you at first." She ruffled his hair. "You've changed."

"So have you." Bending his dark head, he gently kissed her swollen belly.

His exquisite tenderness made her want to weep. She sniffed back tears as questions crowded her mind. "What are you doing here?"

"After helping a friend regain his land, I had decided to go to England to find you." He caressed her cheek, then stole a soft kiss. "What are *you* doing here?"

"I decided to remain in the United States. A friend promised to help me locate you."

He drew back slightly to better read her expression. "You decided to make your home here?" At her puzzled nod, he threw back his head and laughed. "What irony, I was ready to make England my home if it meant our being together."

Then she, too, was laughing, a laughter mingled with tears. As she gazed up at him, her love shone in her eyes. "I want to stay here—with you. Here in your arms is where I belong, where I'm happiest."

"I love you, Gillian du Pré," he whispered softly. "You are my heart, my soul, my life." Luc gathered her close.

Two hearts beat in perfect harmony.

Epilogue

Gillian cradled her infant son in her arms. How strange to be back where it all started. Today Mackinac Island would be officially returned to the Americans. The British, much to Lieutenant-Colonel McDouall's chagrin, would leave the island for good. McDouall could no longer delay the inevitable. Two weeks earlier, Gillian and Luc had arrived on a schooner along with the American troops. Immediately upon arrival, the Americans had lowered the Union Jack and hoisted the Stars and Stripes.

Smiling, she smoothed her son's dark hair. She glanced around the tidy cabin she shared with her husband and son and felt only contentment. The restless, unhappy girl who had longed for London had ceased to exist. Love had changed her entire world.

A knock on the cabin door startled her. She got up

quickly from the rocking chair, hoping their unexpected visitor wouldn't wake the sleeping baby.

"Father!" She gasped in surprise at finding her father standing on her doorstep, his shako in hand. He was resplendent in his scarlet jacket with its shiny brass buttons. His tall black boots were polished to a high gloss.

"Well, Daughter, aren't you going to invite me in?"

She moved aside to allow him entry. This was the first time she had seen him in nearly a year, since the day the Americans had attacked the island.

He gazed around the cabin, then nodded his approval. "I heard your husband accepted a position as agent with John Jacob Astor's fur company. I wish him well."

"Thank you," she replied, aware of the effort that must have cost him. "Luc said Mr. Astor predicts that Mackinac Island will become a business center to equal Detroit or St. Louis."

Randolph Stafford cleared his throat and looked ill at ease. "As you probably know, the British are relinquishing the fort to the Americans. I didn't want to leave without bidding you good-bye. I expect to return to England shortly."

His announcement brought an ache in the region of her heart. "I wish things could have been different between us, Father. I'm sorry to have been such a great disappointment."

He gave her a rueful smile. "I've been a disappointment a time or two myself, but that's all in the past. I haven't had a drink in over three months," he volunteered proudly.

Gillian looked at him more closely and could detect the subtle changes. His eyes were clear, his speech crisp. He carried himself with a stronger sense of pride. "I'm happy for you, Father."

"It's the toughest battle I've ever fought, but one I intend to win."

"Would you like to hold your grandson?" she offered with a smile.

He set aside his shako and gingerly took the baby into his arms. "What's the child's name?" he asked, stroking a battle-scarred finger down the infant's downy cheek.

Emotion clogged her throat as she watched her son wrap tiny fingers around her father's larger one. "His name is Matthieu Stafford du Pré."

"He's as handsome a lad as any I've seen."

She beamed with maternal pride. "He has Luc's dark hair but your eyes. He'll turn plenty of heads when he gets older."

The plaintive notes of a bugle drifted into the cabin. Reluctantly, Randolph returned the baby to Gillian. "It's time for me to go. Take care of the lad. Don't let him forget he's half-English. I want him to be proud of his heritage, just as his father is of his."

"I won't let him forget." Raising on tiptoe, she brushed a kiss across her father's cheek. "Good-bye, Father. God go with you."

Randolph Stafford picked up his shako and started to leave. He had gone half a dozen steps when he stopped and turned back to where his daughter and grandson stood framed in the doorway. He cleared his throat once, then twice. "Don't ever think I don't care about you, Daughter, because I do. Some men have a harder time than others admitting their feelings."

She smiled through her tears. "I love you, too, Father."

Turning, he disappeared down the path leading to the fort.

A short time later, Gillian gathered at the shore along with the other villagers to watch the British depart. Luc, holding Matthieu, stood at her side. Amid the fanfare of rattling drums and the skirl of bagpipes, Lieutenant-Colonel Robert McDouall led his troops through the south sally port for the last time. Gillian immediately spotted her father, shoulders back, chin high, at the head of his regiment. To watch the British retreat one would think them the victors, rather than the vanquished, she mused.

She continued to watch as they clambered into waiting ships and then sailed away. The townspeople gradually dispersed. Soon she and Luc were the only ones still at the shore.

"Do you ever wish you, too, could return home to England?" Luc asked.

She caught his hand and twined her fingers through his. The smile she bestowed on her husband and sleeping son was radiant, serene. "I am home."